THE OTHER EMILY

THE OTHER EMILY

DEAN KOONTZ

THORNDIKE PRESS
A part of Gale, a Cengage Company

Copyright © 2021 by The Koontz Living Trust.
Thorndike Press, a part of Gale, a Cengage Company.

Thorndike Press® Large Print Core.
The text of this Large Print edition is unabridged.
Other aspects of the book may vary from the original edition.
Set in 16 pt. Plantin.

**LIBRARY OF CONGRESS CIP DATA ON FILE.
CATALOGUING IN PUBLICATION FOR THIS BOOK
IS AVAILABLE FROM THE LIBRARY OF CONGRESS.**

ISBN-13: 978-1-4328-8634-9 (hardcover alk. paper)

Published in 2021 by arrangement with Thomas & Mercer.

Printed in Mexico
Print Number: 01   Print Year: 2021

To Gerda, the love of my lives — this one and the next.

PART 1
ALONE AMONG
THE MILLIONS

1

She is lost, and he must find her, but she leaves no trail, no footprints or spoor of any kind, and the way is dark, for she has gone into the forest of the night, where the trees are black and leafless, where the moon and stars do not exist, where the sun will never rise, where the path is ever downward, yet he descends in a desperate search, for she does not belong here among the dead, not when she is so alive in his mind and heart, does not belong here, does not belong here, and although finding her is his only hope of joy, his only reason to exist, there are moments when he senses her within arm's reach in the blinding darkness — *and terror wakes him.*

2

Crystal confetti showered on the city, a final celebration of a winter that, on this twenty-fourth day of March, lingered past its official expiration date.

Scarfed and booted, with his topcoat collar turned up, David Thorne walked the streets of Manhattan, ostensibly in search of inspiration. But his imagination was not stimulated.

The end-of-season storm lacked force. Snow spiraled through windless canyons, as gray as ashes until it fell below the hooded streetlamps and was bleached by the light.

If inspiration was not in fact his goal, if instead he was in need of company, he found none of that, either. The traffic in the streets might as well have been self-driven and without passengers, machines on errands of their own intention. Footprints patterned the inch of snow on the sidewalks. The bitter chill did not dissuade other pedestrians from being out and about, but to David they were as immaterial as ghosts.

By the time he returned to his apartment, he knew that he would soon be leaving for California.

That night he toured a cellar that he had never seen other than in dreams, a maze of half-lit chambers containing abominations from which he woke in a state of terror, his flesh and bones colder than the night beyond his windows.

In the morning, he called his literary

agent, Charlie Placket, to say that he would be going to California for a month or two, until an idea for the next novel fully jelled.

"I have it on my calendar for April fifteenth," Charlie said.

"Have what on your calendar?"

"You and California. It's never been this early before."

"I'm not that predictable, Charlie."

"David, David, you're thirty-seven, I've been representing you for eight years, and every ten months, you're off to Newport Beach for a two-month retreat. Never anywhere else. It's a damn good thing your novels aren't as predictable as your travel schedule."

"The place inspires me, that's all. The sun, the sea. I always come back with an idea for a novel that I absolutely *need* to write."

"So why ever leave there if it inspires you that much?"

Some things were not for sharing, even with a good friend like Charlie Placket. "I heard it said if I could make it here, I could make it anywhere."

"I ask you the same question every time," Charlie said, "and you always have a different bullshit answer."

"I'm a writer. Bullshit is my business."

11

3

Newport Beach luxuriated in spring warmth when David Thorne arrived late on the afternoon of March twenty-sixth. In an otherwise clear sky, a long filigree of white clouds ornamented the west, soon to be gilded by the declining sun.

A taxi brought him from John Wayne Airport to his home in that neighborhood of Newport known as Corona del Mar. His cottage-style single-story residence stood three blocks from the beach and lacked an ocean view, but the lot was of great value. He would not have sold the place for ten times what it was worth.

He had purchased the property with earnings from his first bestseller, when he'd been a twenty-five-year-old wunderkind. He still liked its cottage charm: pale-yellow stucco, windows flanked by white shutters with scalloped slats, a porch with a canary-yellow swing. The house was shaded by palm trees and skirted with hibiscus soon to be laden with huge yellow flowers.

A property-management firm maintained the place in immaculate condition and also looked after his SUV, a white Porsche Cayenne. They would have rented the house when David was in New York; but he didn't allow it to be occupied by others. In spite of its humble style and dimensions, it was something of a shrine.

The urge to return had overcome him in January. But that would have been only seven months since his previous visit, which felt wrong. Self-restraint was required. Always, after he flew back to New York, on landing at the airport, he was seized by a desire to return at once to Newport. He had not yet visited twice in the same year, but he kept the cottage vacant in case one day he could not resist the pull this property exerted on him.

Sometimes he thought he should never have left. Maybe he would be happiest if he lived here full-time.

But intuition argued that to make this his only home would put at risk not just what qualified contentment he had found in the past ten years but also his sanity.

He understood that, in his case, creative talent was twined with a tendency to obsession. He needed to stay in touch with this place, this important period of his past; but if he didn't resist its attraction, he would be consumed by it.

The time he spent here began in denial and hope, but week by week the denial gave way to guilt, and the hope melted into sorrow.

After he had unpacked, he stood for a while staring at the queen-size bed. Then he removed the spread and folded it and put it aside on a bench. His hands trembled when he turned back the sheets.

Later, at a restaurant on the harbor, where the decor was black and silver with blue accents, full-on Art Deco, he had a drink at the bar and then dinner at a window table.

Sailing yachts and motor cruisers plied the waters, returning from an afternoon at sea.

He would dine here most nights. He always did. The food was excellent. If he drank too much, there was strong coffee or a taxi.

He didn't recognize any of the staff from earlier visits. If any remembered him, they didn't say so. That was as he wanted. He preferred anonymity and had no desire to engage in conversation.

At the bar and again as he repaired to a table, an expectation overcame him — of what, whether of good or bad, he couldn't say. Alert, he sat alone at a window table for two, surveying the other patrons, but they were as ordinary as they were well-to-do.

The fleecy clouds alchemized to gold

against an azure sky and then curdled blood-red against a sapphire backdrop. But it wasn't the sunset that filled him with anticipation.

Gradually his presentiment faded as the stars came out. On the dark water of the harbor, reflections of shoreside lights cockled like colorful skeins of rippled-ribbon sugar candy.

He and Emily had come here back in the day, when the decor had been somewhat less glamorous. But she didn't haunt this place, only his heart.

During the ten-minute drive home, he felt that the night was as incomplete as the half-moon.

He dreamed of the many-chambered cellar, that labyrinth of wickedness and cruelty. Although it was a real-world place, he had avoided watching news film of it; but his imagination took him there again in his restless sleep. So vivid were these nightmare images that when he woke at three fifteen, he went into the bathroom and threw up.

4

The following evening, Thursday, the horseshoe-shaped bar was busy early. Well-dressed singles in their twenties and thirties were getting a buzz and on the prowl — but not too obviously — for someone with whom to hook up. Eagerness could be easily misinterpreted as desperation. This was a moneyed crowd that associated desperation with economic rather than emotional need; the men and women alike shied from anyone whose net worth might be tied up in the clothes and jewelry they wore and who might be fishing for a catch.

The bar was too crowded for David. He tipped the hostess for the window table at which he'd dined the previous night. She seated him and saw to it that his waiter brought a glass of Caymus cabernet by the time that he unfolded the napkin and placed it on his lap.

The anticipation that had drawn his nerves taut the previous evening rose in him once more. He expected nothing would come of it. Nothing ever did.

Nearby on the harbor, two twentyish women in bikinis, standing on paddleboards, oared their way past the docks, making progress so effortlessly that they were conducting an animated conversation at the same time and laughing with delight.

They were beautiful and lithe, with tanned and silken limbs, but though they gave rise to a certain need in David, they didn't fill him with true desire.

The swollen sun was still five minutes from immersion in the sea when he glanced toward the noisy bar and saw her. He froze with the wineglass halfway to his mouth and for a moment forgot that it remained in his hand.

She was in that highest rank of beauties that inspired stupid men to commit foolish acts and made wiser men despair for their inadequacies.

He thought he must be wrong about her. Then she looked his way and for a moment met his eyes at a distance, and he put down his glass for fear of spilling the cabernet.

Her gaze didn't linger on David or on anyone. She turned her elegant head to the bartender as he placed a martini before her.

Balanced on the horizon, the fat sun poured apocalyptic light through the huge tinted windows.

The restaurant and bar occupied one enormous space designed to allow patrons to see and be seen by the largest possible audience. Yet as the room filled with the fantastic light of the dying day, David felt as if everyone but he and this woman had been vaporized.

The sun sank, the night rose like a tide,

and the restaurant dimmed to a romantic glow.

Although he considered approaching the woman at the bar, he didn't dare. She surely couldn't be true.

He ordered a second glass of cabernet and the filet mignon, and he watched her surreptitiously for the next hour. She did not glance at him again.

The other unescorted women at the horseshoe bar recognized impossible competition and despised this black-haired blue-eyed beauty.

A few men found the courage to approach her, but she gently turned them away with a minute of conversation and a lovely smile. To a one, they seemed to feel that a courteous rejection from her was a kind of triumph.

Gradually couples paired up and moved to dinner or departed together, and those who were unlucky either amped up their alcohol consumption or moved on to some other watering hole.

She ordered a second martini and then took her dinner at the bar with a glass of red wine. She ate with an appetite and a concentration on her plate that was familiar to David.

The expectation that had possessed him

two nights in a row and that had been fulfilled with this woman's arrival surely counted as something more than mere hope or intuition. There seemed to be some strange destiny unspooling.

He paid his check but carried his unfinished glass of wine to the bar, where he settled on the stool beside hers.

She didn't so much as glance at him, but concentrated on the last of her steak.

David didn't know what to say to her. His throat felt swollen, and he had difficulty swallowing. He was light with hope and heavy with a dread of disappointment.

When she finished and put her fork down and took a sip of her wine, he finally said, "Where have you been all these years?"

She licked her lips, her tongue taking extra care with the right corner of her mouth, as he had known it would.

When she turned her eyes to him, they were striated in two shades of blue, as radiant as jewels.

She said, "I would expect a much better pickup line from a writer."

His heart had felt tight, laboring as though constrained by scar tissue from an old wound. Now it slipped free of those knots and raced like the whole and healthy heart of a boy.

19

"I was afraid . . . afraid you'd say you didn't know me."

"A lot of this crowd probably doesn't read," she said, "but I do. I've always thought you look so different from the kind of thing you write."

The buoyancy that swelled in him now diminished. "That's how you know me — from book-jacket photographs?"

She tilted her head to regard him quizzically, with a half smile. "Well, I didn't see you on TV. I never watch TV."

Her stare was achingly familiar, not just the color of it but the directness.

"You're not playing some game?" he asked.

"Game? No. Are you?"

He bought a moment of silence by taking a sip of wine. "I don't believe in staggering coincidences."

"What coincidence has just staggered you?"

"Emily."

"Excuse me?"

"Your name is Emily."

"My name is Maddison."

"Then you must have a sister named Emily."

"I'm an only child."

"I never knew of a sister," he said.

20

"Because there isn't one."

"This is extraordinary."

"What is?"

She was too young. He saw that now. A decade too young, but otherwise a dead ringer.

"You're too young," he said, though he didn't mean to express that thought aloud.

She sipped her wine and propped an elbow on the bar and cupped her chin in her hand, exactly as Emily had done, and studied him for a long moment. "This has become a much better pickup pitch. It was so lame at the start. 'Where have you been all my life?' "

"It was 'Where have you been all these years?' "

"Whatever. But you've polished it up considerably in subsequent drafts, adding a nice note of mystery."

He felt disoriented. As if he'd been folded into some universe parallel to the one in which he'd been born. "Ten years. She was twenty-five when I last saw her."

"I'm twenty-five."

"But you're not Emily."

"I'm glad we finally agree on that."

He didn't remember finishing his wine, but his glass was empty. "No two people, unrelated, could look so alike. You must

21

have an older sister you don't know about."
He took his smartphone from a jacket
pocket. "May I take your picture?"

"That's all you want of me — a picture?"

That question left him nonplussed.

She said, "What about your younger
brother?"

"I don't have a brother, younger or otherwise."

"Too bad. He might have taken me home
by now."

"You're playing with me. Just like she did."

" 'She' being the fabled Emily, I suppose."

"You wouldn't go home with me if I
asked. She wasn't that easy, and neither are
you."

Maddison shrugged. "As though you
know me. If all you want is a picture, go
ahead and take it."

He took three. "What's your last name?"

"Sutton. Maddison Sutton." As he put the
phone away, she said, "Now what?"

He wasn't smooth at this, not these days,
not since Emily. He said, "There *is* an age
difference."

"Good grief, you're just thirtysomething."

"Thirty-seven."

"I'll call you Grandpa, you can call me
Lolita."

"Okay, it's not a millennium. Will you

22

have dinner with me?"

"I just finished dinner. So did you."

"Tomorrow night."

"I'm free," she said.

"Is this place all right?"

"It's delightfully expensive."

"I'll pick you up at five thirty."

"Let's take it slow. I'll meet you here."

"A moment ago, you were ready to go home with me."

"Not with you," she said. "With your brother."

Although unnerved by her resemblance to Emily, he nevertheless laughed. "Fortunately for me, I'm an only child."

"So you say. Most likely, your brother's cuter."

"You even talk like her."

"Which is how?"

"Always half a step ahead of me."

"Do you like that?"

"I guess I must."

He wanted no more wine. She nursed the last of hers as if to avoid leaving with him and being mistaken for just another meat-market matchup. He said, "Well, okay then, see you tomorrow," and departed.

The night was pleasantly cool, the air soft rather than crisp, appealingly scented with the faint, musky odor of the invading sea that rose and fell and rose ceaselessly within the confines of the harbor.

After retrieving his SUV from the valet, David drove across Pacific Coast Highway and parked in the empty lot of a bank. He had a clear view of the restaurant.

Ten minutes passed before she appeared. At the sight of her, the valet hurried to fetch an ivory-white two-seat Mercedes 450 SL that was at least forty years old but impeccably maintained.

As she stood waiting for the car, bathed in the golden glow of the portico, she seemed to be not the subject of the light but the source of it, radiant.

The sight of her gave rise to that certain need in David, but this time also to desire.

Even though she didn't know what car he drove, he dared to follow her only at a distance. Traffic remained light, and he was never at risk of losing her.

He expected to be led to a house, perhaps one in a gate-guarded community. She went instead to the Island Hotel.

From a distance, he watched her leave the Mercedes with another valet, who stood at the open driver's door to watch her until she had disappeared into the lobby.

David went home, and for five hours he slept as if drugged. He dreamed of searching the Island Hotel for Emily.

The bellmen wore black and carried automatic carbines and refused to help him with his luggage, which didn't matter, because he had no luggage; he wasn't checking in; he was just looking for Emily. The man at the front desk insisted that no one was currently staying in the hotel, and this proved to be true when David went room by room, floor by floor, his sense of urgency growing, seeking someone who might have seen Emily. He thought she must have gone to the bar for a drink. But the bar had been turned into an infirmary, where wounded men were stretched out on rows of cots. Although he didn't recall having been wounded, he found himself on a cot, being attended to by a nurse in a black uniform. Employing a rubber tube as a tourniquet, she used a needle to tap one of his veins and drew blood into a collection tube. Because her uniform was black rather than white, he worried that she wasn't a real nurse, but she assured him that she was a nurse and a trained phlebotomist. "I have much experience of blood," she said. Only then did he realize that she was Emily, and with considerable relief, he said, "At last I've found you," and she said, "You won't remember this. Sleep and forget. You won't remember."

5

He woke and showered during the night.

In a vague sort of way, he remembered the dream in spite of the nurse encouraging him to forget. In the crook of his left arm was a tiny red swelling. A spider bite. Having been bitten in his slumber, he had felt the nip and fashioned part of the dream around it. The sleeping mind was an inventive if strange playwright.

Dawn had not yet broken when he imported the three smartphone snapshots of Maddison Sutton to the computer in the study and printed them on glossy photographic paper.

He put the photos on the kitchen table with the intention of studying them over breakfast. He drank coffee and ate nothing.

The early sun had slowly moved a window shape across the table to the photographs, as if light were tropic to her sublime face.

In the bedroom, he opened the bottom drawer of the highboy and took from it a nine-by-twelve white box. He returned to the kitchen and opened the box and removed an assortment of pictures of Emily Carlino.

He had put them away in the highboy after . . . she was gone. He had not looked at them in years, because the sight of her caused him such pain and longing — and fear.

Although he spent half an hour examining the evidence, he could not see the slightest difference between Maddison and Emily. They were no less alike than identical twins who had formed from one fertilized egg, sharing one amniotic sac and one placenta until they had been delivered into the world.

After he fetched a magnifying glass from the study, further examination of the photos availed him nothing. Her eyes were owlish under the enlarging glass, and she met his stare with her own.

6

Isaac Eisenstein wasn't just a private investigator, a gumshoe with a third-floor walk-up office on a shabby side street. He owned one of the largest security companies in New York City, providing alarm systems and armored vehicles and armed bodyguards. With his staff of licensed PIs, he was able to conduct investigations of any complexity. A valued research source for David's novels, Isaac was also something of a friend. He was in his office at nine o'clock eastern time, when David placed the call.

Standing by the kitchen sink, watching through the window as a ruby-throated hummingbird took its breakfast from the flowers on a red-bark arbutus, David said, "Isaac, I need help."

"So I've told Pazia like a thousand times."

Pazia, his wife, was a psychiatrist with a thriving practice.

"I might actually want to talk to her before this is done. But right now, I'm going to send you six photographs."

"So you're doing lewd selfies like that asshole congressman?"

"No. I wouldn't want to make you feel inadequate."

"Dreamer."

"These are three pictures each of two girls. They look like the same girl, but maybe not. Can you run facial-recognition software, tell me are they the same person?"

"Easy peasy."

"I'm also sending you a California license-plate number from a vintage Mercedes 450 SL. The DMV registration would be helpful. And I'd appreciate a picture of a driver's license issued to Maddison Sutton, age twenty-five." He spelled the name.

"No can do, boychik. This operation is so clean my grandmother would eat off the floor, even though she's a germaphobe."

If Isaac couldn't backdoor every DMV computer system in the country, he knew someone who could. The information would be forthcoming in spite of his denial.

"Well," David said, "I had to ask."

"And I had to say."

"Understood. Some of the photos are straight off my iPhone, but the other three are scans from old black-and-whites."

"Good enough. Listen, kid, are you in trouble out there?"

"Not trouble. Just this weird situation."

"Want to tell me?"

"When I get back to New York."

"Which means never."

"No, I will," David promised.

Isaac sighed. "You play everything so close to your vest, it's like your entire life is one long poker hand."

7

The previous Tuesday, knowing that he was coming west, David Thorne had booked a commuter flight from Orange County's John Wayne Airport to Sacramento. At 9:40 a.m., the plane touched down at Sacramento International.

The rental car had a GPS, but he didn't need it. He'd made this drive to Folsom

State Prison so often he knew the route by heart.

Folsom featured two maximum-security units that housed habitual criminals and violent individuals who posed an extreme risk to the safety of others. The walls encircling the grounds were high and recently topped with concertina wire.

The low sky threatened rain. In the clouds, no shapes could be imagined other than clenched and menacing faces of fierce and inhuman configuration.

In the visitors' receiving area of the most formidable of the maximum-security units, ceiling-mounted cameras watched as David presented photo ID, passed through a metal detector, and submitted to fluoroscopic examination.

Prison authorities, inmate Ronald Lee Jessup, and Jessup's attorney had all approved David for periodic visits. They believed that he was researching a book on Jessup, which he wasn't, but every month, he paid five hundred dollars to Jessup's account, with which the prisoner could buy snacks and paperbacks and other items to make life behind bars more pleasant. As Jessup was otherwise destitute, these contributions alone ensured David's welcome, although making the payments abraded his conscience.

They met in a room set aside for attorney-client conferences. The eight-foot metal table and two benches were bolted to the floor.

Prior to David's arrival, Jessup had been transferred there, shackled to one bench and cuffed to a steel ring in the apron of the table. He could neither stand nor reach out toward his visitor with more than one hand.

An armed guard watched from behind a windowed door that would provide him instant access in the unlikely event of a crisis. The guard was so very still that he looked unreal, as if he were a robot that could be activated only if someone broke the glass behind which he stood.

David sat facing Jessup and put a nine-by-twelve envelope on the table. A guard had earlier inspected the contents.

Ronald Lee Jessup was a big but gentle-looking man with such a suggestion of wit-less kindness in his soft face that he could have played Lennie in Steinbeck's *Of Mice and Men*. The media sometimes said his eyes were yellow, but that wasn't correct. They were warm honey-brown eyes like those that might be sewn to the plush-cloth face of a stuffed-toy bear. They were also like such a bear's eyes because they had

31

little depth.

"Good morning, Mr. Thorne." Jessup's soft, musical voice was always a surprise. "It's so kind of you to come and see old Ronny."

"How are you today, Ronny?"

"I'm good. Are you good?"

"Yes, I'm doing just fine."

"Glad to hear it. And thanks for paying to my account and all."

"Well, that's only what we arranged."

"I bought more of them Louis L'Amour books. You like Westerns, Mr. Thorne?"

"I've not read as many as you have."

Jessup's smile was artless, self-effacing, without irony. "Well, I guess I got more time for it than you do. I like Westerns and all, 'cause the good guys always win, which is how it ought to be but mostly isn't."

Ronny Jessup often expressed gratitude for having been caught and imprisoned. He seemed to be sincere.

"You still making a book about me?" Jessup asked.

"Indeed I am, Ronny."

"It's taking a long time."

"Anything worthwhile generally does."

"I guess that's true. Who do I know, like family and all, that you been interviewing lately?"

32

"I can't tell you, Ronny. People get nervous if they think you know they're talking about you."

"Yeah, I forgot." He shook his burly head. "That's sad. There's nothing I would do to them even if I could. All that's behind me, like it never was."

The house Jessup had inherited from his mother stood on six acres, a quarter of a mile from the nearest neighbor. The original basement had four rooms. A competent carpenter and excellent mason, he had expanded the basement outward from the house until he had eleven subterranean chambers.

When he'd been caught, four of the rooms were occupied by women he had abducted. One prisoner was brain damaged from physical abuse, and another had gone insane. Two were thought salvageable with sufficient time and therapy.

Five of the eleven chambers were cells. Five others were what he called "playrooms," each with a cruel and chilling purpose. In the eleventh space were stored the bodies of nine women whom he had treated with his special concoction of preservatives and wrapped snugly in cotton windings to mummify.

David had never seen that place or even

photographs of it. The architecture of the version in his dreams was unique to him, shaped by his fear and guilt.

Following his apprehension and arrest, Ronny Jessup freely confessed to a total of twenty-seven abductions, fourteen more than the four living women and nine corpses with which he'd been caught. He expressed remorse for his actions and didn't seem to be inflating the figure to make himself more important. The police believed there had indeed been twenty-seven, although Jessup would not name the fourteen bodies that hadn't been found or reveal when and where he had abducted each of them. He said they were his "future queens," and that he alone had the right to their names.

Now David said, "Where are the other fourteen bodies, Ronny? The Jane Does to which you confessed. Are you ready to tell me?"

The big man shrugged and sighed. "You know I can't do that, Mr. Thorne. I pled guilty to them, and that's as much as I can do. I'm sorry and all, but that's as much as I can do."

"You understand you're never getting out of prison. You'll die behind bars."

"That's most likely how it'll be." Lines of distress pleated his soft face, though not

34

because a lifetime of imprisonment caused him to despair. "But what if by some freak chance I do get out? God forbid it happens, but what if it does?"

They had discussed this before, and David had nothing to say.

"Maybe an earthquake breaks open these walls or there's a war and bombs fall, or a guard makes a mistake. If somehow I do end up outside, I don't want to be stealing girls off the highway no more."

"Then don't."

"But I know myself," Jessup said. "I know myself, how weak I can be, and I know I will. Unless I have my fourteen hidden. They'll be enough. I need to have my fourteen hidden, Mr. Thorne, to keep from having to steal new girls."

Jessup sincerely believed in his ability to preserve the dead from decay and in his eventual discovery of a way to reanimate them.

"It can be done with electricity," he declared. "I got it figured out. And when I resurrect them fourteen, I need to be the only one who knows their names. That's just the way it needs to be."

"There's no way it can be done," David disagreed. "No way, not ever. The dead stay dead."

"I don't want to steal no more girls. I got all I need with them fourteen."

David was silent for a while, harnessing his frustration.

The prisoner watched him with bright, flat, button eyes.

The police had used cadaver dogs to search Ronny's six acres and had excavated a few sites without success.

Finally David said, "You told me before that you knew all their names, even if you won't reveal them."

"Sure I did. They meant a lot to me, every one of them pretty girls. But they're mine, waiting to be brung back, and nobody needs to know their names but me. Anyway, I don't got a memory better than anyone's, so there's probably a couple names I forgot."

"Tell me if one of them was Emily Carlino."

She had disappeared ten years earlier, on one of the highways along that stretch of the coast from which Ronny Lee Jessup had snatched many of the other women.

"You asked me that name before."

"I've asked you a lot of names."

"That one more than any other. Why that one more?"

"I don't think I've asked about her more

36

than the others."

"If that's the line you want to sell me, I wonder why."

"I don't want to sell you any line, Ronny. I just want you to help me portray you exactly right in this book."

Jessup nodded. His soft features formed a sad expression, and he hung his head. He sat in silence for a while and then said, "She must've been special to you. See, if I knew more about her than just a name that maybe I could have forgot, if I knew why this one is so special, maybe then there's a chance I could remember."

David dared not allow himself anger. When people were openly angry with Ronny Lee Jessup, his feelings were hurt, and he withdrew into self-pity, maintaining a silence that could last for days or even weeks.

Without any note of accusation, David said, "Ronny, I'm sorry to have to say this, but the problem isn't that you *can't* remember. The problem is that you won't."

The big man raised his head, and unshed tears glimmered in his shallow eyes. "You're such a really nice man, Mr. Thorne. You're the best I ever knew. I don't want you in a world of pain the way you are."

David whispered, "Emily Carlino."

"If I just knew why she's so special, aside

37

from being so pretty, I might remember."

Before David came to Folsom the first time, Dr. Ross Dillon, a specialist in criminal psychology, who possessed personal knowledge of Jessup, had warned him that this killer wasn't a standard-issue sociopath who faked human feelings. He was a homicidal psychopathic sentimentalist whose emotional life was as vivid as it was confused, who was the star of his own soap opera and something of a psychic vampire. His emotions — and the emotions of others on which he fed — were like a mild but continuous orgasm. If he were allowed to feed on David's memories of Emily and on his feelings for her, Jessup would soon be sated on the subject, and he would have no motivation to answer any questions about her. The best way to draw him out was to tease him with the prospect of emotional sharing — but how to do that remained a puzzle.

"I really want to help, Mr. Thorne. It hurts me, knowing you suffer so bad about this girl and all." The tears in his right eye remained contained, but one slipped free from his left and slid down his smooth pink cheek.

8

The encounter with Maddison Sutton had so shaken David Thorne that he was ready to take a step that Dr. Ross Dillon had advised against. He opened the manila envelope that he had put on the table . . . but hesitated to withdraw the contents.

Although he couldn't explain why, with the sudden appearance of Emily Carlino's double, he sensed that getting answers from Jessup was a more urgent matter than it had been twenty-four hours earlier. Maddison's presence in that restaurant was something far stranger and darker than mere co-incidence, and David sensed a pending momentum to events that might sweep him toward a mortal precipice.

The single tear curved down the prisoner's face to one corner of his perpetually pouting lips. The tip of his tongue licked the droplet into his mouth, and he seemed to savor it.

As though some sixth sense made him aware of the intensity of David's emotion, he fixed his attention on the envelope. If he felt he could risk offending, he might have raised his one free hand and torn it away from his visitor.

David produced a photograph, a head

shot of Emily.

A dreaminess came over Jessup's face. His eyelids drooped. His full lips parted, and he breathed through his mouth.

"This was her, Ronny."

A quickening pulse appeared in Jessup's right temple, but he said nothing.

David was loath to allow this man to covet Emily. He felt as though he was betraying her, and he was certainly using her image to inveigle this brutal rapist, this murdering beast, to at last speak what truth he might know about her.

"Tell me, Ronny. Do the right thing. It won't cost you anything to tell me. Is this woman one of the fourteen bodies you've hidden?"

Although he couldn't know what was in the envelope, the killer either intuited what awaited him or could read David's distress with uncanny clarity. "Show me the other one."

After a hesitation, repressing his anger, David removed from the envelope a second eight by ten, this one of Emily on the beach, in a bikini. Her physical form matched the perfection of her face.

He had selected the most erotic photo he had of her, hoping that the impact of it would crack Jessup's reticence and cause him to reveal what happened to her and where her body might be found.

"Pretty girl," said the murderer.

"What happened to her, Ronny?"

"Very pretty girl."

"Where is her body?"

Jessup shook his head. "She can't be dead."

"What do you mean?"

"Such a pretty girl being dead is too sad."

David waited.

With his gaze, Jessup fondled the girl in the photograph.

At last David said, "Her car broke down sometime after midnight on Highway 101, about twenty-two miles north of Santa Barbara."

"She shouldn't ever been out alone so late. Why might a pretty girl like her be driving alone so late?"

Instead of answering that question and revealing the anguish for which the killer thirsted, David said, "It was raining hard that night. A hard, cold rain."

Jessup remained focused on the picture. "What's she driving? What kind of car? Maybe I'd remember the car."

"Don't snark me like that, Ronny. It's not worthy of you. She was a beauty. You'd remember her before the car."

41

"There was a lot of girls, Mr. Thorne, and I kept on stealing them for more than twenty years."

"Twenty-seven isn't so many that you'd forget this one."

Jessup's left eye produced a second tear, his right a first. "I pled to twenty-seven. That's not the all of it. Tell me . . . were she a good girl?"

David answered before he considered the pleasure his reply would give Jessup. "She was the finest person I've ever known."

At last Jessup raised his eyes from the photograph, alert to the settled sorrow in his visitor's statement. "This book of yours — if there is any book — it's going to be about her more than me."

David was determined to maintain his composure and give the killer nothing more to feed upon. "That stretch of highway can be lonely. In those days, cell phone coverage in that area wasn't so good, little chance she could call for help."

"If she was one of my girls, she'd be the first I'd make alive again."

David failed to draw a breath. He saw that Jessup heard that subtle silence, and he breathed again, too late.

"*Is* she one of those bodies you've hidden?"

"Question for question, answer for answer. That's only fair."

"I've answered your questions, Ronny. Unless you mean the car. It was a black Buick sedan."

"The car don't matter. What you didn't answer that matters is — were she a good girl?"

"But I did answer that one. You know I did."

"You answered it the way you heard it, not the way I meant it."

"I don't understand."

The big man wet his ripe lips with his tongue. The steel ring in the table apron, to which his right hand was cuffed, rattled not as though he was making a frustrated effort to break free, but quietly, as if he trembled with need or excitement. "She a good girl, Mr. Thorne? Were she as good as she looks? When you did her, when you was in her, were she tender?"

In all his meetings with this man, David had never given in to anger, for he didn't want to waste the *next* visit assuaging Jessup's hurt feelings and self-pity, repairing their relationship. And there *would be* a next meeting, another beyond that, another and another, as long as Jessup allowed, until he stopped playing games and spoke the verifiable truth, whatever it might be. This was David Thorne's purgatorial passage, his penance, his duty to Emily, and the primary reason that he came to California for two months at a time.

Now he returned the photos to the envelope and closed the clasp and folded his hands on the table and stared at Jessup in silence.

The killer met his stare and produced no more tears. After a while, he said, "If she'd been one of my girls, which I'm not saying she ever were, but if she was and if I could bring her back alive, Mr. Thorne, I wouldn't bring her back for me. I'd bring her back for you. I really would."

Each minute David spent with Ronny Lee Jessup was a test of his own sanity.

He picked up the envelope and got to his feet. "I'll see you in a week. Maybe sooner."

"I always enjoy your visits, Mr. Thorne. They're such a special part of my life."

9

Friday afternoon, David sat in a window seat, southbound from Sacramento under high iron-gray clouds, winging over the San Joaquin Valley, once the most productive farmland in the world, now in places devastated by the state's mismanagement of the water supply: decades-old orchards withered brown; vast fields blackened by recent wildfires. The mountains of the Diablo Range rose in the west, stark and sere. Beyond, the coastal plains lay sunless, and the clouds impressed their somber shapes and shadows on the dark waters.

When Emily disappeared, the world changed overnight, not just his life, not just *his* world, but the very world itself, as if the known universe intersected with another that was unknown, and in that quiet collision, an infinite number of subtle changes occurred. He could not define what was different, could not enumerate the many tweaks and twists, though he could feel the truth of them by the way the world loomed strange around him, by events that were too bizarre for the cosmos as it had been, but that unfurled in this new reality without seeming to amaze or disturb anyone but him.

For perhaps two days he had been in denial, certain that she would be found or would walk through the door with some bright story of comic adventure. On the third day, he realized he would never see her alive again. That he had loved her was not a belated discovery, nor that he had loved her more than he loved himself. They were so young, however, that he had never contemplated — or even imagined — the loss of her. He felt hollowed out and for weeks could not get warm. In his dreams, she wandered fields and forests; he glimpsed her on far hills or between trees, and though she called his name, she never seemed to see him, and she moved always farther away.

They had been together for five years, since he was twenty-two and she was twenty. He had achieved his success with her at his side, *because* she was at his side, because she centered him. In the wake of her disappearance, he couldn't understand why they had not married. They were of a generation that often delayed marriage or even felt it wasn't essential to shaping a life together. But when he had no hope of wedding her, he wanted her to have been his wife, to be able to say that by sanctification they had been as one. He felt that he had failed her by not committing in that fashion. Worse, he found himself lying awake, wondering if being married would have changed their actions, so that she would not have been alone that night and therefore would not have gone missing and, surely, to her death.

When Ronny Lee Jessup had been arrested three years later and his hideous labyrinthine cellar had topped the news, David waited in dread for the coroner to report that one of the nine cadavers the killer had crudely mummified was hers. But she remained missing.

Perhaps he should have found hope in the fact that she wasn't among the living and dead women in those subterranean rooms, but after three years, his capacity for hope had been exhausted. She wasn't out there alive, waiting to be found, not in this strangely altered and steadily darkening world. Like a grotesque insect in human disguise, Jessup stowed her poor body in some secret niche as if it were a chrysalis from which she would in time emerge, her beauty reborn, to submit to his brutality once more.

Friends advised David to move on, and he tried, but he could not. He was haunted by what had been, what might have been, and what could never be. When writing, especially since the loss of Emily, he often became obsessed with the work to the exclusion of all else, so it seemed that if the atmosphere of Earth should suddenly evaporate, he would be sustained by the air of the fictional world he created. He had also become obsessed with one path by which he might find peace of mind: discover the truth of her fate, locate her remains, and bury her in the cemetery nearest to the cottage in Corona del Mar, where they had been so happy, where he would always be able to look after her, as he had failed to do in life. For this reason, for six years, he had been visiting Ronny Lee Jessup in Folsom.

At 2:10 p.m., the turboprop commuter flight began its descent into Orange County. The clouds of the north had withered away south of Santa Barbara. Sun sequined the sea. Vehicles glittered like miniature racers on freeways as undulant as slot-car tracks, and office towers rose to reflect distorted versions of one another in walls of dark glass. In less than four hours, David would have dinner with the impossible woman who could not be Emily Carlino but could not be anyone else.

10

In the Corona del Mar cottage, David switched on his computer and discovered that he already had a response from Isaac Eisenstein in New York. The message was simple: Call me on my personal cell.

Attachments included Maddison Sutton's California driver's license. She was twenty-five, as she claimed, which happened to be

48

the age at which Emily disappeared. Her address was a post office box in Goleta, in Santa Barbara County, which was not far from where Emily's broken-down Buick had been found abandoned on that long-ago night of hard rain.

Also attached, the DMV registration for the ivory-white vintage Mercedes 450 SL identified the owner as Patrick Michael Lynam Corley at the same post office box in Goleta.

The third and last attachment was a death certificate for the same Patrick Michael Lynam Corley, who had passed away on June 22, seven years earlier, at the age of fifty-nine.

David called Isaac's private cell phone, was forwarded to voice mail, and left a message.

The two study windows were fitted with interior shutters. The half-open slats interleaved shadows with bands of sunlight that laddered up one wall.

When Isaac returned the call six minutes later, he said, "Pazia and I are going to dinner at Le Coucou. She's been looking forward to this for a month, so if we're not out the door in twelve minutes, I'll have to eat dinner with an ice pack on my balls."

"Then let's get to it. How can a car be

49

registered to a guy who's been dead seven years?"

"Someone's been renewing it in his name every time it comes due. I don't know who yet, but I'll have more for you tomorrow."

"What do you know about this Corley?"

"He was a contractor and property developer. Built houses in and around Goleta. His wife died five years before him. No children. More tomorrow. Now these photos you sent of Maddison Sutton — my God, she's a looker. Breathtaking. Are you head over heels?"

Isaac knew nothing about Emily Carlino. David spoke of her to no one in his current life. Sorrow, the mystery of her fate, and shame kept him silent.

"It's not about romance, Isaac. And only three of the shots were her. The other three are a different woman."

"So you said, but you're wrong about that. Forty-four-detail comparisons of facial-recognition scans say they're one and the same person, and every photo of the same period."

"No. Those shots were taken ten years apart."

"Somebody's pulling your leg, pal. Faces don't stay the same for a decade. The most highly reliable recognition programs require

50

base images of the subjects on file to be upgraded every seven or eight years. According to her driver's license, she's twenty-five, and the function of our scan that estimates age puts all these photos in her midtwenties."

"But —"

"I haven't been able to get anything on Maddison Sutton, where she works, family, education, anything at all. Such deep anonymity doesn't make sense in Googleworld. We'll dig further. I'll have some follow-up for you tomorrow. And when I have more time, I've got to know what's going on there. 'It's not about romance,' huh? If it's really not, then you're either blind or stupid, and I know you're neither. Now I'm off to Le Coucou."

David hung up. He switched off the computer.

The quiet in the cottage was so deep that the place might have been drifting outside of time, displaced by some quirk of physics. The planet rotated, and on the wall, the ladder of sunshine and shadow skewed somewhat, and the bright bands dimmed. As the light seemed almost to simmer slowly away, steeping the room in mystery, David Thorne wondered what he ought to say to Maddison Sutton at dinner, how he might draw

51

her out yet avoid seeming suspicious — and what he would feel in mind and heart when he touched her.

11

Upon the waters came a multideck party boat, a mere shell of spaces that could be used for banquet rooms and buffet lines and rental casinos and dance floors, bedecked with strings of tiny white lights, with guests of some well-catered event posed at the railings or glimpsed beyond the enormous windows in chambers festooned with cream-white bunting and enormous floral displays of white and yellow blooms. This massive confection of contrived elegance cruised past the windows of the restaurant, moving smoothly through harbor waters glimmering with the first golden light of sunset. It seemed to glide not by the power of its engines but to hydroplane on the music of its big band playing Glenn Miller's "In the Mood."

Maddison had arrived before David. She already sat at the window table where he had dined alone the previous evening. Her martini had been so recently served that it had hardly been touched.

Perhaps she saw his reflection in the glass.

She turned her head to smile just as he approached.

The passing spectacle paled by comparison with this woman. To David, the expensive and lustrous decor of the restaurant became ordinary. The festive clinking of glasses, the ringing of flatware, the laughter of the singles on the hunt at the bar, the animated conversation of the other diners — all of it faded so that even though she spoke softly, her voice was clear and intimate as he settled in the chair across the table from her.

"I've been thinking about Emily," she said.

"Thinking what?"

"How I'm not her."

"We agreed on that."

"Yet that's why we're here."

"Not really, no."

"A girl likes to think she's unique."

"I approached you because you look like her, but that's not why I asked you out."

"Why did you?"

"I liked the way you talk."

"Oops. Last night, you said I talk like her."

"I say a lot of stupid things."

"Few men would admit as much."

The waiter came to take a drink order.

When David and Maddison were alone again, he said, "Maybe I should go home and send my brother."

"Then I would have to dine alone. Anyway, even if he existed, I doubt he'd be cuter than you. Or more entertaining."

He didn't know what to say. He wished he already had a drink.

After taking a sip of her martini, she said, "Which woman in your novels is Emily?"

"I've never written her."

Maddison raised one eyebrow. "You loved her more than life itself, but never wrote about her?"

Although he hadn't spoken to Maddison of his love for Emily, he supposed that she could deduce it from his actions or read his heart as revealed in his eyes.

He said, "Sometimes it takes a lot of distance to be able to fold a piece of your life into a work of fiction."

"Ten years is a lot of distance. Did you leave her?"

"Why would I have left her if I loved her more than life itself?"

"We all do reckless, foolish things. So she left you, just walked out?"

"Yes," he said, and left it there.

"You're afraid of writing about her and getting her wrong. Are you still too angry to be fair to her?"

"I've never been angry with her."

"Then it's pain."

"Is it?"

"Her leaving hurt you so badly that you don't believe you could be fair to her, and you still love her too much to write about her in an unfair way."

"You make me out to be more sensitive and considerate than I am. Are we going to talk about Emily all night?"

"Not all night. But because last night you thought I was Emily and because you still wish I were her, I have more questions. A girl's got to know her competition if she's to have a chance."

"I don't wish you were her."

"That's the second lie you've told me tonight. You're not a guy who lies well, which is to your credit even if you lie."

"Second? What was the first?"

"When you said she left you. Clearly, it was more complicated. She didn't get bored, not with one like you. And you're no brute."

She seemed to be as open and forthright as anyone he had ever known. Yet he sensed that she had been formulating her side of this conversation for much longer than a day — and that his responses did not surprise her.

He said, "More complicated than she just

walked out on me? Do you have a different scenario in mind?"

She met his eyes and seemed to gaze into — rather than merely at — him. "Maybe a moment came when she needed you desperately, and you weren't there. Maybe it haunts you even after all these years. Maybe the guilt you feel for failing her still eats at you like an acid, so that writing about her would be as excruciating as forcing yourself through a mile of razor wire."

He was shocked speechless. He could not break eye contact. Her blue-steel stare pinned him as if he were a butterfly fixed to a specimen board.

After a damning silence, at last he said, "Very dramatic. You think like a novelist."

She smiled and shook her head. "No, no. I have no desire to be a writer and no talent for it. Anyway, sooner or later, you'll tell me the full story."

Her stare no longer chilled him. Her smile was warm. There had been no accusation in what she'd said, only idle speculation. She couldn't know that she had touched an open wound of truth.

Nevertheless, David was relieved that the waiter arrived just then with his glass of Macallan Scotch over ice.

12

Once the golden phase had passed, the sun used only the red and orange spectrum of its palette to paint the sky in advance of the long night of darkness, and by reflection the harbor waters caught fire.

Maddison took an almost childlike delight in the spectacle, and David found pleasure in watching her enjoy the sunset. Emily, too, had been charmed by nature in its ordinary extraordinariness, and he had liked to watch her when she was thus enchanted and unaware that she bewitched his eyes.

This evening, as on the previous night, Maddison dressed well but almost demurely. A tailored sapphire-blue suit that matched the darker striations of her remarkable eyes. A crisp white blouse.

Her form was exquisite, but unlike most of the other young women of her time, she did not advertise her charms with revealed cleavage or with jeans that were in fact leggings.

She needed no makeup and wore little. Her only jewelry was a simple string of pearls. No rings. No wristwatch.

When David gently pressed her to tell him about herself, she responded without apparent evasion. Born in Seattle. An only child of doting parents. Her father, Marcus, an executive at Microsoft. Her mother, Claire, a prosecutor in the district attorney's office. Maddison wasn't married. Not currently in a relationship. Lived now in Goleta. Visiting Orange County on business.

"What line of work are you in?" he asked.

Without hesitation, she said, "I'm an assassin."

"Not of writers, I hope."

"Not of writers," she confirmed. "You're safe with me."

When she did not elucidate, he said, "So 'assassin' is a metaphor for what?"

"It's not a metaphor. Just a synonym for *murderer.* Or more accurately, for *executioner.*"

The waiter stopped by to ask what they would like for dinner.

Maddison ordered a Caesar salad and sea bass, and David ordered the same salad and the rack of lamb, and she said there was no need to order a white wine for her, that she preferred a smooth dry red even with fish. He selected a bottle of Far Niente cabernet.

When the waiter departed, David said, "Your mother being a prosecutor, how does she feel about her daughter the assassin?"

"She's cool with it. I've got very supportive parents."

58

He regarded her with both amusement and impatience. "Okay, last night, I mistakenly thought you were playing games with me when you pretended to know me only by the photos on my books, when you denied being Emily. But now you *are* playing games. What's the joke?"

"No joke. I know that assassins don't usually go around telling people what line of work they're in, but I very much like you and want to get off on the right foot with you, which means being totally honest."

"You're no assassin or murderer or executioner."

She propped an elbow on the table and rested her chin in the cup of her hand, as she'd done the previous night, as Emily had so often done. "So . . . what would you prefer my line of work to be?"

"I don't prefer it to be anything. I'd just like to know what it really is."

Her eyes were as deep as pools that could drown men who had been swimming all their lives. She stared at him with analytic intensity and said, "Do you think I would kill innocent people?"

"I don't think you'd kill anyone."

"Because I only kill extremely wicked people, the truly power-mad bastards who care nothing for others. Or, once in a while, a misguided soul so passionate about one idea or another that he doesn't realize how wicked it is."

David put one hand over his heart. "I feel so much better."

"What troubles you about it? Are you afraid that I might one day turn violent and kill you over some lovers' quarrel?"

"I'm more likely to be eaten by a great white shark, though I never swim in the ocean."

"Then is it the blood, the general messiness of the job? Or some moral compunction, misguided pacifism?"

The waiter arrived with their salads and offered fresh-ground pepper, and they both said yes, and by the time he left the table, the last of the scarlet stain was gone from the sky. The waters of the harbor were jet-black but for the reflections of the shoreside lights that floated upon them like wreaths of radiant flowers cast out to mark some ceremony.

"Do we play this game all the way to the entrée?" he asked.

"Oh, goodness, David, allow me some mystery for a little while. You've certainly got your own share of it. I rather like being an assassin. It's so much more glamorous than being a representative for IBM business systems. Now let's talk about that movie they made from one of your books."

"If you really were an assassin, I could give you a contract for a megalomaniacal film director the world wouldn't miss."

13

Maddison had a profound interest in literature that was unusual in this digital age when the language arts were receding into the mists of the unfashionable along with a knowledge of history, an appreciation for complex music, general civility, and so much else that David valued. In fact, her education was both broad and deep, and consequently their conversation seemed to be a kind of jazz that made three hours pass like one.

Over coffee, when he asked where she'd gone to school, she said, "The University of the Machine," and implied — but would not say — that she was largely self-educated online, as though it might be an embarrassment to her highly educated parents that she had not attended college.

"Given all your interests," David said, "I'm surprised you find it fulfilling to be a sales rep for IBM business systems."

"I'd find it stifling if that's what I was."

"But you said —"

"You inferred, dear. I didn't say or so much as imply IBM. It was just an example of a glamorless career."

"So I'm still supposed to believe you're an assassin."

"And quite a good one."

After the waiter refreshed their coffee, David said, "We've talked nonstop all evening, yet there's a long list of essential things about you that I don't know."

She was about to speak, but her smile became fixed, and her lips parted without producing a word, and her gaze slipped out of focus. She cocked her head as if listening to some voice or siren song that only she could hear.

After perhaps half a minute, he said, "Maddison?"

She blinked, blinked, came back from wherever she'd gone, and said, "Sorry. What did you say?"

"There's a long list of essential things about you that I don't know," he repeated.

Stirring her coffee, she said, "Well, okay — my favorite color is blue, favorite flower the calla lily, favorite time of the day sunrise. Songwriters — Cole Porter, Paul Simon. Dark chocolate, yes. Milk chocolate, no. White chocolate — you've got to be joking.

Red wine, always. White wine, sometimes. Champagne, never, it gives me ghastly headaches. Walks on the beach. Dolphins, whales. Pelicans flying in formation. Hummingbirds. Butterflies. Driving very fast, laughing till I cry, making love. So — lunch on Sunday? Or would you first like to know my favorite textures, smells, and sounds?"

He said, "Why not dinner tomorrow instead of Sunday?"

"You're up early tomorrow and away all day, and you're stressed out about it, whatever it is."

He frowned. "I said that?"

"Only that you're up early and away all day. I inferred the stress. It's very sweet how easy you are to read. If you were an assassin, dear, you'd never be able to get close to your target."

"I'll be back in time for dinner."

"And all knotted up by whatever secret business it is that you have to deal with. I don't know, of course, because you're being as mysterious with me as you say I'm being with you, even though *I* do not know *your* favorite color or favorite flower or position on the issue of driving very fast. Lunch on Sunday, noon, Laguna Beach?" She named a restaurant.

"We'll walk on the beach afterward," he said.

She finished her coffee. "Tour some galleries, cute little shops."

"May I pick you up? Where are you staying?"

"You can pick me up when I'm certain of your position on very fast driving and selected other matters. Sunday, I'll drive myself and meet you there. Don't look bereft. Smile for me. There, that's nice. I love your smile. Especially when it's aimed at me."

Outside, as they waited for the valets to bring their cars, she put one hand against the back of David's head and drew his face down to hers and kissed him warmly, more than chastely, but just once.

He did not follow her to the Island Hotel this time.

14

At home, David emailed Isaac Eisenstein two items for further investigation. Marcus Sutton, executive at Microsoft. Claire Sutton, prosecutor in the Seattle district attorney's office.

Later, lying on his back in bed, David left one lamp on low, staring at the white-painted beam-and-shiplap ceiling, which always before he'd found pleasing to the eye and mind. Now the regularity of those lines and the expertly tight joinery of the boards seemed to mock his confusion and the disorganization that characterized his emotional life.

He could feel her lips on his as if the imprint of them would last a lifetime. The delicacy of her quick tongue. Her warm breath as the kiss ended.

The claim to be an assassin, whatever its purpose, whether to intrigue or merely tease him, did not occupy his thoughts, for he knew she would in time explain why she struck such a pose.

Instead, he focused on the fact that she had known he would be up early tomorrow and away all day. She said he'd told her so. He combed through his memory of the evening but couldn't recall making that revelation. He might have. He just couldn't remember. And it seemed that he *should* remember.

What he *did* remember, and what he kept returning to more than anything else, was what she'd said in response to his complaint that in spite of hours of nonstop conversation, there was still a long list of essential things he didn't know about her. She had charmed him by imitating a schoolgirl and launching into a long list of likes and dislikes.

The first three items he remembered word for word: *My favorite color is blue, favorite flower the calla lily, favorite of the day sunrise.*

Emily Carlino's favorite color had been blue. Her favorite flower was the calla lily. And she loved to be up before sunrise because, as she'd said: *Life is so fragile and uncertain that every daybreak is a miracle, almost a triumph. That first blush in the sky is all the hope of the world distilled into light. I watch the dark fade, and say to myself, "Okay, I'm still here," and the more sunrises I see, the more I feel as if I'll live to see another twenty thousand.*

The seams in the beam-and-shiplap ceiling ran as straight as lasered lines, and each piece fit as tight as in a completed puzzle.

The orderliness of the ceiling annoyed him. He switched off the nightstand lamp.

In the dream of the cellar maze, she came to him out of an unraveling shroud to say, *I am Maddison, who was Emily. Can you love me?* When he replied, *I already do,* he was happier than he had been in a long time — and afraid.

15

In his Porsche Cayenne, David departed Newport Beach at 6:40 Saturday morning and followed Interstate 405 north to Los Angeles. As he had felt in the crush of Manhattan and in Orange County's multitudes, so he also felt when he arrived in the City of Angels and its teeming suburbs at 7:50 — alone among the millions. The city was buzzing, and fast-moving traffic swarmed the freeways. Yet he imagined himself invisible to everyone, not a man at all, but a spirit in denial of his death, racing north in the mere idea of an automobile, a modern ghost motoring from one haunt to another.

Interstate 405 to US Highway 101, then west and northwest toward Oxnard, Ventura . . . Santa Barbara. Inland on State Route 154 to the Santa Ynez Valley, past Lake Cachuma, and then northeast on a county road of sun-fissured blacktop crumbling at the edges.

The six-acre parcel tucked into the low foothills of the San Rafael Mountains. The nearest town, Santa Ynez, lay more than ten miles away. These acres had once been part of a much larger property planted with grapes. The sun-graced valley boasted in excess of a hundred wineries; but for some reason, this enterprise had failed.

Most of the vines were rotted stumps. Others were withered, with looping tangles of dry and barren trailers. Wild mustard and grass and a wide variety of weeds had overtaken the vine rows, the regimented patterns of which could still be discerned, though not many more years would be required to erase what remained of the property's history as a vineyard.

Split-rail fencing, broken down in places by termites and dry rot, encircled the Jessup parcel. A more recent rickety gate of pipe and chain link defended the entrance to the driveway, and the two-story clapboard house stood well back from the county lane, behind a yard that had not been mown in years.

At 11:12, almost twenty minutes prior to his appointment, David parked on the shoulder of the road, near the driveway. Passing the town of Santa Ynez, he had phoned Stuart Ulrich, the current owner of the property, to report that he was in the neighborhood.

Weather had worn much of the paint from the old house. Dirt filmed windows as milky as the eyes of a long-blinded animal. The front porch steps were swaybacked, and balusters were missing from the railing.

In spite of its decrepitude, the house looked formidable and alive with menace, as though the evil done therein had not vacated the premises when Ronny Lee Jessup had been hauled off to prison, but remained and empowered some supernatural entity that took up residence and waited now to possess a visitor.

The horrendous history of the house made the property a hard if not impossible sell. Stuart Ulrich had acquired it for a pittance of unpaid back taxes.

He had for a while conducted tours of the place. A surprising number of curious people with an interest in the macabre had paid for the privilege of inspecting the subterranean rooms where so many innocent women had endured so much terror and misery. Business had been best at Halloween.

The house also made money for Ulrich when a documentary about Ronny was filmed there, and again when a low-budget horror movie used the property for a fictionalized version of the true story.

David figured that those drawn to this house of murder must be sick specimens, yet here he found himself. However, he wasn't drawn by the thrill of the abominations committed in this place. Instead, as the years passed, he had increasingly come to believe — or hope — that something he would see in this cellar maze would either give him a clue to Emily's fate or provide a salient detail that he could use to pry the truth from Ronny Lee Jessup.

Sitting in his SUV, waiting for Ulrich, he realized he'd become desperate for a resolution and a way forward with his life. How long could a man live in desperation, heart riddled with sorrow, before he might become as mad as Poe's grief-pierced narrator in "The Raven"?

Before leaving New York, he'd made arrangements by phone with Ulrich. He had claimed to be writing a book about Jessup. Ronny was old news in this darkening world that produced greater horrors by the week, and the house had long ago ceased to draw the morbid curious. Ulrich smelled a revenue stream and wanted five thousand dollars for a first tour. He settled for twenty-two hundred, which David had wired to the man's account prior to flying west.

Now Ulrich arrived in a Ford pickup and parked in front of David. The driveway lay between their vehicles. They met at the gate.

Ulrich proved to be about forty, maybe two inches short of six feet, lean and sinewy,

70

with a high brow and a low, wide jaw like a scoop. He was as solemn as if he were an animated cadaver. When they shook hands, his was cool and moist.

"Any photos you put in your book, I'll need a separate fee."

"I don't intend to take photographs. I don't have a camera."

"You got yourself a smartphone, sure enough. I'm just sayin', so there's no argument later."

"I understand."

Ulrich keyed open the padlock on the gate. "We'll walk from here. I don't allow no one to drive right up to the house. Too damn easy to sneak some souvenir into their car and drive off with it."

The long, rising driveway was hard-packed earth with embedded gravel, stubbled with weeds that crackled underfoot.

"Not that there's any crap left worth stealin'. Sold off the furniture, dishes, all that. Only thing brought any real money was from the cellar. An armoire, chairs, a few headboards from beds he had down there. Doors from the rooms where he locked them women."

David wondered what kind of dark-minded people wanted items from the abattoir of a rapist-murderer and how Stuart

Ulrich knew where to advertise to attract their attention.

"Had some damn serious offers, could've made good money from his mattresses. But the FBI hauled 'em out to some lab to test 'em for who the hell knows what and never did give 'em back."

Hidden crickets sang in the tall brown grass, and small clouds of midges danced across the ragged lawn, sparkling like specks of glitter in the morning sunlight.

"What's the FBI doin' anyway, bustin' in here after Jessup's been found out and arrested by the sheriff? He weren't a threat to no one by then."

"It was their Critical Incident Response Group," David said. "Behavioral Analysis Units Three and Four. A few times Ronny Jessup crossed state lines to snatch his victims. The Bureau is tasked with putting together the evidence for the federal prosecutor."

As they stepped off the driveway and onto the lawn, moving toward the porch steps, Ulrich said, "Shit, Jessup pleaded guilty. It didn't go to no damn trial. But they never did bring back even one of 'em valuable mattresses."

Seven big crows perched on the ridgeline of the roof, peering down at them, like guardian totems put there not to ward off evil but to repulse whatever forces of good might come to reclaim this place of incalculable abominations.

The loose steps rattled underfoot, and the porch floor creaked.

Ulrich unlocked the deadbolt and pushed the door open. "There's electricity, so there's light. Do whatever it is you need to do. I'll be in my truck when you're done."

In the shade of the porch, the man's gray eyes were bright, direct, and keenly inquisitive.

David had the curious thought that, at night with no light but the moon, Ulrich's stare would shine like those of lantern-eyed coyotes on the hunt.

"If you'll leave me the key, I'll lock up."

Pocketing it, Ulrich said, "I'll do the lockin' myself after you're gone and I've done the usual inspection."

16

Nothing screamed *murder house*. Well-crafted narrow-plank oak floors long in need of refinishing. Dusty moth-eaten draperies, some closed, others open. A long-neglected ill-fitted living room window where years of rain, leaking under the bottom sash, had rotted the sill, stained the wall below, and damaged the flooring. Flowered wallpaper yellowed in swaths where sunshine had traveled past an undraped window. A brick firebox framed with oak columns supporting a carved mantel. Large ceiling fixtures of glass were etched with garlands of ivy, and shadows of those patterns fell in faint reflection on the floors.

David imagined that once there had been wood-legged sofas and armchairs with crocheted antimacassars on the upholstered arms and headrests. A collection of figurines in the recessed shelves that flanked the fireplace. Perhaps a grandfather clock ticking in the hallway.

The mother who had willed this property to Ronny when he was twenty-six had most likely been so genteel that she lacked the experience and capacity to wonder even for a moment if her gentle-giant son might be a monster.

David had no need to explore the second floor. It would be no different from the first. No outrages had been committed up there. The house was like the murderer himself: The horrors were not to be found in the public rooms, but were restricted to the windowless spaces below.

The cellar could be accessed only from

the kitchen. Like all the interior ground-floor doors, this one was made of two-inch-thick solid-core oak. It stood ajar.

The door was hinged on the kitchen side. He opened it wider, pulling it toward him, and saw that the two deadbolt locks were blind set, with no escutcheon, keyhole, or knob on the cellar side. If a captive had escaped her cell, she could not have gotten through this barrier with other than an axe.

David wondered why Ulrich had not sold this door of doors when he'd sold those from the cells below. Perhaps even in this callous and shameless age, there were not sufficient connoisseurs of cruelty with whom to place all the available product.

David stepped onto the landing and flipped the wall switch. Light bloomed on the stairs and below. Ronny Jessup had installed tinted bulbs from which issued a rose-colored glow.

For minutes David stood at the top of the stairs, considering the place below as not a hard passage of his life to be endured, but as a scene in a novel. Writing fiction, he maintained control, had the final decision on what events would occur and what their meaning would be, as in life he nearly never did.

When he felt a calm at the center of his

mind, when the silence of the house became a deeper silence, he went down the stairs.

17

At the foot of the stairs was a steel-bar gate, at the moment standing open. Beyond the gate lay what Ronny Lee Jessup called the "receiving room." He had finished the block walls with plasterboard painted a glossy waterproof white and had applied multiple coats of sealant to the concrete floor to make it easier to clean when one of his games got messy.

He had relied on his physical advantage, his size and great strength, to subdue a woman initially, but then used chloroform to keep her quiescent during transport. He bought acetone from an art supply store, bleaching powder from a janitorial supply, and brewed the chloroform himself from acetone by the reaction of chloride of lime. While maintaining his captive in sedation, Jessup carried her through the house, down the stairs, into the receiving room, where he placed her in a lounge chair.

He had then secured the gate to the stairs with a combination lock to which only he knew the five-digit release code.

If he'd needed to bind the captive's hands

and feet, then as she lay in the lounge chair, he cut those bonds. He applied no more chloroform. He removed her jacket or coat if she wore one, took off her shoes to deny her the chance of delivering an effective crotch kick, and waited for her to awaken.

When she was fully conscious, he explained that her life would now last only as long as she pleased him and was of use to him — unless she was smart enough, in the next fifteen minutes, to find her way out of the cellar maze by the secret exit.

Jessup had told David that, when giving what he called this "orientation speech," he had often wept with the terrified captive, and sometimes wept even when she didn't. *It was such a terribly sad moment, Mr. Thorne, very damn sad and exciting all at once.* This was no doubt true, for he was a homicidal psychopathic sentimentalist with an intense and disorganized emotional life.

It was *not* true, however, that the captive might find a secret exit. There was no secret exit from that prison, only the stairs beyond the gate.

You'd be surprised, Mr. Thorne, how nearly all them believed it, poor things. How much they wanted hope when they should have known there weren't none. Broke my heart every time, it really did.

77

During the fifteen minutes when the woman still might have had hope, he followed close behind her. From time to time, he snared her and removed — or tore off or cut off — another piece of her clothing, until she was naked when her time ran out.

At some point in her desperate search for an exit, she would try locked doors and hear the cries of the women imprisoned behind them. Perhaps her hope then diminished. And if she still held fast to hope in full strength after that, the bleakness of her situation couldn't be entirely denied when she fled into the room where Jessup kept the wrapped bodies of his mummified future harem.

When the house had been heated and cooled, perhaps fresh air moved through this lower realm. But now there was a dank smell and the muskiness of mildew.

Before exploring farther, David returned to the stairs and gazed at the open door at the top. His psychological vulnerability encouraged a sense of physical jeopardy as well.

Whatever he might be, however, Stuart Ulrich was not the serial killer who had ruled this domain for almost twenty years.

Anyway, David had wired the man twenty-two hundred dollars for this tour and had spoken to him more than once on the phone. If he disappeared, there was a trail to follow.

It made no sense to fear that Ulrich would imprison him. The apprehension he felt, the claustrophobia, wasn't occasioned by any risk he faced, but by empathy for the women who had perished here — and by the dread that Emily Carlino might have come awake in this receiving room with the sweet taste of chloroform on her tongue, under the pitying, hungry, honey-brown stare of Ronny Lee Jessup.

The seven rooms that Jessup added to the original four were not connected by one straight hallway, but rather by a warren of narrow passages designed to facilitate exciting chases and tense hunts. The cunning architecture made it difficult for David to know whether he was revisiting a section already inspected. He took a pair of one-dollar bills from his wallet and tore them and dropped small pieces on the floor like Hansel on some macabre search for Gretel.

The rose-colored light bulbs were everywhere. Apparently, to Jessup's eye, his naked prey looked most alluring in rose light.

The labyrinth had supposedly been kept immaculate when the killer played his games here. Now some of the plasterboard featured water stains. In places, mold grew in fractal designs, jet-black in this boudoir light, or webbed a wall in varicose-vein patterns.

Not only the beds and other furniture had been removed, but also whatever instruments or monstrous devices enhanced Jessup's pleasure when using his captives. For that, David was grateful.

According to Jessup, the five cells in which prisoners had been kept plus the mummy chamber had been fitted with doors, though the five "playrooms" had been accessed through open arches. Even if the doors had brought Ulrich a handsome price, he'd sold only five of the six, for David came to one still on its hinges.

The space beyond the threshold was about seventeen feet square and more detailed than other rooms. Sconces provided white light. The walls met at radiused corners rather than ninety-degree angles. In the center of the domed ten-foot ceiling, Jessup had embedded a ceramic tile on which was painted an eye with a bright-blue pupil.

The radiuses and the shallow dome created acoustics different from those of the other rooms. David's footfalls made a hollow sound and echoed along the curved surfaces.

Three walls were painted concrete block, but the back wall appeared to be made of railroad ties from floor to ceiling. Along that entire expanse were three rows of platforms, three platforms per row, the first row a foot off the floor. They were like nine bunk beds, embedded in the wood wall, made of lumber but laminated with white Formica.

He puzzled over them for a moment before realizing that they were catafalques. Here, the nine mummified women had been stored in their windings to await some magical Egyptian reanimation, courtesy of a heretofore unknown resurrecting power of electricity.

There were stains and thin crusts of some unthinkable material on the Formica, though only here and there, not as many as he would have expected. The floor was clean. No mold grew in this room, as though the eye in the dome had the power to forbid its cultivation.

For years he had avoided this man-made hell. He had come today only after ginning up the expectation that he'd recognize a subtle clue to the whereabouts of the additional fourteen mummified victims Jessup claimed to have hidden at some second site separate from this property. *I need to have my fourteen hidden, Mr. Thorne, to keep from*

81

having to steal new girls when I'm free again.
If Emily was among those fourteen, and if
her remains could be identified, she could
be laid to rest at last under a stone that bore
her name. But there was no clue. If there
had been, it would have been found by the
platoons of law enforcement that had
scoured these chambers for evidence. He
had harried himself here to stave off despair,
but had opened his heart to it instead.

18

The quiet calm at the center of David's
mind gave way to a chilling uneasiness. His
ability to set aside his profound personal
interest — the consideration of Emily's fate
— and explore this hideous place as if it
were a scene in a novel began to desert him.

When a character like Ronny Lee Jessup
had been at work here, such a scene in fiction would not have unfolded in silence, but
would have been furnished with grievous
sounds. David was a writer of considerable
imaginative power, and now he heard the
cries of the enslaved women as they cowered
behind their cell doors and listened to
Jessup chase down and violently rape or
murder one of their own.

In a sudden sweat, he exited the mummification room and moved along a narrow passage, anxious to exit this rose-colored realm. He thought he was near the receiving room at the foot of the stairs, but he didn't come to it as quickly as expected. The killer's modest playground seemed to metastasize into a vast and baffling labyrinth of tentacular corridors, undulant and ever changing, torn bits of dollar bills fluttering around his feet, too little treasure for him to buy his Gretel from the ranks of the swaddled dead. It would not have surprised him if he turned a corner and came face-to-face with the hulking form of Ronny Lee Jessup, the past having become the present, the imagined screams now as piercing as if they were real.

He was so relieved when he burst into the receiving room that he let out a cry of his own. He threw open the steel gate, climbed the stairs, and pushed through the upper door into the kitchen.

He leaned against a cabinet, striving to wring from himself a shrinking, anxious fear that anticipated imminent evil. He was in no danger. He had been overwhelmed by the claustrophobic nature of the cellar and by his ability to empathize with the women who'd suffered in those depths. He inhaled deeply through his nose, exhaled through

83

his mouth, and used rhythmic breathing to restore a sense that the world was an orderly place and that he could hold chaos at bay.

According to his wristwatch, he'd been in the basement thirty-five minutes. He remained in the kitchen for ten, until he was calm enough to leave the house and speak with Stuart Ulrich.

He descended the front porch steps and started across the yard toward the driveway but halted and looked back when the crows on the peak of the roof traded silence for raucous cries. They didn't fly from their perch but shrieked at him with seven times the mocking hatred of Poe's one raven, and though they didn't form the word, he knew that their message was the same as the raven's: *Nevermore.*

Stuart Ulrich saw him coming and got out of the Ford pickup. "I thought you'd be a lot longer."

"Enough's enough. It's a wretched, vicious place. You should pour gasoline down there and torch it all."

Ulrich worked his lantern jaw as if David's suggestion struck him as so outrageous that he could find no words to respond. Then: "Easy to say when it wasn't you sank his savin's in the property."

"You got it for nothing but back taxes."

84

"It wasn't nothin' to me, like maybe it would be to them like you that got all they'll ever need."

David didn't want to argue. He said, "I'm sorry, Mr. Ulrich. It just disturbed me more than I expected." But then he couldn't resist pressing an issue that would probably offend the man, even though he didn't make his inquiry in an accusative tone. "You said the doors of the cells sold for good money. If that's the case, why didn't you sell the door to the last room, the one where he kept the mummified women?"

The morning sun found green flecks in Ulrich's gray eyes, and his lips looked bloodless when he skinned them back from yellowing teeth. The virulence of Ulrich's response suggested a man with a short temper — or with something to hide. "What is it to you whether I sell a damn door or don't sell a damn door?"

Against his better judgment, David said, "Seems if you could find five sickos to buy five doors, you could find a sixth."

Ulrich's sinewy body seemed to twist itself tighter, like a length of braided jerky. "My reasons are my reasons, and I've every damn right to 'em. You don't own me or have any more answers comin' for a lousy twenty-two-hundred bucks. Be best for you if you

85

went away now and didn't ever think of comin' back."

By the time David got in his car and started the engine, Ulrich was hiking up the driveway toward the house, and the crows erupted from the roof as if in fright at his approach.

David wondered how long Ulrich would take to inspect the house for vandalism. How long, following that inspection, might he remain in the cellar — and what might he do down there?

19

David drove north on State Route 154 and then west on US Highway 101, which turned south at Gaviota. After several miles, he pulled off the southbound lanes to park where the shoulder widened into a coastal viewpoint capable of accommodating four or five vehicles. At the moment, he had the panoramic vista to himself.

He got out of the car and went to the railing and stood looking at the soft folds of grassland that sloped down a few hundred yards to a white beach. The pacified sea slumbered, hardly rolling in its sleep, stammering quietly on the shore as though whispering of its dreams.

In this lay-by, the highway patrol had found Emily's Buick the day after she disappeared. The key was in the ignition, but the engine would not turn over.

Her purse lay in the footwell that served the front passenger seat. The cash and credit cards hadn't been taken.

In the distance, south of this viewpoint, between the highway and the ocean, lay what seemed to be a horse ranch: a gabled and dormered white house, stables, fenced pastures. An equal distance to the north, a stubby peninsula thrust into the sea, and an impressive stone house stood on that headland, so solid in appearance that it might have been built to withstand the fate of humanity and harbor the last family at the end of time.

Expecting nothing to come of their inquiries, state and federal law enforcement had nevertheless spoken with those who lived in both residences, and their expectations had been fulfilled. Those people had seen nothing. The distance was too great. Furthermore, Emily had been taken from her broken-down Buick at night, in the rain, when visibility was dismal.

David turned from the sea and looked across the divided highway at the foothills of the Santa Ynez Mountains. One residence could be glimpsed far back from the roadway, at a greater distance than the houses on the ocean side.

Traffic sped south, raced north, their wakes of wind shuddering leaves and bits of litter across the viewpoint pavement, whirling up dust devils.

If anyone had seen anything suspicious occurring here that long-ago night, he or she would have been a motorist or a trucker. After midnight, however, the volume of traffic would have been lighter, and the violence of the storm would have further discouraged travel.

Here in the state with the highest population among the fifty, with the bustling northern suburbs of the Los Angeles metroplex less than two hours to the south, this overlook on that rain-swept night would have been not merely lonely, but desolate.

He had been here twice before, a year after she vanished. He'd come just to see the place, first in daylight. He had returned that night, though there had been no rain.

In sunshine and in darkness, with the sea grumbling louder than it did today, he had spoken her name aloud. Not because he expected some miraculous response. Not because he thought she, in some realm of spirits, might hear him. He stood in this terrible place where she had surely known piercing terror, and he spoke her name to shame himself, for that was the least part of the penance he owed for not having been with her on that night.

Now he said her name just once and got in the car and continued south.

He soon passed Goleta, adjacent to Santa Barbara, where Maddison Sutton lived. But he had no street address for her, only the post office box on her driver's license. Anyway, she was not there now, but in Newport Beach, pretending to be an assassin.

He drove fast and counted on the lighter traffic of a Saturday to get back to Orange County while an hour of daylight remained, because he still had tasks to which he must attend.

20

At 5:10 p.m., in Newport Beach, the shadows of the headstones yearned eastward across the gentle slopes and shallow vales of the cemetery, as if the spirits of those interred here had slept through death, only now to wake and wonder at their condition and strain to return to lives lost.

Unto this place David would bring her if

89

ever her remains were found. The memorial park was expensive, and a portion even offered views of the distant ocean, to which it referred in its brochures.

Evidently, for some people, the sting of death might to some extent be ameliorated by the prospect of moldering to bones in a plot of high-end real estate. And why not? No one could make a fool of himself in dying, regardless of his delusions; *life* was the stage for fools, and no one earned mockery by going to his grave.

David had waited seven years before purchasing the plot. Seven years after disappearing without a trace, a person can by law be declared legally dead.

Now he took his time approaching that final resting place, following a roundabout route through the memorial park, as he most often did, steeling himself for the sight of the plot, because the rest that it offered wasn't his yet and would not be his until he could lie there in death.

The previous year, at his request, the cemetery approved the installation of a headstone without names engraved. He didn't know why he felt it was essential to take that step. But he had become increasingly agitated by the absence of a grave marker. When it was completed a week before his birthday, his anxiety abated.

In the first hour after midnight on May 14 of that same year, his birthday, he had awakened from a dream and sat up in bed in his Corona del Mar cottage, struck by the realization that he had wanted the slab of granite erected not because he suspected Emily's remains would be found imminently, but because his own death would occur within a few years, maybe sooner.

In that birthday dream, he had seen himself in a casket, his face painted with a semblance of life by a good mortician, mourners filing past to the strains of somber music. The scene had dissolved to the cemetery, where his casket was lowered into an open grave.

They said no one ever saw his own death in a dream, that the subconscious fiercely denied mortality and would not countenance it even in the worst of nightmares. His subsequent researches seemed to support that contention. Nevertheless, he'd dreamed of his death.

The plot that he'd purchased provided two graves. The memorial stone at the head of it was wide enough for two names, two sets of dates, two epitaphs. If his heart never clarified and healed after Emily, if he never married, his intention always had been to be buried with her at his side, assuming that her body would eventually be found.

He didn't want to die. Somewhere in the depths of his heart, he believed he had earned his death by failing Emily. Nevertheless, he loved life and would hold fast to it as long as he could.

That birthday morning, he'd made an appointment with his attorney for the purpose of redrafting his will. If he should die before Emily was found, he would be buried in this cemetery, in the shade of a graceful California pepper tree, and when her remains were eventually located, they would be interred at his side.

Years earlier, he had been granted conservatorship of her small estate and the power of attorney allowing him to arrange for the disposition of her bones.

If one day his life changed and he married, he could always make different burial arrangements.

But he did not believe that he would ever marry. As vivid as his imagination was, he could not imagine a wedding, a wife.

Had his post-Emily friends known of her and of his fixation on making ready for centuries in the same plot, they would think it macabre and unlike him, an emotional overreaction.

They would be wrong. Since having the stone installed nearly a year earlier, he had been more at peace than at any time since that night of hard rain.

Although no names or dates were chiseled into the marker, an epitaph for both Emily and him had been cut into stone, her favorite lines from Shakespeare's "Sonnet 18": *Rough winds do shake the darling buds of May / And summer's lease hath all too short a date . . . / But thy eternal summer shall not fade.*

Even though she was not in this cemetery yet, he took comfort in each visit when he read those lines.

Now he came at last to his pepper-tree-shaded grave site, where in the branches birds trilled as if in celebration of day's end.

In the plinth on which the gravestone stood, a round recess provided a sleeve in which a container of flowers could be placed.

He had not brought flowers, but someone else had made use of the recess. The milk-glass vase held half a dozen calla lilies, each large white spathe presenting its proud yellow spike, and the bouquet was tied with a length of blue ribbon.

■ ■ ■ ■

PART 2
ONE HEART
BEATING,
ONE HEART STILL

■ ■ ■ ■

21

Though blind, Calista lived in the first-floor apartment in a Balboa Island house with a sweeping view of Newport Harbor. She spent a lot of time on the generous deck that came with her unit, for she enjoyed the smell of the sea and the jasmine that grew in her ceramic pots, the warmth of the sun, the freshness of ocean breezes, the sounds of boat traffic, the chuckle and slap of water against dock pilings, the flight calls of the gulls, the mournful warning note of the channel-entrance foghorn on socked-in nights, and the conversations she engaged in with people who strolled or cycled along the public promenade onto which her deck faced.

When David had bought the house eleven years earlier, he had not told her its location. With Emily, he had walked Calista into the first-floor unit, toured it with her so she could feel the comfort of its rooms, and then escorted her onto the deck, where she first realized that she was on the harbor. If he had not presented the apartment as a fait accompli, she would not have agreed to it. Even so, she had been appalled by what the cost must be, and she could not understand why she deserved such generosity.

"Generosity has nothing to do with it," David had said. "It's what your daughter wants. Without her, I wouldn't be a publishing phenom. I was writing short stories for little pay before she gave me the ideas for my first two novels. I owe her more than what this costs. Anyway, it's a terrific investment."

This evening, he called Calista en route to ask if he could visit, and she invited him for dinner. "Maria cooked a scrumptious brisket and left a rice-and-beans casserole, and as we speak, I'm making a salad."

Maria Alvarez shopped and cooked, her sister Josefa did the cleaning, and one or the other of them looked after Calista for a few hours every day, though the indomitable Mrs. Carlino could otherwise take care of herself. In fact, even after all this time, she complained to David that he was pampering her inexcusably by providing this level of care.

When she answered the door, she was

wearing white athletic shoes and a white kimono with a spare pattern of red hibiscus. She placed a hand on his chest and leaned in unerringly to kiss his cheek. "What a sweet surprise," she said. "I've missed you, child."

"I've missed you, too, Calista. Very much."

When he was in Manhattan, he called her once a week, and when here in Newport, he visited often.

Her blue eyes searched his face as though they could map his features and know his mood by some sense other than sight. "Are you all right, David?"

"I'm fine. I should have called you from New York to let you know I was coming, but events got away from me."

As she welcomed him into the apartment and closed the door, she said, "I was going to eat from my special tray with its separate little compartments, but now that you're here, we can use plates if you'll just set the table. It's warm enough to dine on the deck."

She had a stainless-steel cart with which she wheeled food and utensils to the table where she was taking her meal. He used it to transport plates and napkins and whatnot to the deck and then to convey the salads, rolls, and wine.

She moved with ease about the apartment and onto the deck, the steps between one thing and another counted so often and memorized so completely that she didn't consciously count them anymore, but she knew her way as instinctively as a fish swimming in the depth of a night sea knows what temperatures it must seek and currents it must follow to go where it wishes and find what it needs.

She had been blind since the age of six, when her severely alcoholic mother failed to seek medical treatment for Calista's eye infection and chose instead to treat it with herbal remedies more in line with her faith in holistic healing.

Calista's husband — Emily's father — married with the expectation that a blind woman could be easily controlled, oppressed, abused. Five years later, realizing his error, he abandoned wife and child when Emily was four. Mother and daughter had lived a hardscrabble life for a long time thereafter.

Seated at the table, Calista slid the index finger of her right hand around the curve of the salad plate and then reached for the wineglass where it ought to be. David had put it precisely at one o'clock, as she had known he would.

"A toast," she said. "To the most precious son I never had."

"And to you, dear lady, in memory of the mother I never knew."

His mother had died in childbirth.

She waited for him to clink her glass with his, and then they drank.

"Have we a sunset?" she asked.

"The last of one. Scarlet veined with turquoise in the west, every white yacht in the harbor pinked by reflection, light in the darkling water like garlands of radiant roses floating just below the surface. The birds have gone to their roosts, and the sky in the east is midnight blue, waning to black, diamonded with early stars."

"I suspect you'd describe a wonderful sunset for me even if night had already fallen."

The scene was as he described it; but he hadn't looked away from her face while he painted that word picture. At sixty, she was still quite lovely.

Having gone blind so early in childhood, she had never seen how beautiful she'd been as a young woman, and she had never seen that her daughter, Emily, had been even more beautiful.

As night took dominion, the deck lamps came on automatically, laying down a glow as soft as the scent of the jasmine.

"How is your father?" she asked. "Tell me things have been repaired between you."

"We're cordial," David said. "Better than in past years. But he'll never stop being embarrassed that his only son is a popular novelist rather than an investment banker."

"I don't understand that at all. Your novels are marvelous. I listen to them over and over on audio."

"It's the fact of their popularity that dismays him."

"How perfectly silly."

"Well, he comes from a family of intellectuals. They distrust the taste of the average man and woman. Nothing can be of quality unless it's formed by the right ideas held by the proper people and offensive to the bourgeoisie mind. I have no patience for any of that. The salad is quite good."

During dinner, they caught up with each other's lives, and over coffee, he said, "I was at the cemetery this afternoon."

"There's nothing you can do, David. Nothing either of us can do. Don't torture yourself with the cemetery."

"It's not torture. Really it's not. I find a kind of peace there," he said, which was in fact sometimes the case. "Anyway, I mention it only because someone had recently left flowers."

She frowned. "At a grave without names on the stone?"

"You're the only one who knows what names are intended for it. I thought maybe you sent the flowers."

"Oh, no, dear. I've hoped all these years, I still hope, and I'll continue to hope until the day I die that she'll walk in one morning with an amazing story. I'll never put flowers on her grave until I know beyond doubt that I can't put the bouquet in her arms."

22

When David got home, he checked his emails and found one from Isaac Eisenstein.

According to the private investigator, nobody named Marcus Sutton worked as an executive at Microsoft. The Seattle district attorney's office employed no prosecutor named Claire Sutton.

If Maddison Sutton had been born in Seattle, no record of the event existed, no birth certificate.

No property in either Goleta or adjacent Santa Barbara was owned by Maddison Sutton, but she might be a renter.

The email concluded with: Call me on my

personal cell.

Attached was a photo of Patrick Michael Lynam Corley, who had died seven years earlier and to whom the vintage Mercedes 450 SL was registered. He had been a fresh-faced stocky man with thick white hair and a winning smile.

Although it was midnight in New York, Isaac seldom went to bed before one in the morning. He got by on five hours of sleep a night and sometimes seemed on a sugar high without benefit of sugar.

After pouring brandy into a snifter and settling behind his desk in the study, David placed the call.

Isaac answered on the third ring. "My second-favorite writer."

"Who's number one?"

"Privileged info, boychik. Rest assured, it's not his literary excellence that ranks him above you. He routinely gets himself in the most imaginative kinds of trouble, so he's one of my top twenty billings just about every year. Have you shtupped that stunning girl yet?"

"Privileged info."

"Yeah, so you struck out. Maybe it's just as well."

"How so?"

"Something's not kosher about this cutie.

A valued source of mine says he's ninety-five percent sure her driver's license and the registration for that 450 SL are phantom inserts in the DMV files."

"Which means?"

"They're forgeries that were backdoored into the state system. They'll stand up to any police check, but she never took a driver's test or paid a registration fee for the Mercedes. It was all done with digital finesse."

"Even if he's right, there's still a five percent chance she's on the up-and-up."

"Actually, my guy's ninety-*nine* percent sure they're phantom inserts. I just wanted to give you a little more room to see if you'd leap to defend her. Listen to me, pal. Be careful with this. Think with your head, not your dick."

David swirled the brandy in the snifter. "What if I'm thinking with my heart?"

"Armageddon. Thinking with your dick, pretty much the worst you can get is a curable disease."

David sipped his drink.

"Thinking with your heart," Isaac continued, "you can be ruined forever. What's that, port or brandy?"

"How do you know it's anything? You smell it over the phone?"

"You made a swallowing sound. I know your tastes, and I don't figure you were choked up about my wise advice."

"You're a modern Sherlock."

"I never claimed less."

"Why the photo of Patrick Corley?"

"Patrick Michael Lynam Corley. If a man wants to assert his Irishness with four names, who am I to call him by two? I wanted you to see him so you'd have a reference when I report on him tomorrow."

"Why not report now?"

"I'm still getting feedback from people who knew him. It's not just that this Maddison Sutton is driving a car registered to this guy. Patrick Michael Lynam Corley has taken this investigation into some very weird territory. I don't want to get into that until I've spoken to a couple more people about him."

"How can he take the investigation anywhere, weird or not? He's been dead for seven years."

"Maybe yes. Maybe no. Keep your pants zipped, boychik, until Uncle Isaac tells you otherwise. And if you're listening to your heart again, quickly drink yourself unconscious."

23

The restaurant was a few steps down from the street, funky but clean, romantically lighted even for a Sunday lunch. David arrived first and was seated in a booth in a private back corner of the room.

When Maddison entered in white slacks, matching jacket, and a blouse the precise blue of her eyes, it was as if spring personified had stepped in from the street. She came directly to him and slid into the booth.

"You look refreshed, David. Your Saturday business must have gone well."

"Not as well as I would have liked. And how was *your* Saturday? Did you kill anyone?"

"No, dear. The job is set for this evening."

"I thought we were spending the day together."

"I'd like nothing better, but we have only the afternoon." She winked at him. "The evening is for murder."

"May I ask who the victim will be?"

"If I told you, then you would be an accessory. The last thing I want is to see you in prison. Orange is not your color. Besides, how could our relationship blossom with bars between us?"

The waitress came with menus, and they

ordered glasses of a Meritage.

When they were alone again, David said, "Don't you worry about winding up behind bars yourself?"

Perusing the menu, she said, "Not possible. I'm a ghost in the machine. The blackened halibut is perfection. So are the scallops with fettuccini."

He should have been annoyed that she still maintained this assassin charade, but he wasn't. She intended it as a metaphor. His task was to figure out what she really meant.

After lunch, they followed the bluff path through the long seaside park north of Laguna's main beach, pausing at each viewpoint to watch the waves spill across the tortoiseshell rocks below.

Pelicans glided on air currents without an exertion of wings, dolphins arced in and out of the water, sandpipers strutted along the shore, plein air painters strove to make canvas as luminous as the reality before them, and with Maddison at his side, David felt more a part of the vibrant life of the world than at any time in years.

As they shared the day, he kept thinking about the dozen calla lilies tied with blue ribbon and left in the vase sleeve in the gravestone that as yet was not carved with names.

He didn't want to challenge her, to risk any breach in whatever bond was forming between them. There might be an explanation for the deceptions with which Isaac Eisenstein had charged her, a credible reason that would in the end exonerate her of any ill intent. Good people sometimes told lies out of desperate necessity. Whatever the truth of her, he felt that he owed her the benefit of the doubt. She was too like Emily to harbor true darkness in her heart. Emily had been woven through with light. Maddison might be in a jam, deep in debt to someone — or afraid of someone — who had power over her, but nonetheless as innocent as Emily.

Even as he made excuses for her, David understood his own bent psychology. Ten years earlier, in part by his own fault, he had lost one life as it was meant to be, the one life he most wanted; and now by virtue of this woman's remarkable resemblance to Emily, it seemed as if that ruined life could be restored, the past undone, the lost future regained. He was not enchanted by her looks alone. Her voice, too, was akin to Emily Carlino's, her mannerisms, her sharp wit, her intelligence. Her kiss. She had kissed him only once, outside the restaurant as they waited for the valet to bring her car.

She'd put a hand to the back of his head and drawn his face down to hers, as Emily had done from time to time; her kiss was eerily familiar, deep yet discreet, as if she were taking a taste of some delicacy far too fine for this world.

By the time they reached the north end of the park and were returning along the bluff, holding hands, he broached the subject without mentioning the cemetery. Referring to the grave would be tantamount to asking her if she were researching and stalking him. Therefore, he said simply, "Someone, I don't know who, left flowers for me yesterday."

Neither by the pressure with which her hand gripped his nor by any other tell did she reveal a recognition that his statement was a subtle interrogation. "Didn't they come with a card?"

"No."

"You have a secret admirer."

"I guess I do, strange as it sounds."

"It's supposed to be the girl who gets the flowers."

"I'd have sent you a huge bouquet if I knew where you're staying."

"Well, of course, I'm at the Island Hotel," she said, almost as though she must be aware that he had followed her there on the night they met. "But don't send flowers, David. I might not be staying there much longer, and I'd hate to leave them behind while they're fresh and lovely."

Golden sunlight spangled the sea, as though Midas had gone for a swim and transformed the water into a treasure, and the palm trees cast shadows as royal purple as they were black, and flecks of some mineral sparkled like tiny diamonds in the pathway pavement, as if the park were a king's garden in which a bespelled princess waited to be awakened.

She said, "Maybe the flowers aren't for you. Maybe they were for the girl next door."

"The 'girl' who lives next door is eighty years old."

"If someone loves her, she's still a girl to him."

It occurred to David that by 'girl next door,' she might have meant Emily, for whom half the double-wide gravestone was reserved.

They had parked in the same public lot.

At her car, he said, "When will I see you again?"

"Soon. Very soon. I'll be free for a while after I attend to this evening's unpleasant task."

111

"The assassination."

She smiled, shrugged, and seemed to be acknowledging that they both understood her claim of being an assassin was a mere fantasy, that whatever task awaited her was mundane even if nevertheless unpleasant.

And yet . . . this time she kissed him not on the mouth but on the cheek, with a certain solemnity, as if greater passion were inappropriate with murder in the wind.

He watched her until she drove out of the lot and out of sight.

He was weak with a desire that was more longing than appetite, a craving to set right the great wrong of his past. His heart felt swollen and yet empty in her absence. He told himself that he did not know Maddison well enough to love her, but he felt as if he'd known and cherished her for half his lifetime.

Whatever the answer to the mystery of this woman might be, David Thorne believed that what he felt for her was right and true, that if they couldn't make a future together, he would have no future at all and no reason to want one.

In his SUV, on the way home, his mind filled with memories of Emily, a montage of moments and images. By the time he pulled into his garage, he was irrationally convinced that somehow he had found her, that for Emily time had stood still. If he were invited to undress Maddison Sutton, would he discover a symmetrical, flat, golden birthmark an inch below her navel, the very one that he'd so often kissed, that he had claimed tasted like honey?

24

The night received the day, and the scarlet sunset burned into blackness in the west, leaving the sea to reflect only the lamp of an early moon.

At 6:50 p.m., David was about to drop pasta in a pot of boiling water, preparing a dinner of linguini in butter with roasted pine nuts and Parmesan cheese, broccoli on the side — a meal that Emily had often prepared — when Isaac Eisenstein called from New York.

"Your cutie has a job, such as it is. She's one of the three directors of the Patrick Michael Lynam Corley Foundation. It's not a paid position."

David put down the box of pasta and leaned against the counter. "Which means what? What's this foundation do?"

"Its resources aren't enormous. It's not like the Ford or the Gates Foundations.

They make about a hundred thousand a year in grants to various academics studying the effects of new technology on society."

"They need three directors for that?"

"It's how these things work. Here's an interesting factoid. The other two directors are ghosts. Try to background them, and you find several people with the same names, different SS numbers. None has anything to do with the Corley Foundation. As far as we know, your Maddison is the only director who's a real person."

"What do you make of that?"

"I don't make anything of it, my friend. What it *suggests* to me is that maybe you should forget this lady and use an online dating service. Or join a monastery."

Sinuous curls of steam rose from the boiling water in the pot. They looked like a series of question marks without the dots.

"For the time being," David said, "I'm giving her the benefit of the doubt."

"Have you been hooked and reeled in or what? *Hoo-ha.*"

"There has to be trust in every relationship."

"Hoo-ha!"

"Don't hoo-ha me. Change my mind with facts. Yesterday you said all this had taken a

114

weird turn because of Patrick Corley. You said maybe he's been dead seven years, maybe not."

"A PI from Santa Barbara, Lew Ross, did all the local footwork for me out there. You'll see it on your bill."

David sighed. "Maybe I better write an extra book to pay for this."

"According to Lew, Corley was in a supermarket when he had a massive heart attack. The guy was dead before paramedics got there. Because there was no living family, a director of his foundation signed to release the body from the morgue. Maddison Sutton."

"Seven years ago, she'd have been like eighteen. Can you be a foundation director at eighteen?"

A soft, fluttery tapping drew his attention to the window above the sink. Only darkness beyond the glass. Maybe the sound had been that of a frenzied moth seeking the solace of light.

Isaac said, "More interesting is what happened to Corley's body. She hired Churchill's Funeral Home in Santa Barbara to collect the remains from the morgue, install them in an airtight casket, and deliver them to the Corley Foundation. She didn't want the body to be embalmed or in any way

115

whatsoever prepared for viewing."

"Did they cremate it or what?"

"She didn't explain herself to the mortician. She just claimed a religious objection to modern mortuary practices. And she had this certificate of exemption from state interment laws, granting the foundation the right to bury its founder on its property."

The tapping again. Nothing but darkness at the window above the sink. Only darkness at the window in the door to the back porch.

"What property?" he asked.

"A house and five acres north of Goleta. Lew Ross is pretty sure that's not just the foundation office but also where Maddison Sutton lives."

"With whom?"

" 'With whom,' he asks. You're pathetic, pal. You're lost, gone, bewitched. Might as well buy the ring and change your name to Mr. Sutton."

"With whom?" David persisted.

"Maybe with no one. Like I said, the place is on acreage. No immediate neighbor. No one is currently answering the door. I wish I could say the lady is in a ménage à trois with two bodybuilders who will bust your ass if you touch her, so then I could save you from yourself."

"Maybe *she'll* save me from myself."

After a silence, Isaac said, "You're scaring me, boychik."

"Send me the report you received from Lew Ross."

"As soon as we hang up. Read it and think. The key word is *think.* You need to maybe do more of that. There's another thing you'll find interesting in Lew's report. Patrick Michael Lynam Corley died seven years ago . . . but he's been seen since."

"What does that mean? Seen when, where?"

"Three times. The first was five years ago."

"Where?"

"This guy named Markham was taking a dawn walk on the beach. No one in sight. But then he sees Corley coming the other way, keeping his head down, as if searching for shells. Back in the day, Corley had built Markham's house."

Holding the phone in his right hand, David reached with his left to grip the draw cord and lower the pleated shade over the window above the sink.

"Markham calls out to Corley, but the man keeps going, head down. Markham blocks his way. Turns out this isn't Patrick Michael Lynam himself, but his twin brother, Phelim Kearney Corley, who's

117

visiting the foundation for a few days to familiarize himself with Patrick's legacy."

Letting go of the shade cord, frowning, David said, "Why're you trying to ghost story me, Isaac? You said *Patrick* was seen after his death."

"We can't get any background on this Maddison that checks out. She's a cipher. But Patrick Corley lived his whole life in Goleta and Santa Barbara, and we know everything about him, practically down to what he ate for breakfast every day and how often he had constipation. We know for certain he didn't have a twin brother named Phelim or anything else. He was an only child."

David stared at the window in the back door. He could see his reflection faded like the semitransparent figure of a spirit that had escaped the confines of a casket and the pressing weight of a gravestone. "What am I supposed to make of Markham's story?"

"Besotted with the lady as you are, my friend, I don't know what the hell you'll make of it, except probably too little. What *I* make of it is that, when it comes to this Maddison doll, nothing is what it seems to be. You're reasonably famous and you've got money, so you're a target. Keep that in mind."

"She's not a gold digger."

"You would know that — how?"

David avoided the question. "You said Corley's been seen three times since he died."

Isaac sighed. "It's a weird night in old Manhattan, David. A lot more sirens than usual, even more strange, angry people in the streets than we're accustomed to, one of those nights when you feel these canyons of stone are as fragile as glass, that something's coming and not something good. I just want to lie down with Pazia and go deaf to everything but her. The other two incidents are in Lew Ross's report. I'll send it to you as soon as we hang up."

"I do appreciate your work, Isaac. I know I can always rely on you, and that's a rare thing in this world."

"You're a good friend, David. I care about you. Please don't screw up your life."

David restrained himself from saying, *I already did, a decade ago, before you ever knew me.*

25

After lowering the shade over the back-door window, he sat at the kitchen table with the nine-by-twelve six-inch-deep fabric-covered box that contained his collection of photographs of Emily, some of her alone and others of them together.

Until two nights earlier, he hadn't looked at these pictures in years because the sight of her caused him such pain and longing.

And guilt. He should have been with her on that rainy night. He had failed her before the Buick failed her. He had been a knave and a fool. His weakness had cost Emily her life and had cost him all hope of happiness.

The pain and the longing — and even the guilt — were less acute on this occasion, and David knew why. He wanted to believe the world was shapen to a plan, this layered world of infinite mysteries, that by something akin to a miracle, he was being given a precious second chance. Impossibly, inexplicably, a second chance. He needed to believe no less than he needed to breathe. Although Maddison Sutton was wrapped in mystery, though she sailed into his life on a sea of strangeness through which he would have to chart a course, he was convinced that she meant him no harm. When all was understood, all would be well. Perhaps in some way as yet beyond his comprehension, Emily's fate could be changed.

He sorted through the photographs with solemn tenderness, the past alive again and rising from every image to engulf him. He sat in remembrance for a long while before the familiar fear quickened in him, as it had done in years past when he dared these pictures: the dread that Emily was still alive somewhere, anguished and tormented. She'd never been found. Therefore, it was not beyond possibility that she was alive in some ghastly circumstances, that after a decade, she remained imprisoned and had no surcease from suffering.

This dread became so intolerable that he put away the photos and closed the box.

For the first time since Isaac called, David remembered the pot on the stove. Half the water had boiled away. The linguini was still in the carton.

At the sink, as he refilled the pot, the tapping came again at the shade-covered window before him. The soft, frantic beating of a moth against the glass.

26

Except for the few sounds David made, the small house stood in absolute silence, as though the world outside its walls had ceased to exist, nothing now beyond its doors but eternal darkness and the end of time.

Over dinner, he read and reread the report from the private investigator in Santa Barbara, Lew Ross.

In addition to Samuel Markham, who had met Patrick Corley's nonexistent twin, Phelim, on the beach, two years after Corley had died in the supermarket, Ross had found two others who had seen him vividly alive subsequent to his death, the most recent less than a year previously.

On the second reading, he knew that, sooner or later, he would have to talk to the witnesses, face-to-face, and he did not read the report a third time.

After rinsing the dishes and flatware, after putting them in the dishwasher, he sat at the table with a mug of coffee that he did not drink, staring at the box of photographs that he wanted — and did not want — to review again. He put Lew Ross's report facedown atop the box.

He poured the coffee down the drain. He

filled the mug with ice and Scotch and carried it into the bedroom.

He did not desire music, could not tolerate television. He wanted only what he could not have.

Sitting up in bed, he sipped the whisky in the dark until, halfway through the contents of the mug, he thought he heard the moth again — if it had been a moth before — this time in the room with him. The whispery flutter of gossamer wings, the soft thumping of its body against whatever surface it contested. But there was no light to excite the insect, other than the cold glow of the digital alarm clock. In such blackness, if the bug couldn't fix itself to the small plastic window beyond which the green numbers timed the crawling night, it would settle elsewhere and fold its velvet-dust wings and wait for a brightness to occur. This moth didn't settle but became increasingly frenzied.

The wheels of David's well-oiled imagination spun in silent accompaniment to the tap-tap-tapping, and soon it seemed that the moth wasn't a moth, but a misapprehension, a misinterpretation. The sound wasn't a winged insect frantically throwing itself against an unyielding barrier, but was instead the feeble rapping of a hand, a wordless plea from some exhausted prisoner casketed and buried alive and near the end of her resources.

This was absurd, of course. No casket stood beside his bed, and no one was buried under the foundation of the house. But already his imagination had raced beyond that image conjured by Poe's famous story, "The Premature Burial," which had left an enduring impression on him since he had read it when he was thirteen.

However, neither reason nor the reassurance of Scotch on the rocks could forestall his imagination from proceeding to an even more macabre explanation of the sound. In his mind's eye, he saw again the crypt in Ronny Jessup's cellar, the room with radiused corners, the domed ceiling with one white ceramic tile on which someone had painted a single blue eye that once had gazed down on the mummified bodies of nine women. He saw — could not prevent his mind from tormenting him with — a figure standing in that gloom, under the never-blinking eye, costumed in unraveling white cotton bandages, feebly tapping on the locked door, beyond despair, barely still alive or barely alive *again*. If David listened closely enough, he could hear a sound in addition to the tapping, a faint and half-familiar voice calling his name.

He'd had too much Scotch and too little light. Usually he slept in darkness, but there were nights like this when he couldn't abide it. He turned on the nightstand lamp, switched it to its lowest setting, and got out of bed. He carried the mug into the adjoining bathroom and poured the Scotch and ice into the sink. When he had toileted and washed his hands, he returned to bed.

He saw no moth either in agitation or at rest. The tapping had stopped — and perhaps had never been real, merely an anguished murmur of his troubled heart.

In bed once more, he glanced at the clock. Ten minutes past midnight.

He told himself not to think, to blank his mind, or at least to conjure in his mind's eye a little movie of the sea breaking on the shore. Sometimes a mental image of rhythmic waves could lull him to sleep.

He wondered if Maddison had finished her unpleasant task and whether it involved . . . being with another man. Maybe that's what she meant by *assassination*. Maybe she was in a loveless relationship with a man who had a cruel hold on her; every time she went into his bed, she might feel as if she were killing a small part of herself, so that she was both assassin and victim.

David could not bear the thought of Maddison with another man. He forced himself to concentrate on an image of night surf rolling rhythmically to a moonlit shore, phosphorescent foam surging on a smoothness of sand and fanning out in pale arcs that sparkled like galaxies of stars, that smelled faintly of the sea.

At 1:40 in the morning, she came warm and naked into his bed, smelling neither of the sea nor of any man, but only of herself, whispering his name. "Davey, Davey, my sweet Davey."

27

Even with the confirmation of low lamplight, he thought he must be dreaming, but her kisses woke him to the reality of her presence. Her kisses and her exploring hands. The contours of her body were as familiar as those of his own, but no less exciting for being so well known to him.

He hadn't set the alarm system; he seldom did when he was at home. But he had locked the door. He was pretty sure he had locked the door. However, the moment was so exhilarating, this fulfillment of his most ardent wish so intoxicating, that he didn't question how she'd gotten into the house. It didn't matter. All that mattered was that *she was here.*

"Davey, my sweet Davey." Maddison had not before called him Davey, but Emily often had. Like Emily, Maddison was not meekly submissive but an equal partner, and when joined they were not two in pursuit of their pleasures, but one in rapture. He was lost less in the physical sensations of their coupling than transported by a passion of mind and heart, by delight in her satisfaction, by the wonder of her existence, by astonishment at this reunion. He called her Maddison, but a few times he slipped and spoke Emily's name. When he said that he was sorry, she hushed him and whispered, "It's all right, all right, all right. I'm whoever you need, Davey. I'm me and her — and yours."

The first time wasn't quick, but it wasn't as slow as David wished. However, they were so energized by pent-up yearning that they needed no pause before continuing. There wasn't a single moment of awkwardness to any of it, not one instant of bestial awareness or ugly mechanics, not a surrendering but a sharing, not a taking but a giving, each breathless raveling up followed

127

by a long, silken unraveling. And throughout, he felt the world, which had for so long been wobbling on its axis, now establishing a right rotation, the broken past being repaired moment by moment, his long-lost future resolving into view once more.

A still, small voice within cautioned that this might not be the knitting together of a torn destiny. Not all mysteries, when solved, revealed a world of exquisite design or benign intention. Enigmas of physics, when deciphered, might produce a sublime light, but the answers to mysteries of human behavior seldom resulted in glorious revelations.

He heard this inner voice but discarded the warning that it conveyed. Maybe Maddison was trapped in an oppressive relationship. Maybe someone had a hold on her that required of her actions that she despised, so she felt as though she were killing herself with a thousand self-inflicted wounds, resulting in the unsettling metaphor of assassination. He could have listed a hundred maybes, and every one would have justified his trust in her.

Now he gave himself to her, lost himself in her, and fell asleep with her in his arms.

Sometime later, a continuous rhythmic murmur woke him. Still in a gauze of half sleep, he realized that he was alone in bed, and he raised his head, looking for the source of the voice.

In the soft lamplight, Maddison stood naked before the full-length mirror that hung beside the closet door. Whispering to her reflection, she slowly slid her hands over the voluptuous contours of her body. For all of Emily Carlino's sensuality, modesty had been a fundamental thread of her personality. Although Maddison Sutton could pass for Emily, this delight in her reflection, perhaps more than anything else, confirmed that she was a different person.

If he had not been twice spent, David might have been aroused by her performance, but he was weary, and sleep outbid libido. As he closed his eyes, allowing his mind to fade into dreams, her whisper grew more intense, so that for the first time he clearly could hear the words she spoke to herself.

"This is who you are. This is who you are and who you always will be . . . ."

28

Sunlight slashed through the gaps between the blades of the shutters, and the bedroom was striped with light and shadow when David woke alone shortly after dawn.

He didn't for an instant think the lovemaking had occurred in a dream. The sensation had been too intense and the emotion too overwhelming to have transpired in sleep, where fragmented fantasies of the unconscious mind lacked the continuity and nuance to turn the heart inside out, as his had been turned.

The robe he'd left on the chair was gone. Naked, he got another robe from the closet and put it on and went in search of Maddison.

He found her in the kitchen, barefoot, wearing his robe. Her clothes were scattered across a counter, where perhaps she had left them the previous night, before she'd come into his bed. She stood at the sink, treating her dress with a clear fluid that she squirted in a stream from a squeeze bottle that she had evidently removed from a nearby tote bag.

She was muttering angrily. "Take it, take it, take it, quick and sharp. Damn it, let go, damn it, be done. You want some more? I got more. Take it, be done."

When David arrived at her side, he saw that the pliable plastic bottle contained something called Perky Spotter. Large areas of the pale-yellow dress were wet with it. A

130

protein-eating ingredient in the spot remover metabolized a final stain the size of a hand, instantly sluicing away the color, a moment of alchemical magic so quick and complete in its effect that he could not be certain that the stain he'd seen had been blood.

She didn't look at him. She didn't seem to be aware of him.

"That's better." She was still red-faced though her anger had abated. "That's the way it ought to be." She shuddered violently. "Everything will be so much better now."

"Maddison?"

She stared at the dress. She set aside the spot remover.

"Maddison?" he repeated.

As if returning from some fugue state or mesmerizing memory, she looked at him and blinked, blinked. "Davey. I . . . I love this dress. I'll be just sick if it's not all right when it dries."

She hadn't been merely distressed about the dress. She'd been racked by strong emotion.

As the flush of anger faded from her face, she turned to him and embraced him and held him tightly as she pressed her face to his chest.

Even in these unsettling circumstances,

131

putting his arms around her was as natural as breathing. "What is all this? What's wrong?"

"All the bad that's ever happened," she said, "was made right with you last night."

"It's not just a game you've been playing. I've known it's not. You're in some kind of trouble, and I need to know what it is."

She looked at him. Her stare was direct, her eyes as deep as oceans. "It's not as bad as you might think. Anyway, I'll tell you everything in time. I promise. I swear. Every last little thing."

"Sit down with me here, now. Tell me now."

"Be patient, Davey. Give me breathing room. So very much is happening so very fast. I'm overwhelmed. Give me a few days, and I'll explain everything." She snatched the yellow dress from the counter, where it trailed into the sink. "I've got to hang this in the bathroom while I shower, keep it from wrinkling, let the spot remover evaporate. It's all I've got to wear." She plucked her undergarments from the counter and dropped them into the tote bag, which already contained a pair of white sling-back heels and other items he could not identify. "We belong together, and we will *be* together, and there won't be any secrets

132

between us."

She looked exactly like Emily, sounded like her, had her vivid personality, possessed that powerful *presence* he had never known anyone else to have. And though there had been nothing mysterious about Emily, who was always open and direct, Maddison's secrets only confirmed for him that, if she were not Emily herself, she offered him a way back to Emily. He didn't even know what he meant by that, but he *felt* it profoundly, knew it intuitively. Therefore, arguing with her would be like arguing with Emily, which he had never done, which he could not do, not while still living in the long shadow of the guilt he'd earned by failing her ten years earlier.

"Be patient," she repeated. "I've so much to do today, so much to be finished with. But there are beautiful days ahead of us."

As she picked up the tote and the dress and headed toward the hallway, David said, "Was that blood?"

She halted and glanced back at him. "What — the dress?" A light, seemingly genuine laugh escaped her. "No, no, no. Wine. Just wine."

"You always carry a bottle of spot remover?"

"A lot of the time, yeah. I can be such a klutz."

As far as he had seen, she was grace personified.

"Now I've really got to run," she said, and hurried off to take a shower.

29

On the windowsill by the back door, the house key gleamed in the morning sunlight, a mundane object yet as fateful looking as King Arthur's enchanted sword drawn from a block of stone. It had not been there when David had gone to bed the previous night.

When he picked up the key, it was warm in his hand.

He had not given her a key.

He stepped onto the back porch where two rocking chairs stood with a wrought-iron glass-topped table between them. He overturned one of the chairs and looked at the small key box attached to the frame. He pressed the lid, and it dropped open, revealing an empty container. He replaced the key and clicked the lid shut and put the chair upright.

He had never told her where the spare key was hidden. Emily had known, but Maddison had not.

Standing at the head of the porch steps, he regarded the roses as white as innocence and as red as blood. Barely stirred by a faint breeze, the Australian tree fern in one corner of the property cast a lazily undulant shadow like the wimpling fins of a manta ray.

David crossed the yard to the man-size door that served the two-stall garage. When he peered through the window, just enough light allowed him to see that only his car was parked inside.

He walked around the side of the garage. Her vintage Mercedes wasn't on the brick apron between the big roll-up doors and the alleyway blacktop.

When he went to the front of the house, her car was not parked anywhere along the block.

Once more in the kitchen, less because he wanted coffee than because he needed something to do, he brewed a pot. Like him, she took hers black.

In the hallway, as he carried two mugs to the master bedroom, he heard her talking softly to someone. As he crossed the threshold, she terminated the call and dropped the iPhone in her tote.

"You're a doll," she declared as she accepted the mug that he offered.

135

She wore a bra, panties, camisole, and high heels. She had dried her hair with a towel, but though it was still damp, it fell in an artful shag as black as raven's wings. Breathtakingly erotic, she nevertheless looked vulnerable as well, and suddenly David feared for her.

She took a long drink of the coffee — "Mmmmm" — and another. She carried the mug into the bathroom, put it on the granite countertop. The yellow dress hung from a hook on the back of the door. Maddison slipped it off the hanger and shrugged into it. "Zip me up?"

As he obliged her, he realized that in the night, when she had been naked and his to explore, he had failed to look for the small, flat, golden birthmark an inch below her navel. The light had been dim, and passion had pressed out all thought of satisfying that eccentric curiosity.

Connecting the tiny hook and eye at the apex of the zipper, he told himself there could be no birthmark identical to Emily's, for this wasn't the woman he lost. To believe she'd returned without having aged a day, to think that somehow she was Emily preserved and resurrected . . . Well, it would have been a little creepy to make love to her. No matter how desirable she was, no matter how much he wanted to erase the past ten years, no matter how he had been taken off guard when she slipped into his bed, he wouldn't have melted into her arms so easily if he genuinely embraced the possibility that she was the long-missing and thought-dead Emily.

Besides, no matter what the circumstances of her disappearance, Emily would not have made a mystery of her return to him, would not have toyed with him by claiming to be an assassin, or by leaving the flowers at the grave.

And what did it say about him that he would indulge Maddison's deceits and game playing in the hope that with her he could have at least a semblance, a simulation, of the life he might have had with Emily? Did he see her as a medicine for grief? A cure for guilt? Those were questions he needed to answer, but at the moment could not address. The mere presence of this woman left him without the power of introspection.

Anyway, the mystery of Maddison Sutton was not whether she was Emily Carlino. Her mysteries were many. How could she be a dead ringer for Emily? Why had she contrived to come into his life? She had planned that first encounter in the restaurant; he had no doubt of that. How did she know things that only he or Emily could know — where he kept the spare key, Emily's favorite color and flower and time of day, that a two-plot grave marker waited for names to be cut into the stone. How did she know the way that Emily kissed, as no other woman but Emily had ever kissed him like that?

To answer the questions related to his motives and the state of his heart, he first needed to resolve the mysteries of Maddison and understand with what intention she had come into his life.

When he'd fixed the eye to the hook at the neck of her dress, she turned to him and favored him with a deep and searching kiss.

Leaning back in his arms, she seemed to know his thoughts. "When you sat down next to me at the bar that first night and I realized who you were, I wanted to be part of your life because I'd read and reread your books. I *lived* in them, really, while I read them, and I loved the world you evoked, the way you saw life. I hoped you'd made a world for yourself like the one in your books, that you were what you write. And you are. You're so humble in spite of your success, considerate, funny, tender. I feel not only as though I'm with David Thorne, but as if I'm in a David Thorne novel. It's a wonderful place to be." She kissed him again. "May I come here tonight and cook dinner for you? I'm a very good cook. I'll bring everything I need. Six o'clock?"

"That would be wonderful," he said. "I'd love it."

He walked with her to the front door. He didn't ask where she parked her car or if someone was coming to pick her up, someone whom she'd called while he'd been preparing the coffee. As he opened the door, however, he said, "I'm so glad you found the spare key — but how did you know where to look for it?"

Cocking her head like a beautiful bird regarding a curiosity, she said, "You don't really remember?"

"I'm baffled."

She cited one of his novels: *The Last Flight Out.*

She had so unsettled — and so satiated — him that his mind was flaccid, empty, and he could not access any memory of his book, as if it had been written by someone else, a tale he'd read a long time ago and little recalled.

"The lead character, Elijah," she reminded him, "keeps a spare key under one of two rocking chairs on his back porch. Rocking chairs exactly like the two on your porch."

Although the key had no thematic or plot purpose, though it was a small detail of no consequence, the memory of his book coalesced around it as if it were of great meaning akin to that of the green light, in Fitzgerald's classic novel, that Jay Gatsby saw from across the bay, at the end of Daisy Buchanan's dock, a light symbolizing the orgastic future forever beyond his grasp.

If Maddison had committed to memory even such minor moments of David's work, perhaps she might be one of those obsessive fans whose admiration could compromise their reason, drawing him into dark and dangerous territory. But he didn't find it credible that a woman with all her qualities would have a psychological need to obsess about anyone or anything. All the world was an orchard for her to harvest as she chose; she was more likely to be the *object* of obsession.

"The Last Flight Out," he said. "I forgot I gave Elijah my own back-porch rocking chairs."

"I know it was bold of me," she said. "But last evening, after our time in Laguna but before I came here . . . the business I had to take care of was so terrible, depressing, this awful man of such wicked character. There

140

was no way to sleep, and only one antidote to all that. You. And it was right, wasn't it, Davey, so good and so right?"

"Yes," he agreed for many reasons, including because it was true that in spite of all the strangeness of their relationship, Maddison seemed to be healing him. "Yes, it was lovely and real and very right. Listen, I don't have your phone number."

"But you do, sweetie. After I showered, I texted it to you. You'll find it on your phone."

She kissed him lightly, quickly, and opened the door and said, "Six o'clock."

He said, "I might be a little late. Let yourself in and make yourself at home."

"I love you," she said, and hurried off the front porch.

After closing the door, he moved to a window and watched her follow the flagstones to the public sidewalk, where she turned right toward downtown Corona del Mar and the Pacific Coast Highway. He remained at the window until she was out of sight.

He wondered how Maddison had gotten his phone number. It wasn't listed. He hadn't given it to her, and he had certainly never used it as the phone number of a character in a novel.

"I love you, too," he whispered, and wondered why he had not said that to her when she had been with him.

Whether rationally or irrationally, he was in love with her even though he didn't know who she was.

30

After he showered and dressed, David made the bed and stood staring at it. For a decade, his love life, such as it was, had been exclusively in New York. This bed had remained his and Emily's. Now his and Maddison's. The passion that seemed so right the previous night began to feel like disloyalty if not infidelity, which made little sense, considering that Emily had been gone for ten years. Yet he felt a simmering mortification.

Moving briskly, he stripped the bed and then dressed it with fresh sheets and pillowcases, a new blanket. He returned the spread and smoothed it and made everything just right.

For a minute, two minutes, he could not stop staring at his handiwork.

Then, as if he were a hotel maid, he doubled back the spread, doubled it again, draped it on the footboard bench, and he folded back the sheets, as if turning the bed down for the night. He could have laid the sheets back at one side, but he laid them back at both, on the left and right.

It was 7:08 a.m., and he had much to do.

31

At his computer in the study, he visited the countywide law-enforcement site that offered a public-access police blotter for every community as well as for the territories in the sheriff's jurisdiction.

The murder rate among the more than three and a half million residents of Orange County was low, averaging just six per month. The previous year, there had been seventy-one homicides.

If a murder — or call it an execution — had been committed in the past twenty-four hours, it had not been reported yet. But somewhere a body might be lying in coagulated gore, its former resident having been awakened from the dream of life. A door might at any moment be opened, a discovery made.

He didn't bother to check the missing-persons report. Except in the cases involving children, those were usually not filed until the subject had been out of contact for a minimum of twenty-four hours.

Was that blood?

What — the dress? No, no, no. Wine. Just wine.

Most likely, it had been wine. The truth of her would not prove to be as dark as it sometimes seemed. She didn't merely look like Emily, but was also good at heart, as Emily Carlino had been. That was what he believed. Needed to believe.

The business I had to take care of was so terrible, depressing, this awful man of such wicked character.

In the night, she hadn't come into his bed with the scent or substance of another man clinging to her. She had been fresh, clean, and wholesome in her passion. Whatever "business" she conducted with that wicked individual had not involved intimacy. But that didn't mean the only alternative explanation to sex was murder.

After exiting the Orange County police blotter, he accessed that for Santa Barbara County, where Maddison lived, which also had a low homicide rate. He scrolled backward day by day. On the rare occasion when he found a murder, he retreated from the site to review media reports regarding the case. If the murder had been public and witnesses had identified the perpetrator, or if

144

the victim was from society's most power-less class — a homeless person, an illegal immigrant living in one room above some-one's garage — he had no further interest in the case. The word *assassination* implied that the victim must be in a position of power, either in government or the private sector.

He found what he hoped not to find. Four months earlier, in November of the previous year, a husband and wife — Ephraim and Renata Zabdi, high-tech entrepreneurs and generous philanthropists — were murdered in their home in the exclusive community of Montecito, under mysterious circumstances. Since the event, police had never mentioned a suspect, and press stories indicated that the FBI was involved in the case because the Zabdis' company, Quicksilver, had research contracts related to national security and defense. One story quoted the Zabdis' personal attorney, Gilbert Gurion, who said they were "two of the finest people" he had ever known. He suggested that they were the victims of "ignorant people who fear the future," though he apparently never explained what he meant by that.

Before backing out of the internet, David found an address and office phone number for Gurion, in Santa Barbara. Intuition warned that even if the day remained sunny and cloudless, darkness would settle through it long before nightfall.

32

The mortuary office might almost have been the study in a minister's residence: dark wood paneling; heavy furniture; deep-pile carpet and rubescent-velvet draperies to assist in the creation of a reverential quiet, to suppress the sounds of grief and confession; paintings of serene parklands receding into the distance; but no cross or Star of David, because this was an age when certain secular clients often took quick offense at the sight of symbols that they considered to be primitive, regressive influences on a new world aborning.

Paul Hartell, the general manager of the mortuary and cemetery, wore a black suit and tie, but he wasn't by nature grim. When he realized that David Thorne wasn't there to make funeral arrangements for a loved one, his decorous expression proved more plastic than it seemed, and a smile formed out of the solemn folds of flesh. When he recognized David and remembered seeing him match wits with a late-night talk-show host, his manner was not obsequious but comradely. He was delighted to serve as a guide through the cemetery's security video archives, which could be accessed through the computer on his desk.

"Yes, I can see how flowers left at an unmarked stone, at an untenanted grave, would stir the imagination of a novelist." The padded carpet, upholstered furniture, heavily lined draperies, and coffered ceiling soaked up his new boyish enthusiasm. His voice was rendered almost as hushed as if he had been sobbing in grief. "There must be a story in it."

"So it seems to me," David agreed.

Settling before his computer, Hartell said, "Twenty years ago, no one would have conceived of covering our memorial lawns with cameras. And we didn't need a security guard on duty at every hour of the day and night. But the world has changed, hasn't it? Even here in Newport, our little earthly paradise, so much has changed. But we're always vigilant against the threat of vandalism. No need to worry about that, Mr. Thorne."

"I have perfect confidence in your precautions," David said.

"Here, come behind the desk. I've found the right camera."

David went around the desk to stand beside Hartell's chair.

On the screen, his two-plot grave site was identifiable among the many stones and plaques.

"You said sometime between noon and five p.m. last Saturday?" Hartell confirmed.

"As best I can figure, yes."

Hartell fast-forwarded from dawn, returning to standard speed each time that a human form flickered onto the screen. The video was time-stamped.

Maddison Sutton entered the frame at 4:05 p.m. carrying a milk-glass vase containing calla lilies. She didn't appear to search for the right headstone, but went directly to it, as though she had been there before.

In white slacks and a cornflower-blue blouse, she elicited from Paul Hartell an exclamation of approval: "What a lovely woman! Do you know her?"

On the screen, Maddison stooped to place the flowers in the vase sleeve in the base of the gravestone.

"No," David lied. "I've never seen her before."

"The plot thickens, doesn't it? Not just a mystery woman, but a beautiful one! You certainly have a story here, Mr. Thorne."

"Quite a story," David agreed. "Is it possible to follow her back to her car?"

"We'll have to move through maybe three more cameras, but it's doable."

In the golden afternoon sunshine, she seemed less to walk among the grave rows than float like a celestial being, and David half expected her to dissolve into the gilding light.

She had not come to the cemetery in the white Mercedes 450 SL, but in a beige Ford van that was parked in the shade of a tree. She wasn't the driver. A man stood by the vehicle, waiting for her. Even in shadow, he was recognizable. When he stepped into sunlight, there could be no doubt that he was Patrick Michael Lynam Corley, who had died of a massive heart attack at the age of fifty-nine, seven years earlier.

33

Directly from the cemetery, David departed for Santa Barbara. Using phone numbers provided in the report by Lew Ross, the private detective hired by Isaac Eisenstein, he placed two calls before he crossed the Newport Beach city limits, made contact with both subjects, and arranged meetings with them.

Then he phoned the offices of Gilbert Gu-

149

rion, expecting that the lawyer would decline to speak to him on the grounds that even deceased clients, whose estate he might still represent, deserved attorney-client privilege.

As it turned out, however, Gurion was an avid reader and aware of David's novels. "May I assume, Mr. Thorne, you're considering writing about these murders?"

Because anyone with experience of people in the media expected them to claim noble intentions and slather on flattery as thick as mayonnaise, while in fact being deceitful above all things, a blunt and obviously facetious response might disarm a man like Gurion. David said, "If I swear with seeming sincerity that all I want is justice for Ephraim and Renata Zabdi, and if I make an unsecured promise that I'll write a book with nary a single salacious note, will that assure me of a meeting with you?"

Gurion laughed softly and perhaps proved himself a man of some common sense when he said, "It won't hurt." They agreed to meet this same day at noon.

Having set out after the morning rush, David made good time and reached Santa Barbara at 10:16. Almost eight hours remained before he would be late for dinner with Maddison.

Estella Rosewater lived in a large house on an eye-pleasing street shaded by old magnolia trees that the weather and intelligent city arborists had shaped well. In a state that for decades had suffered under politicians who were even more incompetent than they were corrupt, David found it heartening to encounter proof that at least in days past, even if in the misty long ago, government had not only served the people well but had a hand in making beauty.

The tile-roof white-plaster Spanish Mediterranean residence featured a crescent-shaped front porch that hugged an entrance rotunda. A housekeeper in black slacks and white blouse answered the doorbell. David was expected. She led him across the limestone of the rotunda, along a hallway of Santos mahogany, to the back of the house, where a study overlooked a rose garden.

The mahogany continued from the hall and bore upon it a Persian carpet with an intricately figured overall gold-and-red pattern set against an indigo field. Although the study was elegantly furnished, it clearly functioned as a workplace, not merely a room dedicated to afternoon tea or evening brandy.

Estella Rosewater got up from her chair and came around the desk to greet him. She

151

was a slim, attractive woman in her early sixties, with blonde hair fading to white and clear gray-blue eyes. She wore a powder-blue knit suit, a white silk blouse, a simple strand of pearls, and medium heels.

David suspected that during business hours, this woman always dressed for work, even if she worked from home, and that during her leisure time, she was nonetheless so well put together that she could have been photographed for a style magazine. Soft-spoken, composed, with a firm handshake, she seemed a paragon of self-discipline.

She sat forward in an armchair, ankles crossed, hands folded in her lap, and he sat in an identical chair, facing her across a small table on which stood a crystal bowl filled with peach-colored roses.

Although David was neither physically awkward nor carelessly dressed, he felt raw-boned and somehow untidy in her presence.

"You and your husband were friends with Patrick Corley."

"Initially, we were business partners, but the business went so well that friendship inevitably grew from it."

"Your husband was an eye surgeon?"

"Haskell was an *excellent* eye surgeon. He developed numerous surgical techniques and devices that saved the sight of countless people."

Her pride in her late husband brought fresh color to her face, and she sat up even straighter in her chair.

"He was a good man, Mr. Thorne, kind and generous and patient. But although Haskell could make money, he couldn't grow it or even keep much of it. When we married, he trusted me to put his earnings to work, and as it turned out, I have a modest talent for money management. We invested in various things, including financing six custom homes built by Pat Corley, two here in Santa Barbara and four next door in Montecito. Pat had built, I believe, eighteen others before we began working together."

"And Corley was an honest, reliable partner."

"More than that. He was a caring, responsible craftsman. Many general contractors, building custom homes on spec, they cut corners where the cutting is difficult to see, just to line their pockets with a few thousand more. Pat never cut corners and still achieved a handsome profit. We were proud of the homes we built together."

David said, "I believe his wife was an artist."

"Nanette worked in stained glass, in all

kinds of art glass. More Tiffany inspired than either modern or churchy. Nan was very talented and a good friend." She rose, went to a sideboard on which were arranged a dozen or more photographs in decorative frames, and returned with a photo of Patrick and Nanette Corley, which she gave to David before settling in her chair once more. "Nanette worked on construction sites beside Pat, framing in her own windows, hanging her wonderful art-glass chandeliers."

The woman in the photo had an appealing elfin face and a mop of shaggy auburn hair. David said, "She died eleven years ago."

"Pat was devastated. We all were. Nan was such a vivacious, vibrant woman. We thought she'd live forever. The cancer was fourth stage by the time they discovered it. She was gone in just three months. A terrible thing, a terrible time."

In spite of the woman's composure, David could see that the loss of Nanette and no doubt the subsequent death of Patrick Corley still affected her after all these years. And Haskell Rosewater had died only fourteen months earlier. Estella was at that point when friends and loved ones began to pass away ever more frequently. The essential loneliness that was a key thread in the weave of life, which everyone strove not to think about, now became a truth that she could no longer avoid considering.

"I'm sorry to dredge up bad memories," David said.

"Don't concern yourself, young man. I'm no fragile flower. Anyway, to get to what brought you here, it's necessary to do a little dredging first."

He set the framed photo on the table between them. "After his wife died, I understand Patrick more or less . . . withdrew."

"He was nearly finished with the last house we did together. He wrapped it, we sold it, and he retreated to his place like a man going to a bunker to ride out Armageddon."

David recited the address from Lew Ross's report. "Nine Rock Point Lane."

"Yes. The last house on the street. The only house. He bought the land a long time ago, a rare buildable tract on the coast, where he eventually meant to construct eight other houses after he built his own, but there's only the one. After Nanette passed, he closed his business, retired. Everyone who cared about him invited him to dinner, to cards, to one thing or another, but he rarely accepted. Within a year he stopped socializing altogether. We all knew how close he and Nanette were, but we thought in time he'd get over the loss of her. He never did."

"Sometimes it's hard," David said. "Sometimes there's really no getting over it."

Her mouth tightened. She nodded and looked down at her hands, and he knew she was thinking about her husband.

After giving Estella a moment to collect herself, which she might not have required, David said, "Five years following Nanette's . . . passing, Patrick died of a heart attack in a supermarket."

She looked up and unfolded her hands from her lap and put her arms on the arms of the chair. "Yes."

"There's no doubt he died."

"I know the manager of the market, Brenda Ainsley. She gave him CPR. She said the paramedics were there in three minutes. They also gave him CPR. No one could revive him. It was that heart attack they call the widow-maker, but he was already a widower."

"There was no funeral."

"No. After Nanette died, Pat formed this charitable foundation that would inherit his entire estate. I never really understood its mission. Anyway, five years later, when he

156

died, he was buried on the grounds of the foundation, out there somewhere on Rock Point Lane. If there was a ceremony, no one was invited. Nanette is buried here in Santa Barbara. None of us who knew those two can understand why he wasn't buried beside her. Surely he wanted that."

In his mind's eye, David saw the double-plot gravestone in the cemetery in Newport Beach. He wondered if he was destined to come to rest there alone, with no name on the other half of the polished granite marker — and if he might be consigned to the earth sooner than later.

"Have you ever met Maddison Sutton?" he asked.

Estella frowned. "Who?"

"She's the primary director of Patrick Corley's foundation."

Estella shook her head. "I never heard of her. Whoever they are out there at Rock Point, they're standoffish. I don't know anyone who's met any of them."

They had come to the purpose of his visit, to a discussion of the impossible. He would once have found the subject risible, but his life seemed to be sliding sideways from a world of pure reason into a dimension where what had once been fantastic became more credible day by day.

"Long after his death, you encountered Patrick Corley."

"My one *X-Files* moment."

"When was this?"

"Ten months ago, the eighteenth of August. I'd lost Haskell the previous April, and I was hurting. I went up to Menlo Park to stay with my daughter and her family for a few weeks."

Menlo Park lay more than three hundred miles north of Santa Barbara, south of San Francisco, near the southern end of the bay. It was one of those towns where cutting-edge technology firms were booming and, in the process of raking in historic profits, were also fast changing the world.

Estella's arms remained on the arms of the chair, but her hands were no longer relaxed. Her fingers clenched the upholstery as if she were aboard a jet and afraid of flying.

34

The creeping sun had found the tall western windows of Estella Rosewater's study, slowly extending grid patterns of glass light and muntin shadow across the gleaming mahogany floor and Persian carpet.

Her voice remained soft and steady, and

she avoided dramatics as she spoke of the remarkable encounter on the eighteenth day of the previous August.

She had been in the second week of a visit to her daughter, Rachel, and for the first day since arriving in Menlo Park, she'd been on her own. Rachel had a prior obligation. Her husband was at work. Estella decided to treat herself to lunch at La Convenable, a restaurant at which they had enjoyed dinner a few nights earlier.

Seated at a table for two, by the front window, she overlooked a patio shaded by a striped awning, with the sidewalk and the busy suburban street beyond. This was a white-tablecloth establishment, but cozy and welcoming: a black-and-white-checkered tile floor, black wainscoting, white walls, a patterned tin ceiling, black chairs with bright-yellow cushions.

The customers were a varied bunch. La Convenable was such a perfect place for people watching that Estella never opened the book she had brought to read.

"I looked up from my salad and saw him coming forward through the restaurant, returning from the hall that led to the lavatories."

When Estella seemed to be lost in the memory, David said, "Patrick Corley."

"Yes. I had no doubt that it was him. He was identical to Pat in every detail."

David played devil's advocate. "This was — what? — six years after his death. Memory fades."

"Not mine," she said. "Not after all those years of wonderful friendship, doing business together. Anyway, though he hadn't seen me when he went to the men's room, and though I hadn't noticed him earlier, he saw me as he returned, and he knew me."

"He reacted at once to you," David said, recalling Lew Ross's report.

"He looked shocked at the sight of me. He halted in the middle of the restaurant, froze for a moment, staring, then turned and hurried back the way he'd come."

"You went after him."

"I surprised myself, how quickly I reacted. It wasn't what you might think, not astonishment or curiosity. In retrospect, I realize it was anger that drove me up from my chair. Why would he have faked his death, caused such pain and grief for his friends? What selfish purpose would have motivated him to do such an outrageous thing?"

"But he *didn't* fake his death. He really died. Your friend the supermarket manager attested to that. And the coroner."

Her eyes, the gray-blue of hawk's-eye

quartz, seemed to focus on something at a great distance. Only when her stare returned to David did she reply. "Yes. They attested to it. However, when I saw him and when he reacted to me, I put aside everything I knew. It all became only what I *thought* I knew — it was no longer reliable. Instead of returning to the lavatory hallway, he pushed through a swinging door into the restaurant kitchen. By the time I followed, he was exiting a service door at the back. I barged right through the kitchen staff, went after him, and came out in an alleyway. He was nowhere in sight. The restaurant sits midblock. He could have gone around the south corner or the north, or through a back entrance to a business on the farther side of the alley."

She noticed how fiercely her fingers clutched the arms of the chair, and she relaxed them.

"You returned to your table?" David prompted.

"In something of a daze, assuring the hostess that I was fine, apologizing for the commotion I caused. By the time I got to my chair, shaken and confused, a scene was underway on the patio. This waiter delivering appetizers, and this young woman refusing them but throwing money down to pay.

161

Two glasses of wine hardly touched. Two rolls uneaten on the bread plates. She rushed off the patio, onto the sidewalk, just as a van pulled to the curb. She boarded it. I had a clear view of the driver, and I've no doubt that he was Pat Corley. Then they were off. I wasn't able to get a license number."

"What color was the van?"

"Sort of tan, I think. A Ford. I sat down and finished lunch. I ate very slowly, poring through the whole encounter again and again, so I wouldn't forget any detail."

David wondered if Pat Corley built this house. In moments like this, when he waited for Estella to continue, the room was as silent as a mausoleum, the structure so well insulated that no sound seemed able to penetrate from the street, as though the world beyond these walls had been vacated by humanity, while Nature, with all her power and creatures, had settled into stasis.

"How many people have you told about this?" he asked.

"Just two. Well, four now that I've told Mr. Ross and you. My daughter was the first. Rachel is a dear soul and good to me. But I didn't have her until I was thirty-five. I'm sixty-three now, and she's twenty-eight. She's of a generation that thinks itself wise, that doesn't even intuit its massive ignorance. She was kind when I shared the story, but she had a dozen explanations that made sense to her. I was only sixty-two when this happened, but I could tell she worried I might be in an early stage of dementia, so I relented and accepted one of her explanations, feeble as it was. When I got back to Santa Barbara, I told my best friend, Marsha Gasparelli. Marsha is three years older than I am and has no patience for anyone who thinks that old age inevitably involves a mental decline. She believed me implicitly, but neither of us has been able to imagine what it all means."

Withdrawing his smartphone from an inside jacket pocket, David said, "It was Marsha who mentioned your story to Sam Markham."

"I knew Sam casually, but I'd never heard about him meeting Pat Corley on the beach near Rock Point, two years after Pat died."

"And over four years before you saw Corley in Menlo Park."

"Yes. Apparently, Sam wasn't shy about telling his little ghost story about the twin who never was. Mr. Ross found him, and Harry referred him to Marsha and me."

David rose from his chair and circled the small table and stooped beside Estella. He

163

showed her the photo he had summoned on his phone. "Do you recognize this woman?"

"That's her! The girl on the restaurant patio. The one who went away in the van with Pat."

"You're sure?"

"Who forgets a face that striking? Men dream of it and women envy."

He smiled. "You've nothing to envy."

She placed a hand on his arm. "You're a gentleman, Mr. Thorne. Maybe I turned a few heads in my day, though year by year it seems less likely it ever happened. Who is she? What is this all about?"

"That's what I want to know. I'm no less baffled than you."

"It's impossible Pat's alive. Yet he's out there somewhere. Which means he never died. And after all, the body *was* handled somewhat unconventionally, buried on the foundation grounds. And no memorial service." She shook her head and sighed. "If ever you find the truth, you will share it with me?"

"You'll be among the first I tell."

She insisted on seeing him out rather than calling for the housekeeper to escort him. In the rotunda, when they reached a starburst of sapphire-blue quartzite inlaid in the limestone floor, she stopped and put a hand on his shoulder. "Sometimes, since last August, I wake in the middle of the night afraid."

"Of what?"

"The Pat I saw in Menlo Park didn't act like an old friend. He behaved like a man with something important to hide. People with something to hide, something as strange as this . . . Well, I wake in the night, expecting to find him in the house, not as a friend come to explain himself, but as my enemy here to make sure I never speak of it again. Do you think that's a foolish fear, Mr. Thorne?"

He hesitated to answer, but he wouldn't offer her reassurance that he knew to be without substance. "You have a security system?"

"Yes."

"You might want to employ it religiously. And a gun?"

"Oh, yes. I practice at the shooting range."

"I don't mean to alarm you . . ."

She laughed softly. "Too late."

"But I think you're wise to take precautions. Whether or not this man you saw is your friend from the past or something else altogether, even if he means you no harm, there are plenty of others in the world who

165

mean harm to anyone who doesn't have his guard up."

They continued across the rotunda. She opened the door and said, "Woman's intuition tells me . . ."

After crossing the threshold, he turned to her. "Tells you?"

"It's not the mystery of Pat Corley you're chasing down. It's that splendid-looking girl."

"Both," he acknowledged.

Her smile was as lovely as her eyes were admonitory. "I hope you find both, Mr. Thorne — and that nothing bites you before the hunt is over."

35

The house in Montecito stood on five walled acres. The ten-foot-high bronze gates hung from square stone columns, decorative rails and scrollwork radiating from a central cartouche bearing the letter *Z*, evidently for Zabdi.

David braked at the call box, put down his window, looked into the camera lens, and pushed the button below it. Perhaps because Gilbert Gurion knew his face from book-jacket photos, he wasn't asked to identify himself.

The massive gates swung open with dramatic grace and silence, as if in fact the *Z* stood for Zion, and David was, in error, being admitted to Heaven. He followed a two-lane cobblestone driveway past broad manicured lawns and ancient live oaks with great limbs of an elegance that proved Nature was the finest of all sculptors.

David's father, the investment banker from whom he was long estranged, lived well, though by comparison to this property, the old man's house was unremarkable. In his youth, David often had been uncomfortable with his family's affluence, and he couldn't imagine living on an estate this grand. Even if the cottage-style bungalow that he called home in Corona del Mar hadn't been a shrine to Emily, rich with memories, he would have lived nowhere else in California.

The driveway ended in a circle that surrounded a fountain. He parked behind a Lexus SUV.

Clad in limestone, the Beaux Arts mansion combined elements of Georgian and French Renaissance styles. Broad steps led up to a portico, where a man in a dark suit waited.

With thinning gray hair, the pink face of an aging cupid, and pale-blue eyes, Gilbert

Gurion might have passed for a volunteer with the local historical society, a docent waiting to conduct an informed tour of this storied residence. His handshake was firm but not aggressive.

"It's a pleasure to meet you, Mr. Thorne. I genuinely am an admirer of your writing."

"Thank you, Mr. Gurion. However, considering that pounding out stories is the only thing that I can do at all, I think I should be able to do it better. And please call me David."

"I'm Gilbert. Gil to friends." His tentative smile and a subtle beseeching quality in his stare suggested that in his youth he had been shy, perhaps painfully so, and had worked hard to overcome a natural reserve. "Whatever your intent — and I'm not asking you to spell it out — I hope you might indeed write about Ephraim and dear Renata. They were kind and gentle and blindingly intelligent. It's terrible, what happened here. They were only forty-four. High school sweethearts married twenty-four years, born poor and made their way to the top with sheer brainpower."

David knew only what little he'd read on the internet, but he didn't want Gurion to think his interest was related to anything other than the tragic story of the Zabdis. "I never know that I'm committed to a subject until interest becomes obsession. But the material in this case is undeniably gripping and the Zabdis are the most sympathetic of figures." He admired the magnificent facade of the house. "You said on the phone that the place is as they left it, as it was when they . . . died."

"Except for the master bedroom and bath, nothing inside has been touched. The gruesome nature of the double homicide, not a single suspect yet identified, the mystery of how the killers gained entrance when there was a security system worthy of Fort Knox, how the security-camera archives could have been wiped clean — all that makes the place impossible to sell for the time being."

"The heirs must be frustrated."

"There aren't any. Ephraim and Renata weren't able to have children, and they took good care of family and friends while alive. Their fortune — every dime, including this property — has passed to their tax-free charitable foundation."

David turned to survey the sweeping lawns and gardens and stately oaks. But for birdsong, the quiet was such that this might have been an English manor house on hundreds of acres rather than just five. "Then no one stood to gain financially from their death. Except perhaps the directors of the foundation."

"Out of respect for Ephraim and Renata, we serve without compensation, and we're not reimbursed for expenses."

"I intended no offense," David said.

Gurion smiled and nodded. "None taken. Many foundations with multibillion-dollar endowments do indeed attract those who're greedy but not industrious enough to earn their own fortune — or political types who're eager to spend it all on utopian schemes that ensure dystopia. The Zabdi Foundation is different."

"What's its mission?"

With what might have been pride in the vision of his deceased friends, yet speaking more softly and breaking eye contact, as if he wished to avoid giving the impression that he deserved credit for serving as a director, Gurion said, "It provides free medical care to children with cancer and other potentially mortal illnesses, as well as funding development of technologically advanced options to complement traditional treatments. Currently, the Zabdi Foundation pays for the care of four hundred and thirty-six young patients of all races and creeds. It's a blessing . . . really amazing to be part of it."

Having once engaged in deceit that would haunt him all the days of his life, David had an ear for deception and an eye for its many telltales. Gurion's self-effacement seemed genuine, a modesty that was uncommon among those with his achievements.

"We could liquidate the antiques, the collections," the lawyer said, "but dealers would push prices up by touting the connection to the murders. That's the sorry kind of world we live in now. Valuable provenance can include being associated with horror. We just can't do that to Ephraim and Renata. We'll wait a year or two. There's so much violence these days, so much for the media to sensationalize, that even cases as awful as this one are soon old news that no one cares about, the injustice accepted and the victims forgotten."

"Maybe I can write something to ensure they're remembered," David said, and he wasn't pleased to hear himself so convincingly imply that he was serious about addressing the Zabdi case in a book, when he had no such intention.

"I'll show you the place," said Gurion, and they went inside.

36

On the ground floor, the large rooms were brought into human scale by antique jewel-tone Persian rugs; Japanese screens and bronzes; Chinese ceramics and painted cabinets; Art Deco furniture, sculpture, paintings by Tamara de Lempicka and Jean Dunand: an eclectic mix that should not have worked, but did.

"It must take quite a staff to maintain this."

"Yes, it does," Gurion said. "An even larger staff when . . . when it was lived in."

"And no one heard anything the night of the murders?"

"The place is so solidly built that sound barely travels from room to room let alone beyond the walls. The estate manager lived in a bungalow at the very back of the property, a significant distance from here. Because Ephraim and Renata valued their privacy, the rest of the staff came to work at eight o'clock every morning and left at five, and no one worked on weekends unless there was a dinner party or other event. The murders occurred on a Saturday."

A hotel-size elevator served all levels of the residence, but they climbed the long arc of stairs, shoe leather softly shushing them as if they were in a place made sacred by the lives sacrificed under its roof.

The master bedroom, where the bodies had been found, was a large and barren chamber stripped of the rug, furniture, art, and draperies. With nothing to absorb and soften sound, the limestone floors and bare walls lent a hollow ring to their voices, as though they weren't on the highest floor but deep in a catacomb.

The air was cooler here than elsewhere, suggesting that spirits lingered.

"Even after scoping the place for fingerprints and vacuuming for hairs and such," Gilbert Gurion said, "the FBI took everything from the bedroom, retreat, and bath for further analysis at their lab, an extraordinary step. They still haven't returned anything."

"The FBI? Didn't the local police have jurisdiction?"

"As far as the public was aware, yes. But they were quietly relieved of jurisdiction and cooperated with the Bureau. Ephraim and Renata's company had some defense contracts with national-security issues. The press covered it as a typical tabloid murder case, with wild speculations of sex parties, other grotesque nonsense. But the feds think the Zabdis were tortured into revealing vital information about certain sensitive projects. They say this wasn't just murder, David. They say it was an operation by foreign agents, most likely a team of four. Not mere murder, but a double assassination."

As David stood at a window with a view of the parklike grounds, the previously still air was troubled by a cool draft that chilled the nape of his neck, as though a lurking revenant had breathed it out when Gurion spoke the word *assassination.*

"Did they suggest what country?"

"Country?"

"What country these four foreign agents might be from?"

"No. That's all they said. They were otherwise closemouthed."

"Gil . . . ?"

"Yes, David?"

"Quicksilver is mostly into developing . . . not drugs but medical products. Is that right?"

"Medical technology. It's more correct to think of it as a biotech firm that has grown in related directions."

"As I understand it, Quicksilver owns numerous patents for bioprinting technology."

"That's right. Many, many patents."

"I'm not sure I understand what bioprinting is."

"It involves bioinks. They contain cells and collagen and other stuff to print layers of artificial tissues, even organs, especially capillaries. Before Ephraim and Renata, capillaries were almost impossible to print."

"Sounds like sci-fi."

"It's not. Quicksilver also has key patents on processes to recellularize donor organs before they're transplanted."

"Give it to me in English."

"I'm trying my best. It's a little Greek to me, too. The way I understand it — they strip the cells out of an organ, say a kidney or a heart, and repopulate it with new cells from the person receiving the transplant. Far less chance of the organ being rejected."

The grounds beyond the window now appeared less like a park, more like a cemetery where flat plaques marked the graves.

Gurion said, "Organs once unsuitable for transplant can now be used. The decellularized organ is like a natural scaffold for the new cells. Bioprinting is maybe more important because applications of the technology are . . . well, stunning, revolutionary. Some people think certain biotech developments, like those related to AI, are a little Frankenstein, but that's just ignorance. This science has great potential to alleviate human suffering."

Turning from the window, David harked back to something that the attorney had said earlier. "They were tortured? For a fact?"

Looking toward where the bed had most likely stood, Gurion clamped his lower lip between his teeth as if to bite back a strong wave of emotion. His pale-blue eyes glimmered with unshed tears. When he spoke, his voice was steady but strained. "I'm the one who found them. My wife and I were invited for Sunday brunch at ten thirty. Just the four of us. Renata and Ephraim loved to cook. They could lay out quite a spread, just the two of them, no help from staff. They usually started on it at five in the morning, making a big production of it, but always having fun, the two of them like chefs on some lighthearted Home and Garden Channel cooking show."

The attorney fell silent and seemed lost in grim thought, and David said, "The press reported they were stabbed to death."

"That's what the FBI wanted to say. Keep the truth for court if there's ever a prosecution."

"What was done to them? The torture, I mean."

"I've told no one. Not even my wife."

"If you're constrained by the FBI or you'd just rather not —"

"It's all right," Gurion said. "If you're going to consider writing about them, you need to know. What they suffered."

Shamed by his ongoing deception, David waited.

Gurion went to the open door to the bath and stood there with his back to the bedroom, as if he could not bear the sight of it even now that it had been emptied. "They were faceup. His ankles were zip tied together. So were hers. Ropes tethered each of them to a different footpost of the bed. Their hands were cuffed, too. Other ropes pulled their arms out over their heads, linking the cuffs to the headrail."

David was able to picture it. He didn't want to, but he could. Locks and alarms had failed them. Overpowered in their sleep, they were totally vulnerable once secured.

"Both were . . . disfigured."

"How?"

"Horribly. Their faces. Even with all the blood . . . it looked like slow and careful carving."

"Maybe they were already dead when that was done."

"Not according to the Bureau's medical

examiner." He continued to stand at the threshold of the bathroom, staring through the open door. "And I don't think they were tortured for information."

When the attorney's silence grew extended, David said, "Then what do you think it was about?"

"Vicious hatred. The psychotic hatred of killers whose souls were long ago extinguished. Ephraim and Renata were kind and giving, the last people to inspire homicidal rage. But their killers must have hated them. Only people consumed by demonic hatred could do that, all that, to other human beings."

"Do you have any theories of your own? Suspects? Someone other than foreign agents?"

Gurion seemed reluctant to face the bedroom, as if by facing it he would invite ghastly images to surge in memory. He turned with the caution of a man on a high wire. "No theories. No suspects. But it changed me. I'd never owned a gun. I bought one the next day. And a second, for my wife, a week later. And then two more, so we would have one close at hand wherever we were in our house. I underwent training and got a license to carry." He drew aside a panel of his suit coat to reveal a shoulder holster. "Are you licensed to carry, David?"

"No."

"I recommend it," Gilbert Gurion said. "Especially if you're going to write about Ephraim and Renata. But even if you're not, I recommend it."

37

Half a mile from the Zabdi estate, David pulled to the curb and shifted the SUV into park. He adjusted the dashboard vents to direct the outflow of cold air more directly on his face.

He sat for a few minutes, thinking and trying not to think, alternating between the two.

Whoever invaded the house that Saturday night had possessed the knowledge and technology to override the alarm and, later, to erase all archived video from the security system. That suggested well-funded professional operatives, rather than just a woman who was the director of a small foundation and seemed to enjoy playing at being a femme fatale.

According to Gilbert Gurion, the FBI had estimated that it would have taken a team of four to foil the security system, enter the house undetected, and overpower Ephraim and Renata. If Estella Rosewater was right about Patrick Corley, that his death had been faked somehow and that he was still alive, Corley might have been Maddison's partner that bloody night. But then who were the other two? She hadn't heretofore been seen with anyone else.

She'd lied about her father being a Microsoft executive, about her mother being a Seattle prosecutor. But if she *was* Emily, then her lies were quid pro quo, because he had lied more egregiously to her back in the day, before she had disappeared, and his lies had a greater consequence than hers. He couldn't hold her to a standard that, when it counted most, he'd been unable to meet.

And if she wasn't Emily . . . ? Consciously, he knew that she might not be — logically could not be — the woman he had loved and lost. However, what we perceive consciously is not the fullness of reality. On deeper levels, subconsciously and instinctively, he was convinced that Maddison must somehow be Emily. Down even deeper in the matrix of himself, his soul perceived with conviction what his mind alone could not entirely admit or understand: that she *was* Emily Carlino, the one and only, the same that he had loved.

And being Emily, she was incapable of killing anyone. Emily was gentle, loving, kind, wise to the ways of humanity but also faithful to the expectations of God. Whatever game she was playing with him, she was not really an assassin. She would not have been capable of committing the atrocities that Gilbert Gurion had described, would not have been able even to stand by and watch as others wielded the knives that disfigured and ultimately killed Ephraim and Renata. The Zabdi murders had nothing to do with Emily, with Emily pretending to be Maddison or with Maddison pretending to be Emily. The case was a distraction, a red herring, a blind alley, and David dismissed it from further consideration.

As surely as he understood the psychology of any character in one of his novels, he understood his own. His every action arose inevitably from two emotions that had trumped all others for more than ten years, that were the bedrock of his identity: grief that had become a terrible settled sorrow, and acidic guilt that grew more caustic year by year. There could be no relief from either sorrow or guilt if Emily was indeed dead. Maddison's appearance in his life had given him the first hope that he'd known in a decade, and he couldn't let go of it. One moment he admitted Maddison was not Emily, but the next moment insisted that she was. His heart wanted what it wanted, and his heart rejected what might confound its desire, rejected logic and reason.

He supposed he had gone somewhat mad, but a little madness was preferable to unending despair.

He released the emergency brake and put the car in gear and drove to his third interview of the day.

38

Lacking tires, jacked up on concrete blocks, sun-faded and dust-coated, the old travel trailer stood on scrubland beyond the city limits of Goleta. Neither a patio nor a lawn graced the place, but not far from the trailer door, a pair of outdoor chairs, the blue-vinyl webbing shaggy with wear, flanked a table formed from a large spool around which had once been wound a thousand feet of cable. A square of white melamine had been fixed to one end of the spool to serve as a tabletop, and it was crusted with a variety of substances that not even ants seemed to find appealing. Half a dozen crumpled beer cans were scattered across the dirt and the tramped-flat weeds in front of the table.

An air-conditioning unit, inexpertly fitted in a window at the back of the trailer, rattled against the frame and grumbled like some robot with low-level artificial intelligence that had gotten stuck while attempting burglary.

David rapped loudly on the door, was aware of curtains parting at a window to his right, and after half a minute rapped again.

Farther from an ocean influence than Estella Rosewater's house or the Zabdi estate, this place was hotter, the sun glare conducive to a squint in the absence of tree shade.

The door creaked open, and a twenty-something guy peered down at David. His sandy-brown hair was tangled as though he'd awakened from a long, bad dream. He had a pleasant, beardless, boyish face, but his eyes seemed twice as old as his face, filled with suspicion so long entertained that his stare was toxic, suggesting a capacity for anger and meanness.

"What do you want?"

"Are you Richard Mathers?"

"Who wants to know?"

"I'm David Thorne. Recently you talked to a man, a private investigator, named Lew Ross —"

"Maybe I did, maybe I didn't."

"Mr. Ross was working for me."

"You can't get your money back."

Mathers had insisted on being paid to be interviewed about his experiences related to the Corley Foundation. He and Lew Ross had agreed on three hundred dollars.

"I don't want my money back, Mr. Mathers. I'm here to talk to you about what you told Mr. Ross."

"I said everything I had to say. I got no more."

"I just need to confirm a few things, hear it unfiltered, in your own words. You wouldn't let Mr. Ross record you."

"Nobody records me, you neither. Get your ass outta here."

"I don't want to record you. And I'll pay. Again."

Mathers chewed on his lower lip, from which curled shreds of dry skin. "This must be something bigger than I thought. So maybe I need like a thousand bucks."

"It's not *that* big. I'll pay five hundred cash. Not a dime more."

Mathers thought about it. He turned his head to look back at someone or something in the trailer. Maybe he had a girl in there. Maybe he was packaging drugs for resale.

"I don't got all day," he said. "You get like

fifteen minutes for five hundred."

Mathers stepped down the stacked rail-road ties that served as stairs, pulling the door shut behind him.

He was about five feet ten, lean but solid. Red sneakers, faded jeans, and a T-shirt emblazoned with the word Resistance.

After counting out the five hundred dollars and giving it to Mathers, indicating the T-shirt, David said, "Resistance to what?"

"To everything. To the whole freakin' world. To every shitty thing. You got a phone? Let me see your phone."

David took his smartphone from a jacket pocket.

"You can record with that. Go put it in the car, and so I can see you do it." He dropped onto one of the lawn chairs, in the shade of the trailer.

When David returned from the Porsche, a snub-nosed revolver lay on the makeshift table. His host must have drawn it from an ankle holster or from the small of his back.

"I'm not gonna mess with you," Mathers said. "But I can't see what's really in your heart, can I? The gun is just insurance."

Without comment, David used one hand to cast debris off the second chair.

Mathers issued a snort of derisive laughter. With one finger, he tapped his wristwatch. "Your fifteen minutes started, dude."

Settling in the chair, David said, "This thing that happened — it was about a year and a half ago?"

"Labor Day weekend. I'd been watching the place on and off for like two weeks. No one ever seemed to be there."

"We're talking about the Corley Foundation, the house at the end of Rock Point Lane?"

"Yeah. I'd gone in close several times. Scoping it out, you know. Looking through windows, that kind of shit. There's furniture and stuff, but I never see no one. No sign of an alarm system."

"So you broke in on Labor Day."

"Broke in? Hell, no. It was just a bad window."

"Bad window?"

Mathers shrugged. "It broke itself. So I go in for a look around. I got a big curiosity. That's all I'm saying."

"Okay. I understand."

"There's food in the fridge, but the place don't feel lived in. No dirty dishes. No laundry to be done. Nothing out of place. It's like a furniture showroom set up neat to get you to buy shit."

"Jewelry? Money?" When his host's eyes narrowed with suspicion, David said, "I'm

just curious. Like you, I have a big curiosity."

"Some jewelry in a woman's closet. Nothing special. No money anywhere. Not even
a coin jar where like they collect pocket
change. No safe." Mathers's brow pleated,
his mouth tightened, and his face grew dark
in the shade. He glanced at the revolver on
the table, but he didn't reach for it. "The
place creeped me out, dude."

"You told Lew Ross the house is —"

"I know what I told him," Mathers inter-
rupted. "He gave me a down-the-nose look
I didn't like. Nobody makes me out a fool."

"And I have no intention of doing so."

"And I have no intention of doing so,"
Mathers quoted, mocking David's diction.
"You got too much damn school in you."

"I agree. Half the time I spent in college
was a waste."

Mathers' double-barreled stare sought
some sign of sarcasm, but he evidently
didn't detect any. "I told the bitch I'm with,
and she thought it was bullshit, you know,
like I'm a little kid needs to make up stories.
I got her mind right, quick enough."

David wanted to ask if she still had all her
teeth, but he restrained himself.

Wagging one finger as if to say, *You listen*

to me and you listen good, Mathers declared, "That fucking house is haunted."

39

A fat beetle as big as a bumblebee, with an iridescent green shell and translucent sour-yellow wings, flew past Richard Mathers and settled on the grip of the revolver that lay on the makeshift table.

Leaning forward in his lawn chair, Mathers met David's eyes, intensely recounting his experience at Nine Rock Point Lane. "So I go upstairs. There're like three bedrooms being used. One has a closet full of a man's clothes. The second has like only a lot of, you know, girl stuff. The third is for a bitch, too, and damn if she isn't there, sitting in this armchair. The chair faces away from the door, so I don't see her till I'm deep in the room. Right then I almost split, but I realize she don't see me, don't hear me, she's staring into space like she's fucking hypnotized or something. She's so still, I think maybe she's dead, but then I see she's breathing. And once in a while, her eyes blink. When I talk to her, she don't answer. It's like I'm invisible to her, dude."

David thought of a strange moment on the first night that he and Maddison had

188

dinner together in the harborside restaurant. She had fallen silent; her smile became fixed; her gaze slipped out of focus; and for half a minute, maybe longer, she didn't seem to be there with him.

"This girl in the armchair — what did she look like?"

"What did she look like? Shit, man, she was this spooky bitch staring into space, zombified. Like a freakin' cyborg. I got the hell out of there."

"Blonde hair or black hair? Blue eyes or brown? Young or old?"

Mathers shifted his gaze from David to the iridescent beetle on the revolver. "I don't know. I don't remember. Young, I guess, but not a kid. Young and creepy as shit, so I just quick got the hell out of there, into the upstairs hallway, headed toward the stairs, which is when all this freaky shit happened, everything got weird."

"What got weird?"

"The hallway, dude. It was the same hallway and it wasn't. I mean, it was like tweaked. Like it was the same hallway, but *bent*."

Mathers seemed as earnest as he was incoherent.

"Bent? What's that mean?"

"Bent means *bent*. All the angles was

wrong, walls and ceiling, like it was — I don't know — all sort of rubbery."

"How long did this last?"

"Maybe a minute. I'm like dizzy from it. Unbalanced."

"Anything like that ever happen to you before?"

Mathers frowned. In his boyish face, his frown was close to a pout. "Why would it happen to me before?"

"Some medical conditions have similar symptoms. Like ocular migraines."

"I didn't have no headache."

"Ocular migraines aren't painful. They're characterized by strange visual stimuli."

"Characterized, huh?" The insinuation that he might be less than a perfect physical specimen greatly offended Mathers. "I eat high protein, low carbs. Pump iron every other day. Resting heart rate like sixty. BP is a hundred ten over seventy. I can hammer nails with my dick. I got no medical conditions, asshole."

"Good for you."

Mathers slitted his eyes as thin as razor cuts. "What's that supposed to mean?"

"It means I'm glad you're in good health. I'm happy for you."

"Bullshit, dude. Nobody's happy for nobody but themselves."

The inquisitive iridescent beetle crawled past the loading gate of the revolver, onto the hammer, and started forward over the top strap toward the barrel.

"Back to the bent hallway," David said. "All the angles wrong. What happened then?"

"Heavy footsteps. It's a wood floor. Someone's coming toward me. Gotta be some big sonofabitch, those footsteps so heavy, booming off the walls, like he's wearing lead boots. But nobody's there."

"Footsteps in another room," David suggested. "Or maybe not footsteps at all."

"You was there, huh? You want to tell it? You can tell it better than me?"

"Sorry. Go on."

Mathers took another jab to pay back the imagined insult. "They teach you in college how you know everything, but you don't know nothing. You don't know jack shit."

David placated him with silence.

"The footsteps seem to stop in front of me. Like some guy's right in my face, but I can't see him. Then the bent hallway snaps back like it should be, and I get my balance. But it's suddenly as cold as a witch's tit, so cold I can see my breath all frosty. I want outta there. So I'm down the stairs to the front door, unlock it. But the damn door is stuck, swollen in the frame or something. So I go back through the damn house, you know, but it's the same with the kitchen door. There's this second like dining room off the kitchen, littler than the real dining room. You hoity types maybe call it a breakfast room. It's where the window was broke, except all the furniture is gone, table and chairs and all the other shit, even the pictures on the walls. No way someone could move all that outta there so fast and me hear nothing, but it's *gone.* And the broke window isn't broke no more. I'm freaked out, dude. So I hold my piece by the barrel, smash the window, and I'm gone."

The beetle had proceeded along the barrel of the revolver to the muzzle, where it perched on the rim, flexing its wings.

David had no way of determining the value of the story he'd just been told. He wanted to ask if Mathers dropped acid from time to time or had a relationship with exotic mushrooms, but any such question was certain to trigger the man's trip-wire temper.

As if privy to David's thoughts, Mathers said, "I'm totally native organic. I don't put chemicals in my body. I don't do nothing but California weed, and I hadn't even done no weed before I went in that house."

"According to Lew Ross, what happened at Rock Point Lane wasn't the end of it."

Mathers's face clenched again. He looked as if he wanted to spit at someone, and then he turned his head and *did* spit toward the door of his trailer. "It's like the next day. Kendra she's at work, and I come back from a thing I had going. Trailer's locked, but this sick piece of shit is waiting inside. He jumps me before I know what the hell's happening. I could've busted him up good in a fair fight, but he clubs me down before I know he's there, and then he's kicking me. He's wearing these steel-toed construction boots and doing this gestapo number on me, you know, he's got fists like concrete blocks. He's old, but he's solid, and he keeps shouting at me to stay out of his house, never go back there. He racked me up real good."

"This was Patrick Corley."

"You want to say it wasn't?"

"I'm just asking."

"When I was seventeen, the first job I did was construction-site tear out, cleanup. I worked for that prick, he thought his shit didn't stink."

"This Rock Point Lane business happened a year and a half ago."

193

"I said so, didn't I?"

"You know Patrick Corley's been dead seven years."

For the first time, Mathers looked pleased about something. "He croaked in the fruit aisle at the market, pulled a shitload of kiwis down on himself when he fell. Kiwis. I heard about it, I laughed my ass off."

The beetle began to explore the bore of the revolver, peering into it as if it seemed like a suitable place to construct a nest.

David said, "So the Patrick Corley who beat on you — he was a ghost or what?"

Mathers watched the beetle squirm into the bore of the gun. "Ghost, demon, zombie — I don't know what the hell he was, dude. He just *was*. He came down on me like an avalanche. I wasn't right for two weeks."

"When Kendra came home, found you half-conscious, you told her he was a ghost."

Mathers closed his eyes and summoned a long-suffering look. "I told her not to tell no one, 'cause then people would start asking did I see Bigfoot in a flying saucer with Elvis. But Kendra she just can't keep her damn mouth shut no more than she can keep her legs together. I don't know why I still hang with that bitch. There are some mega-hot pumps out there who got an eye for me. I got choices. Plenty of options. I

194

don't know why I don't kick Kendra's ass out of here."

David said, "Maybe it's love."

Mathers laughed and opened his eyes and shook his head. "You're one crazy dude. You should like record yourself, listen to yourself sometime. You'd be amazed, all the shit you talk."

His laugh was like that of a snarky, arrogant adolescent.

He plucked the revolver off the table, aimed well over David's head, and squeezed the trigger, launching pulverized beetle far into the vista of scrubland.

He pointed the weapon at David. "You got five hundred more in your wallet, college boy?"

Having had some experience of a genuine homicidal sociopath during his many conversations with Ronny Jessup in that conference room at Folsom, David did not react as Mathers wanted. "Why? Do you have more story to tell?"

"What's five hundred to you, anyway? I'm damn sure you don't live in a shitcan trailer."

"You're right about that."

"We're in a lonely place, college boy. That Porsche will bring a nice price from a chop shop. And there wouldn't be no headstone to say *Here lies David Thorne.*"

"You'd have to dig the grave. Hard work. The lovely Kendra can't do the job all by herself."

Most of his life, Richard Mathers had used a low-flashpoint temper to intimidate people, and maybe he hadn't been accustomed to pushback until he'd taken a beating at the hands of Patrick Corley or Corley's ghost or whoever/whatever was waiting for him that day in his trailer. If his attitude had once been highly effective, he had lost some of his mojo after being beaten.

"You dissing my lady?" Mathers asked, leaning forward in his chair, resorting again to that Spaghetti Western tough-guy squint.

"No, not her," David said, and rose to his feet. "After you got the shit kicked out of you, I guess you never went back to the house on Rock Point Lane."

"Maybe I did. I got a big curiosity."

Ignoring the revolver, David met Mathers's stare and finally said, "No, you didn't. And I don't pay for bullshit."

He walked away. He was sure that Mathers had never returned to that house. He was also certain the man had withheld something from him, something related to the spellbound girl in the armchair, but whatever secret he kept, no amount of money

196

would loosen his tongue.

David anticipated the second shot and expected it to be well wide of him. If he ran or ducked or merely flinched, Mathers would feel triumphant, and what critters hadn't been chased out of the brush by the gunshots would flee the snarky adolescent laughter. The crack of the gun echoed through the low hills, then again.

David suspected that, on some level, his courage might be less admirable, might be a capitulation to fate. If he misjudged Mathers and if the creep shot him in the back, maybe that was the overdue justice he had earned by his behavior ten years earlier, that he had been expecting ever since. He got into his car and pulled the door shut and started the engine and drove away from there.

40

From the high north, a slow avalanche of clouds slid down the tilted sky, smothering the sun. The Pacific gradually darkened as it rose out of the curve of the earth in menacing ranks and pounded the shore as if to break it.

At 1:04 p.m., on US Highway 101, north of Goleta and south of Gaviota, David parked at the familiar scenic viewpoint.

Again, his was the only vehicle in a space that could accommodate four or five.

Across the meadow that sloped and rolled shoreward from the railing, the tall grass trembled as though Nature shared David's anticipation of some wicked revelation.

Northwest, where the stubby peninsula thrust into the sea, on the headland stood the impressive stone house, which he now knew to be the former home of Patrick Michael Lynam Corley and the current quarters of the Corley Foundation.

Subsequent to Emily Carlino's disappearance, authorities had interviewed the residents of the houses that were within sight of the viewpoint. Corley's wife, Nanette, had died of cancer two years prior to that rainy night, and Patrick had lived alone since then. Like others in the area, he'd said that he'd seen nothing of Emily. Evidently because he was a well-known county resident of good reputation, the police had seen no reason to disbelieve him.

Three years later, Patrick had died of a heart attack. And seven years after his death, behind the wheel of a beige Ford van, he had driven Maddison Sutton to the cemetery in Newport Beach, where she had placed a bouquet of calla lilies on a certain grave.

David left the viewpoint and walked north along the graveled shoulder of the highway. Southbound traffic raced past on his right, the vehicle slipstreams tossing his hair and harrying him with waves and whirling funnels of dust. His state of mind was such that, although reputably dressed, he imagined that he resembled a wild-eyed vagrant, an itinerant Bible-thumper on a messianic mission, slouching door-to-door to announce the impending Apocalypse.

Rock Point Lane branched off the coastal highway a hundred yards north of where he'd left his SUV. The one-car width of blacktop led through wild grass and weeds, flanked by eighty- and hundred-foot Monterey pines shaped by the wind into tortured configurations that were nonetheless poetry in wood and foliage.

The lane was a private street, serving only Corley's five acres. Although the property wasn't fenced or walled, a low steel-pipe gate between two stone columns barred entrance to what was in essence a long driveway. A sign on the gate made no reference to the Corley Foundation but promised that trespassers would be prosecuted. A call box with speaker invited visitors to announce themselves.

David walked around the gate and followed the blacktop toward the house on the headland.

The two-story residence and four-car garage featured walls of native stone under a slate roof. The lawn was mown, the building well maintained.

He went directly to the front door, an artful work of oak and bronze, and he rang the bell. He could hear chimes echo through the interior stillness. He waited. Rang again. No response.

Maddison was in Newport Beach. Patrick Corley — alive or dead, a twin or a miraculous resurrection — must be there as well.

David went around to the back of the house, which stood about seventy feet from the rocky bluff and fifty feet above the sea. Two clusters of Chinese fan palms added interest to the yard, rustling in the softly hissing wind.

The big back porch was furnished with only two rocking chairs and a table that stood between. The chairs and the wrought-iron glass-topped table were identical to those on David's smaller porch in Corona del Mar.

For a long moment, he stood staring at the tableau. In the wind, the chairs moved back and forth in shallow arcs, as though occupied by people he could not see.

He turned one of the rockers upside down and found the key box fastened to the frame, where he'd known it would be. He clicked the lid of the box, which fell open, and the key dropped into the palm of his right hand.

The feeling that overcame him was eerier than déjà vu. He felt as if he were living through a novel that he had read years before and only half remembered, a work of fiction to which reality was in the process of conforming.

He knew that he should return the key to the box and latch the lid and walk away, that he was being manipulated, to what end he could not guess. Nothing good was likely to come of this.

However, he was incapable of heeding that warning voice that whispered from a place deeper than the mere subconscious, from the marrowed cavities of his bones and from the iron-rich cells of his blood, where a thousand generations of human experience had inlaid instinct. For ten years, he had lived with the mystery of Emily Carlino's fate. Answers — however strange they might be — seemed at last within his reach. He could no more retreat than he could undo the error of his ways that resulted in Emily being alone on that night ten years previously. Instinct be damned. Whatever peril might lie ahead, he had earned it and the understanding that might come with it.

The key fit the lock. The deadbolt turned. He opened the back door to the house.

41

The kitchen appliances weren't of the most recent vintage, yet everything looked as though it had been installed only yesterday. The limestone floor appeared spotless, the polished granite counters as timeless as the planet from which they had been quarried.

The contents of the cabinets, the refrigerator, and the pantry were as ordered and aligned as if they had been stocked by a robot that, by sight alone, could measure precisely to a sixteenth of an inch. The dishwasher and trash compacter were empty.

Evidently there had been a recent power outage. The digital clocks — on the double ovens, on the microwave — were blinking zeros.

In the adjacent breakfast room stood a table with four chairs and a sideboard. Three large, spectacular light-filled nature paintings were in the style of Albert Bierstadt.

This was the room where, eighteen months earlier, Richard Mathers had broken a window to gain entrance — and a short while later supposedly had broken the same window to escape. He claimed that all the furniture had been removed between his arrival and departure. The table was a heavy disc of pine on a solid central plinth, the captain's chairs substantial, the sideboard eight feet long. The room could not have been quickly or silently emptied.

The laundry room, the casual family room, the formal dining room, the living room, the large study, the closets, the half bath — nothing on the ground floor seemed in any way odd or suspicious, nor suggested supernatural presences.

Everywhere were exquisite stained-glass lamps of which Tiffany would have been proud. Three walls of the study were lined with books, nearly all science fiction — Bradbury, Heinlein, Sturgeon, Dick, Zelazny, Delaney, Scalzi, Gibson — and the entire fourth wall featured a backlighted stained-glass triptych of flowering trees framing a view of golden meadows beyond, obviously crafted by Nanette Corley.

The residence was immaculate, which indicated nothing more sinister than someone who had an ingrained habit of cleanliness.

David wondered if the truth was that Mathers had broken into the house and someone — Patrick Corley, who had somehow faked his death, or a twin who really *did* exist — had given him a beating during his intrusion, not a day later in his trailer. Humiliated, Mathers might have invented a story to tell the gullible Kendra, embellishing it with the supernatural. His claim to being chemical-free and "native organic" in his use of only locally grown marijuana was probably another lie. Most likely, he sampled a smorgasbord of drugs and drew on past experiences with hallucinogens to concoct the otherworldly events he claimed had occurred in this residence.

As David stood in the foyer, at the foot of the stairs, he became aware of the deep silence that pooled in the house. Through the sidelights that flanked the front door, he saw trees thrashed by the wind, but he couldn't hear even a whisper of that tumult.

On the second floor were a well-equipped home gym and three spacious bedrooms, each with an en suite bath and walk-in closet. All three bedrooms were being used, as Mathers had reported.

David first explored a closet full of men's

clothing and then the bathroom cabinets. He found nothing extraordinary. In the associated bedroom, there was nothing on the nightstand other than lamps, and nothing whatsoever in the drawers.

In the first woman's bedroom, he discovered a gallery of photographs, thirty-two framed pictures, in every one of which he appeared.

42

The collection was arranged on both nightstands and across the top of the dresser. A variety of sizes. Each in a unique silver or gold-plated or white-enameled frame. A lot of them were publicity photographs from the back of his book jackets or had been used to accompany newspaper and magazine interviews. They could have been downloaded from his website. He only now realized that he had never smiled in a publicity shot, that without calculation, he had always looked solemn, intense — even haunted.

In addition to the many professional portraits, there were ten snapshots, six of him alone, in which he was smiling at the camera. He recognized some of the locations: a bench overlooking the ocean at

Inspiration Point, a few blocks from his house; another bench in that same park along Ocean Boulevard, where he was back-dropped by the breakwater at the Newport Harbor entrance; sitting at a patio table at a cozy neighborhood restaurant.

In all these photos, he was in his early twenties. They were from his personal collection, taken by Emily, with her camera.

In the remaining four snapshots, she was with him. They were from the same period, before she disappeared. He couldn't remember who had taken them, probably friends from those days.

How had they ended up here? Had Maddison stolen them? If so, when? Not just the previous night, because she was still in Orange County, and these pictures were here, framed with such care.

Last night was the first time that she'd been in his house. He dared to believe that only Emily could have had these photographs, that Maddison's possession of them suggested — proved — that she was in fact Emily.

One other object had caught his attention: A fine gold chain hung from a nail in the wall above the bed. At the end of the chain was a glass ampule containing perhaps an ounce of what appeared to be a red fluid.

He leaned over the bed, reached to the ampule, held it in his hand to take a closer look. He was all but certain that it contained blood.

He released the ampule and watched it swing like a pendulum until it became still. He used his smartphone to photograph it.

Whose blood? What did it mean to her? What did it represent?

David surveyed the photographs again. He didn't know what he should think of this collection. He didn't want to think of it at all. He yearned to be with Emily, a desire that could perhaps never be fulfilled. And in the enduring absence of Emily, he wanted to be with Maddison, Emily's uncanny duplicate — who might be Emily herself under a new name — to be with her 24/7, now and forever, until they were old and wizened and white haired, to be with her in a condition of total acceptance, without any suspicion, without *reason* for suspicion, without being consumed by the puzzle of her existence.

Of course this Gordian knot of mysteries was so extraordinary that denial was impossible. He had no viable option other than to continue his investigation. And his only hope of happiness was to resolve every hitch in this tangle of enigmas and discover, at the end of all discoveries, that Maddison was an innocent rather than a villain, that she was somehow Emily returned or reborn.

He searched the closet and the bathroom, but discovered nothing further of interest in either.

In the study on the ground floor, he looked for records of the Corley Foundation, but he found none.

And then he went into the garage.

43

Fluorescent tubes casting bleak light through frosted plastic panels. Cold rising off the concrete floor and off poured-in-place concrete walls painted white and mottled with water stains that vaguely resembled enormous crawling insects.

The immaculate condition of the house did not extend to the garage. Although the two double-wide roll-up doors were closed, in-blown debris littered the floor: dead leaves; loose feathers; the fragile skeletons of perhaps twenty birds, the flesh long stripped from their bones and eyeless skulls. Improbably elaborate spiderwebs, their creators dead or gone to other hunting grounds, trailed in tatters from the rafters, as if fragments of ghosts had snagged on the splintered edges of the beams and the exposed nail heads.

Because Corley had been a general contractor, David expected a home workshop, but there wasn't one. Backboards bolted to two walls suggested that cabinetry had once been hung there but had been torn out and carried away. No vehicles were present. The large space felt hollowed out and decades older than the well-kept house.

The stillness here was equal to that in the residence. Maybe the wind had blown itself into exhaustion.

Leaves crunched underfoot and a smell of mold issued from the carpet of litter. He avoided the avian skeletons; some of the larger ones, as big as owls, seemed to be tortured constructions like the skeletal architecture of a winged menace in a dream.

In addition to the roll-ups, there were three man-size doors: the one from the kitchen, another that led outside, and one set in an interior wall. He went to the third and found it locked.

From a pocket of his pants he retrieved the key he had taken from beneath the rocking chair on the back porch. It fit the keyway and turned the deadbolt.

When he opened the door, he saw stairs descending into darkness from which rose a faint but unpleasant chemical odor. He felt for a switch, found it, flipped it, but no lights came on below.

The basement was not steeped in silence like the garage. The lower realm secreted a faint electronic hum woven from several frequencies and a soft rhythmic throbbing felt as much as heard.

No such noises had issued from the cellar in the Jessup house, where homicidal Ronny had kept his stolen girls, both the living and the mummified. Nevertheless, David grew convinced that something in these depths would prove no less disturbing than what he'd seen at the Jessup place — which was only forty minutes from here.

He needed a flashlight. He went into the house to find one.

As he searched through kitchen drawers, he heard what might have been a door slam upstairs. He froze and listened. Perhaps someone had come into the house while he had been in the garage.

Silence returned, perfect but for his soft breathing.

Then another door slammed, as though a rightful resident was searching rooms for an intruder, angered by the need to do so.

David was not prepared for a confrontation. Besides, he was at risk of being charged with housebreaking.

He stepped onto the back porch and locked the door. He quickly replaced the key in the little box that was fixed to the underside of the rocking chair.

The wind, which had not relented, tossed his hair, flapped the panels of his sport coat, and brought to him the scent of the sea. The gray clouds spilling out of the north had flooded three-quarters of the sky, roiling like smoke from a vast, uncontainable fire.

As he hurried around the side of the house, at least twenty shrieking crows cascaded from the roof as though the building had expelled them. They swooped low over David and arced off toward the Monterey pines, like a scrolling line of ciphers in a coded message.

Proceeding along the driveway, David glanced back a few times, but he never saw a face or figure at any of the windows.

In his SUV once more, he sat thinking about what he'd found in the Rock Point house. As ordinary as most of the rooms had been at the time he explored them, in retrospect the place seemed almost as weird as Richard Mathers had portrayed it. The silence had been uncanny, surely the result of something more than mere construction techniques. The condition of the garage, the lightless basement, the subtle electronic hum rising from below, along with the slow bass throbbing like the heart of some leviathan — all that now creped the skin on the nape of his neck.

His mind's eye kept returning to the collection of photographs in Maddison's bedroom, which seemed to suggest that she must be obsessed with him. God knows, *he* was obsessed with *her,* and any man might be flattered to find himself the object of such a woman's adulation. But over the years, David had endured the obsession of two disturbed fans of his books, one young man and a young woman, and in each case serious security issues had required the hiring of private investigators and bodyguards for the duration of the threat. In spite of Maddison's fantasy of being an assassin, David found it impossible to fear her, for she was the very image of the lost woman whom he had loved so long and passionately. On the other hand, the existence of that collection of photographs seemed proof enough that she'd schemed to meet him last Wednesday evening in the restaurant.

He started the engine, put the car in gear, and pulled out onto the highway, heading south toward home.

Never before had he been so emotionally conflicted. He didn't know what to do next. As he brooded without profit on what course he ought to take, he finally decided he had no choice but to follow Maddison's lead. She was the author of this play. Sooner than later, she'd say something or do something that would give him direction and lead him closer to the cloistered heart of the mystery.

44

He had outrun the leading edge of the southbound clouds, and the beetling vehicles on the freeways cast racing shadows stranger than themselves as sunlight slanted through the afternoon, the rays seeming to distort as much as illuminate.

David's hands-free phone rang as he crossed into Los Angeles, and he activated it with a voice command.

Calista Carlino said, "Sweetheart, I hope I'm not interrupting anything. If I'm interrupting something, call me back whenever."

"No, nothing. I'm in LA, on the 405, coming home."

"Do you have an hour to stop by and see me?"

"Of course." For the first time since head-

213

ing south, he glanced at the car clock and was surprised to see that it was only 2:29 p.m. He thought he'd spent at least half an hour in the house, more like forty minutes. It should be at least half an hour later than this. Evidently, while he'd brooded about Maddison and what might lie ahead for them, he must have greatly exceeded the speed limit from Goleta. "Depending on traffic, I'll probably be there around four o'clock. What's up?"

"I had the most incredible experience this morning. I can't stop thinking about it. I'm *consumed* by it, and I just don't know what to make of it."

"Nothing wrong, I hope."

"No, no, dear. It was quite wonderful but very strange."

"You should be a writer, Calista. You certainly know how to set a narrative hook. Give me a hint of what comes next?"

She was silent a moment. Then she said, "We've never spoken of the subject, perhaps afraid of sounding frivolous. I'm not sure how I feel about it, really. But you, David — do you believe in ghosts?"

He knew at once that whatever had happened, it had involved Maddison Sutton.

"I don't *dis*believe in them," he said cautiously. "I have an open mind, though I've

214

never seen one. Sounds like I might need a drink to go with this tale of yours."

"Josefa is here today. She'll fix you whatever you want, and you'll find me on the deck."

"You're really all right?"

"I'm splendid, dear boy. I'm ebullient!"

"Fourish," he promised, and they disconnected.

In its determination not to keep still, in its fever, humanity surged south and north across eight or ten lanes of traffic, eager to get to one future or another, as if the future wouldn't find all of them on its own, minute by fateful minute.

■ ■ ■ ■

PART 3
THE LAST OF
ALL SILENCES

■ ■ ■ ■

45

At 4:12 p.m., Josefa Alvarez answered the backstreet door and led David into the kitchen, where he agreed to a glass of cabernet. She was a doll-faced dumpling of a woman, just five feet tall but with a mighty heart. Her sweet appearance and air of perpetual gratitude for the very fact of life seemed to be the truth of her.

As she poured the wine, she reported on Calista. "Our Calie has been in such high spirits all day. She had an unexpected visitor at breakfast, before I came to work, and I swear she hasn't stopped smiling since."

"What visitor?"

"That's the strangest part. You know how open she is about just everything. But not this. She says she's saving the story for you, and she might never tell anyone else. I'm all cat with my curiosity, but if she never tells me, that's okay. It's enough to see her so happy."

David carried his glass of wine across the dining area and living room, through the open door to the deck overlooking the public promenade that encircled Balboa Island.

The sea itself was swimming, each of the millions of ripples on its surface like a small fish schooling, withdrawing from the harbor as if to follow the sun westward. As the tide slowly went out, the dock pilings appeared taller as more of their length became exposed, and the belayed boats, big and little, rode low beyond the island seawall, beyond the sand that the receding tide had revealed.

Wearing a sapphire-blue kimono with a pattern of white storks in flight, Calista sat at the table, a glass of wine before her.

Although David moved quietly, she heard him and somehow knew that he was not Josefa. She turned her head and favored him with a warm smile, her blind eyes full of refracted sunlight. "Twice in one week. I love it when you're living on this coast, dear. I wish there wasn't a New York City."

He bent to kiss her on the cheek. "I'm thinking of looking for a larger place and staying here all year."

Until he spoke, he didn't realize that he had been drifting toward such a major decision, but it was true. Either Maddison would explain herself to him, as she had promised when she'd ask for his patience, or he would learn the truth of her on his own. In spite of all the strangeness associated with her, he believed in her, in the rightness of her, and he yearned for — *ached* for — a domestic life with her at his side and perhaps one day children. No mystery in this world was so complicated or so dark that love could not solve it; and because he felt that he knew her heart, he believed no sin she had committed could be so great that love could not pay penance for it. He was not an author of misanthropic fiction. Although he was no Pollyanna, he had considerable faith in people, in humanity's capacity for good and in its future. He had been foolish ten years earlier and, by his foolishness, had lost a shining future of his own. He would not lose this one. He would cling to Maddison through whatever might come, believe in her, be faithful to her through all challenges and revelations.

"Move here full-time!" Calista declared as he settled at the table, in the chair immediately to her right. "Oh, child, how lovely that would be. You always say this place inspires you, gives you ideas for your books. Living here, the writing will come more easily, too. I'm sure it will, dear."

"Whatever has you so buoyant?" he asked. "You look as if you might soar up out of the chair like a helium balloon."

"I had a visitor at breakfast. I'm almost afraid to tell you, as if the telling will take all the magic out of it."

"Someone visited and talked about ghosts."

"Not exactly, no."

Calista sipped her wine, put the glass down, and crossed her arms over her breasts, as though to compose herself and restrain herself from babbling out the story in torrents of words that might somehow diminish it.

After a pause, she said, "I was sitting right here, just where I am now, listening to the harbor, enjoying the early sun, eating a morning roll and having coffee. This girl spoke to me from the promenade, said she thought my kimono was beautiful, and just like that, we were chatting as if we were old friends. I invited her in, and she came through the gate and sat where you're sitting now. I offered her coffee, but she said she needed nothing."

Balboa Island and Little Balboa were connected by a bridge, and a promenade encircled each of them. People walked the islands at all hours, and locals frequently stopped to visit.

"I thought I recognized her voice, but she wasn't a local. She said she'd been here when she was younger but hadn't been back in a long time."

After fifty-four years of blindness, Calista's ear for voices was uncanny. When a passing local called out a greeting to her, she nearly always answered with the person's name — and rarely ever got it wrong.

"She said her name was Maddison. She was here more than an hour, and we were like old friends from the get-go. David, I can't describe how fluid our conversation was, from the serious to the silly, back to serious, each of us so easy with the other. It was like . . . maybe you remember . . . like Emily and I were together."

"I remember," he said.

"It was exactly like Emily and me. And gradually . . ."

"Gradually, what?"

She searched his face with her sightless eyes. "I don't want you to think I'm a crazy old woman."

"You're the farthest thing from that."

"Gradually, I realized I *did* know that voice, knew it as well as I know my own, even though I hadn't heard it in ten years.

She sounded just like my Emily."

Her voice broke on the last few words, and she turned her head from David to gaze out at the harbor as though she could see the prows of three small sailboats cleaving the water as they raced up the channel.

He gave her a long moment to recover and then said, "But her name was Maddison."

"Yes. And when I first recognized the voice, I thought it was only coincidence, a remarkable soundalike. However, the longer we talked, the more I became convinced that something extraordinary was happening. Her attitudes on so many things were the same as Emily's. Her sense of humor, that quick wit, the way she would reach out and touch my hand and tap it three times with one finger. She used to do that, the three taps, and with each tap she'd say a word. 'I. Love. You.' "

"Did she say that this time?"

"No. It was just now and then the reaching out and the tapping while we talked."

He wondered how Maddison could have known to do such a thing. Unless Maddison *was* Emily. "Fascinating. But do ghosts talk?"

Calista found her wineglass but didn't raise it from the table. "If they exist, why couldn't they?"

"I don't know. I'm not a ghostologist or whatever. I guess so."

"A lot of islanders, neighbors, passed us and called out to me, but none of them spoke to her or mentioned her."

"What — you think they couldn't see her?"

She shook her head. "I don't know what to think. But that's not all, David. That's by no means all. I became quite bold. I asked if I could feel her face to know what she looked like."

He could not fathom Maddison's intentions for this visit. Unless she was Emily.

"David, she looked like Emily."

He said, "Felt. Felt like Emily. It's not the same."

"Before . . . before we lost her, I felt my daughter's face countless times. My fingertips learned her face as surely as I learned Braille."

"But why would she call herself Maddison if she was really Emily?" He hoped Calista would have the answer that eluded him.

"Maybe she thought she would shock me too much, scare me, if she started out right away telling me who she was, what she was. In fact, I'm sure I'd have been angry with her, called her a charlatan, and asked her to leave. She needed to . . . to bring me along slowly to the truth. She *was* Emily, David. Somehow, she was."

David didn't know what to say, though for reasons different from those that Calista no doubt imagined.

After waiting for a cacophony of seagulls to wheel through the sky, Calista said, "You *do* think I'm losing it, early dementia."

"No, not at all. Really, I don't. It's mystifying, but I'm sure it happened just as you say. So did you mention Emily, did you tell this Maddison about the similarity, that you recognized her?"

She had been turning her glass between thumb and forefinger. Now she lifted it from the table and sipped and sipped again before putting it down. "I was afraid to broach the subject."

"Afraid . . . ?"

"I thought . . . oh, I don't know . . . I guess I thought if I mentioned it, the spell would be broken and she would be gone."

As the westering sun slowly felled long shadows from the tree-tall masts of those sailing yachts moored nearby, Calista recounted things that Maddison had said, and there was no doubt that many if not all of them were observations that Emily would have made and in much the same language.

"When she said the time had come to go,"

Calista recalled, "I urged her to stay a little while. That was when she said something that makes no sense coming from a stranger named Maddison, but that makes perfect sense if . . . if somehow she was Emily."

David brought his glass to his lips and discovered that he had finished the cabernet without realizing he'd been drinking it.

"Maddison took one of my hands in both of hers and said, 'I've come back just for this one visit, so you will know that I'm happy and beyond all pain, and to tell you . . . be not afraid of whatever comes next, because I'll be with you always.' And then she raised my hand to her lips and kissed it three times and . . . and she said 'I love you.' "

For a long moment Calista and David sat in silence. Her silence was necessitated by the depth of her tenderest emotions. His was the result of desperate hope but also of astonishment, bewilderment, and anxiety.

"I was speechless," Calista said, "and before I could think what to say, she let go of my hand and was gone. Just gone. I don't know whether . . . whether I was so stunned by what she'd said that my senses failed me, but I didn't hear her chair scoot back on the deck or her footsteps or the gate creak like it always does. She was there and then just gone."

A long, sleek racing boat motored by at the harbor speed limit, its big engine throbbing with pent-up power, suggestive of a demonic entity barely restrained from wreaking havoc.

Aware that Calista needed reassurance, he said, "Remarkable. But the word *ghost* seems inadequate. Too pulp fiction. If she wasn't real, maybe *spirit* is a better word. This wasn't a haunting, after all. It was much more of a manifestation . . . a visitation."

"But you do believe me?"

"Of course. You're not delusional and, just like Emily, you'd as soon bite off your tongue as tell a lie."

And there is *a Maddison,* he thought. *Whatever her purpose might be, whyever she felt the need to do this, there* is *a Maddison.*

He continued, "I've read some about visitations, research for a novel I once thought I might write. I don't claim to understand them. Personally, I don't find any organized religion's explanation fully convincing, and in fact many religions deny the existence of ghosts or the ability of spirits to return. It all seems stranger and more complex than doctrinal explanations. I need to do some reading. I need to think about this."

Calista reached out and unerringly found his hand and squeezed it. "You read, child, you think. I *know*. She was here, she was my Emily. As strange as it was, it nevertheless gave me greater peace than I've known in ten years."

"That makes me happy, Calista. You can't know how happy. Life is full of mysteries, isn't it? And maybe we don't always need to know the answers to them. Each thing we don't understand is a wall, and we spend our lives throwing ourselves against those walls, with little to show for it in the end. Maybe sometimes it's just best to accept the limitations of our understanding, accept that some things will be forever beyond our knowledge."

He realized that he was debating with himself, not with any intention of convincing Calista, who didn't need to be convinced. Further, he knew that he was not capable of taking his own advice.

The sun had mined a golden treasure from the western sky, and in Calista's face, fortune's light turned back the effects of time, so that she appeared young again, her smile that of a girl to whom the sorrows of the world were as yet unrevealed.

46

From Balboa Island, David Thorne didn't drive directly home, but curbed his car on Ocean Boulevard in Corona del Mar and walked through the park to Inspiration Point. He stood at the railing, staring out to sea. The vast, deep waters seemed to wash to shore even as in fact they were receding from it.

Whatever reason Maddison might have for temporarily keeping secrets from him —

Be patient, Davey. Give me breathing room . . . Give me a few days, and I'll explain everything.

— whatever justification she might rightly have for teasing him with claims of being an assassin, he nevertheless felt that she had crossed a line by introducing herself to Emily's mother. Unless she *was* Emily. Calista Carlino was sacrosanct. With uncommon grace, she had endured a life of afflictions: a drunken and unloving mother; poverty; blindness since childhood; a cruel husband who abandoned her; the loss of her only child. David couldn't tolerate Calista being drawn into whatever web of fantasy Maddison might be spinning around herself . . . if Maddison wasn't Emily.

True, Maddison's visit had enchanted

Calista, lifted her heart. But it could as easily have frightened her or disturbed her so that she would have been robbed of the peace that she'd found during the past decade.

And what was he to make of some of the last words Maddison had spoken to Calista?

I've come back just for this one visit . . .

Only that morning, before Maddison left the house, before David had gone off to the cemetery and then to points north, she promised him a future together.

We belong together, and we will be together, and there won't be any secrets between us . . . there are beautiful days ahead of us.

Was that promise a lie? How could she tell Calista that she had come for one visit — and subsequently become a part of David's life, therefore a fixture in Calista's as well?

How could she make a pretense of being Emily's spirit — but then later reappear as flesh-and-blood Maddison?

I've come back just for this one visit, so you will know that I'm happy and beyond all pain . . .

Maybe Maddison acted out of compassion, but if that were the case, her actions were misguided. Unless . . . Unless . . .

The mystery of this woman didn't fade

with every new thing he learned about her, but instead grew more impenetrable.

He wasn't angry with Maddison. Long ago, by his own descent into deceit, he had forfeited the right to be angered by the deceit of others. He did not have it in him to confront her in righteous indignation, any more than one thief deserved the right to lecture another thief about his larceny.

As he'd stood at the railing, the sun became a wound as it met the sharp horizon line of the sea, and an artery opened in the sky, spilling scarlet light across the west.

When he returned home, if he pressed Maddison to explain why she had visited Calista, he would surely open the door to questions about what *he* had been doing during the day, prior to responding to Calista's phone call.

If she discovered that he had been probing into her background, both on his own hook and with the help of Isaac Eisenstein and Lew Ross, her reaction might be one that he couldn't manage and would regret. She had asked for his patience and had promised an end to all secrets soon. By his actions and his words, by his acceptance of the gift of her passion, he'd appeared to accept that bargain, even as he continued to investigate her.

He believed in her goodness, the goodness of Emily inexplicably reborn. He despaired at the thought that she might leave him, as if to lose her, as he'd lost Emily, would establish a cycle of losses that would repeat through all his life.

The wounded sky pressed its image on the sea, and the sea, too, was red, and the air between the sky and the sea was as fiery as that in a furnace, as if all of nature would be consumed before night could quench the blaze.

47

When David arrived home at 5:48, Maddison's vintage sports car was in the garage. He parked beside it.

When he entered the kitchen, he found two place settings on the table, a small vase of red roses, and three cut-crystal holders with candles not yet lit. A bottle of chardonnay, in a clear-glass ice bucket, stood open on a counter, with two glasses ready at its side.

In black jeans and a white shirt with an embroidered blue-and-yellow butterfly on the breast pocket, Maddison was busy with what seemed to be half a dozen culinary tasks simultaneously.

She looked ravishing, as always. She paused in the process of dividing the curd of a cauliflower into sprigs, put her arms around him and kissed him. Her mouth was sweet with the flavor of carrots, which she evidently had been slicing and sampling earlier. He did not deserve this, shouldn't accept it until he knew everything about her. But reckless abandon was an aspect of his madness, and he became lost in the kiss for a long moment.

Returning to the cauliflower, she said, "I came at three o'clock because there were groceries to unpack, so many preparations to make. It's a small but wonderfully functional kitchen, so cozy."

"We could have gone out to dinner."

"No, no, no! I want to do this for you, for us, a lovely little dinner at home, without a waiter interrupting to ask if everything is to our taste — I assure you, it will be — if he can pour more water, if he can pour more wine. I want you to myself this evening, no other women's eyes on you."

"I wasn't aware that women took notice of me."

"They all do, Davey. But not tonight. Tonight, you're just mine. How was your day?"

"I knocked around here and there. Looked

234

into a thing or two, this and that."

"Research?" she asked.

He flinched at the question, rattling the ice in the glass bucket as he withdrew the bottle of wine. Belatedly he realized that she meant research for a book.

"Oh, I'm not working now. This is a vacation, a winding down before I get wound up for the next book. How was *your* day?"

"Excellent. I've wrapped up everything I had to do here in Orange County. I'm free, free, free."

"No more assassinations, bodies to dispose of?"

She grinned and winked at him, which he took to mean that it had all been a joke. "Not a one. Got away with it scot-free. I've nothing to do tonight but be your chef — and later something better."

He put her glass of chardonnay near the cutting board at which she had been working.

She paused to slip on an oven mitt, open a warming drawer, and retrieve a platter of *zucchini dorati.* The thick-sliced courgettes had been lightly coated with flour, dipped in an egg-and-cheese mixture, and panfried in olive oil.

"A little something to whet the appetite," she said.

They were delicious. Exactly as Emily had made them.

48

Three golden halos of light quivering on the kitchen ceiling, reflections of the candles below. Wineglasses and polished flatware glimmering on the table. Soft piano solos dialed low to allow easy conversation. A symphony of mouthwatering aromas.

She served dinner at seven o'clock, starting with aubergine salad dressed with a sweet-and-sour sauce. The main course of *sogliole al marsala,* fillets of sole in a thin but delicious batter, was accompanied by *tortellini alla panna* with freshly grated nutmeg, carrots with tarragon, and *cavolfiore alla Siciliana.* For dessert, narrow slices of paradise cake flavored with lemon.

Every dish was exquisitely prepared — as they had been when Emily had cooked them.

David praised Maddison's culinary talent but did not remark that dinner was eerily like others that Emily had created.

She supposedly knew nothing more about Emily Carlino than what he had told her: that she greatly resembled Emily, that he and Emily had once been lovers but that she had "left" him. Yet Maddison knew of the grave meant for Emily — even though the headstone lacked that precious name — and knew of Calista. She sounded like Emily, moved like Emily, cooked like Emily, made love like Emily . . .

With such a cloud of mysteries weighing down on the evening like thunderheads swollen with cold rain and armed with ten thousand lightning bolts, the conversation should have stumbled repeatedly as they avoided tripping over the countless deceptions and evasions in which they had engaged since the night they met. Instead, she was a charming, funny, intelligent companion, and David held his own with her, and the conversation flowed as ever it had between him and Emily, until at ten o'clock they had been three hours at the table.

He suggested that they clean up the kitchen together, but she said, "I'll do it in the morning. I've moved out of the hotel and brought all my luggage here to stay awhile. Why don't you provide the *second* dessert and take me to bed?"

Although he wanted nothing more than to do what she asked, the weirdness of the situation so troubled him that he thought they had best avoid intimacy until all secrets were revealed, according to her promise. He couldn't say as much without in the end disclosing where he'd spent the day, and he was worried that if Maddison knew of his investigation, if she viewed it as distrust of her, the floor might fall out from under their relationship.

He said, "You shouldn't have stuffed me like a fat Italian sausage. I'll be a whale in bed."

"Nonsense. It was a light meal, and you'll be what you were last night, which is everything a girl could ask."

"But it's been a long, warm, sticky day. I'm a poster boy for the tragedy of body odor."

She plucked her napkin off her lap and set it aside and got up from her chair and rounded the table and sat on his lap. "That's easily fixed. We'll take a shower together, soap each other up, and go to bed as fresh as ever we were." She held his face between her hands and kissed him. "Let's not waste an evening, Davey. Let's never say 'tomorrow,' because all we ever have is the moment. People think there's a future, but there really isn't, not if we want to be totally honest with ourselves. There's the past, which we might wish desperately that we can change, and there's *now*. If we don't seize the now with all our might, it becomes just another part of the past that we end up wishing we could change."

She kissed him again and led him to the shower. He convinced himself there was no reason to resist; this was the only way things could be; this was good and true, as much an expression of trust and hope as it was a surrender to need. If she was right and this moment was all they really had, then it was precious beyond valuing. But if what he wished for might come to pass, if all of the mysteries would clarify and the suspicions prove unwarranted, if they could have a few decades together, then this was a commitment to their future.

No less than in Montecito, earlier in the day, on a profound level deeper than the subconscious, deeper than mere intuition or instinct, David knew that she was somehow Emily. His soul recognized hers, and doubt had no place in matters spiritual.

In the act, when they were one, when the fresh scent of her was all that he could smell, when the sight of her was the only reality that his eyes would admit, when there was no sound in all the world but her quickening breath and small cries of rapture, when his senses were saturated with her, he said three times aloud what he had not previously been able to say to Maddison — "I love you" — and in so saying, spoke the truth of his heart.

He had told Emily that he loved her and had meant it no less than he meant it now. But he had been immature then and too callow to grasp how the world would test his vows. He hadn't understood that the ignorance and inexperience of youth provided fertile ground for self-delusion and vanity, which could lead him to betray his best intentions. These years later, he knew the heart was deceitful above all things and required constant self-judgment; all hope and happiness depended on never lying to himself and at all costs being faithful to the vows he made.

With "I love you," he was pledged to this woman beyond reason, no longer primarily driven to find the truth of her, but to prove that the truth of her was benign. Intuition, that primary form of knowledge, coming before all learning and reasoning, told him she was fundamentally good, innocent, and a victim of someone, not a victimizer. His investigation of her would now be an investigation *on her behalf,* an unstinting effort to vindicate her, to free her from those to whom she might in some way be indentured.

He was no longer driven by reasoned

suspicion, which had availed him little. He was motivated instead by pure and powerful emotion, which was a dangerous but exhilarating path to follow.

49

Afterward, Maddison switched off the lamp and pressed against him, her head on his chest.

Neither of them spoke for a while. Sometimes no words could translate and well express the language of the heart.

David listened to a night breeze winging down the roof and warbling like doves nesting in the pockets of the eaves.

In a voice hardly louder than a whisper, Maddison said, "I'm a needy creature, Davey."

"We all are," he said.

"Me more than most. I need affection. I need it like air. I need to be loved."

"You are. I love you. I love you very much."

"I need to be loved every day, every hour. I know so well the loneliness of being unloved. Until you, I've been starved for love all my life."

"Surely not."

"But I have. Starved. And now I can't get

my fill. Until you, life was . . . a horror."

The word unsettled him because she spoke with such sincerity.

"Horror? For a girl with your mind, your heart, your charm? How could that ever be?"

For a while, she seemed to be listening to his heart. Then she said, "Loneliness, enduring fear, a sense that society has gone mad and I'm falling, falling through the madness of it. That's horror enough for me."

He thought of the thirty-two photographs in her bedroom in the house on Rock Point Lane, which had seemed like evidence of a fan's obsession. In the light of the word *horror* and what else she had just said, he wondered if that collection might be something else altogether, something cleaner than obsession, instead an expression of desperate hope. A coldness coiled through David, a chill of responsibility, that she should vest in him all her aspirations.

"I feel safe here," she said. "Only here. With you. I feel so safe. Tell me it's forever."

"I'll never leave you. This is what I want. It's all I want."

"So then say it."

"Say what?"

She raised her head from his chest to look at him. "Say this is forever, you and me."

242

"This is forever."

"Say it again."

"This is forever."

"It better be."

"It is."

She searched his eyes. Lowered her head to his chest once more. "It better be. I won't have anything less. It better be forever."

Her breathing changed as she drifted off to sleep.

He loved her. He needed her no less than she needed him. Even if there would be no end to the mysteries of her, even if the truth of her remained beyond knowing, she was his destiny. He had sworn his love for her, and he was no longer a callow and confused youth who failed to understand what accommodations and sacrifices a vow demanded. There could be no going back on such a promise, not if he hoped to repair his damaged self-respect. From this night forward, even the most startling revelations must be absorbed, adjusted to.

The latest discovery, during their lovemaking, was that Maddison — though a decade too young to be Emily — had a perfectly symmetrical, flat, golden birthmark the size of a quarter about an inch below her navel.

He remained awake for another troubling hour as Monday became Tuesday, as the world turned through more darknesses than the mere absence of the sun. And then he dreamed.

He is in the house on Rock Point Lane, where the digital clocks in the kitchen appliances are blinking zeros. Suddenly he's stricken by a fear that the clocks have been counting down to the moment of his death, that his time is up, that a black-robed Reaper will at any moment appear to harvest his life. When he consults his watch, the face of it is blank, without numbers or checks, and the hands are still, pointing to where the number 12 should be, though it is neither noon nor midnight. His heart racing, he hurries room to room through the ground floor, seeking clocks with time still on them, but there are none. Surely there will be bedside alarm clocks. He climbs the stairs, searches the three bedrooms. They are clockless. In Maddison's room, she stands naked by the bed, regarding him solemnly, and she wears no wristwatch. The thirty-two frames contain no pictures of him, as if he has never existed to be photographed. In terror, he flees the house and is in his Porsche, southbound. He glances at the dashboard clock, which is blinking zeros. When he looks up, no highway lies ahead, only a terrible blackness, a night without moon or stars or sky, and he acceler-

ates into oblivion.

He sat up in bed, a cry caught in his throat, heart hammering.

Maddison slept undisturbed.

When his breath returned to him, David lowered his head to the pillow.

Something about the nightmare was more disturbing than the presentiment of his death. He didn't need long to understand what else unsettled him. His unconscious mind had called to his attention things that he had seen but not properly considered, had found a strange consistency of absences.

The kitchen-appliance clocks at Rock Point had in fact been flashing zeros, which he had attributed to a recent interruption of electrical power — and indeed there were no bedside clocks, a detail he had noticed almost subconsciously.

He'd been in the house half an hour or forty minutes, but after he hit the road and drove south, he was nearer to Los Angeles than he ought to have been, as if his visit had lasted but a minute. He thought he must have been exceeding the speed limit all the way from Rock Point Lane, while preoccupied by thoughts of what he found there. But was that the correct explanation?

The first night that he'd had dinner with Maddison, her only jewelry had been a simple string of pearls. No rings. No wristwatch.

Had she worn a watch on any subsequent occasion? He didn't think so. As if she must be always intimately aware of the time.

But what did any of this mean, if it meant anything at all?

Although he remained awake for another half hour, he could puzzle no meaning from those curious facts.

50

After five hours of sleep, David woke. He was alone in bed.

He pulled on a robe and went in search of Maddison and found her in the kitchen, in a robe of her own, cleaning up from the previous night's dinner.

"I'll help you," he said.

"Not a chance, Galahad. My gift to you was dinner *and* dealing with the wreckage."

Putting his arms around her as she stood at the sink, he kissed the nape of her neck. "Your gift to me was far more than that."

She said, "As gorgeous and sweet as you are, even cute with bed hair and beard stubble, not even you can spread a gloss of romance over congealed leftovers and a garbage disposal. I'll attend to all this, you get your shower, and there'll be hot coffee when you come back presentable."

When he returned forty minutes later, the kitchen gleamed. Maddison kissed him on her way to the shower.

The easy domesticity between them soothed him and supported his conviction that the intuitive emotional commitment he'd made to her was the best of all possible options he could have chosen.

He carried a mug of coffee into his study and switched on his computer. He visited the law-enforcement site that offered a public-access police blotter for every community in the county.

When he felt a twinge of guilt, he reminded himself that this was no longer an investigation *of* Maddison, but an investigation *on her behalf.* To help her and to ensure their future, he needed to separate fantasy from reality and, one by one, resolve all of his unanswered questions.

There had been a gang shooting in Santa Ana, two dead, but the incident had occurred the previous evening when he and Maddison had been having dinner in the kitchen.

Among the missing-persons reports, a new name appeared: Lukas Eugene Ockland of Irvine, California. His wife had reported

247

him missing at 11:10 p.m., and police protocols allowed for the posting of his name only now, Tuesday morning.

Sunday evening, following their afternoon together in Laguna Beach, Maddison had left David alone so that she could attend to some "terrible, depressing" business involving an "awful man of such wicked character."

He googled Lukas Eugene Ockland, who turned out to be a twenty-eight-year-old mathematician, microbiologist, and entrepreneur of considerable accomplishment. He was a figure of some controversy and had been called everything from "a genius, one of the most profound thinkers of his time" to "a wicked piece of work." There was a wife named Linette but no children. With a little effort, David located an address.

The water was still running in the shower.

He wrote a love note to Maddison. Beneath the lines of romance adapted from Shakespeare, he claimed a morning appointment with his lawyer and promised to return by noon.

He backed his car out of the garage and angled east in the alleyway serving the houses that abutted it on both sides. He drove to the end of the block and turned right into the street.

The morning was clear, sunny, and unknowable.

51

Irvine was one of the earliest planned communities, designed from end to end, nothing left to happenstance. The streets were wide and tree-lined, the shopping centers sized and placed to match the population density of each district, the residential neighborhoods graced with numerous parks and greenbelts, the houses in harmony with one another but generally avoiding a cookie-cutter sameness. Year after year, Irvine landed at or near the top of the list of America's most desirable and safest cities. Advertisements for new tracts of homes there had often been headlined ANOTHER PERFECT DAY IN PARADISE, and some might think that Death took a holiday in Irvine, that no one died there — or went missing.

Although located in an expensive neighborhood, the Ockland residence was an indifferent Spanish-style house with a brick front walkway bordered by red and purple impatiens. The woman who answered the doorbell was also expensive, though not indifferent, and more trouble than David expected to find on another perfect day in paradise.

In her Facebook photo, Linette Ockland looked like innocence personified, with a direct wide-eyed stare and a sweet face. In reality her eyes were wide with continuous calculation, and she was neither guileless nor uncorrupted. Although twenty-three, she had the lithe, slender body of a precocious fifteen-year-old and a face that seemed even younger. She wore platform sandals with two-inch cork heels, low-riding denim short shorts, and a cutoff T-shirt that bared her midriff and was emblazoned with the words POP PRINCESS.

"Mrs. Ockland?"

"Yeah?"

"My name's David Thorne. I have an appointment for an interview with Mr. Ockland."

"Here, not at his lab on campus?"

"Lukas wanted to keep our project separate from his work at the university."

"Yeah, well, he never told me shit about you."

"I'm a writer. We're considering a book project together."

"Why would he tell me, anyway?"

"Excuse me?"

250

"He doesn't tell me half the shit he's doing. He probably doesn't want to meet you on campus because he doesn't want the university to take its slice of this. Is it a big-money book?"

"We're at the early stages of the concept. Until we lock down the scope of it, I can't say what potential it has."

Her look was sullen, suspicious. "Can't or won't?"

David wondered what impression she would make at a faculty tea. She most likely didn't attend such functions. Probably Lukas didn't, either. From what David had read, the man savored his reputation for being a rebel as both an academic and a scientist.

"I think it'll do well," he said. "I've had some prior success. Is Lukas available?"

A large German shepherd appeared at her side, ears pricked, its fixed stare intimidating.

"This is Wolfman," she said. "It's a stupid name. Lukas named him. He won't hurt you as long as you don't try to touch him."

Although Linette wore hardly more than a bikini and favored a provocative hip-shot stance, David knew that she was warning him not just to avoid touching the dog but also to keep his hands off her or suffer a savage bite.

"Come in," she said, and she stepped back from the door as the dog, too, relented to allow him entrance.

She escorted David to a large living room that was furnished less like an adult residence than like a room in a fraternity house. An enormous flat-screen TV. A poker table with six chairs in one corner. A Harley-Davidson Rocker with a fully chromed conversion package stood against one wall, like a piece of sculpture. Books and magazines were scattered about. There were armchairs and a sofa and plenty of evidence that the housekeeper who came in one day a week didn't know where to start.

Linette motioned David to an armchair, and she sat in another that faced him. She propped her feet on a footstool, sitting with her long coltish legs spread. The dog sat beside her, almost as still as a life-size ceramic canine meant to ornament a garden.

David waited for the woman to say something, but she only stared at him until he spoke. "Is Lukas here? I hope he remembered our meeting."

She said, "Lukas is dead, the selfish sonofabitch."

52

Because Linette Ockland wasn't behaving like a grieving widow, and because the police blotter listed her husband as merely missing, David assumed her announcement was a weird bit of macabre humor. "I guess there's a punch line. He's quite a joker."

She tilted her head to regard him quizzically. "He is? Do we know the same Lukas? I've never known him to be a lot of laughs. I reported him missing Sunday night, and the cops are finally getting off their fat asses and taking it half seriously. But whatever they think, I know he's dead."

"You're serious?"

"Don't I look serious?"

She looked about as serious as a blow-up sex doll.

"But if he's only missing, how do you know . . . it's something worse?"

"We've been married four years. We have this arrangement. He always lives by it. He knows he damn well better. Then suddenly he doesn't."

"What arrangement — if I may ask?"

"He humps anyone he wants, eighteen or older, but he has to be home by midnight, his curfew."

That statement was so ludicrous that it

sounded like a joke, too, but David no longer assumed that apparent humor was the real thing. "And he didn't come home Sunday night?"

"Or last night. And he didn't call. There are certain times he calls, checks in. That's part of our arrangement, too. He'll hump anything that moves. I told him a thousand times, sooner or later he's going to stick his dick in some psycho bitch, and *she's* going to stick a long knife in him. If he staggered in here right now, bleeding, I'd half want to finish him off, the idiot, risking everything he's been building in partnership with the university and with his company, his patents, risking it all for another piece of tail. Part of that 'everything' was mine. Now what do I have?"

Evidently, something had gone badly wrong with academia since the last time David had been on a college campus.

"How much success?" she asked.

"What?"

"You said you're a writer. You said you've had some success. How much success?"

"Several bestselling novels. A few were number one."

Wolfman got to his four feet, shook himself, and slunk across the room to the poker table.

"You think there's a big book in my story?" Linette asked.

"Well, I don't know your story."

"Being married to the eccentric super genius with the permanent stiffie."

None of this had gone in any way as he expected. However, he had come here to learn whatever he could, so he adapted, pretended that he saw nothing peculiar about this place or she who ruled it. He drew her out. "It probably depends on how outrageous his sex life was. There's always a market for that kind of thing."

"As outrageous as it gets. He was a narcissistic bastard, a sex addict, an encyclopedia of fetishes."

Wolfman sniffed around the poker table, apparently hoping to find a bit of dropped potato chip or pretzel previously overlooked, but paused now and then to glare across the room at their visitor.

David almost apologized for the question he was about to ask, but then he decided that apologies would seem quaint to this woman, who could so easily speak in the crudest terms of the most personal things to a stranger who came to her door. "If he's so obnoxious, why did you marry him?"

"I could see how smart he was, above the rest, how he was going to make billions if

255

he didn't self-destruct. I'm not stupid. I'm the farthest thing from stupid, whether you believe that or not. I could see his potential. He was my ticket, and I was the control that he needed. He couldn't hold it together without me, and he knew it."

"Control?"

"He was a sick sonofabitch. His ideal sex goddess was like thirteen, fourteen."

The disorder of the house apparently reflected the disordered morality of the man who lived there. "A pedophile."

"He could have been. He got himself in some bad trouble once and barely squeezed out of it. I've got this perfect body if you're really into adolescent girls, and I've got this face like I'm still in middle school. When Lukas couldn't keep his Humbert Humbert under control, we did a little role-playing. Sometimes he seduced little Linette, sometimes he tore my clothes off and forced himself on me and I fought and he made me do the most humiliating, disgusting things he could think of. He could be tedious, really, a crushing bore, but you wouldn't have to write it that way."

Wolfman returned from the poker table and stood six or seven feet from David, staring intently, as though he might attack if the slightest expression of distaste was addressed to his mistress.

"We had rules," she said. "He accepted and obeyed them. He was a year, two at most, from the big breakthrough, the thing that would have made us billionaires when he took the company public. Then he goes out and hooks up with some psycho bitch who slits his throat or cuts his dick off. I hate the selfish asshole. He was so brilliant and so stupid at the same time."

"Maybe you're wrong about what's happened. He might show up."

"Yeah, and maybe there's life on Mars with good pizza shops and bowling alleys and everything."

Wolfman's hackles were up, and he growled low in his throat, as if he could read David's mind. His mistress called him to her. With some reluctance, the dog went to sit beside her chair once more.

"As I understand it, your husband's primary work involves something called archaea."

"Yeah. Particularly those archaea that have the capacity to affect HGT."

"I'm afraid it's all over my head."

She swung her feet off the footstool and sat forward on the armchair, suddenly less the pop princess that her T-shirt declared and more like a ninth-grade science geek.

"There are three domains of animal life on Earth. Eukaryotes, which is us and all the higher animals. Then bacteria. You know bacteria. And then microbes called archaea. Until like 1978, archaea were thought to be bacteria. But bacteria are ester based, and archaea are ether based, very stable compared to bacteria, and with all sorts of properties that bacteria don't have."

"You're really into this," David said, surprised.

"I am *totally* into it. I'm the boy toy the dickhead wanted me to be, but I'm also who I am. You got that?"

"I've got it. What does HGT stand for?"

"Horizontal gene transfer. It used to be thought genes can be passed only vertically, from parents to their offspring, and that's by far the primary route. But thanks to molecular phylogenetics, we can compare nucleic acids — DNA and RNA — from different species and track the origin. Archaea can fuck with your genome and insert material from another species, from other animals, even from plants. That sounds like a shitcan horror movie, but it's only nature at work, it happens all the time. There are a lot of ways this thing can revolutionize human life for the better if it can be harnessed. Lukas, the stupid sleazy tail-chasing perv, was a hundred miles ahead of everyone else who's racing for this particular finish line."

"For the better — how?" David asked.

She eased even farther forward on her chair. "Are you looking *at* me, like you were before, or are you finally looking *into* me, at the me inside this bod? You see me clear?"

"Yes."

"You asked 'better how'? Among other things, life extension and the reversal of the effects of aging. Lukas wanted to live forever and be always young, always stiff, the idiot. Maybe archaea HGT will be used to import genes that extend the human life span to two hundred years with a youthful appearance, which isn't forever, but it's a fucking big deal. Do you realize the *billions upon billions* that would flood to the company that makes the breakthrough?" She was so agitated that she could not remain in the chair. She got up to pace. "You see what I've lost because my genius perv husband couldn't keep his pants zipped, because he thought every woman wanted him, because he couldn't even *conceive* that he might hook up with some crazy bitch who wouldn't adore him, who'd instead gut him like the pig he was? Without his guidance, the research goes on, but half-assed and slow. He was *that* smart. So not two years anymore. Maybe ten. Maybe never. There's some value in his patents, but I'll have to fight the shitty university, which has an interest in them. The administration there is a band of thieves, and they have all the money in the world to fight me in court, the bloodsucking leeches."

David floated some optimism at her again. "Just because he broke the rules doesn't mean he's dead. There could be another explanation."

Her phone rang.

She plucked it off the table that stood beside her armchair. "Yeah? Yeah, speaking." She listened and then said, "Man, this sucks. Where was this?" Maybe she hadn't received the worst news, but it wasn't good. She stood pouting like a child. "Was he alone?" Her pout turned into a scowl, and Wolfman whimpered, psychically sharing her distress. "So did you get him out of there?" The answer was lengthy, and Linette grew impatient with the caller, evidently interrupting. "Listen . . . no, you listen to me. You better believe there's a crazy bitch in this somewhere. He's into edgy situations with sluts who have a screw loose. You better operate on that assumption." Wolfman slumped onto his side and continued whimpering. "I want to know who the bitch was.

You find her or I'll be all over your ass in the media, I'll never stop. This is a damn outrage. It takes thirty-six hours to get to this, to *this*? Thirty-six hours, when I told you it was a life-or-death emergency already Sunday night?"

She didn't wait for a reply, but terminated the call and threw the phone across the room. It cracked off a wall and rattled to the floor.

David got to his feet. The atmosphere in the house and this woman's unrelenting attitude were oppressive. He felt trapped.

Anger failed to age Linette's middle-school face but made her look even younger, like a petulant child in the flush of a tantrum. "Police. The shitheads found his car in a canyon off the Ortega Highway, two hundred feet below the road, totally racked up. He's as dead as dead gets. What the hell was he doing way the hell out there on the damn Ortega Highway, middle of nowhere? Being killed, that's what he was doing. You know what I think? I think some crazy bitch killed him somewhere else and drove his body out there and pushed the car over the edge to make it look like an accident. When they do an autopsy, they'll find a dozen stab wounds or a slit throat, or all of that plus his balls are missing." She picked up an eight-inch-tall crystal obelisk from a side-board and threw it at a wall.

The dog ran to hide under the poker table, and as if listening from another room, David heard himself offer his condolences to the woman. "I'm sorry for your loss."

"Billions!" she declared. "I'm so pissed, I wish I'd killed the sonofabitch years ago instead of wasting all this time on him."

"I'll just let myself out."

When she followed David to the front door, he felt pursued, not just by Linette but also by his fear of what the news about Lukas Ockland might portend.

"I am so screwed," she said. "This is a total shitstorm. Give me your card."

"What?"

"Your card, your card. We've got to plan our book. It'll be the tell-all of tell-alls. I'll rat out that perverted creep, scandalize the university pooh-bahs who enabled him, they're a bunch of chicken hawks and coke-heads, and those geek legions of fanboy bio-techies who idolize Lukas on their circle-jerk websites."

To placate her, he fumbled a card from his wallet. It bore a number that he gave to contacts when doing book research. He never answered that line. All calls went to voice mail, and he returned them when he saw fit. "I'll give you a call Monday," he lied, "when you've had time to" — *grieve* was not just the wrong word, but also absurd — "when you've had time to deal with all this."

He opened the door and stepped outside, into a suburbia that seemed to have subtly tilted while he'd been in the Ockland place, each house and identical mailbox and street sign and meticulously pruned tree ever-so-slightly aslant from all the others, as if a former unity was on the brink of fragmentation.

Linette followed him onto the stoop. "Your last name — is it spelled with an *e* or not?"

"With an *e*, like on the card."

"I'm going to get your books, check out your style. But I already know you're a really bright guy. I feel like we'll mesh, like we can get this on and do it right, make something big of it. You'll call me Monday?"

"Definitely. We'll meet. We'll get this going."

"It'll be fucking great, the book of the year."

"Monday," he lied, and he made his way through a world out of kilter, to his car at the curb.

53

David drove two blocks to the nearest park and got out of his car and walked to a lake and sat on a bench and stared out at the water, which mirrored the heavens. Sky above, sky below. As if he had come unmoored from the earth. Which was in fact how he'd begun to feel while in the Ockland house.

Lukas Ockland, first missing but now dead, might have been murdered. But he might not have been. An autopsy would eventually establish the truth.

If he had been murdered, his killer wasn't necessarily Maddison Sutton. By the testimony of his wife, he was sexually reckless, with a special fondness for edgy situations with women who perhaps were not mentally sound. Linette had half expected that he would sooner or later encounter a violent lover.

But a woman alone could not likely have killed him and loaded him in his car and sent it plunging into a canyon. And even if she had done that herself, she would have been without a vehicle, on a lonely stretch of the Ortega Highway.

Unless she had an accomplice. Someone like Patrick Michael Lynam Corley. No.

David had committed to her, pledged his heart to her, had told her that he loved her. If life had taught him one lesson above all others, it was that happiness did not proceed from the breaking of vows. She did not deserve his suspicion. She needed his help. She was under someone's thumb; she had said as much. And if he truly loved her, he needed to be focused on freeing her.

She was Emily. Somehow. Figuratively if not literally. Magically. Emily. She had to be. He could endure nothing else.

Sky above, sky below, and a question for a man adrift: Could the golden birthmark below Maddison's navel have been a tattoo?

No. He vividly recalled the texture of it under his finger and tongue. It was not perfectly flat but slightly raised, as had been Emily's. Tattoos had no dimension. This spot hadn't been prickled into her skin with needles and ink. It had been real, hers since she had entered the world.

She was either Emily, incredibly untouched by time, and for whatever reason could not reveal her true identity to him, or she was in some way an avatar of Emily, embodying her mind and spirit. He had no clue how such an avatar could exist. His ever-spinning imagination couldn't produce even a fragile thread of explanation. In either case, Emily or avatar, it was a matter of magic, in which he did not believe. And in either case, she was essentially Emily.

I'm a needy creature, Davey. I need to be loved every day, every hour. I know so well the loneliness of being unloved. Until you, I've been starved for love all my life.

Surely not.

But I have. Starved. And now I can't get my fill. Until you, life was . . . a horror.

Horror? For a girl with your mind, your heart, your charm? How could that ever be?

Loneliness, enduring fear, a sense that society has gone mad and I'm falling, falling through the madness of it. That's horror enough for me.

In memory, he could hear the haunting quality of her voice, which grew more marked in the last two sentences and which he did not believe she could have faked. She had lived through something horrific, and her heart and mind were scarred by it.

I feel safe here. Only here. With you. I feel so safe. Tell me it's forever.

If Maddison had only him, it was equally the case that he had only her. She was his to save, and in the saving of her, he might save himself.

Doubt had no place in a true love knot, and suspicion could not untie it.

A great egret, snow-white with long black legs and a wingspan of at least four feet, issued as if out of nowhere and flew low across the lake, seeming luminous, other-worldly, and its reflection in the water was a doubling of the miracle of its sudden appearance, so that David's heart was lifted.

He was about to get up from the bench when his phone rang. It was Josefa Alvarez, who took care of Calista Carlino. She was at a hospital and in tears. "Calie's had a stroke. Please come, come quickly, David, she's dying."

54

When David arrived at the hospital's intensive-care unit, Emily's mother had already passed. Weeping, Josefa Alvarez held fast to him for consolation.

He couldn't tell if the small room was warm or not, for cold radiated outward from his marrow. He wasn't able to stop trembling. White ceiling and walls, white floor, white bedsheets, white fluorescent light: It was a room in an ice palace.

Deep in grief, Josefa went home while David remained at Calista's bedside, waiting for the attending physician who, he'd been promised, would shortly speak with him.

The lady lay as though sleeping, her mouth and eyes closed. Although she was pale, death had not lined her face or left her with a tortured expression. She was still lovely and appeared to be in perfect health, though she would not ever open her eyes or speak to break this last of all silences.

David gripped the bed railing to steady himself. His legs were weak. He recalled what Maddison said about feeling as though society had gone mad, as if she were in free fall through all the madness. After the events of the past six days, especially after the bizarre experience in the Ockland residence with the venomous Linette, David was filled with foreboding, with the conviction that he was on the verge of a long fall into an abyss.

He blamed himself for failing Calista just as he had failed Emily. On the one hand, this sense of guilt was irrational. On the other hand . . . he knew why perhaps he should feel at fault, though he was afraid to consider the issue too closely. Not here, not yet.

A nurse entered the room and expressed her condolences as she gently drew the sheet over Calista's face.

Pushing a gurney, an orderly followed close behind the nurse.

"Where are you taking her?"

"Down to the holding room in the basement. Whatever mortician you make arrangements with can assume custody of the body there."

David wanted to slow things down, take time to accommodate himself to this terrible turn of events, to get his mind around how his life had changed, take time to catch his breath. Calista's death had been so sudden, and now the haste with which she was being moved to the hospital morgue seemed to dishonor her.

As the nurse opened the door for the orderly with his gurney, Dr. Theodore Goshen entered. He was dressed in green scrubs. Fiftyish, with a thickening waist and thinning blond hair, he had the weary look of a man who'd seen more death than he had bargained for when the romance of the healer's profession had long ago lured him into medical school.

Josefa had reported the cause of death as a stroke, a blood clot. But Dr. Goshen corrected that misapprehension.

"Not a blood clot. Cerebral aneurysm. The weakened wall of an artery gave way, resulting in a subarachnoid hemorrhage."

"I visited her late yesterday afternoon," David said. "She was in high spirits. She

269

seemed in perfect health."

Nodding as if accustomed to such protests against the mortal facts, Goshen said, "A cerebral aneurysm generally doesn't cause any symptoms until it either ruptures or begins leaking. Then there's a sudden, severe headache and stiff neck. Subsequently there can be vomiting, breathing problems, trouble swallowing, an inability to speak, but there were none of those conditions in this case. She had some slight confusion on admission, but she could breathe and speak, at least initially."

Calista's body had been removed.

The ICU cubicle lay in a hush.

Into David's silence, Dr. Goshen said, "Something?"

David said, "Could there have been . . ."

"Been what?" Goshen asked.

"This sounds melodramatic, but could there have been foul play? Poison, a drug, something to cause . . ."

With a puzzled expression, Goshen seemed to consider not the question so much as David himself, before he said, "No, not at all, not possible. Aneurysms are either congenital or develop later in life. They're a naturally occurring physiological weakness. She received supportive measures immediately on her arrival here and went straight to a CT scan for diagnostic evaluation. The scan was actually underway when the leaking aneurysm burst. The bleeding was massive, there was no time to ameliorate it, no time to prepare her for surgery."

Those were the assurances David had hoped to receive. He was relieved, although less because of the doctor's words than because he *wanted* to be relieved, to banish all suspicion.

"Is there some reason," Dr. Goshen asked, "some circumstance, that might make you wonder about foul play?"

"No, not really," David lied. "Just that, like I said, only yesterday she was in such high spirits, seemed so healthy — then this."

"She was special to you."

"Very special. Yes. Calista was a great lady. Blind since childhood, but she saw things more clearly than I did, more clearly than most of us ever do."

"You're the son-in-law, I believe."

"That's right," David said, rather than explain the painful truth of his and Calista's relationship.

"Her daughter's name is Emily?"

"Yes."

Dr. Goshen hesitated. "The slight confusion she exhibited on admission — it involved her daughter. She believed Emily was

271

at her side. She kept her right hand locked as if holding hands with her daughter, and she carried on a conversation with her."

For a moment, David couldn't speak. Then he said, "They were extremely close."

"Has Emily been notified?"

"Emily . . . Emily is dead."

Genuine sympathy seemed to inform the doctor's eyes, his face. "Ah. One loss after another. I'm so sorry, Mr. Thorne."

"Calista and I helped each other through it. I couldn't have made it without her."

There were papers to sign, acknowledgments and releases.

Calista had brought nothing with her. There were no personal effects to gather.

Although David had been in the hospital less than half an hour, when he stepped outside, he was surprised to find himself in warm morning light, for he had expected a bleak darkness to match his mood.

55

In the parking lot that served the cemetery and mortuary, shaded by the spreading boughs of an old water gum tree, David sat behind the wheel of his SUV, the windows open to receive the breath of the morning.

The tree was the one under which the

beige van had been parked in the security video, the shade the same in which the late Patrick Corley had stood waiting, inexplicably solid for a ghost, while Maddison Sutton had delivered the calla lilies to a grave that was not her own.

The flowers had been for Emily, the girl next door, but maybe they had also been for Calista as well. Maddison had known Calista would die soon. That conclusion was inescapable.

Yesterday, according to Calista, Maddison had visited her, had spent an hour in her company. In parting, she kissed Calista's hand three times and said, *I . . . love . . . you.*

Maddison's words, as recalled by Calista, echoed now in David's memory: *I've come back just for this one visit, so you will know that I'm happy and beyond all pain, and to tell you . . . be not afraid of whatever comes next, because I'll be with you always.*

Whatever comes next. Twenty-four hours later came a cerebral aneurysm. A severe headache, stiff neck, confusion, inevitably fear.

. . . be not afraid of whatever comes next . . .

And according to Dr. Goshen, Calista had not appeared to be afraid, only lightly confused.

. . . because I'll be with you always.

Because of that encounter and the encouragement Calista had taken from it, her bleeding brain evidently conjured a vision of Maddison — Emily — at her side as she'd been taken for a CT scan in the final minutes of her life.

Yesterday, David had been shocked and mystified that Maddison had visited Calista, that she had pretended to be Emily. When he'd come home, where Maddison was busy whipping up dinner, he had been reluctant to ask what motivated her to do such a thing, because he worried that their conversation would lead to the revelation that he'd been investigating her, that she would then withdraw from him.

He had assumed that her motivation had been ill-conceived if not even somehow suggestive of ill intent.

However, it now seemed that Maddison had visited Calista on a mission of mercy, to lift her heart and prepare her to endure the impending crisis of the aneurysm without fear.

Which meant Maddison had known Calista would soon die. Of an undetected, unsuspected, entirely natural arterial weakness.

How could she know? She couldn't.

274

The morning breeze, wafting through the car from window to window, brought no answer to his question. Neither did the soft whispering of the water gum tree.

David put up the car windows and went into the funeral home to make arrangements for the disposition of the body, as well as to purchase a single plot and a headstone.

Later, he would need to plan a memorial service for Calista's many friends, find a date two or three weeks hence. She had never wanted a traditional viewing and funeral with casket, which she'd thought too depressing. *I'd rather be remembered with a wake, lots of wine and upbeat music and laughter.*

When he came out of the funeral home following his appointment with Paul Hartell, the otherwise clear sky was scored by three thick white contrails, perfectly parallel from east to west, as though three celestial chariots had just passed over, escorting Calista's spirit home.

And on the green lawn of memorials sloping up from the parking area, perhaps fifty feet away, stood Patrick Michael Lynam Corley, seven years dead but as solid as David himself. The contractor was a big man, with broad shoulders and a barrel chest.

His glower, his stance, his hands fisted at his sides — the very fact of his presence — suggested malevolent intention. They stared at each other for a long moment. Then Corley turned away and ascended among the graves.

After a hesitation, David followed him.

56

By nature, David Thorne was not confrontational. Normally, if in anger another man braced him about anything, he would have stood his ground, but he wouldn't have taken a first step toward conflict. If a potential adversary had second thoughts and walked away, David would not usually have pursued.

But these were not normal times. After all that happened in the past five days, after this morning's bizarre encounter with Linette Ockland and the news of her husband's possible murder, after Calista Carlino's sudden death, David felt as if he were drowning in mysteries, suffocating in a quicksand of secrets.

Patrick Corley — or whoever this might be — following him, boldly watching him, represented a threat that suddenly seemed intolerable.

Through sunlight and tree shadows, along avenues of the dead, up mortal slopes, across the considerable acreage, Corley moved as quickly as a young man. He disappeared over the top of a hill.

When David reached the crest, beyond the last graves, he came to a gate in a chain-link fence. A sign identified the property beyond as being FUTURE DEVELOPMENT for the memorial park.

Groundskeeping equipment occupied a corrugated-metal building where two double-wide garage doors were raised. At a larger, similar structure, a man-size door stood open. Neither Corley nor anyone else was in sight.

David went to the second building and peered inside. Pale light revealed metal racks of landscaping supplies on both sides. Toward the back of the room, a door stood ajar, a brighter space beyond it, luring him.

He passed bags of fertilizer, boxes of grass seed, cans of insecticide and fungicide. Eased open the second door. An office. Maybe that of the head groundskeeper. Nobody. A door to a bathroom was open wide. No one in there.

When David turned from the threshold to leave, he came face-to-face with Patrick Corley, who crowded him backward into the office. "Stay away from her."

"Hey, hey, back off," David warned.

Estella Rosewater had described Corley as gentle, kind; but the contractor's face was wrenched by demonic anger, his teeth bared as though to bite. If he'd died in that supermarket, which he obviously had not, he was alive now, energized by rage, his eyes glinting like eviscerating blades. "You don't know who she is, what she is. You don't know *anything.*"

"And *you* don't own her. My God, you're old enough to be her grandfather."

Corley shoved hard, and David staggered backward, almost fell, grabbed at the desk to steady himself. The guy was *strong.*

"This isn't about sex, shithead. This isn't about that at all. This is something bigger than you'll ever understand, Thorne. Stay away from her or you're finished, I'm finished, she's finished. If she doesn't stay focused on her work, we're all dead."

As he loomed closer, Corley withdrew something from beneath his jacket and thrust it at David.

Knife!

No. Evidently it was some kind of Taser. Every nerve fascicle in David's body short-circuited. Bright pain scissored through him, and he collapsed. As he thought, *The sonofabitch isn't wearing a watch,* darkness washed over him.

When he woke, he tasted blood. He had bitten his tongue.

He was alone in the office.

His strength returned. He got onto his hands and knees, rose to his feet, and stood swaying until a brief dizziness passed.

Warily, he made his way out of the office, through the storage room, outside. He went to the chain-link fence. No sign of Corley.

He passed through the gate, into the cemetery, and descended the long green slope. Whatever Patrick Corley might be to Maddison Sutton, he was not an inspiring example to the residents of the cemetery, who did not rise in imitation of his resurrection.

57

When David pulled into the garage at forty minutes past noon, Maddison's Mercedes sports car was not in the second stall. After getting out of the shower and finding his note about an appointment with his attorney, she must have gone off on errands of her own.

After the events of the day, David felt disoriented, no nearer clarity than he'd been when his investigation had begun with a call to Isaac Eisenstein the previous Friday. No matter what Corley might insist, David belonged to Maddison, and she had given herself to him, not just physically but emotionally, and he feared both losing what he had won and somehow failing her. Yet again he would delay bracing her face-to-face with what he had thus far discovered. He hoped that further inquiries might bring a resolution of these mysteries, proof of her innocence in all things, and peace of mind.

A handwritten note lay on the kitchen table:

My sweet Davey,
I can't be with you for a while. It's too dangerous for both of us in the current atmosphere. I must persuade them, negotiate. Soon, but not yet. Be patient and believe in me. I promised you many wonderful days together, and we will have them perhaps sooner than later. I love you. I live for you. Please wait for me.

She had not signed the note, as though to say that he must decide for himself whether she was Maddison or Emily, or both.

As if the message must be a forgery or a

prank, he went through the small house, urgently calling her name, but she didn't answer.

Only the previous afternoon, she had left her luggage in the bedroom with the intention of moving in for at least a few days. Those bags were no longer there. No clothing of hers hung in the closet. Nothing belonging to her remained in the bathroom.

Had she left voluntarily?

Or had Corley taken her away by force?

Stunned immobile, David stood in the silence of the house, which was alike unto the hush of the ICU cubicle when he had waited there alone with Calista's lifeless body, the silence of death, the last of all silences, and he waited for a sound that might prove that he wasn't as dead as he felt, that might start his life moving again.

■ ■ ■ ■

PART 4
THE THORN
IN THE HEART

■ ■ ■ ■

58

As he stood in the bedroom, the ringtone broke the sepulchral silence and brought him to life. He withdrew his smartphone from a jacket pocket, his link to life renewed, certain that the caller must be Maddison. However, his editor in New York, Constance, was calling to report that first-pass proofs of his next novel had just been emailed to him and that he had two weeks to read them and correct any errors that had occurred in typesetting.

He forced himself to sit on the edge of the bed and gossip for fifteen minutes, as he and Connie often did. Either he didn't sound as despondent as he felt or she failed to hear the deep current of discouragement beneath his bright chatter.

When they disconnected, David entered the phone number that Maddison had given him. He was sent directly to voice mail and left a message. "I'm confused. I don't understand. Call me."

In the kitchen once more, he read the note she had left, read it a third time. He wasn't concerned about her warning of danger to him. What obsessed him was the implication that she must be under the thumb of some cruel master, Corley or others whom Corley served, being used in one way or another.

I must persuade them, negotiate.

His heart felt compressed by his breastbone, as though the sense of inadequacy that settled on him had real, crushing weight.

He phoned her again and was sent to voice mail. "*Confused* was the wrong word, Maddison. I'm bereft, I feel lost, and I'm afraid for you. I love you. Whatever your situation is, I know I can help. Give me a chance to help. Please, please, call me."

For more than an hour, he restlessly toured the house, as though he would come across something else she'd left behind, other than the note, some cryptic clue that, with sufficient study, would reveal more about the truth of her than he had yet uncovered. He stood at one window after another, gazing out at the day, but the day offered him nothing, not even the comfort of familiarity. The street and the neighboring residences and the courtyard between his house and garage appeared shot through with a subtle but disturbing strangeness. One by one, he took books from the shelves in his study and focused intently on a page of this, a paragraph of that, and put them back without remembering a word of what he'd read.

Eventually, when Maddison did not respond to his phone calls, indignation rose in him, a sense of righteous offense, which became resentment, which grew into anger. He stalked into the bedroom and stared at the bed they had shared. She'd hidden the truth of herself from him, and she'd walked out on him. He couldn't abide sleeping with the sheets in which were enfolded even the faintest scent of her. He tore the bedclothes off the bed and carried them to the laundry room and put them in the washing machine.

But the indignation and resentment and anger were not real, only fabricated feelings with which to mask from himself his hurt and fear. He could not sustain the faux outrage.

He started to phone her again, but stopped before he pressed CALL. She had asked for his patience and faith. He owed her nothing less than what she requested.

He printed the proofs of his forthcoming

novel, which Connie had sent earlier. But he could not concentrate on the text.

At 3:20, although he rarely drank before dinner, he opened a bottle of cabernet sauvignon and poured a generous portion and took solace in the smoothness of the grape.

He decided that in the morning, if he had not heard from her, he would drive to the house on Rock Point Lane. If his life really was at risk, the danger would likely be greater there than anywhere else, but he was in a mood to walk ledges and high wires.

When he was in New York, the management company that cared for this house also collected his mail at the street and sent it to him once a week. But it was now his to collect, which he hadn't done for the past few days. Among the envelopes that he brought in from the mailbox, he found one from Ronny Lee Jessup, posted from Folsom State Prison, stamped with a warning that the contents were from a prisoner of a maximum-security facility.

According to the postmark, the letter had been mailed at 5:00 p.m. Friday, the afternoon of the day that David had visited Ronny. He sat at the kitchen table to read it.

Dear Mr. Thorne,

Since you left a few hours ago, a thing has happened that changes my mind. If you come to see old Ronny, we can maybe work something out so I can tell you what you want so bad to know. I hope you are well and happy and all. I am good, but not as happy as usual.

> Your friend,
> Ronny Lee

David phoned his contact at Folsom and was able to arrange a visit for ten o'clock Thursday morning. Then he booked a commuter flight to Sacramento for Wednesday afternoon — the next day.

The Rock Point Lane house would have to wait. He had spent years trying to get Ronny Jessup to reveal where he had stashed the missing fourteen women whom he had killed and whose bodies he preserved by some arcane form of mummification. He needed to seize this opportunity before the killer changed his mind.

59

The vase of roses Maddison had bought remained on the table with the three candles in cut-crystal holders.

David microwaved leftover *tortellini alla panna,* carrots with tarragon, and cauliflower Sicilian style, which Maddison had cooked the previous evening. Everything tasted good, but even if it had not held its quality from a day earlier, he would have taken pleasure in the food because she had prepared it with her own hands, which made him feel close to her even in her absence.

As he ate and as he sipped the cabernet, he studied the photo of the blood-filled amulet that hung from a gold chain in Maddison's Rock Point Lane bedroom, which earlier he had printed on glossy photographic paper.

Ever since he had seen that strange pendant above her bed, the previous day, it had troubled him because it stirred an echo in his memory, resonated off an event in the past that he couldn't recall.

At first it had seemed to be an icon with some sacred meaning, akin to a crucifix, but David was not able to sustain that simple interpretation.

If you were superstitious enough to believe in vampires, you might hang a clove of garlic over your bed. But what creature would you intend to ward off with an ampule of blood?

It's too dangerous for both of us . . .

He became aware that darkness pressed at the windows. He got up to lower the pleated shades. Sometimes he failed to set the alarm at night, and he never employed it prior to going to bed. Now, however, he crossed the room to the security-system panel next to the back door, and he pressed the button to engage the at-home mode.

After he finished eating and rinsed the dishes and put them in the dishwasher, he poured the last of the cabernet and carried his glass and the photograph into his study. He emailed the picture to Isaac Eisenstein with a short message inquiring if he'd ever seen anything like the pendant, if it suggested a cult of any kind. He didn't say where it had been hanging when he'd seen it.

Because he had drunk the bottle of wine over three and a half hours, he was only mildly inebriated. Maddison had not returned his calls, and he suspected that she was in all ways out of his life for an extended period. What if forever? He wasn't usually a man who, when despondent, drank to excess, but he *was* that man tonight, for he knew he would not sleep, even to dream of her, if he didn't have the assistance of cabernet.

He opened a second bottle, only for one

last full glass. He sat at the kitchen table to drink, watching the candles gradually gutter in their crystal cups, their lambent glow lapping the velvet petals of the deep-red roses, which seemed to swell with pleasure at the gentle licking of the light.

60

The door to the underworld is in an ordinary kitchen, a two-inch-thick slab of local oak hung from sturdy iron hinges. No fiery-eyed hounds with serpent fangs guard the entrance, because everyone who wishes to descend may do so unimpeded; such is the all-welcoming nature of Hell. The wood stairs speak his footfalls to the realm below as he makes his way down through the rose-colored light and through the open steel-bar gate into the receiving room. Hades, the god of the underworld, is nowhere to be seen, but the bargain has already been made, and there are no papers to be signed either in ink or blood. If he can find her, he will be allowed to lead her out, out and up into the world of the living, although if he once looks back at her while they ascend, she will be lost to him, lost forever. Through narrow winding corridors that might have been eaten from the earth by some monstrous maze-making worm, he seeks Emily, softly calling her name, softly, softly, so as not to summon other presences that might tear out his soul, like smoking sweetbreads, and greedily consume his immortality. With increasing urgency, he searches these tunnels of rose light, passing doorless rooms like aneurysms swollen off the artery through which he moves, catacombs where bodies should lie in wait of resurrection, but there are no bodies, neither dead nor living. Urgency becomes a frantic exigency, panic, for though this place should be outside of time, he feels time running out. Then in answer to his calling of her name, he hears his name spoken — "Davey" — and he stops, turns, discovers that she has heard, has come, is following him. The Egyptian windings have begun to unravel from her, revealing her eyes, her mouth and chin. Even from what little he can see of her, he knows that before him stands Emily, vivid and uncorrupted after all these years, her luminous blue stare beseeching him to rescue her. Now that he has found her, he must never look back at her again until they have ascended to the world of the living. That is the bargain. He hurries forward through claustrophobic wormholes, serpent tunnels, in a mist of rose light that is a mockery of romance, trusting her to remain behind him. It seems that he will never find his way through the labyrinth, but at last he comes into the receiving room, passes through the steel gate without glancing back. He begins to climb the steep plank steps, although an enormous weight presses on him, as if he is a deep-sea diver making way under a thousand feet of ocean. On the third of twelve steps, a voice speaks to him from within, that voice of doubt that lives in every human heart and labors to deceive: "Is she still close behind you or have you moved too quickly for her to keep up?" But he does not look back. On the sixth step, the voice inquires, "Is she truly Emily, or have you mistaken another for Calista's daughter?" His gaze remains fixed on the open door at the stairhead. On the ninth step, the voice warns, "If she is Maddison, then you have left Emily among the dead forever." He answers that they are one and the same, Emily and Maddison, and if they are not one and the same, nevertheless he loves them both. But that is not an adequate justification for such an error as the one of which he's being accused. On the twelfth step, with only the landing ahead, the voice within his heart asks, "Is it not a betrayal of your Emily, yet another betrayal, to mistake Maddison for her, leave her among the dead, and embrace her imposter, all in the interest of your own happiness?" Ten gravities pin him to the final step, and he can't lift a foot to the landing, can't reach the threshold at the open door while unsure of whom he's led this far. He turns his head. The interment windings have continued to unravel. She stands further revealed, two steps below him, and she is Emily, no doubt of that, Emily unique. But before his eyes, ten years of death, until now held at bay, abruptly take their toll, and as corruption seethes through her flesh, she says, "I loved you," and she falls away from him, a figure of such horror that his scream comes from him as a silent cry.

David did not wake.

He groaned and muttered in the sweat-soaked sheets.

In sleep, he kept writing new drafts of the dream, but in every one, he was Orpheus from the Greek legend, and she was Eurydice, and he betrayed her with a forbidden glance.

61

Wednesday morning, David was weary of sleep and in need of a bottomless cup of black coffee.

He switched on the TV to cable news. The day was already a dark carnival of the political pandemonium and media hysteria that had become too much the norm. Plus a nightclub shooting in Miami with twenty dead. Riots in Chicago. Churchgoers shotgunned in Memphis. Thirty dead in a terrorist attack on a synagogue in Israel. Two wars in the Middle East. He turned it off.

At the computer in his study, he accessed the law-enforcement website with the countywide police blotter.

Lukas Ockland's name had been removed from the list of missing persons. Two others had been added: a thirteen-year-old girl named Reagan Ausbock, and a seventy-nine-year-old man, Juan Pedro Flores. Neither seemed a likely target for an assassin.

The list of homicides included no new names. Lukas Ockland had not been added, although perhaps the results of an autopsy remained to be revealed.

He recalled Estella Rosewater's account of seeing the late Patrick Corley with Maddison on the eighteenth of August, just the previous year, at a restaurant in Menlo Park.

Menlo Park was in San Mateo County. When David searched, he found that San Mateo also offered a law-enforcement website with a countywide police blotter.

The archives were accessible, and within minutes he discovered that a murder had been committed in Menlo Park on August nineteenth. The victim was the wealthy thirty-year-old cofounder of a company intent on developing virtual-reality recreations of real crimes to facilitate police investigations and criminal prosecutions, whatever that might mean. The murder had been intimate. A stiletto had been slipped between his ribs and into his heart, and he had been found naked in bed. More than seven months later, the police still had no leads.

David exited the website.

He switched off the computer and sat staring at the dead screen for a long while.

Later, he packed a suitcase for an overnighter in Sacramento. He included pictures of Emily, which he might need to share with Ronny Lee Jessup.

62

At 2:25 p.m., as David sat at the desk in his study, struggling to concentrate on the first-pass proofs of his latest novel, Isaac Eisenstein called from New York.

"I keep looking at those photos of your cutie, and it's beauty and the beast, though King Kong was handsomer than you. She must see something in you that I don't, boychik. Have you ignored my sterling advice? Have you shtupped her yet?"

"None of your business."

"*Hoo-ha!* You have. 'None of your business' is a flat-out no-argument admission. Any detective worth his salt knows what 'none of your business' means. Having seen so many pictures of her, I wonder if you're man enough for this, my friend. I sincerely worry that you are going to end up a mere husk of your former self, drained beyond replenishment."

"Damn it, Isaac, she's more than just a looker. She's smart, funny, charming. She's sweet and vulnerable. She's not just some hot piece of tail, so don't talk about her that way."

After a silence, Isaac said, "Hey, listen, David, I'm sorry. I didn't realize it's so serious. I was just, you know, being the lovable asshole that I am."

David's face flushed hot. His heart beat fast. "You don't have anything to apologize for, Isaac. You didn't know. Hell, *I* didn't know. It's only been a week since we met. She's really bowled me over."

"When you get back to New York, you can kick my ass all the way to Gramercy Tavern, and I'll pay for lunch."

"Forget it. I never should have snapped at you."

"Have you told her?"

"That I love her? Yes."

"That, too. But have you told her you hired the nation's finest shamus to investigate her?"

David grimaced with guilt. "Not yet."

"Have you asked her to explain herself, to clear up all the mysteries?"

"I will." Then he lied: "Anyway, many of the mysteries have cleared up by themselves over the past couple days."

"I'm glad to hear that. But talk to her, tell her. If you feel this strongly about her, you owe it to her to be transparent."

"I shouldn't have snapped at you."

"De nada."

"Well, I shouldn't have snapped because I still want you to tell me what you think. I don't want you holding back about her, just to avoid offending me."

"Sounds like you love her but you're conflicted."

" 'Conflicted' is one word for it."

"Maybe you don't need to be. I didn't call you just to report on that charming vial-of-blood necklace. Pazia made me call you about something else."

299

"How did she like Le Coucou, by the way?"

"Loved it. I am her hero. But even heroes do stupid things. I told you to dump this Maddison and use an online dating service — or join a monastery. Pazia says I was wrong, and I think she's right. I don't even know your girl. Listen, the world is going to hell. Maybe it's always been going to hell, but it's sliding down faster on a steeper slope than before. There's so much insanity these days, so much hatred and violence. The internet, social media, seems like a poison that makes some people crazy, it's all about power, everyone wanting to tell everyone else what to think, how to live. It won't end well. If you've got a chance at happiness with this Maddison, then, by God, grab it. We don't get that chance so often that we can afford to turn down something good with the hope something perfect is right around the corner. Not that this gorgeous girl of yours isn't perfect. I'm sure she's perfect. Don't take my head off."

Even in his loneliness and confusion and simmering fear, David found a laugh. "That was quite a speech."

"A private dick is supposed to be a strong, silent type, as terse as a Mickey Spillane character. But when you're married long enough to a psychiatrist, you start babbling like a therapist and philosopher. I love Pazia, she's a peach, but she'll eventually ruin my business."

"So what about the pendant? Ever see anything like it?"

"Where did you find it? Who does it belong to?"

"It belongs to me now," David lied. "I saw it in a thrift shop, and I thought there has to be a story in it, maybe something I can write."

"Who runs this thrift shop? Satan? There's a South American gang, as violent as MS-13, their motto is 'rape, rob, and kill for justice.' Each of them wears blood from his first victim. But this isn't that. The chain's too girly. Only guys allowed in this gang, and they put the blood in an empty rifle cartridge and seal it, not in a glass ampule."

"That's all you've got?"

"Believe it or not, neither Cartier nor Tiffany has a line of blood jewelry. Back in the day, there were those two movie stars, Billy Bob Thornton and Angelina Jolie, they wore little vials of each other's blood on pendants, but for some reason the marriage didn't last. Maybe you've found a genuine Hollywood treasure."

David glanced at his wristwatch. "I've got

an appointment. But I'll look forward to coming back to New York and kicking your ass all the way to Gramercy Tavern."

As he terminated the call, the elusive memory wimpled through the deeper waters of his mind, the incident that he couldn't quite recall and that somehow seemed related to the pendant hanging above Maddison's bed.

He pushed aside the page proofs and carried his empty coffee mug to the kitchen and washed it and put it away.

He tucked his suitcase in the car and drove to John Wayne Airport to catch the commuter flight to Sacramento.

On takeoff, when the tarmac dropped away, a quiver of dread passed through him, and he thought perhaps he would never walk the earth again.

Though alive on touchdown in Sacramento, he felt insubstantial, as if chasing after ghosts might be wearing him away, until soon he would be a mere spirit.

In the rental car, on his way from Sacramento International to his hotel, he wanted to reverse course, fly south, return home, and live in the quiet behind the pleated shades of his sweet bungalow, where the madness of the world would not intrude, and wait for her to call him, if she ever did.

He did not want to go to Folsom in the morning. He did not want to talk with Ronny Lee Jessup. He did not want to go down among the fourteen stolen girls, wherever they might be. What he didn't want didn't matter. That very descent had been his destiny for ten years.

63

The table and benches were bolted to the floor, as if David's eerie sense of reality warping around him had become manifest, the laws of physics inverted, so that the furniture might float to the ceiling. Bear-big gentle-looking Ronny Lee Jessup, with his ever-warm smile and honey-brown eyes glimmering with plush-toy sympathy, sat shackled to a bench and cuff to a steel ring in the apron of the table, as if some grave injustice had cast into prison an innocent host of a Saturday morning TV show for children. The armed guard watched from behind a windowed door.

In a voice as warm and honeyed as his eyes, the killer said, "I guess you got my letter. The postal service does a good job. I often think I could've been a postman. You meet a lot of pretty girls and all on a mail route, I guess, and you see where they live.

Thank you for coming to visit old Ronny, Mr. Thorne."

From the farther side of the wide table, David said, "I hope you haven't brought me here just to toy with me further."

A carefully constructed sadness reshaped Ronny's expressive face. "I always been honest with you, Mr. Thorne. I couldn't tell you where my girls are hid, because if maybe one day I got out of here and needed them. But everything else, I always been true with you. You're a nice man, been fair to me. Now a thing has happened so where the girls are hid isn't a secret I need to keep no more."

"What happened?"

With his eyes and a tip of his head, Ronny indicated his right hand, which was heavily bandaged. "They mostly keep me solitary, you know. So I won't hurt no prisoners, as if I got an interest in men, which is plain silly. But they also keep me mostly to myself also to keep me safe. There's some in here, all bad men, bad as me but can't admit it to themselves, which is their shortcoming, and they think what I done to my girls makes me unfit company. They want to prove themselves better than me by doing me damage. So one cut me with a makeshift knife. He don't have it no more. He don't

304

have a left eye, neither. My hand will heal okay, but this thing happening made me see there's no way I'll have my girls no more. My days are numbered, thanks to some bent guard or another, which is all right, being as how I earned my end because of what I did. Old Ronny is weak when it comes to pretty girls, shamefully weak, and this here isn't no world for the weak."

"Bent guard?" David asked.

Ronny shrugged his big shoulders. "It weren't no accident how he got near me. And nobody here has no makeshift knife that big and sharp unless someone on the other side of the bars wants him to have it. Sad as it is to say, I think maybe one of them newer guards here is from a family where I stole one of my girls. Busy as I was when I was having all my fun, there's bound to be lots of family members out there. This had to happen sooner or later. And it'll happen again. I see that now. Old Ronny might have a month, maybe a year, but he don't have no lifetime, Mr. Thorne. So what I want is you and me do a deal."

"What deal?"

"You know I'm an indigent. It embarrasses me to say, but I got nothing to my name, I'm poor as dirt."

"I send five hundred a month to your account."

Tears, as though of gratitude, welled in Ronny Jessup's eyes and slid down his cheeks. "You do, Mr. Thorne. Like clockwork every month, and life would be dreary without it. I'm forever grateful for your generosity. If you could see your way to making it a thousand, old Ronny's last days would be better than he deserves. It wouldn't be no long obligation. Like I said, my days are numbered, a year at most. If you could agree to do such a very Christian thing for me, then I'll pay you back with what you want to know."

David closed his eyes and took slow deep breaths to repress his anger. Ronny Jessup's feelings were easily hurt. If he felt abused, he would withdraw for days, weeks, nursing his bruised feelings. David didn't have weeks. Maddison, in the grip of some cruel master whom she had no choice but to obey, also perhaps didn't have weeks. He couldn't learn the truth of Maddison until he knew the truth of what had happened to Emily. He felt the vise of fate closing its jaws around him, around him *and* her.

"All right. A thousand a month to your account. But how do you know I'll keep my promise once you've told me?"

Ronny's tear-slick face formed into a broad smile worthy of that superb character actor, Thomas Mitchell, from the era of great films. "Bless you, Mr. Thorne, but I know your word is gold. You're not like me, you keep your promises. You're a good man."

The obsequious flattery offended David, but he didn't say as much. "Where have you hidden them?"

The quality of the killer's smile changed from faux gratitude to genuine delight in his cleverness. He leaned a little forward in his chair, as much as his restraints allowed, and he whispered, although in this private conference room used by attorneys, no recordings were made. "Them pretty girls are hid under the house, Mr. Thorne, right under the noses of all the so-smart police that looked for them and didn't find them."

"But surely they wouldn't have missed them," David objected. "The police used cadaver dogs. They fluoroscoped the ground for hollow spaces in addition to the eleven rooms that were your . . . playground."

The smile grew sly and more offensive, as if they were cronies. Jessup winked. "The one more room, with fourteen girls treated and wrapped and waiting for a new life, isn't part of the basement and isn't outlying from it. That special room is *under* the basement, Mr. Thorne, direct under where they found my nine wrapped girls."

David found himself leaning forward conspiratorially. "Under the room with the blue eye that looks down from the center of the domed ceiling?"

Jessup nodded vigorously. "The very room where you yourself stood, Mr. Thorne. Under that very room."

For a moment, the importance of what the killer said eluded David, and then his gut clutched as understanding hit him. He had not visited the murder house yet when he had most recently paid a call on Jessup, the previous Friday, and he hadn't revealed to this man that he had any intention of going there.

"Ronny . . ."

"Yes, Mr. Thorne?"

"How do you know I went to your old house?"

"Oh, when you visited me last Friday, I already knew you was going there come Saturday. For some reason, you didn't say, and I didn't want to make a thing about it."

"But how did you know?"

Jessup leaned back in his chair. "Mr. Ulrich wrote me about it back when you paid him to see the place."

"Stuart Ulrich?"

"Yeah. Him that bought the place for taxes. He practically got it for nothing. Fact is, I'd call it stealing."

In his mind's eye, David saw Ulrich's face, a visage straight out of some Blumhouse movie, with his high bulbous brow, the low wide jaw like a scoop, the gray eyes as bright as honed steel and every bit as probing as scalpels.

"Ulrich writes to you?"

"From time to time. Mr. Ulrich is a curious man. He wants to know a thousand things — each thing me and them girls did with each other, how I felt when I did it to them girls, what them pretty girls said to me, how I killed them, how I preserved the ones I killed, where the hidden are hid. But don't worry none, Mr. Thorne, I never told him nothing. He stole the house for taxes, but he won't give me a dime for my needs. He don't care I'm indigent, the way you care. He's no Christian."

64

The painted eye on the ceramic tile inset in the domed ceiling of the chamber of mummification was the key to accessing the secret crypt under that room. With evident pride in his carpentry, masonry skills, and mechanical ingenuity, Ronny Jessup explained to David how the tile could be used to reach "my pretty future queens," and described the explosive trap he had laid in the stairs that led down to them.

When David felt confident that he understood, he put on the table the manila envelope containing photos of Emily, including those that he had shown Jessup on his previous visit.

The prisoner stared at this offering with keen interest and licked his lips as if wetting the way for some delectable morsel.

"Ronny, will you swear to me that the missing fourteen are in that hidden room?"

"On my honor, Mr. Thorne."

"In your freely given confession, you claimed to have abducted twenty-seven and murdered twenty-three."

"That's right. That's what I confessed. They caught me fair and square. No reason to lie."

"Of the twenty-seven, thirteen were found."

"Yes, sir."

"Among those fourteen in the secret chamber, is one of them Emily Carlino?"

Jessup raised his stare from the envelope and met David's eyes. "That's the one was so special to you."

"Is one of them Emily Carlino?" David pressed.

A homicidal psychopathic sentimentalist with a vivid emotional life, a psychic vampire who fed on the emotions of others, which were for him a mild continuous orgasm, Jessup wanted this visitor to share the pain and grief, so that he might consume it and revel in it, and satisfy his appetite.

David was about to lay out a banquet for him.

"I can't rightly say whether some Emily Carlino is among them. Like I told you last time you come here, my memory's been getting kind of fuzzy. Maybe I remember nine or ten names of them fourteen. I don't remember no Emily. Problem is, I had to kill some of them before I got a lot of use out of them. Some just didn't have the right attitude, wasn't fun enough. If I killed them too quick after bringing them home, if I didn't get a lot of use of them, I don't remember them so well, no matter how good they looked. But when they open that lower room, Mr. Thorne, they'll know, 'cause I painted each pretty girl's name on the slab where she lays wrapped, so I could resurrect them according to what I might have a taste for."

Jessup turned his attention again to the envelope.

Although David opened the clasp, he did not withdraw the ten photographs. "You told me the last time there were others in addition to the twenty-seven in your confession."

"That's only the truth."

"If Emily Carlino turns out not to be in that lower room, could she have been among those murders to which you didn't confess?"

"No."

"How can you answer so quickly? Your memory isn't what it once was. That's what you told me, Ronny."

When the killer looked up, his gaze had a far harder, sharper quality than before. "She weren't ever one of the others, and that's all I'll say."

"How many others were there?"

"She weren't one of them."

Time to push hard. No more playing by Ronny's rules.

"I'm in a very bad place, Ronny, a desperate place. I don't have time to fence with you. If you want that extra five hundred each month — hell, if you want to continue receiving the first five hundred every month — you've got to tell me everything, nothing can be withheld. I'm at my wit's end, I'm on a ledge, a cliff, and I'm not going to take your shit anymore. I can't. I'm sorry if this makes you angry or hurts your feelings, but that's the way it is. Besides the twenty-seven, *how many others were there?*"

Blood rose in Jessup's face even though his lips paled. He was angry. But this wasn't a pure anger; it was alloyed with something else that David couldn't identify. With evident reluctance, Jessup said, "Two."

"Two others in addition to the twenty-seven."

"Yes."

"Are they dead?"

"Yes."

"Was one of them Emily Carlino?"

"No."

"Who were they?"

Jessup closed his eyes. His jaws clenched. His pulse became visible in his temples. When he spoke, no anger colored his voice, only self-pity. "You're embarrassing me here."

Incredulous, David asked, "How am I embarrassing you?"

Shaking his head, Jessup said nothing.

David withdrew the ten photographs of Emily from the envelope and arranged them on the table, facing the killer. In addition to the two that he'd brought previously, including the one of her in a bikini, he had chosen eight others that he felt conveyed her charm, her warmth, the intelligence that shone in the clarity of her eyes, the character evident in the directness of her stare, the tenderness that would have made her some child's cherished mother.

"What I'm going to do now, Ronny, is embarrass myself, shame myself. I'm cutting open my heart for you, so you can see just what a stupid, deceitful, selfish shit I've been. I give this to you, I know it's the kind of thing you like. I know you get off on other people's anguish. So I give it to you — and in return, you tell me whatever it is you're ashamed of, whatever it is that's keeping you from answering my questions as fully as I need them to be answered."

Jessup opened his eyes and scanned the photographs arrayed in front of him. His bright button eyes were now half-lidded, and his tongue moved slowly between his lips like that of a blood-thinned lizard languishing in the hot sun.

"You see this woman, Ronny?"

"The real pretty one you showed me before. That is some girl, Mr. Thorne."

"Emily Carlino. I loved her, Ronny. I loved her more than I can put into words, loved

314

her so much more than I even realized at the time. I adored Emily. She wasn't just the most beautiful woman I've ever seen, she was also the finest *person* I've ever known. She was honest, caring, good to the bone. She completed me. We were together more than five years, and I never cheated on her, never even *thought* of cheating on her, never had the slightest urge — and then I did."

65

Raising his fevered eyes from the photographs, Ronny Jessup said, "Cheated on her? Who with? Did she know, did she cry?"

"Shut up, Ronny. Just shut up and listen. I'll tell it my way, it's my little walk through Hell. She had this good girlfriend who lived in San Luis Obispo. Name was Nina. Nina had this sudden cancer scare, as young as Emily, just twenty-five, and so afraid. Emily wanted to go to San Luis to be with Nina through the tests and exploratory surgery, just four or five days. She wanted me to go with her to keep *her* spirits up so she could be the best possible cheerleader for Nina. Usually I'd have gone. We went everywhere together, everywhere. It was only maybe two hundred fifty miles up the coast. But this time there was this other . . . this situation."

Jessup nodded sagely and opened his pouting lips to say, "You had this other girl you wanted to bang. Tell me who, Mr. Thorne. Did Emily know her? Was she another good friend of Emily's? Did you fuck one of her friends?"

David wanted to punch him in the face, but he deserved this opprobrium no matter who it came from, even from this monster. For a moment he was unable to continue.

With his free hand, Jessup turned one of the ten photos to face David, but David couldn't look at it and still finish his story.

"I had adapted a screenplay from my first novel. The film was in preproduction, almost ready to roll. I thought it was such a big deal. But it was just a movie. It wasn't anything that mattered, not in the long run. Some of the actors wanted to talk to me about their roles. Sometimes, if the director is just a shooter, just interested in the visuals, the actors want to talk to the screenwriter. I was in and out of LA. Mainly it was the female lead. She was only a few years older than me, but she was a huge star, beautiful. She came on to me a little. Then more than a little. I knew . . . knew I could have her, be with her."

By the intensity with which he listened, by

the fierce tension in his shackled body, Jessup demanded eye contact. David met his stare as the big man said, "I know who she is, Dave. Since you and me become friends, I learned all about you, read up on you, your big career. I know the movie, the star. She's hot. She a good girl? Were she slick when you was in her?"

David shuddered with revulsion. He took a few deep breaths to steady himself.

Jessup's ripe mouth formed a lazy crescent, the smile of a demon dreaming, and he turned another of the photos so that Emily faced David.

Get it over with.

"Just before Emily got the call from Nina, the actress phoned to invite me to dinner the next evening at her home in Bel Air, to discuss the motivation of her character, maybe to slightly massage some dialogue. I told Emily the call was from the director, I needed to go to LA for a couple days, it was important to the picture, I couldn't drive with her up to San Luis Obispo. Emily understood. She always understood. She was always supportive."

Turning a third photo toward David, Jessup said, "She didn't really understand, Dave. She didn't understand how you was lying your ass off to her."

317

David looked over Ronny Jessup's head at a high window screened and barred even though it was out of reach. A white bird perched on the outer sill, peering in and down at them as though it must be an augury of some portentous event impending.

He said, "She went to Nina by herself, stayed four days, started home in the afternoon, and ran into worse weather than she was expecting. And then her car broke down. I never . . . I never saw her again."

Jessup shook his head. "That don't do it, Dave. You skipped the best part. You skipped the actress part. It weren't just dinner. You stayed the night, I bet."

"Two nights. All these years later, I still don't understand myself, why I did it, what I was thinking. The fact that she was famous, that every man I knew would have envied me if they'd known? The glamour?" A short, bitter laugh escaped him. "It was about as glamorous as mud wrestling. She drank too much. So did I, though I never had before. She did cocaine, and I didn't. She was beautiful, but not as beautiful as Emily. She was uninhibited, yeah, but to an extent that scared me, that sickened me, the things she wanted, and in spite of all that, she was boring, self-absorbed. No real wit, no great intelligence, no genuine warmth but plenty of the method-acting kind."

"Tell me what you done with her and all, what sickened you," Jessup said. "Tell me, Dave. You got to look me in the eyes, look me straight in the eyes, Dave, don't shy away, and tell old Ronny . . . if then you want me to tell you."

When you made a deal with the devil, you had to expect there was fine print that, in your eagerness to descend, you failed to read but by which you were obligated to abide.

They sat eye to eye through David's disclosures. The longer he met Jessup's cobra stare, the more he was spell-caught by it, unable to look away. An ineffable connection arose between them, a seeming psychic wire. Word by word, David sensed not that something vital might be draining from him, which the term *psychic vampire* could have predisposed him to feel, but instead that Ronny Jessup strove to transmit some essential part of himself into his visitor, as though, at the end of this, David would find himself shackled and trapped in Jessup's body, while Jessup walked free as David Thorne.

And then it was done. He had withheld nothing, had fully shamed himself in front of this beast — and felt no better for it.

The killer's eyes brimmed with unshed tears. "You're a torn man, Dave. You're all torn up and hurting, and I sorrow to see it. You and me had self-control problems, we sure did, best to fess up to it. Make no excuses. That's the way. Now we got no one, neither of us, me cut and sure to die in prison, you all torn up and still tearing at yourself. It's a hard road we been on, Dave, a hard damn road. What worries me, Dave, because you're my friend, maybe my only friend in the whole world, so what worries me is the way you won't let go of this Emily. She's gone wherever, but you won't let go, and that's not healthy. You can only tear at yourself so long, and then one day you just fall apart. The way you won't let this go, Dave, I think you're falling apart, and I sorrow about that."

David didn't interrupt. He waited for Jessup to wind down. It took a while. Then he said, "In addition to the twenty-seven, there were two others you didn't confess to. They're dead."

"Just what I said."

"Who were they?"

"Neither of them poor souls were your Emily."

"Who were they?" David insisted. "If you

320

want one more dollar from me, answer my questions."

Jessup nodded. "Tit for tat. Tit for tat. We had us a tit-for-tat understanding. Old Ronny keeps his word. They was my first two, Dave. Children. A little boy, a littler girl. It felt all wrong. It weren't right, and it weren't fun enough. So I stopped for a while, till I figured out what would be better. If this was known by the bad men in here, I would've been cut dead long ago. In here, no one ranks lower on the totem pole than us misguided souls who did little children, no matter how we regret it. You now got my life in your hands, Dave. I trust you'll keep my secret, like I'll keep yours about how you humped the movie star while maybe Emily was dying."

Too exhausted for anger and many years beyond a capacity for self-righteousness, David merely said, "Were there any others?"

"Only them two. Like I told."

"You're sure there's no one you forgot?"

"Only a few names, Dave. Some faces. But I remember the number right enough. The number torments me, all the damage I done, all the families whose hearts I broke. Did Emily have a family?"

"Just her mother."

"You ever tell her mom how you was drilling the movie star when Emily was on the road alone?"

David took a deep breath, and his chest ached with the inflow.

"No. I didn't. I couldn't."

"You should, Dave. You should tell her mom. One thing I learned is it feels good to confess and all. You confess, have a good cry together, and then it's all behind you. Tell her mom, Dave, and then you won't keep forever tearing at yourself about it."

66

The white bird had flown from the high window.

Gathering up the photos to put them away, David had a final question for Ronny Lee Jessup. "Were there any women who escaped?"

"Not from the house, not how tight I built my playground."

"I mean when you tried to abduct them."

"Two. One got clean away. But I wore a mask, so she couldn't describe me. She looked juicy. I couldn't stop thinking about her, how juicy wet she would be. You know how it is. She looked sort of like your movie star. I bided my time, went back six months later, and got her good the second time."

322

"What about the other one?"

Jessup grimaced. "She were a nasty bitch. It's unkind to say, but true. She weren't no lady. Before I could use chloroform, she had this pry bar she swung at me, broke a couple ribs. Pissed me off. Old Ronny used to have a temper when some bitch fought back. I'm not proud of that, but it's the honest truth. Her and me got into it hard and fast, and I had to knife her a few times. After that, she weren't worth bringing home."

"You left her for dead?"

"I didn't leave her *for* dead. She *were* dead already."

"When was this?"

"Long ago. I never kept no diary, Dave."

"Could it have been ten years ago?"

The gravity of sadness drew Jessup's features long. "Farther back than ten, I think. I kept at the game twenty years. I wish I could say ten, wish I could tell you it were your special girl, so you'd be at peace." As David was about to slide the last of the ten photos into the envelope, Jessup said, "Wait. Show me her again."

David held up the photo.

As he studied Emily's face, Jessup slowly assumed a frown. "Did she maybe wear a little necklace thing?"

"She wore a gold locket."

323

"What'd it look like?"

"In the shape of a heart, inset with a rare red diamond. I had it designed for her. When you opened the locket, there was a gold thorn fixed in it."

"Thorn because of your name. That's very tender, Dave. That touches my own heart." He closed his eyes and raised his free hand to massage his forehead with his fingertips, as if to encourage a submerged memory to surface. When he lowered his hand and opened his eyes, he said, "I never opened the locket. I never saw no thorn. I don't clearly remember your Emily because she had such attitude. One of them nothing-but-trouble types. I didn't get much good use of her before I killed her." He met David's eyes. "They'll find her in that secret room, I think. Your peace is near, Dave. You don't got to keep tearing at yourself no more. Once they find her and you know, then you can be done with this, move on, be happy — and happy in a way you don't expect you ever can be."

67

David felt wrung out. He thought he should want to kill Ronny Jessup, but he didn't care about this hateful creature any longer. Even if there had been no guard watching through the windowed door, even if he could have done the deed and gotten away with it, he would not have wrought violence here. He didn't believe that killing this monster would be wrong, even though the state's highest-ranking officials, in their ever-more-outrageous virtue signaling, might equate the execution with the crimes that Jessup committed. Anyway, although Ronny had once been a juggernaut of horror, he was now an empty vessel adrift, and he would be so for the remainder of his miserable life. Striking out at this man would be nothing more than a vulgar, pathetic attempt at self-exoneration, when in fact he had no authority to exonerate himself.

As David closed the clasp on the envelope full of photographs, Ronny Jessup said, "When they open that room, Dave, when they find them pretty girls, don't you let them go and bury your Emily. She might look dead, and by some measurements she might be dead, but she's not really dead, not forever."

David got to his feet.

"What I said about bringing all them beauties back to life with electricity — that part were a big crock of shit, Dave. Just one more thing to get the law thinking 'by reason of insanity.' No court is gonna treat old Ronny too hard if I don't know real from fiction, if I think all that electricity shit in Frankenstein movies is true."

David stared down at him.

"But none of them girls is really full dead. Them girls is preserved good as hams or sausages or canned pears or anything in any supermarket, neither spoiled nor withered, preserved by ancient chemical formulas, creams and elixirs of life, smoothed on them pretty bodies and injected. But that's not all." He smiled and shook his head, pleased with himself, proud of his accomplishments. His gentle, musical voice might romance a listener into lending a measure of credibility even to his most irrational claims. "Softest creams and powerful elixirs according to ancient formulas, but there's also big magic in it, Dave. True magic in it."

David looked up at the high window, from which the bird had flown. The winged watcher had not returned. He didn't believe it would return even if he stood there for the rest of his life, watching for it.

"There's real magic in that deep secret room," Jessup repeated. "You don't need no electricity, Dave. All you need to do is whisper her name in her ear and peel back the bandage from her mouth and kiss her.

Kiss her good, and she'll be woke and ready."

David regarded Jessup in silence.

"Kiss her good, Dave, and she'll be yours again." When David turned away from the table, Jessup said, "Thousand a month now. Old Ronny done right by you, like I promised."

"You get nothing more. Not a penny."

Jessup spoke quietly, with equanimity, with seeming confidence that the threat of defunding him would not be fulfilled. "Don't go breaking your promises, Dave. You know how that turns out. You know how that turned out for sweet Emily, you breaking your promises. You break your promise to Ronny, it'll turn out worse for you than me."

At the door opposite the one at which the guard stood, David pressed a call button to summon an escort to accompany him out of maximum security.

"Old Ronny knows more than you do, Dave. Old Ronny hasn't told it all. You'll come back when you understand. You'll come back to hear more, but there won't be no more without you pay my account."

68

In the rental GMC Terrain Denali. Interstate 80 west from Sacramento and then south to Oakland, across the Bay Bridge to San Francisco. The city was dressed in a ragged shroud of fog less white than it should have been, as if the mist had not come off the ocean but had issued out of the soiled streets where in recent years human waste had become such a problem that the government provided maps denoting areas to avoid for health reasons. Then out of the fog and south on US Highway 101.

David Thorne knew where he was going, what he intended to do, but if he did it, he would risk venturing further across the border of sanity than he'd already gone. After his visit to the Zabdi house in Montecito, he'd descended into denial that was a kind of madness, born of love and desperate hope. But to descend farther was perhaps to have no way back. Nevertheless . . .

If he reported to the authorities what Jessup had told him, they would act, but with bureaucratic sluggishness. They would take a week, a month, perhaps longer, to mount the effort to revisit the former Jessup residence and descend into the secret chamber. After all, from their perspective, there was no emergency. Jessup had been imprisoned for years. His reign of terror was long at an end. None of the women he preserved was in danger, for none was alive.

Before they acted on David's information, they would talk to Jessup. Angry at having his income cut off, he might very well lie, say he'd never told David any such thing. That would add a few days of delay. As might Stuart Ulrich, the current owner of the property, who would argue for guarantees against damage and for remuneration.

No one but David would have any sense of urgency.

Maddison had still not called. Nothing in voice mail.

It's too dangerous for both of us in the current atmosphere.

Whom did she fear? Patrick Corley?

Or was Corley no less a victim than Maddison?

This is something bigger than you'll ever understand, Thorne. Stay away from her or you're finished, I'm finished, she's finished. If she doesn't stay focused on her work, we're all dead.

What might be happening to Maddison *right now*?

How could she be Emily down to the birthmark below her navel?

That didn't matter for the moment. The answer to that would come later. All that mattered now was not losing her.

The only place to look for her was the stone house on Rock Point Lane, which Richard Mathers had called haunted and which David had found decidedly strange.

However, Maddison had warned him against seeking her.

He could not be patient, as she had advised. He had lost Emily, and he felt that he was losing Maddison — somehow Emily reborn — and he would not survive that second loss, not psychologically.

If it was dangerous to approach the house on the coast, if he would be putting her life and his own at extreme risk, then before he went there, he needed answers to at least a few of the mysteries that had swept him out of his ordinary life and left him now at sea.

Maybe there were no answers in the former Jessup house. Maybe everything Ronny told him was a lie. But if he went there and saw for himself, he wouldn't know *less* than he did now, and he might uncover a clue, a stunning truth, with which pieces of the puzzle would interlock, bringing him at least a modicum of understanding.

Highway 101 south to San Jose, to Salinas, to Soledad, to Paso Robles . . . The entire trip from Folsom to Santa Barbara required eight hours, and he arrived at the latter city at 7:04 p.m.

The Santa Ynez Mountains to the east were cauldron black and dragon backed against the midnight-blue sky, and the sea to the west lay darker, no moon yet mirrored on it. The city glimmering across the flats and foothills seemed sinister. This was a town he had often visited and enjoyed, but not this night.

If Santa Barbara seemed acrawl with something malignant, perhaps there was no place on earth at this moment that would *not* feel sinister to David.

In a hardware store, he purchased a four-rung step stool and other items that he would need. He found a sporting goods store, where he bought a small backpack and a pair of hiking boots.

He wanted to drive into the Santa Ynez Valley that very night, to the Jessup house, and do the grisly job that needed to be done. But he was strung out, grainy eyed, too weary to cope with what he knew lay ahead and also meet what unknowns he might encounter.

In a supermarket, as he ordered a thick Reuben sandwich and a container of potato salad at the deli section, he felt that he was being watched. He saw no one suspicious among the other customers.

He also bought a large, cold bottle of Coke and a pint bottle of Absolut. He knew that he wouldn't sleep without the ministrations of the goddess vodka.

The three-star motor inn was nothing fancy, but it was clean and comfortable. As he carried his luggage into his room and again as he filled a plastic ice bucket in the vending machine alcove, he sensed that he was under observation.

No one else was on the open-air promenade, and the cars in the immediate parking area all appeared unoccupied.

After the interview with Ronny Jessup, he felt filthy, as he always did post-Folsom. He mixed a drink in one of the motel's plastic glasses and drank half before he took a long, hot shower.

He was toweling off when he thought he heard someone in the other room. He was certain that he had locked the outer door.

He pulled on a pair of briefs and went into the bedroom. The sliding, mirrored closet door stood open, but he had left it that way.

The deadbolt on the exterior door was locked. He believed that he had engaged the security chain, as well, but it hung loose from the jamb plate.

He was exhausted and jumpy. The most logical explanation was that he had forgotten the chain. If anyone had entered with ill intent, the intruder would have come at him when he stepped out of the bathroom, if not before.

He slipped the security-chain slide bolt into the door plate. Anyway, the chain didn't provide much protection; the deadbolt was the true barrier.

After he pulled on pajamas and finished his first drink, he added ice to the glass and mixed a second vodka and Coke.

As he ate at a small table by the only window, he tried not to think about the horror that awaited him in the foothills of the San Rafael Mountains, under the house where Ronny Jessup had for twenty years ruled his demonic kingdom.

69

The oblivion that David sought in vodka proved to be imperfect. For years, his sleep had been tortured by vivid dreams that were saturated with horror and guilt, but none had been half as strange as the one in which he became mired in that Santa Barbara motel room.

As never before, he appeared only briefly

in his own nightmare, and for the most part watched helplessly from within the mind and body of Emily, on that hateful night of rain and ruin. And unlike other dreams, this one unspooled with eerie and terrible coherence, as if it must be the truth that he would be condemned to relive again and again through eternity.

The windshield wipers fling gouts of water off the glass, but the night gives it back in greater volume. She drives at a reduced speed, wary of the poor visibility. When a noisy knocking arises from under the hood, the true risk proves to be not a collision, but a mechanical breakdown. Seconds later, the Buick starts to shimmy, the steering wheel twitches, the car surges and shudders, surges and shudders. Oh, shit. Now what, Carlino? Do you have your degree in American literature handy? What the hell were you thinking? Why not a trade-school course in auto mechanics?

Worried that she might be stranded in traffic and vulnerable to a high-speed back-ending, she pilots the Buick another quarter of a mile, which seems like forever, until she sees the viewpoint lay-by and pulls off the road. No sooner has she braked to a stop than the engine fails. Simultaneously, the battery dies or a mechanical failure doesn't allow what juice it contains to be distributed to the lights and heater.

The wind gusts with such fury that it rocks the Buick. Torrents shatter on the roof, spill down all sides of the car, and the rain-drizzled windows present a night distorted. The lights of passing traffic reveal nothing, but instead add to the sense of a formless and chaotic landscape.

When she tries to use her cell phone to call the AAA emergency number, she discovers there is no service, either because of the horrendous weather or because this section of the coast is rather remote. Beam me up, Scotty.

She feels foolish for setting out so late, in expectation of a milder rain. She could have waited for tomorrow. But she has been away from home for four days, and she misses their little bungalow in Corona del Mar. And David. God, she misses David. Their life is blessed. Sometimes she marvels at how she has become so domestic that she cares little for nightlife or lengthy travel, preferring the quaint pleasures of home. Lately, she's been thinking about kids, too. Her mom prods her about it from time to time. Mom wants grandkids. Two, maybe three. "I'm blind, Emily, and I took the risk anyway, wound up with you, but maybe you'll luck into a kid who's better behaved." Ha, ha, ha. You keep needling me, Mommy dearest, and I will give you a noogie you'll never forget. So Nina's cancer scare has proved to be just that, a scare, and she'll be well. But the trip hasn't been for nothing; an act of friendship is never for nothing. Nonetheless, Emily's been too eager to get home, and now she must deal with the inconvenience of being broken down at night in a storm.

She considers getting out and trying to flag a passing trucker. You never know who might be in a car or SUV. You might be calling trouble to your side. However, truckers are known to be largely reliable — aren't they? — and willing to help a stranded motorist.

But the weather is atrocious. She'll be soaked in two minutes. And there's no guarantee that anyone will stop, not in these days of few Samaritans. Anyway, because of the weather, there's a lot less traffic than usual, less likelihood that some helpful soul will pass and take notice of her. Better to wait for a highway patrol officer to see the dark car and possibly stop to check it out. Yeah. That's what any CHP trooper will do, and one will pass sooner than later. She has faith in the police. Her mom likes police-procedural novels, and Emily has read at least two hundred of them to Calista over the years.

The cops don't always get their man in real life, the way they do in books, because there's no writer setting up the chain of clues for them, but most of them try their best. She's sure that they try their best and that one will be coming along shortly.

Inland, lights glimmer high in the hills, too far to walk to them. Through the screening storm, she can see no lights to the west and assumes there aren't any homes in the vicinity. If you've got to break down, always do it in the equivalent of the Hindu Kush or the Australian outback, where it's so much more adventurous.

"There's a horse ranch to the south, along the coast," David tells her from the back seat of the car. "Go to the horse ranch, go now, quick," but she does not hear him. A sudden coldness on his forehead steals his voice from him, and he is no longer in the back seat, but once more behind Emily's eyes.

The lack of a heater isn't a problem. She's warm enough. She wouldn't mind some music, but there's no way to get any. She has a bottle of water and a PowerBar. She'll be all right. Tough it out. It's not like being shipwrecked on a desert island, not going to have to live on coconuts and raw rats for a year, not going to have to drink her own urine or anything like that. Suck it up, Carlino.

Maybe it's premonition or perhaps the fierce and unrelenting storm is getting on her nerves, but slowly her sense of isolation becomes a sense of danger. She's a stranger to paranoia, an eternal optimist. When she was a child, her mother called her Little Miss Sunshine. Fortunately never in front of other kids. Little Miss Sunshine could use some sunshine now. But she's okay. She's been through worse. She's not a fragile snowflake. By the time an hour passes, however, she is deeply uneasy. There's seldom lightning in storms along this coast, but of course tonight the sky crackles with fireworks, layering on the atmospherics, so the damsel in distress will be sure to feel adequately distressed. There's zero chance that a bolt will strike the car. Zero point zero. Isn't that right? What does your degree in American literature tell you on that subject? Did Twain or Hemingway or Philip Roth have anything instructive to say about the perils of lightning? Anyway, she's sitting on four rubber tires, well insulated from shock. Yet she feels increasingly threatened. She's seriously annoyed by this apprehension. It's not who she is. She's pissed off at herself for being a nervous Nellie. However, there's nothing she can do about it. It is what it is. No point spanking herself. Spanking never worked when her mom did it back in the day. Psychologically, she is spankproof.

She plucks the key from the ignition, throws open the door, scrambles out into the rain. She hurries around to the back of the Buick and pops the trunk lid and retrieves the tire iron: a lug wrench on one end, pry bar on the other. When she gets back into the driver's seat, she's seriously wet, although not soaked to the skin.

Now she has a weapon. It's not exactly Thor's hammer, but it's something.

She slides low in the seat. Better that someone passing doesn't get a glimpse of her and realize she's a woman alone. Unless he's a highway patrolman, of course. A patrolman will stop whether he sees someone in the car or not. In fact, where is Mr. CHiP? He's overdue.

For a while, she shivers, but gradually her body heat dries some of the rain from her clothes. Anyway, it's a chilly night, but it's not really, really cold.

As forty minutes pass without incident and as her shivering subsides, she begins to be mildly amused by her moment of alarm. The tire iron resting against her seat and angled into the footwell is an awkward weapon. She was never good at softball, can't imagine swinging hard enough to knock a would-be assailant out of the park.

Just then the white, paneled van pulls off the southbound lanes and parks parallel to her. When she'd come to a stop, the car hadn't been nose to the viewpoint railing, hadn't been facing the sea. She is parallel to the highway. This larger vehicle pretty much prevents passing traffic from seeing her. The side of the van doesn't bear a company name. She doesn't like how it blocks her from Highway 101.

The guy who gets out of the van is wearing a hooded raincoat, not one of those yellow slickers, but a dark and roomy garment, so it almost looks as if he's wearing a cape. There is no Dracula. Keep that in mind, Carlino. Just a guy in a raincoat. He has left his headlights on, and the viewpoint parking area isn't pitch-black as before. He comes to the window in the driver's door and peers in at her. He has a nice face, like a furless teddy bear, and he looks very concerned when he says, "You broke down, Miss?"

In the front passenger seat, David looks past Emily to Ronny Jessup's face in the side window, and terror electrifies him as if lightning has penetrated the car and struck him. He reaches for the tire iron in the driver's footwell, but his hand closes around an emptiness, as if either he or the iron isn't real. When he looks at the window, Jessup's face is that of Patrick Corley, but an icy coldness against his forehead transforms the face into that of Ronny Jessup, and once more David is looking out through Emily's eyes.

As nice as this guy looks and as sweet as his smile might be, he is nonetheless a big man, humongous, and his size makes Emily uncomfortable. She speaks through the closed window. "I've called the triple A, they have a tow truck on the way."

He raises his voice above the storm. "Hard night for a tow-truck driver. Lots of folks stuck. Maybe hours before he gets here. You want, I'll give you a lift into Goleta, then you deal with this here in the morning."

"Thank you," she says, her words lightly fogging the window. "Thanks, but I'll wait for the tow truck. He'll be here any minute now. I don't want him to come and then I'm not here, and so he doesn't tow the car."

She's talking too much. The guy's staring at her, and she's giving him a thank-you-but-go-away smile, but he's probably reading the anxiety in her eyes. She should look away from him. But maybe not be the first to look away. Don't appear to be intimidated. What is this — a staring contest?

The big man steps to the door behind hers and peers into the car. Why is he looking into the back seat?

341

And now he's moving to the back of the car, now coming around to the starboard side. He arrives at the front passenger door and tries it and finds it locked.

"Get away from here!" she shouts. "I've got a gun. Get away!" He doesn't believe the gun business. He's got something like a ball-peen hammer. He smashes the window in the passenger door. Wind and rain rush past him, into the Buick. Oh, shit. Oh, Jesus God. He reaches inside and pulls up the door handle, he's opening the door, the sonofabitch is going to come inside.

Nothing to do now but open the driver's door and get out, taking the tire iron with her. Don't even think about fighting him, he's too big, a giant. Just sprint around the van, onto the highway, risk the traffic, maybe be run down, but that's better than what this piece of shit has in mind. He won't follow onto the highway. He'll get in his van and split.

Oh, but he's fast for a man his size, quick as a cat. She's at the back of the van. No license plate, he took it off, which isn't good, because maybe he's been cruising for this, just this, wanting to be anonymous, and maybe he's done it before, gotten away with it before. She makes for 101, but he snares her jacket and nearly jerks her off her feet and swings her around, and she expects the ball-peen hammer to come down on her head. But that isn't what he wants, he doesn't want to damage her, he bluntly tells her what he wants, shouts it in her face, the *C* word, shouts it and shouts it as he slams her against one of the double doors on the back of his van, punches her in the gut, knocking the wind out of her, pain radiating through her chest, giving himself time to fumble with the handle on the other door, intending to shove her inside and climb in after her and subdue her, take her away, and then she'll be finished, gone forever.

During all this, a car passes, an SUV, a truck, and no one stops, no one even seems to slow down, no one blows a horn to spook the rapist bastard. The wind is shrieking, torrents of rain lashing, sky blazing, shadows leaping, thin scarves of fog whipping past from the sea, but surely one of the motorists saw them, at least one, yet they are gone, see no evil, and at the moment the southbound lanes are deserted. She is alone, it's all up to her, and in spite of the punch she took, she hasn't dropped the tire iron, which she swings up from the ground, straight between his legs. It's a hard crotch shot, not as hard as she would have liked, but he's bad enough hurt to gasp and relent and stagger backward two or three steps.

David cries out, "Run, run, run while you can!" But the storm is louder than his voice. He rolls his head from side to side in anguish and opens his eyes and sees the motel bed reflected in the mirrored closet door, the night-stand lamp aglow, a man sitting bedside on the straight-backed chair that has been moved from the small writing desk. The man is Ronny Jessup. No. No, he's Patrick Corley. Patrick Corley for real. No dream. He leans forward. Something in his hand. He presses the object to David's forehead. It's icy cold. The motel room becomes the storm-swept night again.

Emily's got to go for it, there's no other choice. If she dashes onto the highway, some see-no-evil type will run her down, sure as shit. So she moves on her attacker and swings the tire iron, swings for the bleachers, and scores a hit on his right side. The raincoat cushions the blow, but he cries out. She's damaged him. She's exhilarated! She swings again, going for his head, a smaller target, a chance she has to take. The wet steel slips through her dripping hands. The iron spins over his head and clatters on the pavement behind him. Oh, Lord God, help me. There's nothing now but to run. She's moving fast toward the west, toward the railing and the meadows below. He can't run as quick as she can, not in his condition. She runs for exercise, she's a gazelle, while he's a lumbering beast. The dark meadows offer not only escape, but also places to hide, and beyond lies a beach where she can run flat out.

Maybe it's his rage, his rage and insanity, but he finds enough strength to plunge after her and grab her again and throw her down against the railing. He swings his massive fist at the side of her head. The blow brings pain and a darkness deeper than the night.

Oh, Davey, Davey, Davey!

She's twenty-five. It can't end here, not with a mother who relies on her, not with children needing to be conceived and born and raised, not with Davey waiting. The beast hits her again, and she is gone. She wakes briefly, realizes she's being dragged across the black-top, passes out, wakes to find herself in the back of his van, restrained with zip ties. Then unrelenting darkness.

In that palpable dark, a voice whispers insistently, "Emily is gone forever, she is gone forever, she is gone forever, and Maddison is but a walking corpse, a walking corpse . . ."

Other ghastly dreams tormented David throughout the night, but unlike the first, they were as amorphous as the molten wax in a lava lamp. He had drunk far less of the vodka than he intended, and the dreams

345

were not conceived in the womb of inebriation. On waking at 8:40 a.m. Friday, he suffered no hangover, although the dread coiling in him was a blunted bramble entwining all his nerves.

He sat on the edge of the bed and stared at his reflection in the mirrored closet door.

He examined the bed and the floor around it, but he found nothing out of the ordinary.

The straight-backed chair was tucked into the kneehole of the desk, where it belonged.

This unit had no connecting door to another.

The high window in the bathroom was small. No one could have come and gone by that route.

He went to the exterior door. The deadbolt was engaged, but not the security chain. He was certain that the chain had been in place when he'd gone to bed.

Whether Maddison was truly Emily or someone else, she couldn't know he had a room at this motel. Neither could Patrick Corley.

David had felt watched the previous evening. He had called it paranoia, nothing more. And yet the chain dangled . . .

Maddison couldn't have known that he had gone to Folsom to speak with the killer. She didn't even know about Ronny Jessup.

Unless . . . Unless she was somehow Emily and therefore knew who had killed her.

And how crazy was *that* thought? As crazy as Jessup himself.

As David dressed, as he went out to find a restaurant, as he ate breakfast, as he contemplated the grim task ahead of him, as his dread did not relent, he decided that the extraordinary dream from Emily's perspective must be either a product of his growing despair — or had somehow been induced by others. The latter explanation made no sense, but he considered it, anyway.

Supposing that the dream had been crafted and in some fashion inserted into his mind during sleep, using a technology he couldn't comprehend, then it must be meant to dispirit him. If he could be convinced that Emily had been taken away by Ronny Jessup and was among the mummified remains of those fourteen who had never been found, and if he could be made to think of Maddison as some unclean thing, the equivalent of an animated cadaver, then he might be less likely to persist in his efforts to find her.

Assuming they knew about his connection with Jessup, assuming they even knew he'd gone to Folsom the previous day, they weren't omniscient. They couldn't know

347

what Ronny Lee Jessup had said to him in the privacy of that consultation room, that he had revealed where to find the remains of the missing fourteen women.

Whether the dream was born of despair or induced with some arcane technology, it was a propellant driving David back to the Jessup house. His conscience and his subconscious demanded that he return to the labyrinth.

He would need a different car. If they had known in advance of his intention to go to Folsom, they could have hidden a GPS in his Terrain Denali while it was in the prison parking lot.

And he needed a weapon. Something better than a tire iron.

····

PART 5
DOWN AMONG THE
DEAD GIRLS

····

70

David owned a pistol. He had left it in a nightstand drawer at home. He wasn't inclined to spend seven hours driving to and from Corona del Mar to arm himself.

He could get dog-repellent pepper spray in a pet store, but that seemed less of a weapon than a preventative. If he had to face someone who had a gun, pepper spray wouldn't serve him well.

The best alternative to a handgun was a knife. From his book research, he knew that the number of people killed each year by knives was five times greater than the number killed by guns.

He was an obsessive researcher. To be sure the details were correct in his books, he'd undergone a five-day combat-handgun and combat-shotgun training course in Nevada, spent ten days learning wilderness survival techniques in Honduran jungles with two former Navy SEALs as tutors, had ridden as an observer on numerous police patrols in several cities, and embedded himself in other interesting and sometimes dangerous professions.

But he was a little squeamish about stabbing someone, which would be repellently intimate. He couldn't quite see himself doing the deed.

However, this wasn't about his fastidious sensibilities. This might be about survival. And not just his survival. Also Maddison's.

After breakfast, he walked downtown Santa Barbara and found a high-end culinary shop with a wide variety of merchandise. The clerk was pleased to show him a selection of the finest chef's knives. He purchased two that were made of laminate cobalt steel with maroon Micarta handles. The first featured a 6.1-inch blade, with an overall length of eleven inches. The second, with a 7.8-inch blade, measured thirteen inches end to end. He also purchased an electric blade sharpener, though the clerk advised that it was best to send the cutlery to the manufacturer every five to seven years for a professional sharpening.

When he exited the store, the scattered clouds of dawn were gradually knitting together into thin gray shawls. Although the sun hadn't yet reached its apex and although it ruled the sky, its light had a cold, unnatural quality, as if the city were a laboratory lighted by banks of fluorescent tubes, and all life within it an experiment.

In a department store, he bought a large handbag of supple calfskin, suggesting that it was a gift for his wife, a zippered leather tote bag, and a travel clock with a digital readout.

In a drugstore, he purchased cord-style shoelaces and dental floss.

In a craft store, he acquired leather shears and a hole punch.

In an electronics store, he bought items that a lead character in one of his novels had procured in order to construct a detonator.

In a public park near his motel, he sat on a bench and placed a call to Estella Rosewater to report that he was making progress on the matter about which he'd come to see her a few days earlier. He had a favor to ask of her. Estella's curiosity was so keen that his promise eventually to share with her everything he had learned was all that she needed to grant his request.

Throughout the morning's activities, David tried to imagine against whom, under what circumstances, he might have to defend himself. But the world had rotated into a parallel universe where laws were plastic and effect sometimes seemed to come before cause, so that nothing could be predicted with assurance.

71

For a few hours, David remained sequestered in his motel room, first using the electric grinder to whet the knife blades to razor edges. Sitting at the desk, using the leather shears, he cut sheath patterns from the handbag, created eyelets with the punch, folded the sheaths to create blade pockets, and stitched the edges with the cord laces.

Using items from the electronics store and the clock, he constructed the detonator, which featured a trigger that would activate a one-minute countdown timer or enable an instantaneous detonation. Book research had never served him so well.

Periodically, he glanced at the mirrored sliding doors on the closet and thought of the moment in the dream when he had seemed to come half-awake and had seen a reflection of himself lying abed. Patrick Corley sitting bedside. In the desk chair that David now occupied. Something in his hand. Something that when pressed against David's forehead sent icy waves through his skull, dropping him back into the dream as it unfolded from Emily's point of view.

Each time that he looked up from his current work and toward the mirror, he half expected to see himself in the bed and Corley in attendance. The past few days had felt like a long dream, sometimes blithe fantasy and sometimes a nightmare, cause and effect replaced by wild chance, every hour warped by surreal effects and unexpected juxtapositions, the dead alive again, the living lost in a maze of meaning.

At two o'clock, after a late lunch that would also be his dinner, he put his loaded backpack in the Terrain Denali, in which he'd left the stepladder the previous evening. Assuming that a tracking device had been fixed to the car, he drove to a church lot six blocks from the Rosewater house and abandoned the vehicle. Wearing the backpack, carrying the stepladder and the tote, he walked to Estella's place by a roundabout route, alert for an observer. He saw no one suspicious.

The Ford Explorer Sport stood in the driveway, where she had promised he would find it. He opened the tailgate and put both the ladder and the backpack in the cargo hold. When he settled in the driver's seat, he found the key in the cup holder.

At 2:40, he set out inland on State Route 154 to the Santa Ynez Valley. Past Lake Cachuma. Past the town of Santa Ynez. He turned northeast on a lonely stress-cracked two-lane blacktop, into the lower foothills of the San Rafael Mountains.

When he cruised by it at 3:55, the weathered old house with filth-clouded windows gazed down at the road as though aware of who passed, patiently awaiting the evening's visitor. Seven huge crows stood on the ridgeline of the roof, as solemn and still as black-robed judges viewing everything below and beyond them with contempt.

David drove two miles farther, looking for a suitable turnoff, and found a rough dirt track to his right, which snaked between two hills and descended out of sight of the county road. It led between vine rows — some dead, others gone wild and producing only bitter fruit — and it ended at a half-collapsed barn that might have once stored the vineyardist's equipment. Judging by appearances, no one had been here in a long time.

Stuart Ulrich lived in Santa Ynez, about ten miles from the notorious residence. Now that the public's interest in Ronny Lee and his crimes had faded in the wake of the countless other electrifying abominations born of the culture of self and sensation, few if any of the morbidly curious would prowl around the property. Ulrich had less reason to keep a close watch over the place. Nevertheless, if he happened past and saw a strange vehicle parked in front of the house or along the road in the immediate vicinity, he would be on the hunt for nonpaying trespassers.

Standing beside the Ford Explorer, David slipped his arms through the loops of the small backpack that contained the gear he needed. He cinched the strap across his chest. He tied the sheath with the larger chef's knife to his belt and secured it with a cord that he knotted around his right thigh. The smaller knife depended from his belt on his left side and hung loose in its sheath. He retrieved the four-rung folding stepladder from the back seat.

When he returned, stealth wouldn't be necessary. No need to come overland. His grisly task would have been completed. He could follow the county road and with flashlight make his way along the dirt track.

The bearded sky had blinded the sun. The once regimented fields of the abandoned vineyard were as brown and gray as they were green. Woody vines sprawled like uncoiled spools of concertina wire. Blue oat grass bristled. An early growth of mustard plant bloomed yellow.

The slopes of the foothills at first seemed to roll under his feet, so that he lurched a few times and staggered, the stepladder knocking against his side.

But the problem wasn't the land or his sense of balance. The fault lay in his state of mind. Doubt troubled him, and he wondered if he had misjudged the degree of aberrant behavior to which recent events had driven him.

He halted, alarmed by his rapid breathing and the throb of blood in his temples. A tinnitus of terror hummed in his ears, and his heart quickened absurdly, considering that he was nowhere near his destination, with nothing yet at risk. He tried to calm himself.

He'd been willing to acknowledge that lately he was in the firm grip of mania, which he'd once researched for a novel and which he understood to be unnatural fixation on some emotion or situation, accompanied by melancholy. His guilt about Emily, his enduring grief, the sudden hope represented by Maddison, the deep mystery of death, the impossibility of resurrection: All that had come together to unbalance him mentally. Yes, all right, mania. Mania came and went, like a hurricane wind; it seldom wrecked a man for life. But as he listened to his breathing grow more rapid and ragged, as his heart knocked against his rib cage, he thought also of lunacy and madness and the difference between them. Lunacy described what was insanely foolish, madness what was insanely desperate, and once a man surrendered to either condition, there might be no escape.

If he was being carried away from the shore of sanity on a tide of madness, there was one thing with which to moor himself and stop the drift. Maddison. Whoever she was, whatever the explanation for her existence, he loved her as he'd loved only one other, and she was in serious trouble. He dared not fail her as he'd failed Emily.

A wind came out of the northwest, and the stilled world around him rose into motion: the grass shivering, the vines lashing, a few feeding birds harried from the ground to roosts in distant trees. It was a cool wind. He faced into it, taking slow deep breaths, *willing* himself to overcome this fear of derangement.

At Folsom, eye to eye with Ronny Jessup, David had felt as if the killer's intense stare were a psychic wire, transmitting his essence into his visitor. The overwhelming emotion of that encounter had evidently rattled David more than he'd realized, leading to this moment of crippling doubt.

Maddison needed him. Doubt had no place in a true love knot, and neither suspicion nor fear could untie it. He was a better man than he had been ten years earlier. He knew what a commitment meant and the price of not keeping it.

He quieted his heart, his breathing. Recovered his balance.

He made his way across the rolling land. In the last quarter hour of light, he ascended to the crown of a hill and looked down on the murder house.

72

He lay flat on the ground, glassing the house with binoculars that he took from his backpack. No one at a window. No movement but the wind and what it stirred.

Beyond the Santa Ynez Mountains in the west, behind the masking clouds, the hidden sun descended. The gray overcast drew lower and scudded southward as a storm marshaled its forces in the northwest.

In the dimming light, David carried the stepladder down through the meadow that had reclaimed the land from the ruins of the old vine rows. He took up a position behind a bushy mass of mountain Pieris, about twenty yards from the house, and waited there until night had fully settled.

When after fifteen minutes no light appeared in the residence — he had expected none — he carried the stepladder to the back porch and put it down near the door.

He was reluctant to smash a window and leave evidence of his visit. Anyway, it might not be necessary. He went around to the west side of the house. The previous Saturday, after Ulrich had admitted him, as David had stood in the living room, getting a feel for the place, he noticed a long-neglected ill-fitted window. Years of rain, leaking under the bottom sash, had rotted the sill and damaged the floor below. It was unlikely that such a warped window could be locked.

It wasn't. The meeting rails of the upper and lower sashes were so far out of alignment that the swivel latch could not be engaged.

Nothing remained here worth stealing, and Ulrich had no reason to install a security system. Nonetheless David steeled himself for a siren when he raised the bottom sash, but there was no alarm. He clambered into the living room, wind billowing the rotted draperies around him, and closed the sash as best he could.

He stood listening to the vacant rooms. Because the night was moonless and the stars were bedded behind a thick layer of woolpack, the windows could hardly be discerned, limned by a vague ghost light reminiscent of the barely visible glow that sometimes haunts a screen for a short while after a TV has been turned off. Darkness seemed to pool deeper in this place than elsewhere, a distilled blackness, but that was a false perception arising from what he knew of the house's evil history.

From a side pocket of his backpack, he removed one of his three flashlights. Masking part of the lens with two fingers, he switched it on. The room resolved in its remembered drabness, and he made his way to the kitchen. He brought the stepladder in from the porch and locked the back door.

The two-inch-thick door to the cellar stood ajar, as it had been when he'd taken the tour for which he had paid Ulrich. The two deadbolts were blind set and, once locked, could not be opened from the cellar side.

He wanted to search the ground floor and upstairs before going to the lower realm, to be certain no one lurked at his back. But if someone waited in the house, he ought to have responded to the noise David made. Anyway, a search would take too long and abrade nerves already raw; the sooner that he was out of this place, the better.

He preferred not to pull the cellar door shut behind him. It might be impossible for one of the deadbolts to slip a fraction of an inch into the striker plate on the doorframe, accidentally trapping him. On the other hand, seemingly impossible things had recently happened with some frequency.

Although only a pale glow would rise into the kitchen from below, and although Stuart Ulrich was unlikely to cruise by at just the wrong moment and notice a faint radiance in the house, David did not intend to use the electric lights in the cellar. He would rely on his flashlights.

He stepped onto the landing and hesitated.

Maybe he would find Emily's body in its Egyptian windings, among the fourteen stolen girls, and would know beyond all doubt that she was long dead. But that would not explain Maddison.

Maybe Emily's remains wouldn't be found here. In that case, nothing whatsoever would be resolved.

In any event, mysteries would remain.

But what else was there to do but descend and see? Nothing else. This maze had brought him to a turn where, for once, there were no other paths to take.

He went down the stairs, carrying the folded stepladder. The steel-bar gate at the bottom stood open as before. He proceeded into what Ronny Jessup called the "receiving room."

He withdrew his fingers from the lens, providing more light, although not enough to warm his chilled blood.

73

The maze of Ronny Jessup's dark erotic dreams of absolute power was also the labyrinth of David Thorne's nightmares. In this cochlea of eerie silence, the narrow serpentine passageways, with their low ceilings and walls patterned by creeping mold, testified to the seed of evil in the human heart — dormant in some, flourishing in others. Where it flourished, there was the narcissistic certainty of being superior and the associated insatiable lust for power from which all other wickedness grew. The need to control others and use them, to intimidate and abuse them, forcing them to submit until eventually they submitted with self-negating eagerness. In the twisting warrens of Jessup's mind, which were here made manifest, all the varied gods of human history were dead and catacombed and powerless, leaving the new god, Ronny, whose one commandment was *Do as I tell you,* whose love was insatiable lust, whose grace was terror, whose promise was death everlasting.

Here and there, the flashlight beam played over a fragment of the dollar bill that, on his first tour, David had torn into pieces and used to mark the route that he had followed, so that he would not waste time revisiting places he had already explored.

On the previous visit, his understanding of what had occurred here over two decades had filled him with excruciating anguish that grew into physical terror, moral panic. He thought that experience had inoculated him against the dread this place could inspire; but it had not. A shrinking fear, in expectation of impending violence, caused him to hesitate at every turn and fork in the passageways before he finally came to the mummification room.

He opened the door, crossed the threshold, and probed with the flashlight. Cleaner than the rest of this hateful playground, almost immaculate. No mold. No spiderwebs. The nine white catafalques in three rows along the entire back wall, stacked like bunk beds. The radiused corners of the room. The domed ten-foot ceiling.

He placed the stepladder below the white ceramic tile with the blue ever-staring eye. He put the flashlight on the pail rest.

After taking off his backpack, he retrieved two Bell and Howell Tac Lights from it, switched them on, twisted them to spread their beams as wide as possible, and stood them on end. The light splashed the ceiling and washed down the walls. Some of it would leak across the threshold and into the passageway, although not as far as the receiving room and certainly not all the way up to the ground floor.

With the flashlight he'd left on the pail rest, he went to the catafalques and studied how they were cantilevered from the railroad ties. Even now that he knew what to look for, he couldn't see any evidence of what Jessup described. Either the design was devilishly clever and the workmanship exceptional — or the killer lied to him.

One way to find out.

He climbed the four steps of the short ladder, reached high, and felt the edges of the round ceramic tile. The four-inch-diameter disc did not set flush to the ceiling, but offered a recess around its entire perimeter into which fingers could be inserted to get a workable grip. It was a knob meant to be turned.

At first, he couldn't twist it, and he worried that during the seven years since Jessup was arrested, the mechanism had corroded and seized up. But he strained harder, and abruptly the knob moved, grudgingly at first and then more easily.

Noise arose in the ceiling: gears turning, cams rotating, rods sliding, whatever. Jessup hadn't explained the mechanics, and David lacked the knowledge to imagine how such a mechanism might work.

The more that he twisted the ceramic knob, with the blue eye blinkless against his palm, the easier the task became and the faster he was able to turn it. The noises in the ceiling moved across the room.

A grinding sound drew his attention to the catafalques. The three in the center were receding with the section of wall from which they were cantilevered. The entire mass slid backward into a heretofore secret space.

When the ceramic knob reached a stop and would turn no more, David got down from the ladder and crossed to the opening that the retreating catafalques had revealed. A flight of wood stairs, about five feet wide, led to a lower chamber.

Jessup's voice rose in memory: *They'll find her in that secret room. Your peace is near, Dave.*

There would be no peace. He realized that now, as he stared at the steps dwindling into darkness. There might be answers, a degree of resolution, but there would be no peace. Resignation, acceptance at last, but no peace. Maybe a way forward, a life to be lived, with less anguish, even with good times, but always that underlying sense of fault and the sorrow of an enduring loss.

Your peace is near, Dave. You don't got to keep tearing at yourself no more.

Shaking, David stood transfixed, unable to proceed. The crisp white beam of the flashlight shuddered across the landing and the top step, and at the periphery of the light, the darkness jittered. These were not tremors of fear as much as they were born of grief, the raw grief that he had thought long behind him, that seemed to have been diluted by the passage of time, but that now surged back in its full power, as devastating as it had been when Emily had gone missing and he'd first admitted that she was lost to him forever.

His vision blurred.

His face was hot and wet.

He tasted salt.

He turned away from the stairs and returned to the center of the room and stood gazing up at the blue eye. Never speaking aloud, he confessed his fault and failures, as he had often done before, revealed the depth of his sorrow, pled also to the truth of his undying love for her, and begged her forgiveness.

From mere mania into madness. Coming here, surely he'd crossed the line of sanity that he'd been walking with the fear of losing his balance.

Once here, however, he could not go back until he explored the chamber below. This horror he had earned, this and more, and he was still man enough not to flee from the consequences of his deceit.

He put down the flashlight, retrieved one of the more powerful Tac Lights, took a screwdriver from the backpack, and went once more to the head of the secret stairs.

He knelt on the landing and studied the first step and saw that it was held in place by four screws, as Ronny Jessup had described. David removed the screws and put them aside. He lifted the loose tread, revealing a hollow space.

Tucked in that niche were two one-kilogram bricks of a plastic explosive. The

369

second was plugged into the first, and the first was plugged into a standard electrical outlet that featured a hot slot and a neutral slot parallel to each other, separated by a smaller ground slot.

According to Jessup, the green grounding wire and the white neutral wire were active, but an interrupter switch prevented the black hot wire from powering the outlet. Each of the first two stair treads was designed with sufficient give so that, when stepped on, it would trigger the interrupter switch, power the outlet, and detonate the plastic explosive.

If crazy Ronny couldn't have his secret stash of fourteen pretty girls, he was determined that no one else would wake them and be pleasured by them. The two bricks, composed of nitrocellulose and nitroglycerin, would not only obliterate any intruder, but would also destroy the entire house and the warren under it.

David extracted the wires from the first one-kilogram charge and then pulled the plug from the outlet. He took the two bricks into the mummification room and put them on the floor beside his backpack.

The plastic explosive might have deteriorated over the past seven years, might even be unstable. But Ronny Jessup was sure that it could still get the job done.

David returned to the secret stairs and knelt on the landing and replaced the wooden tread and reattached it with four screws. This was unnecessary. He could have stepped over the open first step. Restoring it was nothing but an excuse to delay going down among the dead girls and taking inventory.

You're a torn man, Dave. You're all torn up and hurting, and I sorrow to see it. You and me had self-control problems, we sure did, best to fess up to it. Make no excuses. That's the way.

Following the beam of the Tac Light, David descended into the lower crypt.

74

The air here was not damp, as he expected, but as dry as that in an oven, and yet colder than in the room above. Instead of the anticipated stench of corruption, a pungent chemical smell burned his nasal passages, though under it lay a ripe and more organic scent that might have been offensive if it had not been masked.

Equipped with a backhoe and other construction equipment, Ronny Jessup had labored with little rest during the two years between his mother's death and the abduction of his first victim, adding the seven higher rooms and this one to the existing basement. *I had a dream,* he'd once told David, *and a man can do just about any damn thing if his dream is big and he wants it bad enough.* This chamber was smaller than the one above, maybe fourteen feet on a side, with seamless plasterboard ceiling and walls that were painted white and pale blue in geometric designs like those in some peculiar two-tone kaleidoscope. The ceramic tile floor had been laid on a concrete base, not in orderly squares but in thousands of little pieces of many sizes and shapes, forming white-and-blue patterns; David was reminded of photographs he had seen of voodoo veves made with flour and powdered chalk and blue cornmeal, and he wondered if this was part of the magic that Jessup had fantasized.

On each wall were six catafalques, two ascending rows of three each, eighteen in all, fourteen occupied. The remains were wound about with strips of bandage, immense cocoons in which dead women, preserved by an obsessed madman, waited for rebirth, though they would never emerge like butterflies cloaked in greater beauty.

The layered cotton dressings appeared

unstained, as if what waited within them had survived uncorrupted. But whatever Jessup might have learned about the art of mummification, death could not be undone by chemicals and creams and elixirs any more than by a jolt of electricity.

The crazy hateful bastard had done it, but to no meaningful end. The soft-spoken honey-eyed god of this grim underworld could no more resurrect beauty than he could create it.

Nevertheless, as the beam of the Tac Light slid across the bodies on the catafalques, David startled when something moved in the shadows of its wake. More than once, he twitched and swung the light back to the corpse it had revealed a moment earlier, but each time the threat proved to be a phantom conjured by his imagination.

With obvious care and calculated flourishes, a name was painted on the edge of each catafalque. For the moment, however, David was too emotional to go closer and read them.

In the center of the room stood a four-foot-square table, and on it lay a collection of personal objects that apparently belonged to these fourteen victims, arranged as if the deceased had offered their small treasures to the cruel deity of this domain. Perhaps

Jessup intended to ornament the women on their revival as they had been in their first life. Dust seemed not to intrude in this realm; the rings and bracelets and necklaces and brooches still glittered. Wristwatches, hair barrettes, gold chains, pop beads, scarves.

And a gold locket in the shape of a heart, inlaid with a rare red diamond.

At the sight of it, David could not get his breath. Although he had resigned himself to what he would discover here, he felt as if his heart had been pierced by a thorn immensely larger than the tiny one surely contained within this locket.

His hands shook so badly that he almost dropped the pendant, and he fumbled interminably with the clasp. When he opened it at last, the thorn was fixed therein, just as it had been when he had given the piece to Emily so many years earlier, before he discovered that a nettle of deceit waited in his own heart.

He tucked the bright locket into a pocket of his jeans and played the light across the catafalques and murmured, "Oh God, oh God," as the task awaiting him almost brought him to his knees.

75

He had no choice but to circle the room, reading the names that Jessup had painted in a calligraphic script on the leading edge of each catafalque.

There's real magic in that deep secret room. You don't need no electricity, Dave. All you need to do is whisper her name in her ear and peel back the bandage from her mouth and kiss her. Kiss her good, and she'll be woke and ready.

David had no intention of kissing a corpse. When he found her, she would not be Sleeping Beauty, bewitched by a spell that a kiss could undo.

However, he would need to do something almost as terrible. He would unwind the bandages from her face to be sure that the name on the catafalque belonged to she who lay at rest thereon. Unwind or cut. He had brought scissors. One way or the other, he would do it. The unsoiled appearance of the cotton winding, the dry air, and the eye-watering chemical smell suggested that Jessup had to some degree preserved the bodies. But Emily would be at least withered, her once glowing skin now heavily creped and gray, her face drawn tight on her skull, as the faces of mummies usually were, her lips a thinness of flesh shaped to the teeth beneath them, her eyes sunken in their sockets. The sight of her in that condition — if not in one worse — would shrink his already shrunken soul, but he must look because there would likely be enough resemblance to confirm her identity, and because this was his duty.

As David moved from corpse to corpse, reading names, he heard himself saying, "I'll take you out of here, Emily. I'll take you out of here tonight and home to Newport. I have a place for you in the shade of a lovely pepper tree, overhung by those cascading boughs you always liked so much."

If he wasn't mad, he *sounded* mad. He didn't care. The world had gone insane, and madmen belonged here more than those who had held fast to their sanity. He would carry her out in his arms, and to hell with the law.

"I've had the stone engraved with lines from your favorite sonnet. 'Rough winds do shake the darling buds of May / And summer's lease hath all too short a date . . . / But thy eternal summer shall not fade.' "

Corpse by corpse, David Thorne circled the chamber and came heartsick to the fourteenth and final body. As with the previous thirteen, the name on the catafalque

376

was not that of the woman he had lost. Not Emily Carlino.

Perplexed, he extracted the locket from his jeans and held it in his cupped right hand. It had been a custom order, crafted to his design. There couldn't be another like it in all the world.

David swept the light around the room, from victim to victim. Could Jessup have misnamed one of them? No, not likely. He had so painstakingly painted their names, each letter artfully crafted. Ronny was an obsessive, with great attention to detail, which was one reason he'd been able to abduct so many women over so many years before he'd been caught. Furthermore, he believed in his powers of preservation and resurrection, and he fully expected to return here one day to enjoy his hidden harem; therefore, he would have taken special care in the wrapping and naming of each.

If Emily wasn't in this lower crypt, and considering that she had not been found in the higher crypt years earlier, when Jessup was arrested, how had the killer come into possession of her locket?

Maybe he had stalked her unsuccessfully, *meant* to possess her, and regretted that he hadn't been able to include her among the "stolen girls" in this room. If he had been lying when he said he didn't know her name and didn't recognize her from the photographs, if he'd been toying with David just for the emotional charge it gave him . . . then where was Emily?

Jessup had asked about the locket shortly after he'd spoken of the two women who escaped. He'd gone after one of them again, six months after she fled, and he'd gotten her on his second try.

The other one supposedly had fought him, hurt him, had broken a couple of his ribs with a pry bar.

Her and me got into it hard and fast, and I had to knife her a few times. After that, she weren't worth bringing home.

Could she have been Emily? Could the locket have been torn from her in the struggle, and could Jessup have taken it with him when he had left her for dead?

I didn't leave her for dead. She were dead already.

But if she had been dead and he'd left her wherever the assault had taken place, why hadn't her body been found?

Where was Emily Carlino? Might she yet be alive? Might she somehow be Maddison Sutton, after all?

Here among these bundled women who had suffered so grievously, David's spirit did not — could not — soar, but it lifted just enough for his despair to recede.

He became convinced that his dream the previous night, from Emily's point of view, had indeed been induced by whatever means, perhaps with the intention of discouraging him from continuing his search before it led him back to the house on Rock Point Lane. Maybe much in the dream had been true, but she had not been abducted by Ronny Jessup. Maybe the maniac was telling the truth, maybe he had stabbed her and left her for dead. But if she hadn't been dead, maybe she had made her way to Corley's house.

His heart beat faster, spurred by fear and anger, but also encouraged by a fragile hope. He stood for a long moment, cherishing the hope, daring to nurture it.

He returned the locket to a pocket of his jeans once more and went to the stairs and climbed into the upper chamber.

The blue eye gazed down at the stepladder, on the pail rest of which one flashlight waited. The other Tac Light stood where he had left it, focused on the ceiling.

The space was sufficiently illuminated for him to see the scrap of paper skitter out of the passageway, through the open door, and across the concrete. A piece of the dollar bill that he had torn and dropped on his previous visit. Carried on a low draft, it fluttered six or eight feet into the room before it came to rest, quivering.

Until now, the stillness here had been complete. The cellar lacked windows. If there had once been air circulation through the venting, the heating-cooling system had not functioned in years.

He could imagine but one source of a draft: the door at the head of the cellar steps — and then only if an outside door on the ground floor had been opened, admitting the night wind.

He snatched the flashlight off the pail rest and doused it. He grabbed the Tac Light from the floor, extinguished that one, too, and slipped it into a jacket pocket.

Shielding the lens of the remaining Tac Light with two fingers to provide the minimum visibility he required, David stepped to the open door. He listened intently to a silence so deep that it seemed to deny the threat that the fragment of currency implied.

Abruptly the scrap of paper stopped quivering, as though the door that had admitted the draft had just been closed.

If there were footsteps or other noises upstairs, he couldn't hear them. No surprise. To isolate his stolen girls for all those years, Jessup had no doubt worked considerable sound insulation into the ceiling of this lower realm.

In the room where David stood, the sconces abruptly bloomed with white light. In the passageway before him, in the doorless room across the passageway — and everywhere else — the lights came on, the rose-colored lampglow by which Ronny had played his cruel games.

76

David could assume only that Stuart Ulrich had arrived for whatever purpose, perhaps because the house was equipped with a silent alarm, after all.

With no time to remove evidence of his intrusion, he stepped into the passageway, eased the door shut, pocketed the Tac Light. He turned right, away from the receiving room and the stairs down which Ulrich might even now be descending. He went deeper into the maze.

His recollection of the basement layout was spotty. During his first visit, abhorrence had overwhelmed him, and he'd bolted through the labyrinth's twisting intricacies in a frantic attempt to escape its oppressive atmosphere and lurid history. As had been reported in the press, like the creepiest of fun houses, this maze made clever use of its space, so that it seemed, if not infinite, at least three times its actual size.

And Ronny Jessup's excavations were impressive to begin with, much larger than a carnival spook show. There were apparent dead ends that on close inspection offered, to either the left or right, an eighteen-inch-wide tunnel that must be navigated sidewise in a severe test of the claustrophobic reflex. Recesses were fitted with ascending steps that inspired hope of a way out but curved up only to a blank wall. Full-length shatterproof mirrors were strategically placed to allow the harried prey to see themselves in their naked vulnerability and terror and true helplessness.

In spite of his seeming dull-wittedness and genuine madness, Jessup possessed a certain dark genius, evident in the passageway design, which seemed like one nautilus inserted crosswise into another nautilus, the spirals of the two shells intersecting at unpredictable angles. Any runner of this maze quickly became — and remained — disoriented, but was also overcome by a terrifying sense of having fallen through some dimensional door into an alternate reality where neither the laws of physics nor the truth of nature were what they had been in the previous world.

Moving quickly, quietly along the quirking passageways, relying on what little he recalled from the previous week, David hoped to find the receiving room, which provided two entrances to — or exits from — the maze. To avoid whoever had entered in his wake, he needed to return to that initial chamber by the second route.

He passed empty rooms revealed by soft rose light. Two were among the five that Jessup called his playrooms, once furnished with beds and whatever else a sadist felt he needed to fully express his cruel nature; each had always been doorless, accessible from more than one passageway, thus becoming part of the maze. Two other rooms were former cells, the doors missing because Stuart Ulrich had sold them for serious money to freaks whose reasons for wanting them did not bear contemplation.

Passing a fifth doorway, a former playroom, David glimpsed something from the corner of his eye that didn't compute until he proceeded a few steps past it. Stunned, he halted, then froze.

He told himself that what he'd seen was an illusion born of fright and stress, a grim figment of his novelist's imagination. It might make sense in a world that existed between the gathered pages of a story meant to rattle the reader's comfortable assumption of a benign universe, but it was too extreme a twist to be credible in the real world. Besides, what he thought he'd seen hadn't been there on his previous tour only six days earlier.

He turned. He stepped to the doorless playroom, which last Saturday had been empty of all that it had once contained.

Inside lay a cheap area carpet. On it stood a leather armchair. Box spring and mattress on a bed frame, with a headboard. Fitted bottom sheet. Pillows. A television with a DVD player atop it. A small refrigerator, one of those that in a kitchen would be set under the counter.

David did not want to believe the purpose of the tableau before him. He stood for a long moment in denial.

In the grip of mesmerizing horror, he turned from the furnished room and continued a short distance along the passageway, until he arrived at a door where a door had not been before. This was one of five cells in which Ronny Jessup had kept his stolen girls. Ulrich had sold all those doors. All of them. This door was solid, hinged on the outside, with a shiny new steel escutcheon and knob. Above the knob were the cylinder, core, and keyway of a deadbolt.

Like a sleepwalker with no control of his actions, David tried the knob. The lock wasn't engaged. The door swung inward.

As in the other cells, an open toilet and sink stood to one side. But whereas the other four had been unfurnished when he had been here Saturday and remained unfurnished now, this cell contained a mattress. No bed frame. No box spring. No headboard. No sheets or blanket. A pillow without a pillowcase.

Here she would be kept to wait, perhaps in darkness, to dwell upon her fate, to dread his return when he was ready for another session in the playroom.

In the conference room at Folsom, eye to eye with Jessup, David had felt as if the killer might be able to transmit some essence of himself across a psychic wire and contaminate the mind of a visitor. Not possible. More easily believed, however, was that during his many years in this place, Jessup daily imbued it with his cruelty and wickedness, until the old house was pregnant with evil, either itself having been possessed by a demonic consciousness or serving as a magnet to draw to it others who had the capacity to become another Ronny

385

Lee Jessup.

Stuart Ulrich had heard the call, the siren song of the house, and he had answered it.

The truth about the fate of Emily had seemed to be within David's grasp. Not now. He might die here, where she had not.

77

Ulrich couldn't know of David's presence, but if he opened the door to the mummification room, he would discover the stepladder and the miraculously revealed entrance to the lower crypt. Then he would be on the hunt.

Maybe Ulrich had returned this evening to continue furnishing the cellar for his future crimes. He might want to do that in the dark rather than be seen moving items into the infamous house during the day. In that case, he might be following the route that David had taken, heading for the furnished playroom or this cell, to add some finishing touches.

Fearing that Ulrich might appear at any moment, David pressed forward along the passageway, toward a turn that would take him out of sight of someone approaching from behind. He didn't run. He was acutely aware of the need for silence. At each turn and fork of the maze, he paused and eased his head around the corner and scoped the way ahead.

During the past week, events had unfolded like the petals of a strange, intricate work of origami, a deeply structured fanfold of mysteries that followed one another in dreamlike succession. Now his long-repeating nightmare and the waking world had intersected, and a greater darkness threatened. The maze branched out around him as if it were an organic construct that could grow new passages with frightening speed, defeating all efforts to map it. He alternated between the conviction that he was moving toward the receiving room and the fear that he had already become lost, must be circling back on himself. The ceiling seemed to loom lower, the walls to draw closer, and when he passed one of the shatterproof mirrors, he saw a desperate man, owl-eyed and grimacing.

A sudden, measured series of sounds brought him to a halt: *Thud . . . thud . . . thud . . .*

Like rhythmic hammer blows. *Thud . . .* Like a giant's footsteps on a wood floor, though there were neither wood floors nor headroom for giants down here. *Thud . . .* Like the measured beating of some leviathan's heart. The pounding echoed through the labyrinth, a solemn tolling. David couldn't discern from which direction it originated. The sound seemed to come from everywhere at once, thumping through the corridors, a menacing pulse.

Thud . . . thud . . . thud . . .

After perhaps a dozen repetitions, the noise ceased, and David began moving again, but with even greater caution. Claustrophobia draped its mantle over him, and a primitive sense of the unknown welled up from whatever level of consciousness usually constrained it. He felt as if he were venturing through the waxways of a hive where a hideous horde would be revealed around the next turn or the one after that. He might not have been surprised if, on trading one passageway for another, he had come upon fourteen of the walking dead, trailing their unraveling graveclothes, seeking someone on whom to take revenge, with him the only man present and, according to their view, a justifiable target by virtue of his gender.

To his relief, he reached the end of the maze and came through the back entrance to the receiving room, where he found no one. A hand truck stood in the middle of the space, its restraining straps dangling.

Stuart Ulrich must have used it to bring some heavy item into the cellar. The loud thumps would have been the solid rubber tires, bearing the weight of the cargo, crashing from one stair tread to another. If Ulrich had wheeled the item away and placed it in one room or another, he'd evidently already come back here with the hand truck.

Where was he then?

Had he gone upstairs?

Was it better to go up there, hope to elude him, slip out of the house? Alert the police that he appeared to be planning to take up where Ronny Jessup had left off seven years earlier?

Or wait here until he returned, and take him by surprise?

Opting for the police seemed to be the wiser course.

As he went to the stainless-steel gate, David realized that it was closed. It had been standing open when he'd come down here. Not only closed — also locked. The combination padlock no longer hung from it; Ulrich had installed a deadbolt package.

David looked through the gate, up the steep stairs. The door at the top was closed, as well.

Claustrophobia didn't just mantle him now, but *encased* him. He found it more difficult to breathe, harder to think. A new fear — of burning to death — crept over him. There would be no way to escape and no means with which to quench the flames if a fire broke out.

He remembered advising Ulrich to destroy the house.

It's a wretched, vicious place. You should pour gasoline down there and torch it all.

In retrospect, it seemed as if he had foreseen his death.

His smartphone was in the car, maybe a mile and a half from here. In this hole, far from a town, there wasn't likely to be cell service, anyway.

What if Ulrich didn't come back for a week? Okay, there were the sinks in the cells. He had water. He wouldn't die of thirst.

But what if Ulrich didn't come back for a month, two months? How long did it take a man to starve to death?

On the way here, David had wondered about his sanity. This turn of events seemed to confirm that, like some ill-fated character in the fiction of Edgar Allan Poe, he had slipped loose from the anchor of sanity and was adrift in alien latitudes.

Then he realized that Ulrich had left the lights on. Maybe the heir of Ronny Jessup would be returning soon. Maybe he had forgotten to switch the lights off. Or maybe . . . he was still down here.

From elsewhere in the labyrinth came a muffled cry of distress, of terror. A woman's cry.

Ulrich had not brought a piece of furniture down the stairs on the hand truck. A *woman* had been strapped to it, perhaps unconscious after being sprayed with chloroform, a technique borrowed from Ronny Jessup's playbook.

The world turns and the world changes, but one thing does not change . . . The perpetual struggle of Good and Evil.

78

David put his back to the locked gate and looked from one maze entrance to the other, struggling to clear his fear-fogged mind and *think.*

The confrontation before him would inevitably be violent. There would be no way out of here except by the spilling of blood.

David wasn't a violent man. He had honed a razor's edge to the knives that depended from his belt, but in doing so, he hadn't also sharpened whatever predatory instinct he might have.

The cry came again. It wasn't Emily's cry, wasn't Maddison's. In the end, however, all such cries were one, his responsibility the same in every case.

On that night of hard rain, Emily had encountered Ronny Jessup. They had struggled. He had at some point taken her locket. She had hurt him. Maybe he stabbed her and left her for dead, or that might be a lie. Her body had never been found. Maybe Emily survived. Maybe Emily was Maddison and by some miracle hadn't aged in ten years.

David didn't believe in miracles, at least not for himself. Maybe others experienced them, but he hadn't earned a miracle.

The answer to that mystery wasn't supernatural. A logical explanation existed.

Whether she was Emily or Maddison, whether she would be the death of him or his salvation, he wanted desperately to be with her for whatever time he might have left in this world. And almost as much as the desire to love her and be loved by her, he needed to know how she could exist as she was, why she had said the things she'd said, why she'd done the things she'd done, whether there could be forgiveness for one such as he, and not just forgiveness but perhaps exoneration, absolution, and peace.

But first *this* woman.

The miserable cry came again, louder and attenuated — but was cut off abruptly, as if by a slap.

He had to kill Ulrich not merely to get the keys and escape this dungeon, but also to save whomever the man had abducted. This was a step in his redemption.

David moved to the maze entrance that he had entered when he had first arrived. From its sheath, he drew the knife. The big one.

79

This was not merely the cellar maze crafted by Ronny Jessup, but also the labyrinth below Crete, where the Minotaur prowled and ate the flesh of those who dared enter its realm, but also Grendel's far northern lair where Beowulf ventured, also the huge catacombs beneath the Mountains of Madness, where the Old Ones of Lovecraft's story still waited to be called out of the depths of time or from another dimension, and this was as well the tunnel system under the terraforming atmosphere factories where brave Ripley had gone with a team of high-tech colonial marines on a bug hunt, to learn what happened to the colonists on the planet called LV-426. This was both reality and myth, concrete and symbol, the maze of homicidal desires and lust and hunger for power that spiraled to infinity within the deepest darkness of the human heart, male and female alike, here given dimension and immediacy. It was inhabited by a Grendel named Ulrich and a would-be hero who knew himself to be no hero at all, but only an imperfect man with something to prove to himself.

If he were armed with a gun, he might have advanced through the passageways by one police strategy or another, as he'd learned when doing research for a book: his back to one wall in order to look both ahead and behind, each doorway a danger to be addressed, each room a lair to be cleared, proceeding expeditiously but also with a prudence arising from an appreciation of the enemy's cunning.

But he had no gun, and this was a maze with uncounted ways that his quarry could circle behind him regardless of how carefully he proceeded. Better to move boldly, quietly but with few hesitations.

He had often written about fear, and he had known profound fear in his life, but he had never experienced or imagined terror as raw as this, his gut alternately clenching tight and fluttering, acid refluxing into his throat — *swallow it, keep it down* — his sweat cold and his breath hot. His scalp prickled as if acrawl with pin-legged ants, and he strained to hear more than the booming of his heart that made of him a one-man cortege.

His eyes were wider than they had ever been, the sullen rose-colored light layering a sameness on the maze, increasingly like a fog that obscured rather than illuminated.

He had to guard against recklessness. Boldness was essential, but the situation was not one of mortal urgency.

Ulrich wouldn't be killing her, not immediately after bringing her here, and he wouldn't already be engaged in rape, either. For him, this was about sex, yes, transgressive sex, but it was foremost about power, as it had been for Ronny Jessup, as it always was for such men. For a while, Ulrich would want to savor his authority, his control of her, his absolute dominion.

David needed to get to her in a timely manner, spare her from as many indignities as possible, but not at too great a risk of her life and his. Firefighters found their way around the flames to those entrapped; they didn't forge through the fire to be ignited.

Doorway after doorway, corner by corner,

turn by turn, past the upper mummification room where the door remained closed . . .

He was so high on adrenaline, blood flooding brain and muscles in the fight-or-flight response, that the walls appeared at times to buckle, becoming concave or convex, and the ceiling seemed to swoon.

His claustrophobia intensified, and a demon of doubt spoke of calamity, warning him that he would never see the sky again or feel the sun on his face or breathe air untainted by mold.

He persevered and came to the room that Ulrich had furnished with armchair, bed, TV, fridge. He stood with his back against the wall, to the left of the arched and doorless opening. Listening. No voices. A rattling-clinking. And a sob of frustration.

She was in there.

But what of Ulrich?

In his mind's eye, David saw that face: the high brow unlined by a habit of contemplation, the gray eyes as cold as dirty ice, the slit of a mouth, the lantern jaw that made the man appear as though he regarded everyone and everything with teeth-clenched contempt.

Do it. Do it now. Do it while he still might have the element of surprise on his side. Across the threshold, into the room, the large chef's knife at his side, his arm drawn back, ready to thrust or slash, all squeamishness having evaporated in this mortal moment.

The girl wasn't on the bed, and she wasn't in the armchair. She wasn't real, not in the here and now, but only a tense presence on the television screen. Seventeen or eighteen. Fresh-faced. Lovely. With great caution and feigning terror, she made her way silently through the labyrinth beyond this playroom, through the eerie rose light. As she turned a corner, a sudden eruption of melodramatic music accompanied her shrill scream, and before her loomed Ronny Jessup, grinning maniacally, not the real Ronny but an actor who seemed to be channeling a crazy clown rather than making an effort to portray realistically the demented man who had terrorized and killed so many in this warren. Ulrich was running the cheap horror movie that had been filmed here, perhaps because he thrilled to the screams echoing through the passageways of Jessup's old hunting ground.

Reality and surreality were becoming indistinguishable, fiction and fact folding together in a hallucinatory kaleidoscopic moment.

In a corner of the room, beside the small

refrigerator, were cases of bottled water and beer that hadn't been here earlier. That was what Ulrich had brought down the stairs on the hand truck: beverages. Stocking the playground.

Evidently, no woman was here yet, no prey selected.

Directly across the room from where he'd entered, an archway led to another segment of the maze. Ulrich might return through it or through the entrance David had used.

On the screen, the sobbing girl begged Jessup not to hurt her. His reply — like nothing the real killer would have said — boomed out of the TV, and from elsewhere in the catacombs came Stuart Ulrich's voice, raised to a fierce shout, reciting the corny dialogue along with the actor: "You're my toy now, my toy, and I'm a bad boy who always breaks his toys!"

Before David could retreat, the fanboy styling himself after Ronny Jessup came through the archway, barefoot and bare chested, as if he was at home here, the new master of the murder maze. He wore a belt holster at his right hip. *"You,"* he declared as if David had been a lifelong nemesis who had, for the hundredth time, appeared to thwart Ulrich's intentions. He picked up the remote control from the arm of the chair and clicked off the TV. He threw down the remote and put his right hand on the grip of the holstered pistol.

80

David in the doorway. The locked labyrinth lay behind him, every corridor a dead end.

"You got yourself big trouble," Stuart Ulrich said, halting a few steps into the far end of the room. "What you think you're doin' here besides trespassin'?"

David's racing heart decelerated. A seeming calm overcame him, which was in fact cold expectation, the stabilizing clarity of the survival instinct. "And what're *you* doing here like this, like you are?"

"It's my place, isn't it? I can be here any damn way I want. I don't answer to you or nobody. You answer *me* and quick."

"You said I couldn't come back," David reminded him.

"That need a translation, asshole?"

"I had to do more research. Anyway, I didn't want to pay for the privilege, not at the rates you charge."

"Like you're poor or somethin'. People like you got it all and still pinch every dime. You oughta embarrass yourself."

"So I'll pay."

"You will, huh? Maybe I don't need your money. What you think I'm doing here, dressin' the place up like this?"

David looked at the bed, the TV. "I guess you'll tell me."

"Tour business went away. So if I dress it up, like them real estate agents stage houses, show it like Ronny is still here and all, that's the kind of full experience people are gonna pay for."

"You're talking real showmanship," David said.

"Man's got an asset like this, he can't let it lay fallow."

"Exactly right. So maybe hire some girl to play dead, half-naked, smear her with fake blood. Tourists will pay extra to have their photo taken with one of Ronny's victims."

Ulrich's hatred was palpable. David's skin prickled as if peppered with lethal radiation.

"You make it sound all cheap," Ulrich said, "when it's nothin' worse than history. Maybe you come here to make more history."

David said nothing.

"Why you come here with them knives danglin'? You mean to cut someone?"

The moment was near. Ulrich knew that his story of staging the killing ground for tourists didn't ring true. He probably hoped to encourage David to go upstairs at gunpoint, where he could be more conveniently killed, freeing his murderer from the chore of hauling a corpse up the steps.

Ulrich said, "Maybe you figured to bring someone down here later, have your fun, cut her, and leave me to explain to the cops."

Although David focused on Ulrich's eyes, he was keenly aware of the hand on the grip of the holstered gun. "So . . . what's her name?"

"Whose name?"

"The woman you've targeted. Or the girl. A man like you, she's probably just a girl, easy to grab, easy to terrorize. You're no match for a grown woman."

Ulrich's face was as stiff as a lacquered mask, his mouth a slit from which words issued as if in the voice of a ventriloquist. "Not everyone is sick like you."

"Is she sixteen? Fourteen? Ten? Is she even eight years old, *you sick sonofabitch*?"

As his voice rose to a shout, David reached cross body with his right hand and plucked the smaller knife from its sheath.

Ulrich, a ready-to-be rapist and wannabe killer, flushed with outrage at being accused of child molestation. He drew his pistol.

David tossed the knife with the confidence of a blade master in a carnival act, though he had no such skill. Ulrich took the throw seriously — twisting to his right, almost falling — as if he expected to be skewered through the heart. He squeezed off a shot that went wild.

David pivoted, ducked, and went out through the doorway by which he'd entered.

A second shot, a third. The maze seemed to shake with the roar of the pistol, as if a primordial monster, previously in suspended animation, must be rising from caverns even deeper and stranger than Jessup's labyrinth.

81

Maybe Stuart Ulrich didn't have a second magazine for the pistol. Maybe the weapon's capacity was eight or ten rounds, with five or seven shots remaining. However, a knife against a pistol didn't work either in a dueling field at dawn or in a windowless labyrinth.

Go deeper into the maze and be murdered there. Go back to the receiving room and be murdered there. They weren't choices. They were fates to be avoided.

David prayed that his pursuer, having seen there were two knives, would proceed with

402

caution when clearing the doorway, wasting a few seconds. He made it to the first turn without being shot in the back. Took a fork to the left, another to the right. He hurried toward the receiving room, but went only as far as the upper mummification chamber. There was nowhere else to go.

He stepped inside and closed the door.

The blue eye gazed down at the stepladder.

Eventually Ulrich would come here. In a minute or three or ten.

The door opened inward, but that availed David nothing. Ulrich wouldn't be deceived by a lame hide-behind-the-door ruse. The barren room offered no other place of concealment.

He'd arrived also in a new mental space, mere terror having lost its grip on him. He stood in icy desperation, in energized despair, hope receding in the rearview mirror, with no option other than vigorous, reckless action. Do or die, all or nothing.

David crossed the chamber to the previously concealed entrance to the secret crypt. The space below was lit by sconces, a soft milky light like that in the upper chamber.

He quickly descended the stairs, once more going down among the dead girls, into the chemical stink, the hint of a grim underscent.

A fourteen-foot-square space. The table with jewelry and other personal belongings of the deceased. The three walls of catafalques, six per wall.

The chamber was not as small as a coffin, but it was no larger than a family mausoleum. Although beyond terror, he couldn't shed the clinging claustrophobia. He worried that he wouldn't be able to quiet his panicky breathing.

He sheathed the large knife and chose the wall nearest the foot of the stairs. One of the highest platforms, almost seven feet off the floor, bore the name Isabella Lopez in Ronny Jessup's fancy, painted script.

The catafalque was five feet deep, the body less wide than that. Four feet of clearance between the deceased and the ceiling.

He hesitated, assuring himself that he could do this. If he was beyond terror, he was beyond horror, as well. The survival instinct trumped all. In a moment this extreme, the heart became a stone, temporarily beyond a capacity for emotion, incapable of abhorrence and pity, filled only with the furious determination to live.

Isabella had evidently been petite, her wrapped remains hardly more than five feet long. The shelf on which she rested was about seven feet from end to end.

Standing on the lowest catafalque, gripping the highest with his right hand to steady himself, David used his left hand to tug the body toward one end of the shelf. It moved more easily than he expected. If a flood of adrenaline could empower a mother to lift one end of a wrecked automobile off her trapped child, as had been recorded more than once, David's feat of strength was unremarkable by comparison.

He climbed onto Isabella's catafalque and eeled behind her and then dragged her back into place in front of him, she on her back, he on his left side. She crowded him into the shadows against the back wall. When he raised his head to look across her, he could see the lower half of the flight of steps that led down from the higher crypt.

82

Disturbing the mummified woman had stirred a stronger smell from her, and David lay in that suffusion. The astringent chemical stink remained dominant, but there was no longer a mere suggestion of an underlying organic odor; it was insistent. He would have been less unnerved if the smell had been profoundly foul, but it had a sweetness to it, an *unappealing* sweetness, cloying and spicy, that turned his stomach solely because of its strangeness.

He withdrew the large knife from its sheath. Held it in his right hand. Breathed through his mouth without gagging. Quiet now.

David didn't know himself. Lying concealed behind the wrapped remains of Isabella Lopez, he'd never been more of a stranger to himself, not even when he had lied to Emily and spent two sordid days with the actress. The human heart might be, as they said, deceitful, but it seemed to him that it was no less stoic than deceitful, and glorious in its capacity for charity, devotion, friendship, tenderness, and love. One of his novels had explored three questions. What would you do for love? Would you die? Would you kill? He had thought that he'd found the limits of a man's capacity for sacrifice in that story, but he realized that he had failed to plumb those questions adequately. His answers had been superficial. He knew now that a self-aware and self-critical man, grown past the callowness of youth, would do anything for the object of his love if he felt her to be good and worthy. Not merely die. Not merely kill. But kill and die and go to Hell for his actions, supposing Hell was real and his actions warranted damnation. Stuart Ulrich deserved death, and David would kill him, if he could, not for love, but for self-preservation and for the innocent girl whom Ulrich would eventually imprison. However, having discovered this capacity in himself, he knew that he was also capable of killing for Maddison, not merely to protect her from men like Ulrich, but to ensure her safety, her honor, her happiness. In a world long on hate and short on love, he would stake his soul on the defense of the latter, and though society limited capital punishment to murderers — and often even excused them — he would not. He scared himself, but he could live with whom he was becoming — if he could live at all.

Peering over the mummified body of Isabella Lopez, he saw Ulrich appear on the steps. He lowered his head and waited.

"Holy shit," Ulrich said, "his hidden harem, just like the crazy bastard said, all wrapped tight as Tootsie Rolls."

83

Ulrich stood about five feet ten. The topmost catafalque was perhaps a foot above his head.

He must have decided at a glance that David wouldn't be found here. Besides, the collection of hidden pretties astonished him and perhaps excited him, not necessarily because he would ever do what Jessup had done with these bodies, but because it appealed to his lust for power. According to Ronny Jessup's twisted way of thinking, for a portion of these women's lives, he owned them, and by this act of preservation and storage, he felt that he owned them in death, too, even if they couldn't be called back to life and used. Drawn by admiration for the work of his imprisoned idol, perhaps thrilled to be about to ascend the throne of this underworld and soon begin his vicious rule with a living girl upstairs, Ulrich came off the stairs and into the crypt.

The man was barefoot. David could judge his position only by sound. Fortunately Ulrich muttered his amazement and admiration as he moved past the first wall of catafalques. Trusting his ear, David shoved the mummified body off the platform.

Ulrich cried out as the corpse fell upon him. He staggered back into the table of jewelry and personal effects, and fell.

David slid off the shelf and dropped to the floor, knife in hand, as Ulrich thrashed to get out from under the wrapped cadaver.

The pistol had been knocked from his hand. He scrambled after it, seized it, rolled onto his back, and squeezed off a shot that missed David's head by the width of grace.

Even as the muzzle flared, David slashed, and light glistened liquidly along the arcing blade, which sliced the wrist of his adversary's gun hand.

Ulrich's scream was as shrill as a hog's bleat. No less high on adrenaline than his attacker, he squeezed off another round. But the pistol wobbled in his weakened hand, and the shot went well wide of its target. David fell on him, all his strength and weight behind the knife, driving the big blade into the other's chest, cracking ribs and cleaving the dark heart that clutched around the steel.

The milky light of the sconces painted cataracts on Ulrich's gray eyes. His scoop of a jaw hung open, as if he meant to shout in terror at something he had seen just as the life was cut out of him, something beyond his assailant.

David withdrew the knife from the dead man.

The only significant blood was from the slashed wrist. Because the heart stopped instantly, the chest wound produced only a small dark stain.

A small dark stain and stillness. The stillness of the dead man affected David as might have the violent pitching and yawing of a ship in a storm, for he had been the agent of this solemn fixity.

After the wave of nausea passed, he picked up Ulrich's pistol. An ammo pouch hung from the dead man's belt; David extracted a spare magazine from it. He ejected the partially depleted magazine from the weapon and replaced it with the fully loaded spare. A quick search of Ulrich's pockets turned up a small ring of keys in addition to an electronic key for a vehicle.

He got to his feet.

With his shirt sleeve, he blotted the sweat from his eyes.

He was shaking, though not as badly as he'd been earlier.

From the items on the table, those few belongings of the lost women, he took a folded midnight-blue silk scarf with a pattern of silver stars.

He ascended the stairs to the upper crypt. He climbed the step stool and used the scarf to wipe his prints from the ceramic tile with the never-blinking blue eye.

He folded the stepladder and put it in the passageway outside the door. He inserted all the flashlights and the two bricks of plastic explosive into the backpack and set it beside the ladder. He untied the leather sheaths from his belt and put the knife in the backpack, and then the pistol, as well.

He went a short distance through the maze to the cell that Ulrich had prepared for whatever girl he had intended to capture.

No mirror hung above the white pedestal sink. He was grateful for that.

He washed the blood from his hands and dried them and used the towel to wipe the faucets and, on leaving, the knob on the cell door.

In the passageway, he looked left, right, half expecting Ronny Lee Jessup to lunge at him, which sometimes happened in his dreams.

A rushing sound. Like a flight of dark birds, an enormous flock. But it wasn't birds at all, only the susurration of his own blood eerily audible to him, his life in circulation through his arteries and veins.

84

David retrieved the step stool and backpack from the passageway outside the door of the mummification room.

To his eye, the character of the maze had changed. There was no longer an inherent menace in these passageways, no gathered demonic forces, no evil ineradicable. The place looked foolish, more like a tacky carnival fun house than a genuine den of horror, a construct designed by a puerile mind, concocted by a perpetual adolescent who had achieved adulthood only physically, having otherwise been formed by video games and internet porn.

In spite of all the cruelty and murder that had occurred here, the cellar was not haunted. He felt no ghostly presences. The dead stayed dead. The dead did not return.

Emily had not died here.

If she had died elsewhere, knifed by Ronny Jessup as she fought him off, she had not returned as Maddison Sutton.

There was no defense against time and the toll it took, no turning back the clock and remaining twenty-five, not with the aid of Lukas Ockland and archaea and horizontal gene transfer any more than with expensive creams and lotions advertised on the lesser cable TV networks.

Maddison was Maddison. And yet she was impossibly Emily. If Emily had not died here, perhaps she had never died elsewhere, either. More than ever, the truth seemed to be a Gordian knot that could be neither untied nor severed with a blade.

David had nowhere to go now but to the house on Rock Point Lane. There were no answers anywhere but there. He had no future anywhere but Rock Point Lane. No hope anywhere but Rock Point Lane.

From the playroom, he retrieved the knife he'd thrown at Ulrich. He sheathed it as he had the large knife, one clean and the other tempered with blood. He carried the stepladder and backpack up to the kitchen.

Leaving the lights on behind him and the back door open, he went out into the chilly wind, which had grown in power as shrouded lightning pulsed through clouds to the northwest and distant thunder rolled. He walked the driveway to the county road, turned northeast. He hurried along the blacktop and then along the dirt track, at the end of which he'd left Estella Rosewater's Ford Explorer Sport.

He opened the tailgate, slid the step stool into the back of the SUV. He shrugged out of the backpack and placed it in the Explorer and took the two kilos of plastic explosive from it and set them aside.

He hadn't worn his sport coat to the Jessup house because it would have overhung the knives depending from his belt. Now he took it from the back of the Explorer and pulled it on.

After retrieving the explosives, he closed the tailgate. He got in behind the wheel and put the two kilos on the passenger seat.

He sped past Santa Ynez on State Route 154, bound for US Highway 101. As he drove through the San Marcos Pass and out of the Santa Ynez Mountains, the sky broke, and a heavy rain shattered through the night.

Even in torrential downpours, lightning rarely troubled the sky along the California coast. But the heavens were electrified on this occasion, and great blazing spears struck down to sizzle on the surface of the black and tossing sea.

PART 6
A BRIDGE TO
THE PAST

85

Although the thunder and the hard rain drumming on the metal roof of the travel trailer would mask the sound of the Explorer, David nevertheless killed the engine and the headlights at the top of the hill and coasted at least two hundred yards, coming to a stop about twenty feet from the shitcan where Richard Mathers smoked his native, organic weed and made a girl named Kendra miserable and lived what he called a life.

Lamplight glowed at the windows, though none of the curtains parted when David got out of the SUV. He ran through the downpour to the trailer and stepped onto the first of the stacked railroad ties that served as stairs. With Ulrich's pistol, he fired two rounds into the crappy lock, the muzzle flash lending brief color to the falling rain. He topped the steps and threw open the door and rushed inside with no concern for his safety. If Mathers had his revolver close at hand, this might be the end of everything.

The stoner slouched in front of a TV, watching a soft-core erotic vampire movie: flashing teeth, the full bare breasts of a would-be victim. He was drinking a can of beer and spilled it on himself as he struggled up from an armchair with duct-tape-repaired upholstery, hampered by a mismatched ottoman. Wherever his revolver might be, it wasn't within reach.

David went at him fast, while Mathers was off balance, lashed with the pistol, breaking some ear cartilage. The front sight tore the tender tissue, and bright blood dripped from the lobe. Mathers cried out in pain and lost his footing and fell back into the chair.

"Where's Kendra?" David demanded.

Mathers could have looked no more shocked and terrified if the vampire had come at him from out of the TV. "What the hell, man, what are you doing, are you fucking crazy?"

"Where's Kendra?" David repeated, looming over him, the pistol at arm's length, giving the stoner a dead-on view of the muzzle. "Is she in the bedroom, the bathroom?"

"She's not here, dude."

"Where is she?"

"Why do you give a shit about Kendra?"

"When is she coming back?"

"Hey, the dumb bitch don't live here no more. I threw her lazy ass out."

"More likely, she came to her senses."

Mathers winced as he put one hand to his bloody ear. "This is so wrong, man, this is deep shit you stepped in, you'll do serious damn time for this."

"I was never here," David said. "Your word against mine. Guess who they'll believe."

"I'll maybe go deaf from this, man. You disabled me for life, you piece of shit."

Because of the rataplan of rain on the roof, the TV was turned loud. Spooky music swelled from it, and David shot the screen.

"Hey, hey, hey! That's big bucks, dude."

"No money, Richie. I'm done paying for information. Don't have time for you to jerk me around anymore. Before I go back to Rock Point, I need to know what you withheld from me. I need to know *right now.*"

"You got more than you paid for, asshole. I didn't withhold nothing."

"The girl sitting in that bedroom, the girl who was in a trance or whatever."

Although he'd been glaring at David, challenging him, Mathers looked away now. Some emotion in addition to fear and anger welled in him; it might have been one degree or another of embarrassment, maybe even humiliation.

"I told you about her. There's no more to tell."

"I don't believe you. You're as transparent as window glass."

"I'm bleeding like a pig here."

"As if I care. Talk to me."

Lightning flashed and thunder rolled and wind drove shatters of rain through the open door.

"I'm gonna have major water damage here. This isn't you, man. This isn't how you are. What's happened to you? What's *wrong* with you?"

"You've got three minutes to spill everything. If you don't," David lied, "I'll kill you. I'm in a bad place you can't begin to understand. I've got nothing to lose, Richie. So talk or die. Was she pretty?"

"Was who pretty?"

David fired a round into the ottoman between Mathers's feet.

"Holy shit!" The stoner pulled his legs onto the armchair as thin smoke curled out of the hole in the vinyl. "Yeah, she was a looker. Hotter than hot. So what? Are you horny? You need a date?"

"Black hair, blue eyes?"

420

"If you already knew, why come here and ask?"

From a hip pocket, David withdrew a photograph of Emily and unfolded it and showed it to Mathers. "Is this her?"

"Yeah, yeah, that's the bitch." Greater fear darkened his expression. "Is she something to you?"

Returning the photo to his pocket, the pistol still trained on Mathers, David said, "What did you do to her?"

"What shit are you talking? What's that supposed to mean?"

"You know what it means. Your first minute is almost up."

Richard Mathers continued to avoid meeting David's eyes. "That amazing face. I'm only human, aren't I?"

"I haven't seen any evidence of it."

"Hey, I only did what any guy would do."

"Any pervert. *Tell me.*"

"She was all alone in the house, just sitting there staring, totally out of it, like hypnotized or maybe some autistic person, maybe having a seizure, maybe some kind of deep stupid. I don't know. I'm no freakin' doctor."

"Go on."

"It was creepy, you know, like crazy weird, but she had this super nice rack, and I could see she wasn't wearing no bra."

"You unbuttoned her blouse."

"It was a sweater. I pulled it off, right over her head, and she just sat there like some blow-up doll, like she was saying you could do anything to her and she'd be cool with it."

"And?"

"Give me a break. You don't need to ask."

"And?"

"I hate your guts, man. Okay, all right, I took her head in my hands, you know, just to put it where I needed it to be."

"Dirtbag."

"Like you wouldn't have done the same. But before I could do what I wanted, I felt this thing through her hair, in the back of her head."

David frowned. "What thing?"

"Like a recess, very shallow, like a sixteenth-inch deep. You could hardly detect it, except it was perfectly round, which felt really weird. Creepy. I bent her head farther forward, pulled her hair out of the way, and there was this shiny metal cap, like the size of a quarter, in her skull."

"Cap?"

"A cap or maybe the flat end of something that was like plugged into a socket."

"A socket in the back of her skull? I'm

supposed to believe that? How many weed brownies did you eat today?"

"Hey, save a bullet, I'm only telling you what I saw, what I thought it might be. It might've been something else. How would I know? It was weird shit, whatever it was. Maybe some totally out-there medical condition. All kinds of crazy shit is happening in biotech these days. I watch them science shows, they got stuff going on Frankenstein never would've thought of."

"So what happened when you found this thing in the back of her head?"

"Not what I wanted, for damn sure. I'm fingering the cap or socket, whatever it is, suddenly the bitch comes out of her trance, raises her head, looks me straight in the eyes, coming to life like some cyborg just got its battery charged. Scares the bejesus out of me. She shouts, 'Who are you? What're you doing here? Get out, get out.' I run into the hallway, which was when it tweaks. It bent, dude, like I told you about before."

"Did she follow you?"

"Only into the hall, not when I ran downstairs to get out."

"And that's everything?"

As if chilled, Mathers tucked his legs farther under himself and wrapped his arms around his torso. He looked far younger than he was, like a dissolute twelve-year-old. "Isn't that enough for you? It was enough weird shit for me."

David lowered the pistol. "Don't even think about following me, Richie."

Mathers's boyish face crimped with self-pity. "That's it? I'm bleeding, got no TV no more, a hole in my ottoman, door lock busted, more water damage by the minute, and you just walk out with no offer of compensation?"

"That's it," David agreed and left the trailer.

If Mathers considered getting his revolver and following, he thought better of it.

86

David parked in the viewpoint lot, facing the Pacific.

He didn't know what to make of what Richard Mathers told him. The stoner wasn't the most reliable witness; the freak might have misunderstood what he'd seen. David had thought Mathers must be withholding something that would help unravel the truth of Rock Point Lane, but his revelation had only tied more knots in the mystery.

In two nights of intimacy with Maddison, David had not felt the indentation that Mathers claimed to have seen. However, perhaps he had never touched the right place on the back of her head.

Maybe she'd suffered a blow to the skull, damaged bone that required a metal plate. A head injury would explain why she might sometimes lose focus, drift away. But wouldn't skin have been grafted over it?

Life was getting weirder year by year, but was the world really sliding into an extended episode of *Stranger Things*? He didn't think so. He didn't *want* to think so.

Richard Mathers's voice came back to David: *All kinds of crazy shit is happening in biotech these days. I watch them science shows, they got stuff going on Frankenstein never would've thought of.*

Those words stirred from memory something that Gilbert Gurion, the attorney handling the estate of Ephraim and Renata Zabdi, had said in that mansion in Montecito on Monday: *Bioprinting . . . recellularize . . . . Some people think certain biotech developments, like those related to AI, are a little Frankenstein.*

Was that coincidence or something more, that kind of meaningful coincidence called *synchronicity*?

From his wallet, he extracted the card that Gurion had given him. It provided the attorney's phone numbers, including his cell.

Ten years earlier, on the night when Emily vanished, there had been poor cell service along this sparsely populated section of the coast. Now, service was immediate, and Gilbert Gurion took the call.

"I'm sorry to bother you after hours, Gil. I've been thinking about something you said that is of importance to me as I consider this project."

"No problem at all. What was it I said?"

"You were talking about bioprinting, recellularization, about the revolutionary applications of biotech, how fast everything is moving."

"Faster and faster."

"You said that some of this biotech, like that related to AI, is 'a little Frankenstein.' "

"That's not what I think, David. It's a concern of some people who, in my estimation, are simply ignorant."

"Quicksilver's work in bioprinting and all that — it's *medical* research. How does that have anything to do with AI, artificial intelligence? AI is machine learning, right?"

The incessant drumming of rain on the roof of the Explorer was oppressive, as it had been in the vivid dream of Emily alone in the broken-down Buick. It was the sound of isolation, helplessness, and dark destiny.

After a long hesitation, Gurion spoke with evident caution. "I may have been rash, bringing that up. I get emotional every time I visit that house. I'm not sure I should talk about . . ."

When the attorney seemed uncertain how to continue, David said, "I understand that some Quicksilver projects are related to national security. I don't want to put you in a difficult spot."

Again Gurion hesitated before saying, "Quicksilver is of course a metal, bright and liquid at room temperature. Spill some, and it's nearly impossible to contain. Ephraim said quicksilver is a lot like human intelligence and creativity. He said they're as fluid as quicksilver. Intelligence and creativity can't be long restrained, which is why humanity has a hope of solving all its problems. That's what Ephraim and Renata believed."

Phone to his ear, listening to Gurion's breathing — an intimate sound that seemed to summarize the truth of human vulnerability — and the ferocity of the rain pounding on the SUV as though Nature meant to dissolve all works of civilization, David strove to puzzle out what he was to infer from the attorney's words.

David said, "If bioinks and bioprinting can produce flesh, skin, capillaries, eventually organs . . ." He fell silent, troubled by where this line of thought inevitably led. "Does an AI have to be a machine? Or rather . . . does a machine have to be made of inorganic matter? Can a superintelligent AI be a . . . a bioprinted brain of extraordinary complexity?"

"Interesting to speculate," Gurion said. "The technology is certainly possible, although it's far in the future at this point, David. Far in the future. Now if you'll excuse me, I've been helping Georgina, my wife, prepare dinner. I've got to get back to that."

"Of course, Gil. I'm grateful that you took my call."

"I'm not sure I should have," the attorney said, and hung up.

Judging by all evidence, Ephraim and Renata Zabdi had been kind and generous and innocent, acting only with the best intentions. It was possible to conceive, however, that some people might find their dream of an organic AI to be a nightmare. Even so, did that justify their being tortured and murdered? Surely not.

Whether Richard Mathers had seen exactly what he claimed to have seen, or if he gravely misunderstood what he'd seen, or if he hallucinated the entire experience while on peyote, it didn't change the course on which David was embarked.

He had convinced himself that not only must he go to the Rock Point house, but also that Maddison *wanted* him to come there, wanted to be rescued from whatever situation she endured in that place. The note she'd left for him on his kitchen table; what she said about her loneliness and enduring fear, about starving for love: He took all of that as a cry for help to which he must respond.

Maybe it was foolish to go to Rock Point Lane without any idea of what trouble or trap he might be walking into. But if he was a fool, he was a fool for love, which felt better than the various other fools he had played during his thirty-seven years.

He would never claim to be a hero. However, there were moments when you had to show up, be there, assume risks, take bold action, if you still wanted to call yourself a man.

But what in God's name was waiting for him on Rock Point Lane?

87

Beyond the viewpoint railing, the sloping meadow lay barely discernible, like a scratchboard work so lightly etched by the artist that the white clay beneath the black ink was revealed only as pale gray lines that didn't portray gentle folds of descending land as much as suggest them. The sea was as black as blindness until lightning flared, whereupon twelve-foot dark breakers leaped out of the void and attacked the shore, as if they were ancient monsters of the deep returning millennia after their extinction.

David's car was the only one in the viewpoint parking area, as Emily's would have been on that night. Infinite beaded curtains of driving rain reduced visibility, and the lights of traffic passing behind him on 101 seemed more distant than they really were, like the running lights of submersible vehicles motoring on some mission into an oceanic abyss.

From the footwell in front of the passenger seat, he extracted the leather tote bag that he had bought in Santa Barbara earlier in the day and on which he had worked in his motel room. He powered his seat back as far as it would go and put the bag between his legs. He placed the two kilos of explosives in the bag, next to the travel clock, from which he had removed the plastic casing. The clock was powered by two rectangular Duracell D batteries.

A length of insulated wire trailed from the exposed guts of the clock. The rubber coating had been stripped from the end of it to reveal braided copper wires, which he now pressed deeply into one of the bricks of explosive.

He zippered shut the tote bag and returned it to the passenger seat.

He had no rain gear, only the damp sport coat. Even if he'd been attired for the weather, he wouldn't have walked to the end of Rock Point Lane, as before. The strangeness of the house convinced him that no matter how stealthily he approached, Maddison's keepers would know that he had come.

He drove south on 101, crossed over, drove north, crossed to the southbound lanes once more, and turned right onto Rock Point Lane. At the gate between the stacked-stone posts, he put down his window and pressed the button to announce himself.

Expecting to be asked his name and purpose, he intended to say that he had come to see Maddison. But no voice issued

431

from the call-box speaker, and the gate swung open before him.

The Monterey pines shuddered in the wind, and the flailing branches flicked browning needles onto the windshield. He passed under the trees and came to the house and parked as near to the front stoop as the driveway allowed.

Lights glowed throughout both floors of the residence, as if a party must be underway, but draperies and sheers prevented him from seeing who might be inside.

He picked up the pistol from the passenger seat. Six rounds remained in the magazine.

A slack length of dental floss, connected to the travel clock, came out of a hole in the left side of the tote. It was taped to one of the two handles. He picked up the bag, closing his hand over the tape, and got out of the Explorer.

He tucked the gun under his belt, in the small of his back. The sport coat concealed it.

The bomb didn't in the least wear on his nerves. He had nothing to lose. If Emily was dead, if his hopes had been raised only to be dashed, and if he could not learn the truth of Maddison, then he had no life to which he could return. No life worth living.

His mania had progressed beyond obsession, to a desperate and mad compulsion.

A bleak future was guaranteed not just by loneliness but by the fact that he wasn't going to be able to write anymore and would have no purpose. The quality of his work had declined after the loss of Emily, and he had no doubt that it would *plummet* if he lost her — or Maddison — again, if he didn't learn the truth of what lay behind the events of the past week. He was living a story, and stories had to have satisfying endings. If they didn't have satisfying endings, what was the purpose of stories? Since childhood, reading stories had taught him how to reason, how to live, how to hope, how to *be.* Doing research for the stories that he'd written had taught him far more than he had learned in college — not least of all including how to construct a bomb, how to defend himself with a knife. *He had killed a man.* Yes, all right, he'd acted in self-defense, and Stuart Ulrich had been evil, *but he had killed a man.* That was a radical plot twist, considering that he was a character with zero experience of killing, and if he lost his girl again, if he *failed her again,* that killing would have availed him nothing; his story, the story of David Thorne, would be finished, and it would have meant nothing.

He hurried through the rain to the stoop and sheltered under its roof and thumbed the doorbell. Through the oak-and-bronze door, he heard chimes announcing a visitor.

No one responded.

He pressed his thumb to the bell again, again, again.

They knew he was here. They had to know he would not go away. Perhaps they didn't answer because they knew he would get in one way or another, because they knew they couldn't keep him out, in which case maybe they wouldn't even bother to lock the door. He tried it, and it opened.

He stood staring into the foyer, which featured a Tiffany-style chandelier in a wisteria pattern, cascading glass petals in rich shades of blue. Past the foyer, a hallway led to the back of the residence.

No one appeared.

The wind shifted direction, bulleting a barrage of rain against David's back. He stepped across the threshold.

Drawn by the wind, the door crashed shut behind him.

In any other circumstances, he would have called out, would have asked if anyone was at home. But clearly someone waited here for him and knew that he had ventured inside.

88

David stepped farther into the foyer and halted when he heard what he first thought were footsteps. Here and on the upper level, the floors were of tightly joined, darkly stained walnut. The rooms featured replicas of antique Persian carpets, but no carpet runners softened the hallways on either level. These steps were heavy and rhythmic. Then he realized they were not footfalls, after all, but instead the low throbbing that he had heard — and felt — rising from the basement on his previous visit. The sound was much louder this time, insistent. And now the electronic hum, woven from several frequencies, swelled in accompaniment.

The air became chilly. His breath plumed in a cold smoke.

He recalled what Richard Mathers reported about his experiences in this place. Mathers believed that he had been face-to-face with someone or something invisible. David knew better. No spirit roamed the hallway; the noise and the cold rose from whatever machinery lay in the cellar.

He also remembered the dream that had afflicted him in the early hours of Tuesday morning, when recollections of real events, buried in his subconscious, had fashioned a nightmare of timepieces that had run out of time, of clockless rooms, of driving his Porsche into a void, with its digital clock blinking zeroes. He looked now at his wristwatch and saw that the second hand — and surely the other two as well — was frozen, as if there might be no future in this place, only this one moment, eternal.

And yet time passed here. If time were frozen, he would not be able to move, and all within these walls would lie in stasis.

Down the rabbit hole, through the looking glass. Day by day, a sea of weirdness had washed through his life, and now it seemed that a high tide of unreason might sweep him away.

The recollection of one dream reminded him of yet another, which was related to the elusive memory that he had been trying to recall since his previous visit to the house, when he had seen the ampule of blood hanging on a chain above her bed.

The Thursday night when he first met Maddison, he'd come home and slept as if drugged, and he dreamed of seeking her in the Island Hotel. At one point he found himself in a makeshift infirmary, lying on a cot, while a nurse in a black uniform drew his blood, assuring him that she was a phlebotomist. *I have much experience of blood.*

The dream had been one in which he'd at moments thought he was at least half-awake, in a twilight land between sleep's fantasy and reality. The nurse had been Emily. Or Maddison. And hadn't she told him not to remember, to sleep and forget?

If that was the source of the blood in the pendant hanging above her bed, if it was in fact *his* blood, drawn while he slept, drawn by Maddison after she admitted herself to his house a night before their first date, then the truth he sought was going to be more extraordinary and fearsome than anything that even his much exercised novelistic imagination could conceive.

But there could be no going back. He had traveled too far out of the territory of everyday life, had discovered dimensions to the world that he had never imagined, *had killed a man.* If he didn't at least learn the truth about Emily, he had nothing to go back to, nothing but frustrated curiosity and doubt and loneliness that would end in emotional — if not physical — oblivion.

Carrying the tote, he continued along the hall and startled when the living room, which had been brightly lighted, abruptly fell into darkness. He turned to his right,

437

peering into the gloom.

Blazing at the tall windows, an extended barrage of lightning revealed an empty chamber, all the furniture gone, storm flares and storm shadows imprinting a flickering series of kaleidoscopic black-and-white patterns on the floor and walls. The quick strobing light revealed what appeared to be haunting spirits, gossamer ectoplasmic shapes that undulated in midair, but they were instead the tattered remnants of fantastic, elaborately woven spiderwebs hanging from the deeply coffered ceiling, alike to those that he had seen in the garage on his previous visit.

The hallway lights dimmed, brightened, dimmed, as though the power might fail. With each dimming, the suggestion of water stains began to appear on the walls along with fractal patterns of mold, which faded away each time the lights brightened.

David feared nothing and everything. The bomb he carried was a defense against being overpowered, but it was also a commitment to give his life for Emily — or Maddison — if necessary. When a man was willing to die for someone else, *ready* to die, he feared nothing in practice; no threat could deter him. However, he could still dread the unknown, which in this case seemed to be

438

everything: the house, the people in it, and their purpose.

"Stay back, keep away," he said, not sure to whom or what he was speaking. His index finger curled around the slack length of floss that served as a trigger wire.

The hallway lights stopped pulsing, and the living room lights bloomed bright once more, the furniture returning with the sudden illumination.

Somehow the dark living room had not been *this* room now well lit. It had been *another version* of this room in a distant time, though his mind could not process what his intuition told him.

From elsewhere in the house, a voice rose in song. A clear, beautiful soprano. Crystalline notes. A sorrowing Celtic ballad.

David went to the swinging door between the hall and kitchen.

"If my Irish boy is lost / He's the only one I adore / And seven years I'll wait for him / On the bank of the Moorlough shore."

He pushed through the door into the kitchen.

She sat at the table, staring into her teacup as she sang.

"Farewell to Sinclair's castle grand / Farewell to the foggy dew / Where the linen waves like

bleaching silk / And the falling stream runs still."

She appeared to be in her late forties. Under a shaggy mop of auburn hair, her face — lovely, freckled, elfin — known to him. He had seen a photograph of her with her husband, Patrick, when he had visited Estella Rosewater in Santa Barbara. Nanette Corley. Stained-glass artist. She had died of cancer twelve years earlier.

89

The melancholy song had an eerie edge that raised the hairs on the nape of David's neck, and he stood transfixed by the sight of the woman.

Neither surprised by nor concerned about his sudden entrance, she rose from the table and took her cup to the sink and rinsed it under running water and put it aside on the drainboard.

"Near here I spent my youthful days / But alas they are all gone / For cruelty has banished me / Far from Moorlough shore."

As though the song worked a spell of silencing, storm light flared as bright as ever at the window, but no thunder followed.

He said, "You're Nanette Corley."

She turned to him, her stare solemn and

disapproving, her voice cool. "Nanette died of cancer. She's rotting in a grave."

"Then who are you?"

"Technically, I'm nobody. I won't be born for another sixty-seven years."

"What the hell does that mean?" David was frustrated by the endless mysteries, deceptions, and evasions.

"It means you shouldn't have come here. Didn't Richard Mathers tell you this place is haunted?"

"You're no ghost."

"What a keen mind you have. Razor sharp. Penetrating."

This sarcastic woman wasn't the kind and gentle artist whom Estella Rosewater had described.

"Who are you?" David asked. "*What* are you? What is this damn place?"

"It's the last place you'll ever be."

"I'm not afraid of you."

"There's nothing but death for you here."

"Where's Maddison? I'm taking her out of here."

Her laughter was sour with mockery. "Who's taking whom?" She crossed the room to the swinging door. "You're doomed, scribbler. But she's still a fool, putting the mission at risk, and for what? For *you*? As though you wouldn't run screaming if you realized what a monster she really is."

She stepped into the hall, the swinging door whisking the space where she'd been standing, as though it swept her out of existence.

Storm light tore the sky, and fierce demonic faces of white fire flickered in brief witness at the windows.

He'd imagined various things that might happen when he entered the house, but his imagination had failed him. The strangeness of the place, markedly greater than on his first tour, unnerved him.

He would have followed the woman, but the rhythmic throbbing and the electronic hum rose again from under the house, drawing his attention first to the floor and then to the connecting door to the garage. The entrance to the basement was out there, and it seemed to him that the fullest answer to this mystery might lie below.

Moving toward the door, he noticed that the digital clocks on the double ovens and on the microwave were blinking zeros.

The garage wasn't the filthy space that it had been before. Clean. Well ordered. The cabinetry had been restored. Maddison's Mercedes 450 SL and the beige Ford van were parked side by side.

He made his way to the basement door, tried the knob, and found it locked. The key was on the back porch, in a box attached to the bottom of one of the chairs.

"You must want very much to die."

Turning, David discovered Patrick Corley just this side of the door to the house. He looked as powerful and furious as when he had used a Taser in the cemetery groundskeeper's office.

David repeated a question he had asked Nanette, the one that increasingly seemed to be the key to this mystery. "What *are* you?"

Approaching slowly, the long-dead contractor spoke of himself in the third person. "Pat Corley was a reader of science fiction."

"I saw the books in your study. But what —"

Interrupting, Corley said, "He wrote extensively about sci-fi, hundreds of reviews and essays that survived a century in archives on the internet. Will anything you've written survive a century?"

"How would I know? How would you? Don't come any closer."

The big man halted. "Your writing days are over. There is no literary immortality for David Thorne. We will be your life now, if you're to have a life."

"What *are* you?" David repeated.

Corley said of himself, "Pat Corley was chosen because his reading and writing prepared him to accept us and work with us in spite of our . . . appearance. Which he did. He understood our mission. He helped us until he died. And even after he died."

"What work?" David demanded.

"We've come back in time to change the future," Corley said, as though their mission was as simple as that of young Mormons going door-to-door to share the message of the Latter-day Saints.

Following Corley's revelation, something happened akin to what Richard Mathers had lacked the ability to describe adequately. The garage pleated, folded into a brief darkness, then opened like a blooming rose, having reformed into the mold-riddled leaf-littered bone-strewn space from which cabinets had been stripped, where tattered remnants of immense spiderwebs festooned the rafters.

Because of all he'd experienced in the past week, David had become increasingly credulous in matters of the fantastic, possessed of a new willingness to trust that the world was deeply strange.

A new and dire thought came upon him: If this version of the garage with its scattering of large, deformed skeletons of birds wasn't of his time, if it existed in some grim future, and if it failed to return to normal, he might be condemned to haunt this version of the residence, a phantom without an opera.

Perhaps sensing the nature of David's fear, Corley said, "The house is a bridge between then and now, two points a hundred years apart. The bridge is always under terrible stress, so we endure moments of temporal dislocation. They pass. The bridge will not collapse."

Equally in the grip of dread and amazement, David Thorne began to awaken to a previously unthought-of truth, the ramifications of which were devastating and numberless.

The deep throbbing that rose from the cellar and multi-frequency electronic wail were perhaps the voice of time as it protested that its fabric had been tortured, the present and the future stitched together by some technological needle.

"What's in the tote bag?" Corley demanded.

He took a step forward, bird bones crunching under his boots.

"Money," David lied. "Half a million." He dared offer it to Corley. "For Maddison's freedom. I'll pay more if she's released."

Corley's anger soured to scorn. "In every age, idiots like you think money can solve any problem. But money can't buy a future without horror. It can't buy what you want. Emily Carlino is dead."

"You lie," David declared, desperately hoping that was true. "Last night, the dream you somehow inserted while I slept, the dream of Emily and Jessup — maybe it was mostly true, what happened to her, but not the end. Jessup didn't take her away in his van. I found his secret catacomb tonight. Emily wasn't among those fourteen mummified bodies. Jessup stabbed her, left her for dead. But maybe she made her way here through the storm. Maybe somehow she's still alive."

Corley — or whoever he might be — was not a relaxed liar. His hands were fisted at his sides. "She rang the bell that night. We let her in, and she died in the front hall. What little is left of her is the one you know as Maddison."

As the contractor turned away from David and went into the kitchen, the garage fractured, folded, reshaped, became the neat well-lighted space in which the Mercedes and Ford van were parked.

David returned to the house, but Corley

was nowhere to be seen.

He crossed the kitchen, followed the downstairs hallway past rooms where the windows flared as if a revelation were about to melt the world and reveal the reality behind it. The roar of thunder was as loud as an entire mountainside calving off a granite range.

Nanette stood at the front door, as if to bar his exit, though he had no intention of leaving. Her face was white and taut with fury, her stare as sharp as crucifying nails. "I'd kill you now if only I had the authority, if I could be sure killing you wouldn't have consequences that make the future even darker than it is."

"Why such rage? I don't mean any harm to anyone."

"In your arrogance, in your obsession to have what you want at any cost, you better know the price might be the world itself."

"I don't make any future but my own — and not much of that."

Her hatred was palpable. "Seemingly insignificant things can have terrible consequences. The horrors coming in the next hundred years are beyond your comprehension, pretty boy."

The stained-glass chandelier and other lights pulsed, and with each dimming, wings of shadow furled and unfurled through the house.

She said, "The catastrophes that people of your time fear — none come to pass. You fear the wrong things. You're all stupid, blind. You're so ignorant, you mistake the real threats as steps to Utopia. But if the future can't be changed, there will be hell on Earth."

He had no time for Nanette's rage and contempt.

The woman whom he had come to set free must be on the second floor. As the lights pulsed and the low throbbing passed through the house again, David climbed the stairs, no less in the grip of dread than in the thrall of hope. He followed the upper hall to her room.

90

The collection of photographs. The ampule of blood hanging by a gold chain.

All in white, she was more radiant than the dress she wore. She stood at the foot of the bed, young and beautiful and so alive, her face as solemn as that of a mystic contemplating eternal mysteries.

He stopped six feet short of her, afraid that what he had come here to learn would not be what he wanted to hear.

The lightning and thunder seemed to have relented, but hard-driven sheets of rain drummed the windows as though some tempest of absolution meant to wash from the world its long, sordid history of wickedness.

When he spoke the names, his voice was reverent but also riven with uncertainty. "Maddison? Emily?"

"Neither," she said. "You should have waited for me, David. You shouldn't have investigated me, shouldn't have come here. I asked you to have patience, but it's too late for that now. Put the tote down and sit with me. Understand . . . once you know, there is no going back to your old life. You'll have to pledge to me."

Although she remained radiant, she lacked the warmth that had previously marked her treatment of him, that had been a fundamental aspect of Emily's personality.

. . . there was this shiny metal cap, like the size of a quarter, in her skull.

What he said now was the truth but also an effort to placate her, to draw her out. "I don't have a life worth going back to. Not now that I've been filled with so many . . . expectations."

She sat on the edge of the bed and extended one hand to him. "Put the tote down and sit here."

If the tote contained only money, there would be no reason to refuse to put it aside. He placed it on an armchair, sat next to her, and took her offered hand.

She smiled at him, but this was not the lover's smile with which she favored him in recent days. He couldn't read her mood as clearly as he'd read it before, but that smile seemed reptilian.

"What did you mean 'neither'?" he asked. "How can you be neither Maddison nor Emily?"

"My future, a century from now, is a place of technological wonders — but also horrors without equal in history. Your generation and others, enchanted by change, welcomed their enslavement without realizing the hell they'd bring on themselves by their trust in unconsidered 'progress.' When change occurs at warp speed, some technological dreams become nightmares."

A sinking, sickening feeling overcame him as his hope shrank. "But if you're not Emily or Maddison, who are you?"

"My name is Anna. My body is in the basement, in a control pod that transmits my consciousness into this clone of Emily."

"Clone." The word felt like a stone in his mouth.

"The clone is my avatar. I operate it, I see through its eyes, I feel through its senses. With a DNA sample, we can grow a clone to maturation in four to six weeks. Three of us are on this mission. Pat Corley worked with us until he died, and now one of us operates a clone of him. Nanette was cloned from a lock of her hair that Pat, a sentimental man, clipped while she lay dying."

The Emily that Richard Mathers had found sitting in an armchair as if spellbound, *this* Emily, had been a clone whose operator had been at the time withdrawn, occupied elsewhere.

He thought of the love they had made during the two nights she had been with him, and ripples of nausea washed through him. He had not lost himself in the woman he loved, but in some crafted *thing,* some mindless biomachine controlled by someone whom Nanette had called a monster.

He managed to say, "Why clones?"

"Because of how we look, what we are, what human beings have become in our blighted time. We can't pass secretly among you as ourselves. We're too . . . different. We'd inspire disgust and terror."

David looked into her singular blue eyes

and felt that he was meeting the stare of an animated mannequin or robot or some alien life-form mimicking Emily.

At the moment, he had no capacity for amazement and wonder. His grief was resurgent, and under it swelled a rising anger. He felt that he had been the victim of an unconscionable deception.

Striving not to reveal his anger, sensing it would be dangerous to do so, he said, "You came back in time a year after Nanette died. That's eleven years ago."

"Yes."

"For eleven years you've been trying to change the course of history through highly selective assassinations."

"History shows us who the fanatics are, the sociopaths and narcissists who wanted to change the world at any cost. Who *have* changed it so much for the worse."

"You've had success?"

"Some. Not much. Time is a hard river to divert. The future wants to continue being what the past made it. When we eliminate an historical threat, it often recurs in a different way, driven by a different person from the one we cut out of the fabric of history. Sometimes it's a misguided obsessive with no malicious intent, like Ephraim and Renata Zabdi. But often it's a fanatic seeking power."

Her hand in his felt like a claw. Yet when he looked at her, he couldn't hate her, because he had loved that face for half his life.

If he couldn't hate her, he was gradually coming to fear her.

Her recent words were sinister in memory:

I feel safe here. Only here. With you. I feel so safe. Tell me it's forever.

I'll never leave you. This is what I want. It's all I want.

So then say it.

Say what?

Say this is forever, you and me.

This is forever.

Say it again.

This is forever.

It better be.

In recollection, those last three words that she had spoken in bed, with her head resting on his chest, sounded menacing now, which they had not at the time.

He got up from the bed and went to the window and gazed into the storm. If he walked out into the night, if he retraced the route that Emily had taken ten years earlier, off the headland and across the meadows and to the viewpoint, perhaps some arbiter of justice behind the veil of nature would finish him with a bolt of lightning and put an end to his yearning.

With the ultimate truth revealed, nothing else mattered. Yet he wondered, and in his wondering, he asked, "It wasn't by chance that we met that night in the restaurant, was it, Anna?"

"No."

"You drew me into all this."

"Yes."

"Why?"

She was silent.

He turned from the window. "Why?"

"Because I have experienced hours and hours, weeks and weeks of the memory scan we made of Emily as she lay dying. We possess the technology to copy anyone's memory as if it were just a long digital document, upload it to the cloud, and experience it as our own. In my way, I have lived the years she was with you, from the day you met. Your courtship of her, the romance you shared with her — all of that is now a part of my experience, my heart. She loved you more than she loved herself, and I came to love you, too."

91

Cold to the bone, David regarded the collection of thirty-two photographs.

In the white dress of innocence but in fact a pretender, Anna had risen from the bed. "For years I loved you from a distance, but that became intolerable. From Emily's memory scan, I knew what it felt like to love and be loved. I have never been loved as you loved her, as she loved you. There is little love in the brutal future from which I come. Much despair, hatred, self-loathing, fear. So I yearned to know such love from more than another's memory scan. And at long last, I contrived to meet you, to bring Emily back to you. From that scan, I know her, I can be her. I take such *delight* in being her."

Distraught, discomposed, David turned away from her, once more facing the night beyond the window, to which the storm's fireworks had returned. The lightning was a promise of release from a life that had spiraled into a darkness from which he saw no way out but vanishment into a storm, as Emily had vanished.

"What do you expect now?" he asked, dreading her answer.

"I have my mission, my work, but I don't

see why I can't also still have you, why we can't have each other."

He was incredulous. "You don't see why?"

"I'm an equal member of the mission. I can do what's best for me, and the others must conform to new arrangements. You and I can be happy, David. You've been very happy during the time we've spent together. Happier than you've been since you lost Emily. Don't throw away that happiness. You'll regret it. You will deeply regret it."

He remembered too well what she said before she'd gone away:

Say it again.

This is forever.

It better be.

It is.

It better be. I won't have anything less. It better be forever.

A thought occurred to him, a desperate hope. He knew it would be dangerous to raise this issue, but he had no choice. "To change the future, you change the past. So change the past. If you love me, really love me, change the past for me."

After an icy silence, she asked what he meant, though he was sure she must know.

He could see her ghostly form in the window as she came nearer to him and stood close behind his right shoulder.

He spoke to her reflection. "Go back to that night. Take a gun. You're an assassin, after all. Go back to that rotten night and take a gun and blow Ronny Jessup's head off when he steps out of the van, before he can touch her."

92

The quality of Anna's silence was such that David knew she would deny him.

When she spoke, his intuition was confirmed. "I wish I could, David. For you, I wish I could. But it's not possible."

He couldn't bear to look at her directly, couldn't allow himself to love the sight of her, couldn't permit himself to hate anyone who looked like her. "You could if you wanted."

"You don't understand the expense and the effort needed to create the bridge between this house in my time and yours. It was a revolutionary, Herculean effort. The year at this end of the bridge was carefully chosen for the work we need to do. It's only a bridge, not a time machine, just a bridge between this house in different centuries. I can't return to yesterday, let alone ten years to that awful night. I'm a prisoner of the present, just like you are, with no power to move anywhere but forward."

They stood in a long mutual silence as the rain ceaselessly washed the darkness toward a distant dreary dawn.

Softly she said, "Thy eternal summer shall not fade."

Part of the epitaph on the double-wide gravestone marker. From Emily's favorite of Shakespeare's sonnets.

"David, I'm a needy creature. I need affection. I need so much to be loved, and so do you. Until you, I've been starved for love all my life. I'm Anna, hideous to behold in my true state, a monster by any standard. I was born of normal parents, sent as an infant to a sanitarium for freaks, as the first of us were, until there were too many of us, until every child was a freak, though every child a unique horror. Human biology was upended by fanatical narcissists grasping for immortality through genetic manipulation. And that's only one of the horrors. One of many. The world was already dark and cruel, a hard place, off the rails, before we freaks began to be born. I'm fortunate I wasn't killed. Many were murdered out of fear and ignorance. I was beaten more times than I can remember, mocked and despised and spat on and never loved by anyone. But Emily . . . Emily was beautiful. How glorious it's been to be Emily Carlino and gaze into a mirror at Nature's work as it was meant to be, not as it has been undone by fools. You love her, but you can love me, too, if you will only give yourself the chance to discover it."

She put a hand on his shoulder. He closed his eyes rather than look at the transparent image of her in the window glass.

"Now that you've learned the truth," she prodded, "what relief has it brought you?"

He didn't answer.

"It's brought you none, no relief. Emily died. You can't change that. No one can. And you still blame yourself. You live in torment, and you always will, unless you open your heart to the extraordinary opportunity that lies before you."

Through his eyelids, each flash of lightning remained visible, dim flickering flares, as though the storm raged not just outside, but also within him. In fact, the one real storm always had been internal; the tempest lashing the California night was a mere reflection of the storm within.

He said, "Because you're from the future and know the past, you knew the day when Calista would die."

The hand on his shoulder gripped tighter, as if she meant to encourage him to proceed with this line of thought. "It was only a matter of reviewing the historical obituaries."

"You made her very happy on her last day, gave her hope."

Anna said, "Emily loved Calista very much. I owed it to Emily to ease her mother's way. Emily's memories taught me what love is. This should prove to you the quality of my heart. I can do what Emily would have done. I am worth loving. I won't accept that I'm not. I won't accept that from you. Ever."

He opened his eyes and looked not at her image in the glass but instead at the windswept night. The headland was dark, the vast sea dark, the sky dark in a sudden absence of lightning, and the future was darker than the scene before him, not just for him but evidently for all humanity.

He turned from the window to face her, and she withdrew her hand from his shoulder. "What if you're wrong?" he asked.

"But I'm not. I know you can love me. You will. You must. There is no choice now."

"I don't mean that. What if all this killing you people have done, eleven years of assassinations, isn't the solution?"

She adopted the tone of an impatient mother with a dull child. "You don't get it, Davey. You can't get it. You're not equipped to understand. You have a naive perspective because, technologically, you come from a primitive culture. Our computers are fifth-stage AI, and their models tell us there is no other solution."

He persisted. "You say you've had little success in changing the future. But what if you're partly the *cause* of that future?"

She grimaced in evident frustration. "You can't understand. You're incapable. Don't be stupid. You're not a stupid man."

"When you traveled here to fix the future, you became part of the past, so surely you became one of the forces that originally shaped the future. Perhaps in ways *you* can't comprehend. If you'd never built your bridge to the past, maybe your horrific future would cure itself. If an AI — or a whole cult of them — is telling you to come here, telling you whom to kill, maybe the AI is using you to ensure the future it wants, which might be the one you have, until eventually humanity becomes extinct."

David saw doubt pass through Anna's eyes, but she could not tolerate it. She clenched her jaws, compressed her lips, and shook her head dismissively. At the moment, she was being Emily only in appearance. A colder personality surfaced.

She said, "That's absurd for so many

461

reasons. Discussing the possibility is pointless, ludicrous. It's childish. You disappoint me. Face the truth. Deal with what *is*. Here I am. *Here I am!* Here is Emily, as close as you'll ever get to her. She's dead, dead and gone to bones, and I'm not. Accept what is, what must be. There's only one thing that can happen."

His fear was so great now that even his heart felt cold, the blood in his veins like currents of the arctic sea.

Whether she was an unwitting tool of oppression or a freedom fighter, she was also a vicious killer. They all were, everyone in the house.

The lightning and thunder had subsided again, but not the unremitting, pounding rain.

She was right when she said there was only one thing that could happen, in the sense that there was only one course he could follow, and it was not the one she insisted upon.

"What happened to Emily's body?" he asked.

Anna's answer sounded practiced. "We couldn't risk calling the police and drawing suspicion of any kind to this house. We worried that we'd be caught if we returned her to the car at the viewpoint and left her to be found. When we had what we needed to clone her, to add her to our inventory of possible identities, we acquired a casket and buried her right here on the property, just as a few years later we would bury Pat Corley."

"Was she left in an unmarked grave?"

"No. We did right by her. There is a stone set flat in the ground. It bears no name. We couldn't risk that. But on it is the word *beauty,* which we all agreed was the truth of her, based on how she looked and what we knew of her from the memory scan."

This sounded fully Disney, a nice bit from a fairy tale, out of place in this darker narrative.

"I want to see the stone. I want to . . . kneel where she is."

Anna hesitated but then said, "I'll take you there when the time is right."

After another silence, he said, "I betrayed her once, and you know the price. I can't betray her again. I can't betray her with you. I won't."

She came close to him and put a hand on his chest, and he did not flinch. "You won't be betraying her. I'll *be* her. With you, I'll be her exactly as she always was."

Whatever else had gone wrong with society a century hence, there seemed to have been a profound collapse in moral judgment, a triumph of fascist thinking that valued clones and human beings and machine intelligence equally — which was to say almost not at all.

The incessant drumming of the rain was like the relentless rush of time that washed away the days and carried all lovers — and hope — toward the same mortal void.

He said, "I'd be living with an assassin. One night you'll come home with blood on your dress and call it wine."

"No, I never will. I'll spare you all knowledge of what I do. To intrigue you, I made the mistake of telling you about my work. I can't untell it. But I won't be in your face with it again."

In an emotional vortex that pulled him toward despair, he said, "It would be madness to do what you want."

He felt her stiffen at his rejection, but she didn't remove her hand from his chest. She slid it to his abdomen. "There is a land of the living and a land of the dead, and the bridge is love . . . the only meaning."

A not unpleasant shiver passed through David, a recognition of the potential of tomorrow in spite of the calamity of today. "That's a quote from Thornton Wilder, from his novel, *The Bridge of San Luis Rey.*

Emily was enthralled by that story."

Sliding her hand to his groin, Anna said, "Yes, I know."

He was afraid to say what must be said next.

After a silence, he pursued his suspicion. "There's a poem by John Keats that I like. Emily liked it, too. It contains two lines that are especially poignant. 'Beauty is truth, truth beauty, that is all —' "

She finished it: "— all ye know on earth, and all ye need to know."

David met her eyes. "Love without truth isn't beautiful. It's not even love."

Her eyes narrowed, and she took her hand away from him.

He said, "The memory scan you made of Emily that night . . . You told me that you learned what love is from her. She knew love is the ultimate beauty. Therefore, love is the ultimate truth of the world. You can't love me and lie to me, not truly love me. That's a lesson I learned at the cost of . . . everything. And if you truly love me, you'll never make me live a lie."

If Anna had been angry with him before, she had largely hidden it well. She couldn't conceal her extreme displeasure now. "Don't do this to me, damn you. Don't be such a piece of shit. Love me like I love you."

"You can't insist on being loved."

"Oh, but I can. I do. I fucking insist on it. Never think I don't. I fucking *insist.*" She smiled to take the edge off what she'd said, but her smile was strained, manic, without charm, a crescent of insanity.

The two fans of his books who had become obsessed with him, who had taken actions requiring him to hire Isaac Eisenstein to provide security at his publicly announced appearances, both shared four characteristics. They were socially awkward. They believed that they were victims of an unjust society. They read his fiction in such a way that they were convinced he understood them and sympathized with them. And they saw his success as based in part on the exploitation of their victimhood; they believed he was writing about them, and therefore he owed them recognition, friendship, money, even love and marriage. One a man, the other a woman, they had been capable of violence, but neither had been a killer with "much experience of blood," as was Anna, alias Maddison.

Nevertheless, David did not relent. "Maybe love can't be fully understood from a memory scan. In fact, I'm sure it can't.

Now, please, Anna, I want to see her grave. And more than merely see it. I want to dig it open. I want to open the casket. I want to see her body. If there is a body."

Judging by her expression, he suspected that with his words he had signed his own execution order.

93

Anna turned from David and went to the dresser and stood reviewing the photographs of him that were arranged there.

David waited, not allowing himself to hope, for it was human nature often to hope for the wrong thing, while thinking it right.

When Anna had been silent so long that he suspected her displeasure might be ripening into a darker and more dangerous passion, he said, "I love how kind you were to Calista on her last day. I love you for enduring so much suffering and not becoming the monster you were accused of being when you were a child. Regardless of what you might look like, regardless of what the hellish future has required you to do, there's goodness in your heart." He was not sure that was true, though he was willing to concede it. "But I can't love you the same way that I love her. I love her entirely, her virtues and her faults, the intricate weave of her, every thread in the pattern that is the *real* Emily Carlino."

The incessant rain at the windows. The expectation that this room might at any moment tweak and fold into a bleak new century. His heartbeat slow, heavy. A stillness without hope. Only anguished anticipation.

Anna picked up one of the photographs.

David spoke to her better nature. "The technology of your time is so advanced, it's like magic to me."

She looked up from the image of David to the reality of him.

He took a deep breath and hesitated and finally said, "Emily had been knifed twice. Maybe she'd lost a lot of blood. Maybe there'd been organ damage. But with your technology, surely she could have been saved."

Holding the photograph to her breast, she said, "You listen to me now, David. You listen close. This is how it is, and it can't be any other way. She's dead, dead, dead, *and it can't be any other way.* Our protocols allow us to kill only those responsible for the horrors that we believe have shaped the world of our time. We are not permitted to kill — *or even to save from death* — anyone else. Because there's no way to know how interference of that kind might reverberate through time and possibly shape an even worse future than the one we have."

In her insistence, he heard deception. He persisted. "Patrick Corley was a sweet, sentimental man. In those days he was alive and working with you, Pat himself, not a clone of him. He was a gentle guy, incapable of killing. Incapable of letting someone die who could be saved, someone innocent like Emily. You needed his continued cooperation, his assistance in concealing what his house had become. In part, by cloning Nanette from a lock of her hair, you bought his cooperation, didn't you? In part. Before you were Emily for me, were you Nanette for him, using her clone as your avatar?"

"I'm only Emily now," Anna declared. "She's my only avatar. Only for you. The others use the Nanette clone, but I never will again."

"A year after giving him his lost wife, Nanette, what did you do that night when he insisted you couldn't let Emily die? What did you do? What did you do that night?"

"You won't listen," she said. "You're deaf to reason."

David pressed her harder. "There's no stone with the word *beauty.* That was a lie.

Wasn't it? There's no stone because there's no grave."

"Don't do this, David," she warned.

"What else is there left for me to do?"

"Accept. Just accept the way it is, the way it will be."

"I can't accept the unacceptable, the unthinkable."

"You won't give up, will you?"

"No."

"You will not have me."

"No. Never again."

"You know too much now. You realize that you know too damn much?"

"Too much," he agreed, "but not quite enough."

"Do you understand the price of such knowledge?"

"Will you prevent me from leaving, keep me here forever? Kill me? Isn't killing me against your protocols?"

She'd been so deeply wounded by rejection that she was capable of regarding him with coldest contempt. "There are rare exceptions to the protocols."

"Now I know the price. You've made it clear. So be it. I want the truth. All of it."

She raised her voice, slashed at him with her words. "You're sick, David. You're obsessed with your guilt, with earning absolution. Get over it. *She's dead!* She's gone to the worms. You aren't Christ Almighty. You can't resurrect her."

"You can."

Anna's face — Emily's face — was clenched with anger and self-pity. "She's dead. The gorgeous bitch is dead. There's me. Take *me,* you selfish bastard. *I'm* gorgeous now. I love you."

"You love me? Really? Or do you just love being loved? Do you love seeing beauty in the mirror? Is what you love just that fine reflection? True beauty is more than that."

Defiantly, she said, "I can have you whether you want me or not." She indicated the ampule of blood hanging above her bed. "I have insurance against rejection. I can clone you. I can have *another* you."

"And call that true love? Two soulless avatars, each operated by a puppeteer? Can that really be love? Or would it be only a squalid passion?"

"I can have another you," she insisted. "If you won't be what I need, I can make what I need."

"Then make him, use him. And tell me what you did that night ten years ago, when Pat Corley insisted you couldn't let Emily die?"

Anna shuddered as if speaking the truth

471

tore something loose in her. "Okay, all right, damn you, *yes*. That night, while she still lived, we took your Emily below."

"Into the basement?"

"Yes."

"And then?"

"We healed her."

I said to my soul, be still, and wait without hope.

"And then?" he asked.

"Your precious bitch is in a stasis chamber, suspended animation, unaware of her condition."

"She . . . she's been there for *ten years*?"

"We promised Patrick, when our work is done, when changing Emily's destiny poses less risk to our mission, we'll release her."

"And if you never succeed in your mission?"

"She remains in suspended animation."

"No. Not any longer. Bring her to me."

Anna looked again at the framed photograph she held. Her face flushed and twisted with a pure hatred of which Emily would never have been capable, a hatred seeded in a childhood of beatings and cruel rejection and perpetual fear. She might want to know what love was, might yearn for it, but she remained a victim of her fallen future and of her twisted physiology. She threw the

472

picture at him, and he ducked, and it knocked against a wall. She swept the other photographs from the dresser to the floor, pivoted toward David, and declared, "All right, deny me! Treat me like shit! Spit on me! I can pull the plug on your precious princess. Then you'll have exactly what you started with — *nothing.*"

He turned away from her, toward the armchair where he had left the tote bag that contained the bomb.

The Corley avatar had quietly entered the room and stood now between David and the chair.

94

She is here. Emily was here, in the realm below, waiting to be awakened from a long, unnatural sleep. She hadn't been lost forever, though he might yet lose her — fail her — again.

As David backed off from the avatar of the dead contractor, which was inhabited now by one of Anna's two nameless comrades, Corley spoke to her. "We should do with him what we did with her. Suspended animation in a stasis chamber. Let them sleep away the century together, while we change it."

"He deserves a harder judgment," Anna said, her Emily face ugly as it never had been before, distorted by bitterness.

"The protocols —"

"Fuck the protocols! Look at him. Handsome and well formed. Like my hateful father. His kind loathed me on sight, sent me away at birth. His kind ran the sanitarium where we were kept. His kind tormented me all my childhood, all my life. Tormented all of us. His kind beat me, reviled me. By their arrogance and stupidity, *people of his era made us the creatures that we are.*" Her fury was white-hot. If she could have killed David with a look, he would already be ashes. "He wants nothing of me even now, even when I walk in Emily, live in Emily, even when I'm as beautiful as she is. Even beauty isn't enough for him. I disgust him. My being her isn't enough for him, he needs me actually to *be* her. I want him dead. Both him and her. Both dead."

"Settle yourself," Corley said sharply. "Your authority is no greater than mine. We live by the protocols. He'll be placed in a stasis chamber to dream through the years."

She took several deep breaths. "There's no justice. There never is. There never has been. Screw it. All right then. But it doesn't end with this. Damn if it does." Anna took a step toward David. "You'll never have her. *Never!* If we fail to change the future for the better, you'll sleep forever or until the stasis chamber fails and you suffocate in it. And if we succeed, if we undo the mess your generation and others have made, the last thing I'll do before we close down the bridge is terminate your precious Emily Carlino and let you wake up without hope. No matter what, you're never getting out of this house with what you came here to get. Have a taste of my despair, David. Take a deep drink of it."

Legions of rain marched across the roof, lightning napalmed the sky, cannonades of thunder rocked the night, and it seemed the earth was a battlefield, pole to pole, where armies clashed ceaselessly, from time immemorial to time's end, good pitched against evil, evil against good, neither able to achieve a permanent triumph. There was no joy, no light, no certitude, no peace except what existed between two hearts that were true to each other and, in being true, found the forgotten Truth of the world.

Do not fail her, not again.

As Corley reached into a pocket, perhaps intending to withdraw the compact Taser-like device that he'd used in the cemetery, David drew Ulrich's pistol from the small of his back, from under his sport coat, and fired two rounds point-blank. An arc of blood slicked through the air. The big man dropped and lay as if he were stone shaped in a human form, his head cracked like a broken melon.

No, neither a man nor a granite monument of one. This was only a thing, a soulless clone being operated long-distance by a twisted specimen of decadent humanity ensconced in a "control pod" in order to experience the world through the senses of an avatar.

Shrieking like a Harpy that would gut him with her talons, Anna came at David so fast that she seemed to fly, clawing viciously at his face, drawing blood from one cheek, going for his eyes, driving him backward until he came up against a wall. He straight-armed her, the butt of his hand slamming her chin, snapping her head back, staggering her, so that he might slip away to the armchair.

She saw his intent and seemed suddenly to know that there was something other than money in the tote. She got to it as he did, and they both seized the handles.

"You killed only the meat machine he was operating," she said. "He'll activate another. There's no way out for you, pretty boy."

476

He was terrified that she would accidently pull the trigger string, all but vaporizing them and bringing the house down on the cellar, in some corner of which Emily waited to be revived.

Face-to-face, breath merging with breath, she sneered at him, at the hesitation inspired in him by her familiar face and form. "I can make one Emily after another and use them as I wish, use them to kill, make whores of them."

He shot her in the abdomen and then the chest, killed this ersatz Emily to save the real woman if he could, and her hand slipped off the handles of the tote as she fell.

Somewhere far below, Anna might already be seeking to control some other avatar.

Movement drew his attention to the door. The third member of the mission, whatever his or her name, appeared in the Nanette avatar. She had a pistol in a two-handed grip.

Before she could open fire, David curled the line of floss around the index finger of the hand with which he held the tote. "This bag contains two kilos of a plastic explosive. I can trigger it in an instant. Shoot me, and I'll trigger it reflexively. If I fail Emily again, I have nothing to live for. I'll gladly die, and take you with me — this house, your mission, the bridge through time across which you came here. *Now bring her to me.*"

95

David stood in the foyer, by the front door, the tote bag in his right hand, the trigger string taut.

The Nanette avatar had wanted him to descend into the basement with her, where Emily lay in suspended animation, but he dared not go. He couldn't know what else waited below, in addition to Emily, and he might be disarmed by some means unforeseeable.

If he pulled the length of floss until he felt the timer switch click over, he would have just sixty seconds until detonation. If he pulled the string hard enough to tear it loose of the switch, the explosion would be instantaneous.

The house lay silent but for the storm without.

What would you do for love? he'd once asked in a novel, written after the loss of Emily. *Would you die? Would you kill?* Yes and yes. The cause better be righteous, however, and in this case he knew it was right to kill these travelers out of time, who themselves had no respect for life. Even in his own time, evil players often did not recognize their own evil, thought themselves paragons of virtue, proclaimed themselves champions of justice to justify violence, with no understanding that justice is often subjective, that the pursuit of justice is not the same, not as worthy, as the pursuit of hard, objective truth; and judging by what he'd learned, it seemed the world a hundred years hence might be a place where most were evil, in a war of all against all, where every murderer thought himself a virtuous victim. David had no stake in such a future and no power to change it. He had only Emily, the hope of saving one life by facing the hard truth of his past betrayal.

He was physically exhausted, emotionally drained, mentally weary. By the grace of adrenaline, desperation, and raw hope, he remained on his feet and alert.

The period of what Corley had called "temporal dislocation" seemed to have passed. The lights maintained a steady glow, and the air remained warm. No hallway from another century folded into this one.

According to whoever operated the Nanette avatar, she required fifteen minutes to release Emily from the stasis chamber and bring her fully conscious.

David couldn't imagine how Emily would cope with what had happened. She would remember Jessup's assault, being stabbed, making her way to this house, collapsing in the front hall, but most likely nothing else. For her, all of that terror had occurred not ten years ago, but only minutes earlier — and yet she had no wounds.

Although she had supposedly remained unconscious in the stasis chamber, perhaps some subtle awareness of her status informed her dreams, if indeed she had dreams. Then she might awaken with a sense that something extraordinary happened. Maybe she even possessed a memory of being healed by miraculous technology before they had subjected her to suspended animation. In that case, upon being resurrected, she might suffer less from shock and fear than from perplexity or even just bewilderment. Whatever her condition, she would come to understand, to accept the ten-year hole in the middle of her life, because she would have him to help her. David would counsel her, guide her, gentle her into her life renewed; he would cherish her, live for her.

His wristwatch did not work in this house. But it felt as though fifteen minutes became sixteen, became eighteen, and then twenty.

He began to wonder if somehow they had gone away with Emily, not out the back door, which would have availed them nothing, but across the bridge between centuries, to the blighted future where David didn't know how to follow them.

And then two figures emerged from the open kitchen door at the farther end of the hallway. The first was Emily Carlino, as glorious as ever she had been. Close behind her was the Nanette avatar.

Emily wore black jeans, a white T-shirt, a black denim jacket — which must have been the outfit she'd been wearing on that terrible long-ago night. At first he thought this might be yet another trick, a second clone previously created and kept ready to serve as an avatar, a control mechanism surgically implanted in its skull. As she drew closer, however, he saw beyond doubt that she was the real woman. If the clone had seemed to move with Emily's grace, David now saw this wasn't in fact the case. The real Emily moved with an ease of action and attitude and posture, with an elegance and harmony, that the cloned avatar had imitated but had not been able to match. Emily was grace personified, while the avatar had been merely comely and striving to be lithe.

His heart swelled at the sight of her, the

true Emily. However, it swelled not just with love and joy, but also with fear for her. In this penultimate moment, seeming triumph could become disaster in more ways than he was able to anticipate. An inch from paradise was no better than a mile in a world ruled by devils.

As she approached him, her expression was one of emotional astonishment chastened with perplexity, hope twined with trembling uncertainty, mystification.

He smiled and made a come-to-me gesture with his left hand, and she glided toward him like a figure in a dream, closing not only the distance between them but crossing time itself, coming forward from the past, across a lost decade, still twenty-five and luminous.

Nanette halted at the midpoint of the hall, regarding them with fury and frustration.

David kept glancing at the staircase. Two clones lay dead in an upstairs room, surely as beyond revival as any ordinary human body in such condition. A brain shattered by a head shot or a heart torn by a bullet couldn't mend magically and begin to function again. Yet he was wary of the stairs.

Emily came to him and put a hand to his face, as though needing to confirm by touch that he was real. "Davey. You're bleeding."

"It's nothing. A scratch. Get out quick. There's an Explorer in front of the house. Key in the cup holder. Start the engine, get in the passenger seat. I'll follow."

She was Emily, daughter of Calista, not just book smart but also street smart. Even in her bewilderment, she didn't hesitate, opened the front door, and went out into the night.

The diminished wind had lost the power to pull the door shut. David stood listening to rain slashing through the trees, pounding the earth, drumming the roof over the front stoop.

At the farther end of the hall, behind the Nanette avatar, something appeared in the kitchen doorway, roughly human though misshapen, a configuration of malformed bones, sloughed facial features, eyes receding under a shelf of brow. She was as fearsome as she was wretched, and as she joined Nanette at the midpoint of the hall, David knew she could be no one but Anna.

The deceitful could know suffering and grief, could be humbled and broken by it, as David well knew. Although he could fear Anna, he couldn't hate her, only pity her.

However, he must not allow pity to cloud his judgment. Anna and the others had their mission, and if it might be misguided, if they

483

were unwittingly serving the very oppression they hated, they were nevertheless committed. Now that the real Patrick Corley had died, now that he was no longer a moderating influence on them, now that his house belonged to a foundation and was theirs forever, they would not continue to grant Emily the mercy with which Corley had forced them to treat her. And they would be merciless with David. They were killers who murdered in the name of humanity; they would be bloodthirsty.

When he heard the Explorer's engine start, he pulled the string just hard enough to engage the timer switch. Now he had one minute.

He didn't want to give Nanette and Anna enough time to get to the tote and zipper it open and jerk the bare wires out of the brick of plastic explosive. The moment he felt the switch click, he began to count the seconds in his head — *one thousand one, one thousand two, one thousand three* — praying that he might be at least ninety percent as accurate as a Rolex.

If clocks in this house could not display time properly, that didn't mean the seconds weren't passing. This was apparently some kind of eddy in the river of time; the river rushed forward; but here, the currents circled in a side pool. This wasn't a pocket of stasis; events still proceeded here in a familiar linear fashion. Therefore, the timer in the bag should count down to detonation. The fact that Nanette and Anna seemed to respect the threat indicated that the device would work. Nevertheless, he broke into a sweat as he considered that he might leave the bomb behind to no effect.

Ten seconds. Twenty. Thirty. Forty. Forty-five.

David put down the tote, stepped out of the house, pulled shut the door, and ran to the nearby Explorer, splashing across the sodden lawn. Emily had left the driver's door open, the headlights blazing. He swung in behind the steering wheel, slammed the door. She hadn't engaged the emergency brake. He needed only to shift the vehicle into drive and tramp on the accelerator.

As they rocketed away from the house, a thousand knuckles of rain rapped the windshield, the safety system loudly warned him that he had not engaged his harness, and he expected bullets. When he glanced at the rearview mirror, it filled with a roiling mass of reflected fire. An instant later, a concussion wave rocked the Explorer on its tires, and the steering wheel stuttered in his hands.

Before they reached Highway 101, another blast wave rattled the tall Monterey pines that flanked the long driveway, shaking loose a whirling mass of dead needles. Sleeping birds, waking from sheltered branches, swooped in front of the racing Explorer and seemed to blow away into the storm, as if they were swatches of celestial fabric torn from the starless night sky.

Third and fourth concussions, each greater than the one before, were not the work of the bomb, but perhaps signified the collapse of whatever elemental power sustained the bridge that linked this troubled century to one more troubled in the future.

96

The night, the rain, the southbound blacktop glistening in the headlights like some magical highway leading to an enchanted land. Emily beside him, untouched by time and by those tormented creatures who had conquered it. She was an impossibility, but real.

She said, "A man . . . he stabbed me."

"Yes."

"I . . . I died."

"Almost. Thank God, not quite."

In his face, she seemed to see the years

that she had lost but he had lived. "How long ago?"

"The man, the knife? Ten years."

Shock silenced Emily for a mile, and then she said, "I dreamed. I didn't realize how very long I was dreaming, Davey. I dreamed of anniversaries, celebrations, journeys, children. I dreamed . . . a life. Davey, what was that place? What happened there?"

For the moment, he had lost the talent to weave a story. He was unable to think where to begin.

Instead, he wondered how they would explain her reappearance, what tale of amnesia they would concoct and how they would anchor it with enough hard facts to satisfy both those who had known her and the authorities — and Isaac Eisenstein. There would be a way. He had no doubt they could do it. Life was a tapestry of stories. People spun stories ceaselessly, every day of their lives, whether they were writers or not.

She respected his silence, as if she understood that he wasn't buying time to deceive, but was struggling to decide how best to lead her through the extraordinary maze of truth that they could never dare to share with anyone.

The rain relented. Santa Barbara glittered

in the darkness, necklaces of light across the hills.

He would not return the Explorer to Estella Rosewater just yet. Call her later. Come north again in a few days to collect his things at the motel and retrieve the rented Terrain Denali. Tonight, they would drive all the way to Corona del Mar. To the yellow bungalow with the white shutters, where the yellow porch swing waited to be swung and yellow hibiscus bloomed in abundance.

At last he said, "You know the legend of Orpheus and Eurydice."

Her eyes were blue gems in the instrument-panel light. "Eurydice treads on a serpent and dies of its bite. Orpheus is a great poet and musician. He descends into the land of the dead, using music to charm his way past Charon and various demons, to rescue his beloved Eurydice."

David said, "Hades allows him to take her, though Orpheus must vow that he won't look back at her until he's led her into the land of the living."

She said, "At the last moment, he breaks the vow, looks back at her, and loses her forever."

"Let's start with that," David said, as clouds began to tatter and beams of moonlight found the sea. "This time, I did not look back."

ABOUT THE AUTHOR

International bestselling author **Dean Koontz** was only a senior in college when he won an *Atlantic Monthly* fiction competition. He has never stopped writing since. Koontz is the author of fourteen number one *New York Times* bestsellers, including *One Door Away from Heaven, From the Corner of His Eye, Midnight, Cold Fire, The Bad Place, Hideaway, Dragon Tears, Intensity, Sole Survivor, The Husband, Odd Hours, Relentless, What the Night Knows,* and *77 Shadow Street.* He's been hailed by *Rolling Stone* as "America's most popular suspense novelist," and his books have been published in thirty-eight languages and have sold over five hundred million copies worldwide. Born and raised in Pennsylvania, he now lives in Southern California with his wife, Gerda, their golden retriever, Elsa, and the enduring spirits of their goldens Trixie and

Anna. For more information, visit his website at www.deankoontz.com.

The employees of Thorndike Press hope you have enjoyed this Large Print book. All our Thorndike, Wheeler, and Kennebec Large Print titles are designed for easy reading, and all our books are made to last. Other Thorndike Press Large Print books are available at your library, through selected bookstores, or directly from us.

For information about titles, please call:
    (800) 223-1244

or visit our website at:
    gale.com/thorndike

To share your comments, please write:
    Publisher
    Thorndike Press
    10 Water St., Suite 310
    Waterville, ME 04901